Lords of Grass and Thunder

Lords of Grass and Thunder

Curt Benjamin

DAW BOOKS, INC.

DONALD A. WOLLHEIM, FOUNDER

375 Hudson Street, New York, NY 10014

**ELIZABETH R. WOLLHEIM
SHEILA E. GILBERT
PUBLISHERS**

http://www.dawbooks.com

First Printing, April 2005

1   2   3   4   5   6   7   8   9   10

DAW TRADEMARK REGISTERED
U.S. PAT. OFF. AND FOREIGN COUNTRIES
—MARCA REGISTRADA
HECHO EN U.S.A.

PRINTED IN THE U.S.A.

ACKNOWLEDGMENTS

Thanks as always to Barb for all the feedback, and Charlotte for all the feeding, and Erik and David and Mom and Dad and the sisters, who keep me going and the cousins, Emily and Sarah and Rachel and Matt, and Stephanie and Jessica and Rodi and Ashley and Kyle and Megan and Bethany and Kaitlin and Madison and Ethan, a never-ending source of inspiration and information.

Thanks to the Free Library of Philadelphia and the Sherwood branch of the Fairfax County Library, to whom I am indebted for everything I know about the Mongols. The ignorance, as usual, is all mine. For those who are curious about such things, I developed my ideas about riddles for this book reading Archer Taylor's 1954 *Annotated Collection of Mongolian Riddles,* a publication of the American Philosophical Society. My favorite version of the Secret History of the Golden Horde is Urgunge Onon's translation as *The Life and History of Chinggis Khan.* (Leiden, Brill, 1990). And the Carlsberg Nomad Research Foundation catalog of Nomad Costume (Henny Harold Hanson. Copenhagen: the Rhodos International Science and Art Publishers, 1993) has the most amazing photographs of Mongol Costumes, including some shaman costumes. I borrowed shamelessly to dress the characters in this book!

Military Command Structure

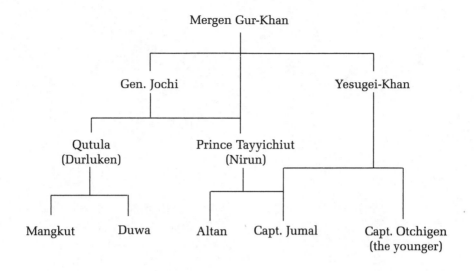

Family Trees

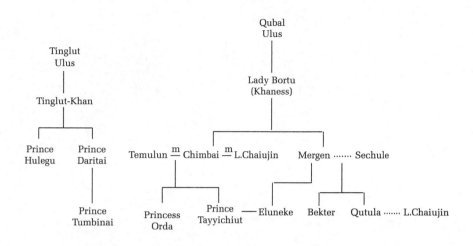

Tinglut
Ulus

Tinglut-Khan

Prince
Hulegu

Prince
Daritai

Prince
Tumbinai

Qubal
Ulus

Lady Bortu
(Khaness)

Temulun — m — Chimbai — m — L.Chaiujin

Mergen ······· Sechule

Princess
Orda

Prince
Tayyichiut

Eluneke

Bekter

Qutula ······· L.Chaiujin

PART ONE

COMING HOME

Chapter One

Four kings with crowns of silver
Rode out of the east
Their steeds more gold than sunlight—
Dragons breathing fire.

QUTULA DIDN'T REMEMBER it that way, and there hadn't been a lot of time to forget. They were riding west at last, across the barren landscape of the mountain plateau of the Cloud Country. Going home. Behind them lay the battle that had united the grasslands and the Shan Empire to free the Cloud Country, called Thebin by its people, and save them all from the end of the world. Or so the prophets had said. So he was very clear on what had happened. "The kings rode horses," he objected. "And only one of the dragons was golden."

"Close enough for poetry," Bekter assured him. "But I'm done for now. The air is too thin for making up songs." He settled his poorly tuned lute at his back and puffed out the cheeks of his broad flat face as if he were storing nuts for the winter. He was short for his kind, the runt in childhood, but he'd grown round with the promise of a strong, deep chest as he entered manhood. His coarse black hair fell in thick braids to the collars of the long-sleeved coat he wore.

Qutula, who was more finely built than his brother, with high cheekbones sharp in a wolflike, pointed face, grunted in halfhearted agreement. "That's why they call it the roof of the world. Be glad no one expects you to fight today." He wished Bekter would carry himself more like the son of a khan and less like a demented squirrel, but complaining hadn't gotten him anywhere in all the time they'd been brothers. For the most part, the khan's court put up with it because, for some reason that he never could figure, people seemed to like Bekter's songs.

"How long, do you think, before we reach the grasslands at this pace?"

Qutula had run a silk cord through a fragment of jade he'd picked up as a token of battle, and he worried his fingers over the spiral incised on it as he considered the question. War had brought them to the Cloud Country at a pitched gallop. Now they made their way home at a leisurely pace to spare both animals and men. "Two weeks, maybe three," he finally decided. "Longer for some." Their army spread out through many li on either side so the horses could forage on the sparse grass. Each squad would reach camp in its own time.

"It can't be soon enough for me," the demented squirrel grumbled through his blown-out cheeks. "I've had enough of exalted realms,"

Bekter cast a backward glance at the mountains, gleaming silver at their tops like the old crowned heads of ancient kings. Qutula's thoughts, however, lingered on different heights. Prince Tayyichiut rode ahead with the khan, so he spoke his mind more freely than he otherwise might.

"Too exalted for the likes of us, it seems, whom no one calls princes." He stroked the spiral rune on the jade at his throat, his gaze fixed on their father's back. Not even Bekter could miss . the hidden meanings tangled in his words. Their father the khan had never married their mother, nor had he seen fit to recognize his sons in front of the clans.

With his personal guard and advisers around him, Mergen-Khan led the gathered army of the Qubal clans down from the mountains that surrounded the Golden City of the Cloud Country. Their cousin, Prince Tayyichiut, took the honored position at his side, a place he had earned as a hero and as his uncle's heir. Victory had confirmed Mergen in the title of khan of the Qubal people, lately conferred on him at the death of his royal brother, Chimbai-Khan. But Prince Tayy, who had journeyed with foreign gods and fought at the side of dragons, had won the hearts of their allies.

Qutula and, in a lesser way, Bekter beside him had entered the fray as untested boys as well, and they likewise returned as blooded warriors. Their father would surely acknowledge them, he'd thought, now that they had proved their worth on the battlefield.

At battle's end, the khan had returned to his encampment outside the high mud wall of Kungol, the Golden City of the Cloud Country, to honor the service of his armies. In the traditional ceremony of their fathers, he would welcome as officers those noble youths with the blood of their first campaign still fresh on their swords.

At the door of the command tent, servants had raised the khan's dais, which remained empty while the army gathered in the parade ground before it. Those advisers and generals who had traveled to battle with the army ranged themselves on either side of a wide grassy lane that led through the camp, past the army, to the foot of the dais.

Anticipation created a stir of voices, but gradually the nervous talk died down. When the field had fallen silent, Mergen-Khan took his place on the dais. In his half-armor, chased and gleaming, and the silver cap of his office, he dazzled the eye like a god in the light of Great Sun. The new khan had led the clans in their first victory under his rule and they showed their approval with a thunder of jubilant cheers from every side. Mergen waited until the storm of sound had rolled over him and subsided, then he raised his hands in the air.

"Soldiers, warriors, generals, I honor you! Dead, wounded, I honor you! Living and blooded, I honor you! Your ancestors will sing your praises in the underworld, and the skies will roll with your names in the thunder!"

The crowd roared again. The ceremony, when the young warriors would present their weapons to the khan in victory, had begun. It should have been the greatest moment in Qutula's life, but memory turned to dust in his mouth.

"Youths went into battle on this land, men come before me now with the blood of the vanquished on their swords!" the khan had declared, and commanded, "Welcome the new warriors among you!"

Again cheers filled the air. That didn't matter to Qutula, of course. Only Mergen mattered, and what he would say to his sons. First in line, however, their cousin Prince Tayyichiut strode forward until he stood just below the dais. Bowing his head, he offered his weapon to his uncle. Of course, Mergen accepted his service. With a kiss on each cheek he welcomed his nephew into the company of men and invited him to take his place once again on the dais.

A little farther back in the line of young officers, Qutula held himself rigidly erect, his chest thrown out in the proud stance of a hero. Beside him, Bekter fidgeted anxiously.

"Do you suppose he will say something? I need to remember everything so I can put it all in a song.'The Great Khan Welcomes his Sons,' I will call it, or 'The Great Khan Rewards his Armies,' if not . . ."

Qutula unbent only enough to jab his brother in the ribs. "Be quiet! Think of my dignity if you have none of your own. Can't you at least try to stand up straight?"

"I'm nervous."

The line moved forward. Bekter settled into his own shambling dignity and soon they stood before their father the khan. He would acknowledge them as his blanket sons, Qutula thought, and then they would be invited to join the prince on the dais. Soon they would supplant the heir. Prince Tayyichiut would find himself among the guardsmen, keeping watch over Qutula's sleep.

"Qutula. Bekter." Mergen-Khan held out his hands, palms up to receive their tribute.

Bowing deeply, each son placed his sword on their father's outstretched palms.

"A grateful people acknowledge your might at arms. For courage in battle, and for the loyalty you have shown your clans and your khan, I name you Captain Qutula, and you Captain Bekter."

Mergen returned their weapons. The ritual formulation accepted their service and promoted them in the name of the khanate. With a gesture at Tayy on his right hand, he added, "Your prince prizes your company among his own picked guard.

May you serve him faithfully after me and take your enemy with you when you die." He gave no sign that they were his sons.

Not acknowledged, and the reference to their cousin struck Qutula as a rebuke. For a moment the shock of the insult froze his hands so that he almost dropped his sword between them. "I am your son," he whispered so that just the two of them could hear.

Mergen had dandled him on a less-royal knee when Qutula was a child. He had favored them while his own brother Chimbai-Khan had lived, urging Qutula and Bekter to the fore among the young warriors in training who had surrounded the young Prince Tayyichiut. It had seemed only natural that Mergen-Khan must recognize his blanket-sons now, when they had shown in battle that they were brave and honorable men.

Mergen, however, returned him a solemn frown. "As defenders of the prince you will share in many honors, good warrior," he said, making no mention of the relationship between them except, "I trust you as I would myself to defend the prince and the Qubal ulus."

"Always," Qutula answered, "I am but a spear in my father's hand."

Still, Mergen-Khan had not acknowledged him. Qutula's heart constricted in his chest when he thought about it. Bekter, however, had shown no hurt from the encounter—not even now, when they could speak with little danger of being overheard in the jangle and plod of an army on the move.

"I saw the dragons with my own eyes!" Enthusiasm spilled out of Bekter's mouth in spite of his lack of breath to speak the words. He had gone on talking while Qutula worried his past like a stone in his boot. "I didn't believe in dragons, to tell the truth. Then I saw this huge green monster gouge a scar deep as a lake into the land with one clawed foot. When he breathed fire, the snow from the mountains melted, filling the new lake with water. I wouldn't be surprised if there were fish in it already."

"And thus are the heavenly creatures of our imagination reduced to public works," Qutula responded sharply. "And the Golden City of Kungol itself turns into mud."

"It was glorious from a distance, even if the tales did prove false," Bekter defended his enthusiasm. Seeing the effect of sunlight on the peculiar yellow plaster that covered all the buildings, travelers had brought back stories of a city made of gold hidden in the mountains. Like most caravan tales, the truth fell short of the telling. Until the Uulgar raiders had invaded the Cloud Country, Kungol had stood as the last great stopping place for caravans on the trade routes to the West. The so-called Golden City lay at the crossroad of the high passes through the Thousand Peaks Mountains, no more hidden than it was made of gold.

Bekter shrugged off reality like a bird shaking dust off its feathers. "I'm a poet," he explained. "It's my job to put the wonder back in, and you can't get any more wonderful than a skyful of dragons."

Qutula scorned the tales and all their spectacle, and he gave his brother's conversation only half his attention. The better part of his thoughts continued to circle round his father, who had rejected his claim in front of the whole court.

"Like kings, the wonders of the world seem marvelous from a distance," he said, and added, "Seen eye to eye, we find them only clay, no more exalted than ourselves."

Even Bekter could not ignore the bitterness of this complaint. He finally seemed to understand they weren't talking about dragons or cities made of gold, but of their own lives.

"Given time, our father will see the value of his sons," he answered mildly. "He seemed interested when I asked his permission to compose a history of his reign, at least. If we find ways to show ourselves faithful to his cause, he'll have to recognize us."

"So you believe." The worm of discontent gnawed at Qutula's heart. "It seems more likely he will choose a fresh young wife as different from our mother as spring is from winter, and build his legacy on sons born above the firebox." Closer to the khan in rank, he meant. Their mother had no claim to nobility.

Better to make history than to record it, he concluded. They would need to act soon, before Mergen made legitimate heirs of his own and the brothers lost even the cursory attention of their royal father. Qutula kept those thoughts to himself. His eyes, however, strayed to the prince who rode beside the khan in Qutula's place.

Prince Tayyichiut, heir to the khanate of the Qubal people, looked back along the road they had traveled with a little shiver. In the language of the clans, Thebin was called the Cloud Country. It had lived up to its name. Even in summer the morning dew spun cobwebs of ice on the sparse grass. At noon Great Sun shed a pale cold light on the mountains, but little warmth touched the army crawling home across the high plateau. He had hoped to catch a last glimmer of the Golden City falling away at the slow pace of their homebound horses, as if to remind himself that his adventures had been real. But the city had disappeared into the folds of the landscape.

The war was over. His mind still shone with the wonders he had seen in the Golden City high in those mountains; like the ferryman, however, marvels demand a fee. He had run away looking for adventures and to save his own life from the conspiracies that seethed around the firebox in the ger-tent palace of the khan. In the aftermath of battle he returned in body to the clans. His heart, however, remained apart from the friends who had been his companions for all of his life.

The time he spent traveling in faraway countries had made him into something new, a hero who had endured great hardship and fought beside creatures of mythic terror: gods and dragons and ghosts and kings. There were questions about his travels that his old companions were afraid to ask. *It's mostly cold and wet and scary*, he would have told them. *And in between it is the unspeakable pain of terrible wounds patched badly in the field.* He didn't have words to describe the parts they were afraid to hear, but the knowledge stood between them as a darkness in his eyes. So the distance grew while all he wished was to return to those days when he knew nothing of faraway countries or conspiracies at home.

Tayy was thinking all of this when he looked back in his saddle to make a last, silent farewell to the friends of his journeys whom he'd left behind with the distant mountains. By chance, his eye fell on his cousins Qutula and Bekter deep in conversation.

"A long road is a short road," Mergen reminded him with a nod in the direction of the brothers. Bolghai the shaman often posed the riddle as a reminder when the clans prepared to move camp. The solution, of course, was conversation, which shortened a long road by relieving the tedium of travel, thus making the time pass more quickly. Mergen had returned his attention to the road ahead so he didn't see Qutula look up then to fix a darkly brooding gaze between the khan's shoulder blades. Tayy saw, however, and a chill settled in his belly, as if the sun had dropped suddenly behind a mountain peak.

"He is my friend and loves his father," he thought, while a tiny whisper of a doubt troubled his confidence.

When he was very young, he thought his own father a perfect example of the cunning and bravery required of a khan. Chimbai-Khan had been murdered by his second wife, the false Lady Chaiujin, however, leaving Prince Tayy an orphan and his people on the brink of war with unholy forces of evil. Tayy had to admit to himself that his father might have made more than one error of judgment along the road to his untimely death. He should not have brought the demon-lady Chaiujin into his camp. And he should not, Tayy suspected, have forbidden his brother Mergen to marry.

Recriminations wouldn't bring his parents back. But Prince Tayy wondered if his uncle didn't follow too closely down the path of Chimbai-Khan's errors. Mergen's wisdom about matters of policy and warfare could not be faulted. But in matters of family politics he relied too much, perhaps, on his great mind and too little on his heart.

Tayy wanted peace. He wished for nothing more than a quiet place to study and grow into his new knowledge. Now, he judged, was not the time to bring such a notion to the khan.

"Your mind seems to be wandering today, nephew. What are you thinking about?"

Prince Tayy gave a start, suddenly afraid that the khan had somehow read his mind. But Mergen turned to him with a wry twist of a smile and he relaxed into his saddle again. Safe in his own thoughts, at least for now, he gave his uncle the smallest part of his truth.

"Hunting. Fishing. Everyday things."

"Tired of adventures already?"

"There is much to be said for a quiet life." Tayy rubbed a hand across his gut, worrying at the scars beneath his clothes. It was becoming a habit and he pulled the hand away to rest it on the pommel of his saddle.

He wasn't quick enough to evade his uncle's sharp eye however. "Not all adventures carry such a heavy cost," Mergen reminded him gently, and asked, "Does it still hurt?"

"Sometimes." Tayy found it easy enough to admit to the physical ache that still plagued him on cold days. The memory hurt more, though, and he couldn't talk about that. He looked away into the distance, remembering. Soon the clans would return to their usual grazing grounds, the scene of his father's murder, and his mother's. Their murderer still breathed, if such as she lived in the way of mortal creatures, and he feared the spirits of his parents would never find rest until he had avenged their deaths.

"Chimbai-Khan would have been proud of you," his uncle said, and Prince Tayy did wonder then if his uncle Mergen could read his mind after all. But then he added a reminder of the ritual of praise and homecoming, "You acquitted yourself with bravery in the field of battle, and brought honor on your house."

Tayy gave his uncle the smile his words demanded, but he doubted honor would be enough.

Chapter Two

WHEN THE SUN BURNED red on the horizon, Mergen called a halt for the night. The less-than-sweet water from a marshy spring nearby would satisfy the thirsty horses and his army would have time to set up their small round campaign tents before nightfall. They needed to light the fires before the hard dark. His own forces had helped to seal the gates of hell that had spilled monsters onto this land, but a few stray imps and goblins still wandered the plateau in search of home. By nature they avoided the light, however. And the smoke from the fires would keep away the mosquitos big as moths that drove an otherwise hardened warrior mad.

While his followers worked to set up the command tent, Prince Tayyichiut, his heir, led his horse aside to tend her needs himself. The khan watched his nephew perform the simple tasks with keen attention.

Tayy looked up as if he felt his uncle's eyes on him and answered with a puzzled smile. "Am I needed elsewhere?" He gestured with the brush in his hands "I can let one of the others rub her down. It's just that she nips if you aren't careful about her sore spots."

"I'll need you beside me soon enough, but not right now. You have time to tend to your lady." Mergen would have done the same, but his new position forbid him such homely tasks.

"No lady," Tayy laughed. "She has a will of her own, but we see eye to eye on most things." He rubbed her nose in a comradely gesture to show that there were no hard feelings between them.

"And so it has been throughout history." Which reminded Mergen of his blanket-son's request. "Bekter has submitted formal petition to record a history of the Qubal court. I told him 'yes,' of course. How could I deny the clans the pleasure of his songs? He plans to create a whole cycle of tales and it would please him to hear your adventures in your own words, with your own commentary."

"I know. He asked me about it when we were still in Kungol, but I wasn't ready then."

"And you are now?"

"I'm not sure." Tayy paused, brush raised for the next stroke. His vision seemed to turn inward as he thought. "Maybe. Soon."

It struck Mergen that the young prince had little experience by which to judge his current feelings, and he offered a bit of his own truth from past wars fought at Chimbai's side. "There's always a letdown after battle."

"I know. I'm fine." The next stroke with the brush came down on a raw spot with more force than the horse liked. She tossed her head and sidled a step away from the hurt. "Sorry, sorry, girl," he said, calming her.

He seemed unwilling to accept any comfort for himself, however. After a long silent moment, Mergen turned for the command tent. "Come when you are ready," he said with a glance over his shoulder, and meant many things by that.

Prince Tayy didn't look up, but his nod seemed to answer all of them.

There was nothing left but to go, and so Mergen did.

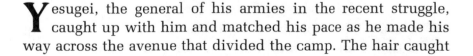

Yesugei, the general of his armies in the recent struggle, caught up with him and matched his pace as he made his way across the avenue that divided the camp. The hair caught at the nape of his neck in the long flat braid of a chieftain was scattered with more gray than before the war. Otherwise he showed no signs of aging, but remained broad in the chest, his thick arms still capable with the sword or the spear. He'd been watching the halting conversation between khan and heir, it seemed, and now spoke up with more understanding than Mergen felt comfortable acknowledging: "He'll be ready when the clans need him."

"I know he will." Mergen had called himself a humble servant of the khan and few knew how deeply felt those words had been. But if he could do this one last service in Chimbai's name, set Chimbai's son on the dais, he'd be free. He just had to keep the prince alive and moving forward. It seemed, for the moment, he had. "The boy has survived when others haven't, a valuable skill in a khan."

"In the present khan as well," Yesugei reminded him. "Where else will a boy learn how to lead?"

They had reached the command tent. Great Sun had set below the horizon, chased to his sleep by little moons Han and Chen. Great Moon Lun would follow her brothers soon to light the night sky. Now, fire painted the side of Yesugei's face crimson and gold as he gave one last word before taking his place among the captains and chieftains at the side of the dais.

"On the dais or whispering in the ear of the heir who takes your place there, your people need you," he reminded the khan. It would have been impertinent, except that his bow, and the cupped hand outstretched in the gesture of a supplicant, made clear that he spoke not as a friend but as a chieftain. A reminder that the clans had elected their khan to be above them for a reason.

"I serve at the will of my people," Mergen answered with a tilt of his head to acknowledge the gentle rebuke. With that he took the dais, calling for his supper so that the others might eat.

The road down from the mountains was hard and the recent battle left all the armies that fought in it exhausted and reel-

ing both from the fighting and from the onslaught of wonders
they had seen. Mergen-Khan therefore kept the court in attendance only until Great Moon Lun had begun her descent. Then
he sent them all to their own tents to sleep as they might until
morning. Bekter was not the only one that night to fall like the
dead on the sheepskin of his saddle pad, under the warm cover
of a low round campaign tent. Qutula, however, remained wide
awake, twisting on his own bed in an excess of feverish energy.
He wanted someone to talk to—not just anyone, but a brother
who shared his interest in bettering their position in the eyes of
their father, the khan.

"Bek," he called across the narrow darkness between them.
 Nothing.

The jade fragment on its silken cord itched at his breast and
Qutula wrapped his hand around it, wishing it to be still. He'd
found it high in the mountains, outside a cave that a demon-
king had used for his den. They had fought a terrible battle
there with imps and minions. He often wondered if the jade
had come from the underworld as part of some vessel used in
that evil court. The demon-king was dead, however. The crack
in the world that had let the horrible creatures escape the land
of the dead into that of the living was closed.

Sometimes, when he thought about it, though, the shard
made him feel strange hungers he didn't understand. He
wanted to devour the world whole, to wield power and control,
to amass a wealth of herds and precious goods and to gather
women to him like fluttering butterflies drawn to their special
tree. Not a few, but all the women. He wanted to tell the wind
to fall and have it do his bidding, or tell the sun to rise at midnight and have the night spin by as nothing. He wasn't sure if
the feelings attracted or repelled him, but he didn't want his
brother to know about them.

"Bek, are you awake?"
"Mrmph."
"We need a plan."
"Mrmph."
Hopeless. Qutula pulled his blanket over his shoulder and
turned his back on his brother.

A stranger was lying in his bed. "You've stumbled into the wrong tent, soldier," he said, keeping his hands and other body parts discreetly to himself.

"Not a soldier," a woman's voice whispered hot breath in his ear. "But an admirer of one."

Qutula froze, uncertain what to do. Such things happened in war, of course. Camp followers always accompanied the traveling hordes to ease the burdens of weary soldiers. The boldest didn't wait to be asked. Mindful of his own parentage, however, he did not as a rule indulge himself so freely. Which was one thing. For another, the camp followers he had known didn't smell like this—like fresh grass and wildflowers and spring on the Onga River. She didn't, he realized, smell like a woman at all.

"Don't you like women?"

Her hand reached under his shirt, scratched at the sparse hairs on his chest. Qutula didn't really need to tell her that yes, he did like women, because his body moved toward her as if his will meant nothing in the matter. She must not think that she could rule him with her body, however, so he held himself a little apart while the sweat bloomed on his forehead and on his nether regions. "I like them well enough," he answered her question, "when I do the choosing."

"Ah. I see." She reached out and took his hand, placed it on her naked breast. "And do you not, then, choose me?"

Her breast . . . her breast felt softer than anything he had ever touched, softer than the wool of a newborn lamb. It molded under his touch, unblemished and fine and he wanted to explore it with his tongue. She reached down between his legs and the distance between them vanished. They were one creature writhing luxuriantly in the dark. His legs tangled with her smooth limbs, his sinewy bones cradled in the welcome softness of her thighs, his hard chest crushing the lush pillows of her breasts between them. Her dark places felt like warm butter on his flesh. She would not let him kiss her, but her tongue flicked out to nuzzle at his neck, at the skin exposed at the collar of his shirt.

"Ahh . . . Ah . . ."

She covered his lips with her hand when he would have cried out, her silent laughter warm against his cheek. "Bekter will hear," she whispered. "Do you want your brother to know?"

No. Torn by shame and greed he wished only to keep even the knowledge of her to himself.

"Who are you?" He reached out with strong arms to hold her close. This time it was she who pulled away, wiping herself fastidiously with a corner of his shirt.

"My name is Lady— But no, not yet. Let us make a bargain."

He thought that she would name her price then. The realization that she was indeed a soldier's whore troubled him because he had begun to build fantasies of magical women drawn to the worth of his blood, if not his rank. When she made her demand, it seemed she read even the dreams of his waking mind.

"A kingdom, for a name. When you bring me the silver cap of the khanate, then will I give you my name."

"How—I will not kill my father," he said, though it was in his mind that he would. But Prince Tayyichiut was heir. Mergen's death would bring Qutula no closer to the dais than he was now.

"Not a patricide." The lady's voice hissed softly against his ear. Her tongue flicked at his throat, where the blood pulsed quick at the angle of his jaw, while her hands wandered freely beneath his clothes. "I could not love a patricide."

Prince Tayy, then, she meant him to murder.

When the serpent poisoned Tayy's father, the prince had been an untried boy with neither the experience to lead nor the confidence of the chieftains who elected the khan. They had chosen the dead khan's brother who had, in turn, redeemed the honor of his word when he named his weak young nephew his heir. Qutula had felt certain that his father would see the error of that decision before it came to fruition. Now, however, Prince Tayyichiut returned from battle as the darling of the khan's advisers and the hero of the army. It gave one pause to wonder how long Mergen himself would live with so popular a candidate waiting for his place on the dais.

In his calculation of the future, Qutula had forgotten that he was not alone until a whisper brought him back to himself with a start.

"Events are not on your side, young prince-as-should-be," she urged him with her words and her body.

She followed his thoughts as a hunter followed its prey, not by visible sign, for it was too dark to see. Somehow she had learned the patterns of his mind: where a thought would take him next and how he would reach the end of any trail. But who could she be? How had she grown so familiar with the workings of his intellect?

"Will you come again?" he asked. He told himself he would use a future visit to ferret out a name, a rank. When he would have rested his hand upon her breast again, however, she withdrew farther from his reach.

"Maybe. If you promise."

To murder his cousin, she meant. As the lady read him, so Qutula learned the pathways of her thoughts. She leaned over him and with her mouth and fingers and her soft, soft thighs, she teased him with her own promises. "Swear it," she whispered.

He was dizzy with her scent, which had deepened with the rich smells of moss and loamy earth and the slightest trace of something less wholesome lurking at the bottom of it all. And sex, of course. She smelled most strongly of the sharp tang of his musk and her own juices, mingled with their sweat in the covers. When she mounted him, he could only groan, "Anything, anything," into the hand she placed over his mouth

She sighed back at him, "Promise, promise," and held him on the brink that way until he said the words.

"I promise."

It seemed the words were all the outpouring he needed. She withdrew from him and he held her only lightly, not wishing to impede her, only to ask a favor, "If not your name, then may I have a small token of your visit, my lady? Or when I wake this will all seem like a dream."

He did not mean his request as a threat to forget his promise, but cold and bitter eyes gleamed out of the dark at him, as if he had betrayed her.

"You already have such a token—"

He didn't understand, or chose not to. "Love marks fade," he answered with a little nip at her shoulder. "I would remember this night forever."

After a moment, she softened toward him.

"Of course."

With that she pressed her lips to his breast, above his heart. He felt the prick of needle-sharp teeth and his heart beat faster in its cage of bone. Death seemed to creep closer, ready to slip inside the low round tent and steal him away, and he didn't seem to mind when she touched him like that . . .

Sense returned with the rising of Great Sun in the morning. Qutula's eyes flew open, the events of the night spinning like a fever in his head.

"Bek!" he called, wanting the evidence of his brother's ears to confirm that it had been no dream. But his brother slept so soundly and so cold upon the ground that he might have died in the night.

"Bekter! Wake up!"

At last his brother did, shaking off the unnatural lethargy with bleary eyes. "My head is killing me," he said. "How can I be so drunk and remember nothing of the feast?"

While his brother's state did nothing to assure him that the events of his own night were true, Qutula discovered he was relieved that the secret remained his alone.

"What's that on your chest?"

The jade he wore on the string; his brother must have seen it. Qutula bristled at the question, but he didn't want to rouse Bekter's suspicions. "Just a broken bit of something I picked up on the battlefield. I thought I showed it to you before." It felt different when he tucked it back into his shirt—the carved spiral that had covered it like a rune had disappeared. Had his night visitor taken the shard he had brought down from the mountains and replaced it with one of her own? It pleased him to think that she had wanted a remembrance of him as he had wanted one from her. But Bekter wasn't looking at the jade.

"Not that. The mark on your chest." Bekter's eyes had begun to focus again, and they had fallen on the very place where the lady had pricked him with her teeth.

"It must have been a spider. A little bite, nothing more." Qutula shrugged off his brother's interest, but Bekter persisted.

"No spider, brother, but a coiled serpent green as grass. You must have been drunker than I, to get the wrong tattoo!"

A tattoo. Idly his fingers passed across the mark that tingled in parts of his body distant from his breast. He had asked her for a token and his lady had left him this. His smile brought a like one to his brother's sickly face.

"A reminder of some lady?" Bekter asked. "Do I know her? Is she pretty? Is she expensive?"

"She's not that kind of lady." Qutula answered his brother with a tart pursing of his lips to discourage further questions. "I can't tell you more."

He made it sound as though he defended the lady's honor with his silence, which he did as any young man would. In this case gallantry hid his ignorance, as well as the promise he had made. Not a serious vow, he assured himself, but a lovers' game for the dark. The tattoo began to burn, however, and did not stop until he admitted to himself that he knew what he must do. Then the gentler warmth returned.

His brother had watched the silent debate cross Qutula's narrow features with interest. "I think there's more of a tale here than meets the eye," Bekter said. "When you're ready to talk, I'll be your willing audience."

"No tale at all for you to turn into a song, but indigestion." Qutula passed off the pain of the tattoo with the same drunken evening that had answered Bekter's curiosity about his headache. But he covered the mark well with his shirt and caftan before he left his tent. A lady's token, like her name, belonged to no one but the man to whom she gave it.

Chapter Three

MUCH LATER, WHEN ASKED what he remembered of that return from war to the great tent city of the Qubal clans, Mergen would say the barking of the dogs as they ran alongside the horses, nipping at the heels of his soldiers. Proud at the head of his army as they rode down the broad avenue, lined on either side by white felt tents of many lattices, he noticed only in passing the flash of Sechule's dark hair moving through the crowd. He had set his gaze on the great ger-tent palace at the head of the avenue, its silver embroidery glowing like Great Moon herself to welcome his first return from battle as the khan.

How would his mother greet him? he wondered. She loved him as a son, but he had not been her first choice as khan. That son, that brother, had died and Mergen had survived. Surely survival must mean something to the old ones waiting for an accounting of this foreign war. In the silver cap of the khanate and the lavishly embroidered silk robes he wore, his magnificence must amaze his people crowding either side of the avenue. But vanity didn't urge him to wonder if he cut a splendid figure on his horse. The clans who had elected him could replace him if they found him lacking.

In such an event, of course, there would be war. The riches he displayed on his horse and his person, the very tilt of his head and the way he held himself in the saddle, warned his adversaries that they had a fight on their hands. Or, if his presence failed to issue the proper warning, assured that they might easily remove him. He had neither the breadth of chest nor the regal stature of Chimbai-Khan who had gone before him, but he believed that the wisdom of his thoughts must show in his solemn carriage. The keen eye he set upon the crowd must prove him a dauntless foe.

If his own looks did not inspire confidence, however, the ten thousand Qubal warriors at his back, and the ten thousand of his conquered enemy who followed in chains, must. Cheered by the solid presence of his armies, Mergen was ready to pay attention to his companions.

Prince Tayyichiut, in the embroidered silks and cone-shaped silver cap of the heir, attended him at his right hand as the youth had so often ridden at the side of his father. The boy had become a hero, but he seemed unable to encompass the thought as yet. He scanned with satisfaction the crowd cheering and throwing flowers as they passed. "The wars have made you popular, uncle," he said as a bluebell tumbled off his cap.

"It's not my name on the lips of the clans, nephew." Mergen had keen hearing, and he knew the limits of his popularity. "The Qubal celebrate their hero-prince."

"No—" Prince Tayyichiut turned in his saddle as if seeking some other prince, some other hero with his name who had captured their love.

"Salute your people," Mergen instructed, "for they are yours indeed, and only in my keeping until I can return them to you."

The dogs running at his side increased the din with their barking, as if in agreement with the khan. The prince seemed less convinced than his hounds, but he'd been raised at the khan's court. When reminded, he squared his jaw and sat straighter in his saddle, raising his hand to greet the crowd as his horse continued its stately walk down the grassy avenue. He would grow into his fame as a hero must, Mergen thought, while those of more subtle skills accepted the burden of rule and the joy of teaching their successor. The crowd already showed that Prince Tayy would make a popular khan. Mergen had to ensure he became a wise one as well.

He turned to share his doubts with General Yesugei, who rode at his left hand, but the general's thoughts were elsewhere. His eye followed the movement of black hair slipping through the crowd. Yesugei had one wife and was looking for a second. Mergen doubted the wisdom of the direction his affection was leading him in, however.

"She will never settle for the place of second wife in your tent," he reminded his friend. Sechule had always put ambition above her heart.

Her beauty had drawn Mergen to her tent against his better sense for more seasons than he cared to think about, so he understood the attraction. But her ambitions had followed Sechule under the blankets, making an uneasy third in their bed. He must put himself forward, she had said; his cunning made him more fit to be khan than his brother. Her complaints had tired him long before their affair had ended.

He could only warn Yesugei, his friend of many battles, what he knew of the woman Sechule. "If the brother of the khan did not satisfy her ambitions, a general who stands a step below the dais can expect to do no better." One who could offer her only second place in his tent in particular stood no chance against Sechule's pride.

Yesugei dismissed his concerns with a breezy wave of his hand, as if sweeping pebbles off the board. "I have many herds and flocks," he reminded the khan. Mergen had served his clan well, but they both knew he had gathered no wealth of his own, increasing his brother's fortunes instead. "Sechule can have her own house in my camp and rule over it as she wishes. She may even keep her sons with her, though they will be looking around them for wives of their own soon enough." Mergen's sons as well, but they would never be called so while they remained unacknowledged.

"She's a haughty woman," the khan reminded him. "And cold when she doesn't get her way."

"I would never criticize my khan—" Yesugei affected a

boastful tone, in jest, "—but some, perhaps, are better at pleasing a woman—her way."

The khan laughed at the ribald joke as he was meant to do, but still he wondered if his friend had heard any of his warnings.

If General Yesugei heard not enough, Prince Tayy's wary expression told Mergen that perhaps his nephew had heard too much. He leaned over in his saddle and gave the prince a reassuring slap on the shoulder, a wicked grin held to his lips with determination.

"Matters of the heart," he said. "You will understand about such things yourself soon enough."

Tayy returned him an uncertain smile. His eyes roved the crowd, but Sechule had gone.

"Too old for you," Mergen joked again, though he had no fear for his nephew on that score. Prince Tayyichiut had come back from his journey a great deal braver than when he set out, but no less cautious. He'd lost a father, after all, and a mother at the hands of a monster wearing a fair face and a stolen name. His nephew would not be parted easily from his good sense for a one-sided love.

They had arrived at the door to the white-and-silver ger-tent palace. Mergen alighted, his fist upraised in a salute to the warriors who quickly filled the practice field behind him with their cries and the thunder of horses' hooves. Prince Tayy and General Yesugei followed amid the recrimination of Tayy's dogs, who chastised their master with their howling for leaving them behind. After Yesugei came their guardsmen. As he entered the palace, Mergen noted with pleasure how closely his own blanket-sons clung to the prince. Bekter and the prince laughed between them as they held off the dogs from entering with the party of men while Qutula looked on with exaggerated dismay at the noisy beasts.

Already Qutula had gathered some small renown, with followers who pledged to serve the prince in his name. Bekter declared himself ready to immortalize their brave deeds in his songs. Their presence at Tayy's side assured him that his blanket-sons would bring honor to their family as chosen guardsmen when their cousin took his rightful place as khan. He hoped, with the hope of one who had lost to death the anda of his boyhood, that they would swear themselves friends of the heart to their young khan, binding them in lifelong alliance of friendship and service. He had sworn so to Chimbai, his brother, as Otchigin had sworn himself to Mergen. Both khan and adviser were dead now, murdered, but the ties of anda held fast even in the underworld. Mergen stilled a shiver that traveled up his spine. It would be different for his nephew, who would reign in peace.

Prince Tayyichiut must decide for himself to accept his cousins as anda, but he had confidence in his nephew. A family so united could only grow richer and more powerful. Satisfied that he had done all he could for now to ensure their future, he led the triumphal procession inside.

The ger-tent palace of the khan was much as Mergen remembered it. Where they showed between the rich hangings on the walls, the polished lattices were hung with decorations of bronze and silver and mirrors to frighten away evil spirits. Painted chests scattered here and there displayed their burdens of family heirlooms and clan treasures. Six hundred clansmen could fit at need within the round, felted walls. Less than half that number settled in their places today, but as always the firebox at the center marked the dividing line of rank and station. Above sat the royal family and those of greatest rank, the most powerful of the clan chieftains and the advisers to the khan. Below the firebox, nearest the door, chieftains and retainers of lesser family and lower standing settled themselves by a separate order.

The khan's guardsmen, and the younger corps who defended the prince, followed only as far as the firebox at the center of the palace. There the greater number split off to take their positions with their backs to the lattices on the perimeter. The chosen few, Qutula and Bekter among them, continued to the dais at a respectful distance. Yesugei at other times had advanced with Mergen's guard, sitting at the khan's back to serve him. Their disagreement over the woman Sechule seemed to have made the general sensitive to his other obligations, however. He left Mergen to join the elders and chieftains of the many clans of the Qubal ulus.

This was no time to hesitate, however. As custom dictated, Mergen strode ahead with his heir a proper pace behind him. Each acknowledged the waiting dignitaries with gracious nods to the left and the right until they reached the dais.

Surrounded by those elders most closely tied to them by blood and marriage, the Lady Bortu, his mother, awaited them. She wore a towering headdress of silver horns from which her hair poured forth on either side of her head. Medallions of figured silver hung with many ornaments dangled from her earlobes. Large beads of coral and turquoise and other jewels strung on silver chains spilled like a waterfall to the shoulders of her heavy yellow silk coats, obscuring all but her eyes. Those eyes, however, read to the very heart of her son, offering welcome as she measured the stature he had gained in his position since she had seen him on the eve of battle.

At the dais, he stopped. Prince Tayy stepped up beside him, equals before their Great Mother and neither of them khan in the camp of the Qubal while the Lady Bortu ruled in Mergen's name. Together they made respectful bows, their elaborate silver caps brushing the soft upturned boots on her feet.

"The sons of the great clans of the Qubal people return to the hearth of the Great Mother," Mergen recited the formula of return. "We bring you slaves, ten thousand in number, who grovel at your feet—" he meant by that the fallen army of the Uulgar, defeated in the battle for the Cloud Country. "Speak only the word and a ruddy river will spring up to rival the Onga, flowing with the treasure of their spilled blood."

"Have these slaves sworn an oath to you, my son the khan?" Old Bortu put her hands on his head as she asked the question.

"They have, Great Mother," he answered. "The evil magician who led them, and the evil demon who held sway over them, have both been destroyed. Their armies have renounced them."

"That pleases us," she approved.

From Mergen's position he could see that she shifted her weight from foot to foot. The right one must hurt where the bunion pinched. She had so formidable a determination he sometimes forgot that age brought with it these small infirmities. Best to finish quickly so that she might sit in comfort among the furs heaped on the dais. She seemed to feel the same, for she stepped back, drawing him with her.

"Assume your rightful place, then, son. The throne is no comfortable seat for an old lady." Her words put the ulus into Mergen's hands again.

"And grandson," she greeted Prince Tayyichiut, "Take your ease with your old grandmother. You will be happy to know that the cooks have watched the dust of your horses drawing nearer since morning!"

As khan, Mergen sat first, one leg tucked up under him and the other with the knee drawn up to his chin in front of him. Prince Tayy followed him and took the heir's seat at his side. The boy could not help but suffer from the memory of times past when his father sat in Mergen's place, with his beloved mother to hand as well. Mother and father both lay murdered now, but the ancient Bortu still greeted her grandson with a hug and a kiss for each cheek.

"You must tell me about your adventures," she said to both her male relatives. "And then we must dispose of these slaves you have brought me. There will be tents in need of men, but not so many. And as you will doubtless soon prove, fighting men require a great deal of feeding."

As she spoke, she clapped her hands. An army of servants waiting only for her signal marched into the great ger-tent carrying huge trays in their arms. Dish followed dish of the feast prepared for them. Mergen helped himself to sour yogurt made from mare's milk, and a tangy cheese from the milk of sheep. Tea with butter followed, and Mergen's favorite kumiss—beer fermented from mare's milk. When Chimbai was khan, the servants had brought out thick-crusted pies filled with fat from the tail of a sheep first, but on this homecoming his mother had arranged for his own more humble favorites, rich with minced roots and meats, to greet him. Only when he had chosen one to his taste did the servants bring out the others, which Tayy preferred.

Bortu laughed at the hopeful look that the prince was quick to hide. "Can you think the Great Mother of the khan would forget how to welcome a hero?" she asked him.

Mergen was pleased to note that, though he colored like old wine, his heir didn't hide his face but smiled to accept the teasing of his grandmother. He'd always been a steady boy. *Your father would be proud of you,* he thought. *Your mother would berate me for not protecting you better.* But such thoughts were better left for the light of Great Moon Lun, when regrets came home to live in dreams. In the warmth of Great Sun came pies that tasted like all the heavens of Bekter's tales, and the company of clan and ulus to hold the questions at bay.

As they ate, newcomers arriving from farther down the line of march took their places among the honorable company. Bolghai the shaman scampered down the aisle in the character of his totem animal, the skins of a dozen stoats flying out from around his neck as he danced. Beating a mischievous tattoo on his drum with a stick made from the thighbone of a roebuck, he asked the company a riddle. "A horse with three legs is whole," he said with a flourish on his drum. The ulus, he meant, crippled without their khan, now healed by his return. Giving Mergen an approving nod, which the khan acknowledged with an answering tilt of his head, the shaman took his place below the dais. There he could enjoy the pies and drink among the second ranks while watching the comings and goings of the court.

Home. Prince Tayy gave Bolghai a preoccupied smile. He owed the shaman a lot—probably his life—but he couldn't quite shake the conversation he'd overheard on the road between General Yesugei and the kahn.

"Something is troubling you, grandson?"

"Nothing important." Tayy gave a little shrug, muttering curses in his head where he hoped his grandmother couldn't hear them. Maintaining his court face while his thoughts wandered where they would used to be as natural as breathing to him. He was pretty sure that he had it in place now—politely attentive, with nothing deeper showing in his eyes than calculating his odds of snagging another pie. Lady Bortu easily saw through the pretense, however.

"You don't have to talk to me," she sniffed. "All I've done in my life is raise two khans from womb to the dais and lead the ulus in their absence for more years than are decent for an old lady to live. How could I have any comfort to offer a young warrior home from his first war?"

When she put it that way, it really did seem like nothing. But he let his glance drift from the khan to his general, which told the perceptive Bortu all that she needed to know.

"Sechule!" she sniffed. "Those two are worse than dogs after the same bitch. If you have any sense in you at all, and I hope you do, you'll let the women choose your wives and leave this sneaking into friendly tents to the foolish."

"We have many allies now. I expect Mergen-Khan will make a political match for me." He knew better than to mention love. His father had grown to love his mother, but it hadn't always been like that. He worried more about a match like the Lady Chaiujin.

Bortu had lost a son just as Tayy had lost a father to that demon-lady, and knew where his thoughts had settled. "Your uncle would not let that happen again. But Mergen holds the place of khan in trust for you. He may suggest a match, but will make no demands that cross your own wishes. If you desire a Qubal girl to wed, he will doubtless defer to clan tradition."

That meant Lady Bortu would put her head together with the Great Mothers of the clans. Between them they would choose a girl who met their high standards for family and form and disposition. And the politics of the ulus, of course. Nothing that happened in the court was free of politics, least of all a royal wedding.

"In the meantime," Bortu continued, "There is no rush to the marriage bed. You have tales to tell and adventures still awaiting you. And you have only just come home. Allow yourself a little time to enjoy the carefree life of a hero in peacetime before you take on the burdens of husband and khan."

Lady Bortu was right. His uncle's woman trouble didn't

seem like much compared to where he had been and what he had seen, the things both wonderful and terrible that had happened to him in the far reaches of the world.

"Home," he agreed, taking in the huge tent around him. Many of the guardsmen who circled the perimeter of the tent in their deep blue coats and cone-shaped hats had stood guard in just this way when his father had been khan. They hadn't saved him from the serpent who crept into his bed and murdered him in his sleep. No, carefree didn't cover it.

Suddenly the walls oppressed him. The riches and heirlooms were like lead weights dragging him down, drowning him in foreboding. Childhood had fled while he schemed to stay alive in this deadly court. Now the ulus needed him to take his place as a man and a hero. His grandmother was right about one thing at least: he wasn't ready yet to give up his freedom to the responsibilities that had killed his father.

Bortu watched his struggles with an answering sorrow in her eyes. "The prattling of an old woman must be tiresome to the young."

"Not at all! Believe that I take your words to heart." He gave an apologetic shrug, unable to share his restlessness with the woman who had lost as much as he and never shirked her duty. "Summer is short." He offered the distraction of sunshine and long grass as an excuse for his fidgeting.

One might, if one chose, take his words as the simple plea of a very young man who wished to enjoy the rare warmth of the day out of doors. He should have known better than to bandy metaphors with his grandmother, however. Too late to unspeak it he saw how much his answer revealed in its riddle form. Life, like summer, was short, and his own moved too swiftly toward the autumn, as he saw it, of adulthood. Bortu, who lived in the snows of age, let the skin around her eyes crinkle with her black-toothed grin.

"Like young stallions, young men should never waste the sunlight of summer among the toothless," she agreed.

"I meant no disrespect." He understood the riddle hidden in her permission to go. A young man's place was out beyond the firebox of home, winning followers to secure his place among his tents. Tayy had helped to win a war already and now he had alliances to build. He couldn't do that sitting at his uncle's knee in the tents of his elders. With a bow to the khan and a kiss on the cheek of his grandmother, he took his leave.

Where once he would have run laughing from the tent he now strode purposefully with his head high and his shoulders set for battle as a hero might. He could have the freedom he wanted for a little while longer, his grandmother seemed to say, provided he acted the part of the hero in a shadow play for the clans. He could do that.

So, with his hand to the hilt of his sword, he made his way toward the door. Below the firebox he picked up those among his own house guard who had accompanied him into the palace, his unacknowledged cousins Qutula and Bekter at their fore. Altan fell in behind them, and Duwa. Others he recognized and some were only lately assigned to fill the places of those lost in the war. Together they made a princely sight, and Tayy thought that Bolghai must approve this change in his bearing. But when he looked to the corner, the shaman encouraged him with a smile more sad than proud. Tayy wondered how he'd got it wrong this time, but he refused to let uneasy questions trouble him. The door was straight ahead.

Chapter Four

SQUATTING AMONG THE DOGS and casting lots with the older guardsmen, the companions of lesser rank waited for them at the side of the door. Tayy counted Jumal there, and Mangkut who, with Duwa, had followed Qutula into his service. Their horses lazily cropped the grass at a little distance but, true to their training, did not stray far from their masters.

"Whew!" Bekter exclaimed with a dramatic wiping of his brow. "I wondered how long they would keep us indoors!"

"Too long," Tayy agreed with an answering grin. His guardsmen never pressed him for his secrets and he'd had more than enough of his grandmother's keen eye.

"At last!"

"Here they are!"

Their companions at the door rose noisily from their games to greet the cousins.

"Halloo!" Tayy answered, then sought out his own two hounds and accepted their doggy welcome with a vigorous rub. They had just been pups when he left them and he'd had little enough of their company before that. The Lady Chaiujin had claimed to fear them, though he figured, now, that she was afraid they had scented her demon form as an emerald green bamboo snake. He'd doubted they would remember him, but the red bitch whined and butted her nose against his leg, demanding his attention. The black dog snarled a warning.

Meeting the creature's red-eyed glare with a glower of his own, Qutula took a step back, which satisfied the beast. "Your dog takes affront at my presence," he said, which all of their companions must surely have noticed. "I don't know what I've done to upset him."

Tayy gave the dog a reassuring rub, which settled him a little, though he continued to regard Qutula with the intense interest he generally applied only to his dinner. "We've been away a long time; he's probably forgotten you and thinks you're a stranger." It had been his own fear, after all. "He'll get used to you again."

The dog lapped a slobbery tongue across his cheek and the prince felt the comfort in the gesture settle his troubled heart. With a last ruffling scratch at the thick hair around the dog's throat he rose from this second homecoming with a challenge for his companions: "Why are you sitting around on your haunches when Great Sun is shining and the warm breezes carry the scent of flowers from the river?"

"Waiting for you, Oh leader of warriors." Among the guardsmen at the door, Jumal answered with an exaggerated bow and a mocking pucker of his lips that aped Qutula's disapproval.

"Watch your tongue!" Qutula snapped, "or I'll cut it out for you."

Tayy laid a warning hand on his cousin's arm. "It's just a joke," he said. "I was no less a prince the last time Jumal poked fun at my station than I am today. Why reward him now with more than the usual groans?"

He knew the answer even if he didn't want to admit it. Jumal's status had fallen with his family's fortunes while Qutula's had, indirectly, risen. Though Tayy continued to favor among his followers the friend and partner in the boyish games of childhood, the politics of rank now gave an uneasy precedence to Mergen's blanket-sons.

Jumal might have meant his joke as an insult to Qutula's birth, an offense that would surely lead to murder between them. But if his friend resented the brothers for taking his place at the prince's side, he never showed it. From childhood, however, Jumal had an abrasive sense of humor which seemed a more likely explanation for his joke than some new resentment.

Picking up his follower's tone like the spear exchanged in a game of jidu, therefore, Tayy answered the jape in a similarly exaggerated style. With all the pomp of his station as Prince Tayyichiut of the Qubal people he issued his edict to enjoy the day.

"Wait no longer, minions, for Great Sun will not wait for you!" Consciously, he mimicked the most imperial tones of Chimbai-Khan as he used to do when his father was alive. He thought it might hurt, the memory of old and loving jokes. But his companions laughed as they were meant to do, and he discovered that he could laugh, too. His father was gone, but he hadn't taken the joy of his living with him into the underworld. It remained in the clear eyes of his son and his straight arm with a bow or the spear. And it remained in the old jokes from boyhood when they had all aspired to be their own parent.

Bekter laughed as loud as any, but Qutula's eyes flared briefly in anger. In childhood he had copied his own father's manner, but with Mergen so raised in station and his own rank still in question, such games were forbidden him.

Tired of picking his way through the nettles of his cousin's feelings, Tayy thought that perhaps all games were best left to childhood after all. "Are we going hunting, or are we going to stand around and argue?" he asked in his own voice.

"Hunting!" his companions shouted with as much relief to have the brewing quarrel ended, he thought, as pleasure at the chase.

His horse waited among the others and came when he whistled. "Come, sweet," he murmured in his mount's ear. In moments he was on her back, flying down the grassy avenue. The dogs knew the hunt and leaped away, barking excitedly, but Tayy called on his uncle's lesser guardsmen to hold them fast. He would stalk the wood for game today; dogs would be more hindrance than help.

The black dog snarled and strained to follow, his eyes wild with longing, but the guardsman tightened his hold. With a nod of thanks, Prince Tayy ducked his head down at the side of his horse's neck, urging her forward. His companions followed and soon flanked him protectively, though they made it a race. They left the palace behind quickly.

The khan's city was huge, tens of thousands of round felt tents with all the women and children and the aged, with the sheep in their pens and the horses who wandered at will both out on the plain and among the camps. But the grand avenue was clear ahead of him and soon the ranks of white tents fell away as well. The companions spread out in the lake attack formation; in close order the young hunters turned in a sweeping curve and headed for the forest that bordered the river.

Qutula preferred hunting from horseback on the open plain, but the heir, Prince Tayyichiut, led them in a hell-bent turn back toward the forest that crowded the banks of the Onga. Just as well. The tattoo on his breast warmed and calmed him to his purpose. Today he would hunt the biggest game of all, and win for himself all that he had wished.

When they reached the line of trees, they leaped from their horses. The prince took only his short bow, a quiver of arrows, and the knife at his belt. A bow could throw an arrow farther than an arm could throw a short spear. It would drive the point of the arrow deeper than an arm might guide a short spear. Close in, however, a spear offered more control for a lethal first strike. Qutula would need that advantage against his human prey.

Satisfaction hummed through his body; warm memories of the mystery woman who had come to him in his sleep clung to his skin. If not for the tattoo over his breast, he might have thought her just a dream. But he had asked for a token and refused to question how she had done it with just the prick of her sharp teeth beneath the fragment of jade he wore around his neck. The mark, in the shape of an emerald green bamboo snake, tingled with the promise of new memories to come if he did just this one thing for her. For himself, really.

Not with his own weapon, however. He fumbled with the ties on his quiver until Bekter raised a quizzical eyebrow.

"Are you coming, brother? It's not like you to lag behind when there's game to be had."

"The ties are loose." Qutula had artfully loosened them, and he showed his brother the quiver, where he was tightening them again. "Go on with the others—I'll catch up in a few minutes."

The rest of their party had already entered the wood, leaving the horses to nibble the leaves from the bushes, but Bekter hesitated. "I can wait."

"No, go." Qutula looked up from his work on the strings with an indulgent smile. "Think of it as a head start, the way we raced as children. I'll wager a dozen arrows I will still bring down the first game between us!"

"In that case I'll match your bet with this bow, and take the advantage!" With a last companionable slap on the shoulder, Bekter headed purposefully into the forest, his clumsy efforts at stealth rustling old leaves as he made his way toward the river.

Qutula watched him go. He wasn't worried that Bekter would actually win the bet, but he liked that bow. He didn't think his brother would accept the prince as fair game, but maybe no one would notice Tayy was missing until he had bagged something for the pot and won the bet. It would give greater credence to his own story as well. *If only I had stayed closer to the prince,* he rehearsed in his head, *if not for that stupid bet, I might have saved him.* That would work.

When he was certain that no one would see him, Qutula glided up to a horse not his own. Hushing her with whispers in her ear, he took the spear from the sheath on Jumal's saddle. Jumal's family had suffered reverses in their fortunes in the years since the prince had made his boyhood friendships. No one would stand up to defend him in the khan's court.

It seemed to Qutula that Jumal truly loved Prince Tayy, and not only for the place his friendship had gained him at court. In grief for the terrible loss of his beloved prince, he might take his skinning knife to his own gut, saving them all the effort of accusations and denials. And if he didn't think of it himself, Qutula would be happy to help him along.

A smile lingered on his lips as he followed his fellow guardsmen into the woods, tracking not the buck or doe of his companions, but the huntsman himself. Prince Tayyichiut.

Light, filtered through the highest branches, fell like hangings of gold in the trees. The thick carpet of rotting leaves and pine needles underfoot swallowed the sound of his companions. Tayy wiped a bloom of cold sweat from his forehead and notched an arrow. The last time he'd been alone in a forest, a magician in the shape of a huge bird had sliced his belly open. He'd almost died and some nights the pain of the healed wound still pulled him from his sleep. So did the nightmares.

The magician was dead, however, and the Onga River itself was the most perilous danger lurking in this familiar wood. He had only to stay away from its banks—a rustle of fallen leaves pulled his head around, listening. There it was.

A roebuck, its antlers in full maturity this late in the summer, stepped delicately between the trees almost close enough for him to touch. For a moment he hesitated, thinking of a friend who had traveled in the shape of just such a creature. Only animal intelligence moved behind these eyes, however. He aligned his body with the target and pulled, his bow hand level with his eye.

From the shadows, hidden among the trees, Qutula watched as the prince nocked his arrow. He had grown used to the idea of killing Mergen's heir. The thought of slipping the point of Jumal's spear between the princely ribs gave him only the slightest twinge of doubt. He hesitated, however, to end his cousin's life until after the taking of his prey. He had his father to lead him to the home of his ancestors, of course, and his mother. But it always helped to bring an offering for the spirits with you. Qutula's hand clenched around the shaft of the spear. He would do it—

A rustle in the underbrush signaled the arrival of his companions. Too soon. If he'd acted, he'd have been caught. Grateful to whatever demons or spirits were looking out for him, Qutula turned to hush whoever had come upon them as they would expect him to do—Tayy still had to take his shot.

"Roooaaaar!"

Oh. Not his fellow guardsmen after all. A great black bear reared on his hind legs. Towering over him, the bear stretched his mouth wide to threaten him with sharp teeth long as his fingers.

Time slowed as it does in battle. Qutula felt the beat of his heart pressing the blood through his veins, heard it pounding in his ears. The tattoo on his breast stirred with anticipation. No time to set an arrow; he pulled back and threw the spear he carried, held his breath as it flew through the air and plunged deeply into the flesh of the bear's shoulder.

"Roooaaaaar!" The black bear dropped on all fours, limping, and shook his head. Maddened slobber frothed at the corners of an old purple scar that cut across his muzzle. He charged, and Qutula reached for the knife at his waist, knowing there was no time to draw it, that it wouldn't stop the beast. *He's mad,* he thought, looking into beady eyes red with ancient rage. *I'm going to die.*

An arrow snapped past his shoulder, so close Qutula felt the breath of its passing against his face. It pierced the beast's eye, penetrating deep into his brain. The power of his dumb limbs kept the bear moving a pace, two, until his body finally realized that he was dead. Then he tumbled forward, crashing over on his side no more than a pace away.

I'm alive, Qutula thought. The terror had gone, leaving a melting lassitude in all his limbs. He hadn't died after all.

"Qutula! Are you hurt?" The prince stood at the ready, a second arrow set to fly. But the bear was dead. "Are you all right?"

"I'm fine. He didn't touch me."

His voice sounded distant, disinterested even to his own ears. Jumal and Bekter crashed through the underbrush then and for a moment he allowed himself the foolish hope that Bekter had made the killing shot. But the newcomers were both out of breath and he recognized the fletching on the arrow.

"You saved my life."

" 'Tula? What's wrong with my brother?" Bekter was still gasping for air. Later, there would be pointed questions, but now he accepted the prince's answer, "Shock. He says he's unhurt."

Jumal had followed Bekter. His eyes were more for the creature when he asked, "What happened?"

That's a bear at my feet with the heir's arrow in its eye. It should be pretty damned obvious what happened.

" 'Tula?"

Qutula looked at his brother, but he couldn't quite make sense of what Bekter wanted from him. He'd heard Tayy's answer, however; it seemed easiest just to repeat it. "Unhurt. Yes, of course." He'd rather be dead than owing a life debt to the man he planned to murder. But he couldn't tell Bekter that. As the lethargy of near-death passed off him, he realized it wasn't really true either. Better the prince had been in his place, and Qutula's own shot missed—how unfortunate!—but being alive was always better than being dead.

More of their companions had joined them, Mangkut and Duwa adding their worried questions to Bekter's. Altan, last to arrive, uttered only a muttered curse as he examined the dead beast. Silence descended quickly, however. They seemed to be waiting not just for the obvious explanations but for some outburst of gratitude—effusive thanks, praise for the hunter's keen eye and steady hand. Death had brushed Qutula too closely for manufactured emotions, however, and his real ones were scarcely fit for public display.

When the silence had stretched beyond enduring, Jumal took a step closer to the bear and examined the fletching on the arrow.

"A fine shot, Prince Tayy. And a fine trophy. Look at his face." He pointed to the scar on the creature's muzzle. "He's fought men before and won. He would have killed Qutula, surely."

His laugh edged with the danger averted, Tayy responded with bravado. "Better to face a bear than to suffer the wrath of my uncle if I had lost a guardsman within shouting distance of his own tents." He might have meant any of them gathered there, but they all understood the implication. Mergen would not suffer the loss of his blanket-son easily.

You're wrong, Qutula thought. *That bear's teeth and claws would have freed my father from the troubling presence of a son he has never wanted.* But the fizz in his blood of life or death was calming. He was starting to think more clearly again. He might use this to his advantage.

"My prince." He dropped to one knee in front of his father's heir and bowed his head, though it was a hard thing to do with the imagined weight of the prince's booted foot upon his neck. "I owe you my life. Let me stand between you and your enemies, let my breast be your shield and my arm be your defense."

A ruse, Qutula thought, as the emerald green bamboo snake painted on his skin bit deep. But pain hot as a brand burned straight through his heart.

"You have always been my strong right arm." Tayy blushed, and tugged at his sleeve. "Now get up. We've been friends too long for so much formality."

Qutula blinked the sweat from his eyes, saw guilt trouble the prince's brow. Interesting. He could use the day to his advantage. Qutula would not sully the bond of an anda with a false pledge, but Tayy must surely take him up now as closely as a sworn blood brother. There would be many opportunities to keep his promise, with less risk of discovery. He remained on one knee, therefore, pressing his advantage.

"I would be first at your side," he insisted with a pointed glance at Jumal, who with the rest of their companions had set themselves to the task of butchering the great beast for its hide and meat. "I would offer my own breast to the arrow meant for yours, my throat to the tooth bared at your throat." *To allay suspicion.* The lady was not pleased with him, however. Blood pooled in his vision and he felt a damp trickle from his nose.

Someone squelched a snicker. Qutula had been thinking about the bear, trying to control the pain his lady sent him at his apparent betrayal. He'd forgotten the damned dogs. It wasn't Tayy who had to worry about the bared tooth. He couldn't stand and he was making a laughingstock of himself in the eyes of the prince's followers, and his own. Tayy seemed not to notice, however, only studying with concern the sudden flush that had suffused his features.

I'll explain, he promised the lady. When he thought he had control over his features, he lifted his head to meet the Prince's gaze with a gravely sincere one of his own. "You have bought my life with the force of your arm, and I would be first to repay that service."

Jumal was listening attentively, his skinning knife poised but not moving. "This is my spear," he noted, his voice neutral. "I carved this device in it myself, for luck."

"**W**e needed it," Tayy acknowledged, thinking of the spear itself, but also the luck carved into its shaft. "It delayed the bear's attack until I could steady a killing shot."

A stray question troubled his thoughts, though. Why Jumal's spear, when Qutula had a perfectly good weapon of his own? It seemed petty to remark upon the pilfering of a trifle when that trifle had done as much as the arrow to save his cousin's life, however. Or he thought it had. Qutula was looking decidedly unwell.

"You said you were unhurt!" he accused his cousin as a drop of blood welled from the corner of his eye. Qutula had paled suddenly; Tayy saw him flinch in spite of his effort to hide his weakness.

"You *are* hurt!" Bekter took a solicitous step toward his brother.

"No—"

Qutula toppled over.

" 'Tula!" Bekter fell to his knees, his ear pressed to his brother's chest.

"How is he?" Tayy asked. He should have known sooner. Had known something was wrong, and had dismissed it when he saw no blood. But there was blood now, leaking from Qutula's nose, and from the corners of his eyes. The last time the prince had seen blood like that from a man with no visible wounds, he had died, murdered by the bite of the venomous Lady Chaiujin in demon form, the emerald green bamboo snake.

"He's breathing—" Bekter shook his head. "I can't find a wound on him, but he's burning up with fever. No. Wait. He's coming round—"

"What happened?" Dislodging his brother, Qutula rested a hand over his heart, as if it ached there. His eyes were still cloudy with pain, or the memory of a fading misery.

"I thought for a moment you had died," Tayy answered. He was still shaky, old memories fueling new fears for his cousin.

"I assure you, my lord prince, that I'm not dead. I fainted, that's all, making more of a fool of myself than I had already."

"No fool," Tayy insisted, "but wounded in some way we cannot see. Do you need a litter?"

"I need nothing but my prince's good opinion and the help of my brother's arm to regain my feet," he said.

"Then I'll get out of your way." Tayy stepped aside, making room for Bekter who held out his arm to his brother.

"When you feel better, you'll have to tell me everything," Bekter insisted. "I'll make a song about the hunt. The great Prince Tayyichiut will be the hero, and you will be his strong right arm, just as you say."

Tayy could see the effort he was making to sound normal, just as he saw the worry that creased the round soft face.

"As for the fainting business, it must have been the dying curse of the bear, which is only now releasing you as the bear's spirit departs. You'll have to talk to Mother about a charm to protect you until we're certain the danger has passed, but it'll make a wonderful song."

"Don't be foolish." Qutula brushed off his brother's praise, but Bekter could not be stopped so easily.

"Are you well enough to ride?"

"Well enough, though I may die of shame if you say another

word." He seemed to be feeling more himself. Bekter must have thought so, too, because he did what he was told for a change.

Tayy refused to let it go at that. "Sometimes even heroes need help," he said.

Qutula seemed on the point of making a sharp retort, but then he shrugged a shoulder, dismissing whatever objection he had planned to make. "And sometimes the only hurt is to their pride. I am no hero, though I doubt we can stop Bekter from composing a song in which I have a far greater part than the facts would tell."

"I think you are exactly hero enough." Clasping his cousin's shoulders between his hands, Prince Tayy kissed him first on his right cheek, then on his left. "If it truly would displease you to hear a song in which we appear side by side as legendary heroes, I'll forbid it." He smiled slyly then. "But I think it would please you very much. And it would certainly please Bekter to write it!"

"Then it is decided," Bekter announced. " 'Prince Tayyichiut the brave against the terrible mad bear, with Qutula his strong right arm at his side.' I will build my history around this moment when the fate of the clans hung in the balance!"

When the fate of the clans hung in the balance indeed. Little did Bekter know how truly he spoke. *It will be better this way,* Qutula promised the lady. *No one will suspect a thing when I kill him.*

Her token subsided, waiting, he knew, to inflict pain or pleasure as he did her will or crossed it. Feeling much better, he brushed the leaves from his clothes and offered his prince a false grin.

"I'm sorry that in rescuing me you lost the roebuck you had within your grasp," he said.

"A bear will serve the pots as well," Tayy answered with a laugh.

Jumal had taken up the direction of the skinning, and at the prince's signal he divided the prize according to custom. "Skin to the prince, for the arrow that brought him down," he said.

"Qutula had the first strike, so the meat is divided between them. As for the liver—"

"A gift to my uncle," Tayy was quick to say, adding only after, "in both our names, as is fitting. I might not have stopped him with my arrow if Qutula had not already wounded him with the spear."

"A gift suited to a khan," Qutula agreed, careful to claim no closer relation to his father.

The liver was large as a saddlebag and nearly didn't fit, but Jumal wrapped it tightly in a piece of doeskin for carrying game and bound it with strips of hide used for that purpose. "We'll stay to finish the butchering and carting," he said, and slung the liver over the haunch of Prince Tayyichiut's horse. "Mergen-Khan will want to hear the tale from your own lips."

"One should never keep a khan—or a poet—-waiting," Tayy agreed, summoning Bekter to return to camp with them.

"Jumal, too," Bekter insisted. "It was his spear, in Qutula's hand, and so the khan will want to show his gratitude to Jumal as well."

Qutula would have hit him if they'd been alone. The last person he wanted in his company just then was Jumal. It seemed the guardsmen felt the same. He would have stayed behind with the others of his guard, but Tayy agreed with his cousin.

"Bolghai will want to hear about this design worked into the shaft for luck," he said, "and my uncle will want to thank you for your part in the adventure." He did not say, "For saving the life of his son," but the unspoken meaning hung in the air like the clinging golden sunlight.

"Of course," Qutula agreed, though it pained him almost as much as the lady's mark to say it. "If I have to suffer the outrage of my brother's song-making, then so should he who carved the spear!"

They all laughed at his mocking display of indignation, which gave Jumal no choice but to join them, leaving the bear in the hands of their lesser companions. When they sorted themselves out for the return to camp, Jumal rode at Bekter's left, as far from Qutula on Tayy's right as he could be. And somehow, Duwa had joined the company with a watchful eye on Jumal as they rode.

Chapter Five

AS THEY MADE THEIR WAY home to the great tent city, Duwa and Jumal regarded each other with suspicion across the backs of their champions. Each had mistrusted the other since some childhood prank—Tayy couldn't remember what had happened—which had set them eternally at odds. They usually put their differences aside for the more important task of defending their prince as his guardsmen. The division of the recent prize, however, seemed to have added chips to the flame of their animosity.

"I'd have thought fighting a war together would have . . ." Tayy started to say to his cousin. But Qutula, who had lately escaped a bloody death at the jaws of the maddened bear, had fallen into a brooding silence that the prince recognized only too well. Like the two quarreling guardsmen, they had been to war together in the Golden City. Fighting hand to hand in the squares and down streets both wide and narrow, they'd had to worry about an arrow in the back or a monster swooping down on them from the air.

On the battlefield, memories of the tent city of the Qubal Khan must have filled Qutula with a sense of safety and warmth just as it had Tayy. Neither of them had expected to find his life hanging in the balance on their own ground. The realization that they would find no safety even here at home heightened battle nerves more happily left behind. The prince took a breath to say some word of sympathy, but his cousin's brooding, closed-in silence rejected any comfort before it could be spoken.

They were passing through the outskirts of the tent city. Qutula's hooded gaze ranged over the camps, smaller and more widely scattered here than they were closer to the ger-tent palace of the khan. Tayy did the same, saw the gaps and absences of a city eroding at its edges as clans with no particular wealth or political connections packed their tents. They would follow the horses grazing afield on the rich grasslands that rolled away from the river in a sea of green and wildflower blue. Soon there would be nothing left but the political center around the khan, and his army of young fighters.

Against these lowering thoughts, only Bekter seemed to have an antidote. He held his bow in the position of a lute and muttered nonsense words under his breath while he fingered imaginary strings, working out a tune. He'd want the story out of his brother before Great Sun set, Tayy suspected; they might have the first performance after the feasting.

"So," he said, directing his comments to Bekter, but speaking loud enough for all his companions to hear. "Do you think our bear is bigger than the one Nogai presented to the khan on his wedding night?"

Qutula looked at him strangely, but Bekter had perked up at the reference to the old story. As Tayy had hoped, he recited the first exaggerated description of the bear that Nogai killed.

> *"Old Brown raised up on his feet*
> *Twice taller than the center pole*
> *On which the silver palace stood,*
> *In girth, wider than the lattices around."*

Songs often called the ger-tent of the khan "the silver palace" for the glittering silver embroideries that covered the white felt. Tayy would have had the recitation end there, with the bear, but Jumal, with his usual absence of tact, picked up the tale where Nogai entered it.

"The khan called Nogai to his side
His eyes aglisten with the dew of tears.
'All I have is yours, good friend, but
find for me what I have lost.' "

"Our own tale reversed!" he said, pleased that he had made the connection. In the tale, the bear had stolen the khan's new bride. Nogai had caught up with the bear and in a savage battle killed it. At the end of the tale he presents his khan with the huge bearskin, in which he has wrapped the rescued bride. "Instead of the friend saving the heir, the heir has saved the friend!"

Qutula glared murderously at his fellow guardsman and Tayy groaned under his breath. He'd have been annoyed enough if Jumal had compared him to the khan's wife. But Jumal meant what happened next. Nine months after her return, the bride had produced a son and heir for the khan, thus Nogai had saved not only the bride, but the heir as well. The Nogai cycle didn't end there, of course. The heir, it turned out, was the true offspring of the bear. When he reached the age of manhood, the bear-boy wreaked vengeance on the Qubal people for the death of his father. Finally Nogai met with him in a great battle fought on the banks of the Onga, where both had died of their wounds.

But that came much later. The story of Nogai's bear was a favorite of childhood and only the coincidental symmetry of their ranks would have brought the end of the cycle to mind at all.

Fortunately, Bekter had his mind on his own version of the song. "Our Prince Tayy killed a smaller bear, of course," he mused, though it went without saying.

"Ah, but consider this," Tayy argued his case, glad to be back on the trail he had meant them to follow from his first mention of Nogai's bear. "Tales always grow in the telling, right? So the bears in them must also grow. How big do you think this bear of ours will grow by the time we are old men?"

Bekter needed only a moment to consider. "Very large," he agreed with a grin. "I think I can guarantee that it will become a very tower among bears."

The clans did not build towers, of course. Cities that stayed in one place had once amazed the prince. In their travels to the Cloud Country, however, the army of the khan had seen great walls and towers built of stone or mud or wood that stood much longer than the life of a man, even a king. So they laughed, as they were meant to do, at the notion of a bear as tall as the great Temple of the Moon at the heart of the Golden City.

"And did I bring down the beast alone with my simple bow? Or did a valiant guardsman come to my aid with a spear carved with a charm for good fortune?" Tayy teased both cousins with the question.

Bekter picked up his tone, fluttering his fingers across the bent bow, mimicking their travel along the strings of his lute. "The young prince will win the day since that is the true history. And, of course, a singer at court always knows where his pies are coming from. Though the friend and guardsman must get in his blows, since brothers are closer than cousins."

"And the rest of his companions? Do they appear as the villains in the piece, or the comic relief?" Jumal rolled his eyes and let his tongue loll out of the corner of his mouth in answer to his own mocking questions.

"They could be led astray by mischievous spirits," Bekter thought out loud. Tayy was relieved that he had taken up his prince's cause to draw his companions out of their dark moods with frivolity. In that vein he offered another end to their tale: "But is it not true that the companions had spread out in the woods, hunting prey and also alert to every danger? Good fortune made the prince a hero, but who would not have bagged the same shaggy prey in his position?"

"Not I," Jumal cast a dark and complex look at the cousin who now rode in his place at Tayy's side. "Qutula had my spear."

"I thought I might need one but discovered a flaw in the shaft of my own. I meant to return it to you, or replace it if it took damage."

"And a good thing you did," Bekter asserted with fervor. Tayy thought he meant because it had helped to save his life, but in the true spirit of a singer, Bekter explained, "It gives me a way to add Jumal as another character in the tale."

"The fool who left his weapon behind?"

They passed through the palisade of carts that marked the boundary of the tent city. As they entered the broad avenue that led to the palace of the khan, Bekter waved his hand to dismiss Jumal's contribution. "That will never work. We must have only heroes in this tale. I think you gave the brave companion Qutula your spear, to replace his damaged one as a token of your regard. And so you are implicated with the prince in saving his life as well."

Jumal seemed on the point of objecting to this version of the tale, which caused Tayy to wonder himself at the histories he had taken for truth all his life. Not the giant bear, of course. Even as a boy he had recognized the rich embroidery of a poet's imagination, but he wondered now what less miraculous truth like his own hid behind the singer's art.

Riding between the round white tents of the city, however, his companions had taken up the decoration of the afternoon with elaborations of their own exploits at the hunt. His objections lost in the laughing contributions of his fellows, Jumal accepted that he would have no say in the part he would play in the coming epic. Which was exactly what Tayy wanted. He laughed with the others, adding his own variant: "Where is the maiden in the tale? How can we have a hero without a maiden?"

Qutula paled alarmingly at the suggestion, but Tayy spread his arm wide to express his generosity when he said, "I will gladly cede my place in the tale to a princess. Perhaps the warrior queen of Pontus may rescue the embattled warrior? Even Qutula could have no objection to such a womanly rescue!"

They had all seen the warrior queen and her women's army in battle, and agreed that she made a more comely heroine than the prince, "Though as likely to skin the brave companion as the bear," Bekter pointed out, which made them all laugh the harder.

"A gentler maiden, then," Jumal suggested, to which Tayy

made one change: "Then she must take your place, good friend, and offer up the charmed spear to the gallant youth."

Jumal flashed his eyelashes, ever the fool for a joke, and Tayy added his own jeering to that of his companions.

Then he saw the girl, conjured, it seemed, by their discussion.

There was nothing outwardly noteworthy about her, he would later admit. Pretty, but in a self-contained way, with none of the obvious allure that Sechule seemed to hold for her suitors. The girl stood with a broom in her hand in the doorway of a tent with ravens embroidered on the flap that closed over the smoke hole. He didn't know why the broom seemed so important—he'd seen enough of them in the hands of slaves and servants. But raven feathers decorated the doorway of the tent the way pelts of stoats hung from Bolghai's burrow. Brooms hung from Bolghai's roof as well. Tayy's friend Llesho, who had turned out to be a mortal god, had danced with a broom to find his totem form. So he wondered if the broom in the hands of the girl had magical properties, too.

She met his gaze, her dark, thoughtful eyes taking his measure, though he couldn't tell what judgment she made about him. She wore the simple dress and hair ornaments of a maiden, but she didn't giggle or hide her face or disappear inside the tent as most girls would do. She didn't call out to him or smile either. Tayy felt turned inside out, with all his guts exposed to view. His thoughts from the deepest to the most frivolous, his feelings from the meanest to the most exalted were suddenly there on the surface for the girl to examine and to judge.

If he'd had a place to hide, he might have done so—except that for some reason he didn't mind the intrusion of her gaze as he might anyone else who looked at him that way. Anyone but Lady Bortu. His grandmother had the same way of reading him to the ground with her glance. He didn't get this funny feeling in the pit of his stomach when Lady Bortu did it, though.

Look your fill, he told the girl with his own gaze. "Scars are the measure of a king."

"Excuse me, my prince. I didn't hear." Qutula asked, polite

attention on his face, while a little behind them, their companions watched expectantly for his answer.

"Nothing—" He must have spoken aloud without realizing. "Nothing, just a riddle my father used to tell. 'Scars are the measure of a king.' "

Chimbai-Khan had laughed at the wounds he took in battle, giving the riddle as his reason. Tayy had thought he meant that a khan was spared the pain of his injuries. Bruised from weapons practice and combat games, he had longed for the day he became khan so that he could laugh at painless cuts as well. Since then, war and death had taught him otherwise. No wound came without its cost. Scars marked not the wounding of a king, but his ability to heal himself, and with it, his people.

Fighting beside Llesho, the god-king, he had grown to understand more about what it meant to rule. People need their gods and shamans, their peaceful lives. But someone had to protect them from the evil of the world, even it if cost him some scars. He figured he'd be good at that now, good at being their khan.

"I was thinking of my father, and hoping that the way I carry my own wounds speaks well of me."

Qutula looked at him strangely and he gave a little shrug, as if to let the words slide off his shoulders. "I hadn't meant to say it out loud."

His cousin's answer, when it came—"All who follow you are honored to serve you"— felt like a line recited from a hero's tale. Tayy ducked his head, feeling foolish. No one but himself cared about his old war wounds. The girl couldn't know about his scars anyway.

Her eyes were very dark and very large, he noticed. She held his gaze while the pink tip of her tongue reached out and delicately touched the corner of her rich, full lip before disappearing again. He didn't know what that revealed of her thoughts about him, but he had a suspicion that he ought to.

Who are you? he wondered. *What clan? What name?*

He dared not stop to ask. Her tent was small, not even two lattices and so far from the palace, indicating a family of low station. He didn't want his companions to mistake his curiosity for interest. Qutula, he thought, might have noticed something, but his cousin made no comment. Tayy was relieved. They moved on and soon the mysterious girl had passed out of sight behind them.

The laughter had died in the strange moment before the raven tent, but the companions resumed their boasting as they neared the center of the camp. Challenges were accepted for wrestling matches and, if they noticed that he didn't join in the merriment, they were discreet and did not remark on it. Left to his own thoughts, the prince considered the wagons heading away from the outskirts of the city. The passage of the peaceful folk meant nothing to the fighters who would stay at the right hand of the khan wherever he raised his tents. But Prince Tayy wondered how he could impel the family of the girl to stay until he had learned more about her. For the sake of curiosity, of course. He did not consider that he might fall in love until his uncle supplied him with a wife.

Mergen picked at the blood itching under his fingernails. The hunt had gone well. For a few hours he had forgotten all about the decisions waiting for him in the ger-tent palace where he served as an uneasy place keeper for his brother's son. The khan understood the value of war, had fought it well enough as a strategist and with the force of his own arm. Stretching out over the neck of his horse, following the baying of the dogs in pursuit of a fleet-footed stag or a wild ram, however, he felt his connections to the earth and the sky and the people of the Qubal clans more keenly than he ever had on the battlefield.

The moment reminded him of what he was beneath his coats, at heart and soul. A man of the grasslands. Harnish, the Tashek mystics named them, for the wind that passed over the grass, never resting. The wind. That's what he was. The wind.

Even an afternoon in summer must end, however. Returning to the tent city with their prey securely tied on the back of

a horse, Mergen joined his companions in their jokes and boasting.

"You have cut short that ram's lazy reign over his harem of
ewes," Mergen praised the skill of his friend Yesugei. "You
must insist that the cooks honor the virility of beast and hunter
with their best recipes."

"Perhaps he can help me with my own harem," Yesugei
agreed. None but the khan knew how deeply from the heart the
general's answering joke had come. Yesugei pined to add
Sechule to his household. She rebuffed him, setting her aim
above him, on the khanate Mergen could not, in conscience,
give her. Like all the rest, however, he passed it off as rueful
boasting to enflame the scandalous jesting insults of their companions.

"Better the one end than the other," someone joked from the
back, and another, "Better the horns of a ram than the egg of a
cuckoo!" This was an old riddle, which could lead to a murderous fight if a man's sons strayed too far from the look of his
own face. But this time they all laughed, knowing it for a harmless joke. If the general had no harem, at least Yesugei's wife
was faithful as Great Moon herself. All his sons and his one
daughter took after their father.

With no cause for insult in his own tent, at least, Yesugei
shifted the boasting attention onto his khan. "If there is a point
to this conversation," he asserted with mock indignation, "then
it is dangling off the head of that fine stag you have yourself
caught."

Their party joined in laughing agreement, slapping the
sides of their horses in goodwill.

"A lover for every branch," they agreed. The many points to
the antlers of the stag must surely indicate something about the
pointed manliness of the hunter who bagged him, after all. "But
a bit hesitant to commit his shot."

Mergen had, in fact, hesitated to let his arrow go. He shuddered a little at the memory of wonders he had seen in the war.
Even a khan had to consider, as he set the arrow, if he aimed at
fair game or a neighbor visiting in his totem form. But the joke

referred more to his lack of a wife. As his brother the khan had wished of him, he did, indeed, enjoy the welcome of many lovers among the clans without bestowing his tents on any one, or two of them.

Beside him, Yesugei said something. He didn't catch it all, but recognized the tag line of another ribald riddle with, perhaps, a knife edge glittering in the folds of its meaning—if he wished to hear it so. With the others of his own generation of guardsmen and counselors around him, however, he chose not to see the nettles among the clover and laughed his raucous appreciation of the jest.

The day, he decided, was perfect. Warm, though, and the hunt was warm work. Sweat beaded on his forehead, and without thinking he wiped at it with the back of his hand. An uneasy silence fell suddenly over his companions. He didn't need to ask what troubled them; he felt the bloody mark smeared across his forehead.

"It's nothing. Wipe your face." Yesugei handed him a scarf and reached to take it back when he had wiped the red streak from his brow.

My tether line, Mergen-Khan thought of his general, who accepted the wonders he had seen without letting them trouble his world. Since Otchigin had died, and then Chimbai-Khan, Mergen had had no friend as sure, no counselor as honest as the chieftain Yesugei. Blood was just blood. Men got it on themselves when hunting. It meant nothing, certainly pointed to no guilt on his part. He'd loved his brother and had no desire for his position.

They all knew that Chimbai-Khan had died of a snake's venomous bite. Fewer knew the snake for Chimbai's second wife, the emerald green bamboo snake demon, but no part of the tale laid any blame on Mergen. Still, he would not return the soiled scarf but tucked it into his own clothes rather than deflect the omen onto his general.

"Isn't that the young Prince Tayyichiut?" One of his guardsmen pointed toward a minor tent as they came onto the wide avenue leading to the ger-tent palace gleaming in the distance.

"The heir has turned to hunting rabbit," Mergen's guardsman pointed out in jest.

With his attention drawn to the modest tent decorated in the raven totem, the khan saw where his heir's hunt had taken him. Prince Tayyichiut had slowed his horse, his eyes fixed on a girl. She had high cheekbones and a mouth a bit too wide, but her solemn dark eyes seemed lit with complex inner life. Long, straight hair fell thick as a horse's tail from her maiden's combs. As he passed with his companions around him, the young prince couldn't take his eyes off her. For her part, she seemed equally fascinated by the sudden appearance of a prince at her door.

"Not rabbit, I think, but larger game," Yesugei amended. He might have meant the doeskin packet strapped to the packhorse. But Mergen, like his hunting party, understood him to mean the girl, and that perhaps the arrow went both ways. The prince seemed spellbound.

Mergen recognized the look. He'd had the same for Sechule in his time, and Yesugei himself often sported it in her presence now. Unfortunately, he also recognized the girl. But what was she doing here, in a shaman's tent so close to the grand avenue leading to the palace? Had her fosterers lost their senses? And why, of all the girls in the camp, did Tayy have that look on his face for this one?

"No lady," a guardsman sniffed with a nudge of his chin at her bare feet. "But she'll do for practice."

A vein throbbed at Mergen's temples as he turned his wrath on the man. He'd spent years hiding the very existence of the girl, but in his temper his hand went to the sword at his side. He would separate the man's head from his body with one stroke and worry about explanations later.

"Not if he has any sense." Another of his guardsmen spoke up. Chahar, one of Bolghai's many sons. Some had followed their father's path and others had chosen the army. One brother had died with Otchigin, fighting stone monsters in the war for the Cloud Country. But they had all grown up wandering in and out of their father's burrowlike tent. Chahar wasn't looking at

Mergen or the sword half drawn from its sheath, but at the broom in the girl's hand.

"That broom has seen little enough of sweeping, and she's holding it wrong way up for earthly chores. She's a shaman, or practicing to be one, with the raven-lady, Toragana, I would guess. If the boy has any sense, he'll wait at least until she can control her spells before approaching her with any suggestion he may want to make."

"I'd have thought the young prince had seen enough wonders in his short life," Yesugei mused. "I'm sure he has no more than a passing curiosity about her, but I'll put a word in Qutula's ear if you wish, my khan. Sometimes young men will listen to each other before they will take the advice of their elders."

Alone of Mergen's companions, Yesugei knew the identity of the girl and the khan's plans for her. Mergen wondered, however, if he only pretended to surprise at the shaman business.

"I'll talk to Qutula." It was time, Mergen thought, to start demonstrating to the court his faith in his sons. Bekter was a poet and the favorite of all, so his place in the palace was already secured. The khan's appreciation of Qutula's more subtle mind must be carefully introduced, however. He wanted to raise no fear among the clans that he planned to establish his own dynasty on Sechule's blanket-sons.

"And I'll make my feelings clear to the prince myself. He may find his way under whatever blanket he wishes as long as he makes his connections for the clans." Mergen had no intention of letting Prince Tayy develop any sort of acquaintance with that particular girl, but he would reveal nothing on that score yet. Soon, though. First, he had to put an end to this shaman nonsense.

The prince led his followers racing the night toward home in a cloud of dust kicked up by their horses' flying hooves. Mergen slowed his own party to a walk so they didn't have to make their greetings in front of all the clans. Mergen let his companions think the fading of the light had put him in a pensive mood. His courtiers knew his temper well enough to cease their joking. Content to raise themselves a little higher in their saddles, they urged their horses to a swaggering gait past rows of round white tents. Yesugei, however, watched him with a sharp eye that didn't escape Mergen's notice.

He was pretty sure that plain dumb luck had brought the prince and the girl together. But the shaman business had to stop. She'd be no use to him at all with a rattle and a drum in her hand.

Chapter Six

"ELUNEKE! COME AWAY FROM the door!" Toragana's high, sharp voice called from inside the tent.

"Coming!" Eluneke answered. Her teacher expected prompt obedience, but still she lingered on the doorsill, watching the bold young lords as they galloped up the wide avenue.

"What is it, girl?" They had no customers that afternoon, so Toragana had come to the door in her everyday coats with a wide apron covering everything from shoulders to ankles. She set a motherly hand on Eluneke's shoulder and craned her neck to discover what her protégée found so interesting. "What did you see?"

Eluneke wanted to answer truthfully, but the truths that vied for release on her tongue confused her. "A dead man," she said, though the same voice said to her heart: "My husband."

"Did you recognize him?" Toragana asked. "Only the sky knows what uneasy spirits have followed the armies down from the mountains. Does Chimbai-Khan himself wander among his tents? Bolghai did what he could, but I have never been satisfied that the khan's soul rested easy. He had unfinished business with the lady who murdered him."

The questions didn't surprise Eluneke. Shaman, who stood guard at the gate to the underworld, regularly talked with the dead. When Eluneke's fosterers had apprenticed her to Tora-

gana, she had already begun to receive such visitations. Her answer was more problematic, however.

"I never saw him before."

Toragana narrowed her eyes and peered down the avenue.
"Was it a hunting accident?"

The boy, she meant. Eluneke shook her head. "I think it will
be murder."

"Will be. And murder, no less. Oh, my. I wonder who it
could be?" The shaman tugged at her sleeve, drawing Eluneke
into the tent they shared as student and teacher.

"I've been able to see the spirits of the dead since I was little," Eluneke objected. She didn't understand Toragana's urgency over this boy—she hadn't even told her the husband part
yet.

"I know, I know." Toragana patted her hand and began to
pace. "The spirits pay a great deal less attention to the niceties
of past and future than the living do," she explained, thinking
it through for herself at the same time. "Still, it's very unusual
for an apprentice who hasn't found her totem yet to have such
sensitivity to the dead, let alone the not-dead-yet. Let me
think."

She circled the firebox at the center of the little tent as she
spoke. Past the little stool by the door for customers and patients she went, between the workbench filled with her herbs
and elixirs and the chest where she stored the ingredients for
the mixable potions. She paced quickly by the furs for their
beds stacked at the far end of the tent, around the firebox to the
door on the far side. Her robes swung on their pegs as she swept
by them, around another set of chests where she kept the things
they used for tea and their stores of flour and honey and sheep
fat for special occasions.

Eluneke thought her teacher was going to trip over the thick
pillows scattered for sitting on the carpeted floor, but she somehow managed to avoid them—and the brooms hanging from the
lattices on strings of sinew—without looking up from her
frowning concentration. As her thoughts grew more troubled,
however, Toragana circled more quickly. The little mirrors
hanging from the spokes of the round ceiling to keep away evil

spirits swung wildly in her wake, and Eluneke thought she could see the old carpets growing thinner with each pass.

Just as she thought her teacher would turn into her totem animal and fly away through the smoke hole, Toragana stopped. "Stay here," she said. "Don't go anywhere. If anyone comes for a prayer or a talisman, tell them I'll be back later. Dispense medicines if you feel confident to do so. The others can come back tomorrow."

While she gave her usual instructions, Toragana flitted about the neat little tent no more slowly than she had a moment before, but with a great deal more purpose. Hanging her apron on a peg, she put on her shaman's robe of doeskin with many cuts in it, sewn everywhere with the feathers of her totem animal, the raven. She put on her shamanic cap of feathers crowned by a stuffed raven whose keen dead eyes pierced the gloom between the worlds.

"I want to ask Bolghai's opinion, but I'll be back before Great Moon rises," she said. "In the meantime, say nothing of what you have seen to anyone. Speaking with the dead is one thing, but predicting death is quite another. Some do it, of course, but no one ever speaks of it, you understand."

"Of course!" Eluneke couldn't hide her indignation. She wouldn't have told her own teacher except that the words seemed to pop out of her mouth of their own will.

"I know. You've always been a good girl." Toragana absently patted her cheek and reached for her drum and the drumstick she had carved from the shin of a sheep. Then she hurried away with long swooping motions to signify the flight of her totem raven.

"I won't tell anyone," Eluneke whispered after her. She went back to the work of becoming acquainted with her broom but could not put out of her mind the image of the death's-head she had seen riding a skeletal horse among his laughing companions.

Her husband. That was the second part of her vision. The dead rider would someday be her husband. She had kept that part to herself. It might, after all, be a trick of mischievous spirits having sport at her expense. She didn't want to look like a fool for listening to them.

Resting her cheek on her hands, which were wrapped around her broom, she thought about the husband that fate— perhaps—had given her. He was very handsome, she decided, or the smooth bronze face that had hovered like a mask over the death's head had seemed so. She wondered who he was. He had ridden like a warrior and had shown no sign of leaving the great avenue among the lesser clans, so he must at least be rich. Probably returned from the wars as well, and a hero of some sort. That didn't mean he had good sense, certainly, which she would wish in a husband. His impending doom seemed even to cast doubt on his judgment. Her own low station didn't trouble her, but Eluneke insisted on intelligence in a husband.

With a sigh she dismissed all thought of the mysterious young huntsman. A girl could change her fate if she was determined. But as prophetic visions went, this one seemed particularly unlikely in all the wrong places. Perhaps the spirits of the underworld were trying to bribe her for her help in keeping him alive.

"It's completely unnecessary," she said out loud in case any of the spirits were listening. "I would save him for the sake of his family and his clans even if he had no money at all. Empty promises just annoy me."

Alone with her thoughts, she set her broom aside and grabbed a polishing rag. On Toragana's workbench stood a chest with designs inlaid in contrasting shades of wood. Eluneke opened the small hinged doors, took out the first nest of feathers in which the shamaness kept her silver charms and amulets. They had begun to tarnish, and she set her rag to work with fervent energy. This one, shaped like a wreath, she knew to foster a good marriage. Aunts bought them, and grandmothers. The supply was running low; war, it seemed, set the old heads to thoughts of ensuring their family line.

Another, in a shape that made her blush, was meant to ensure a couple's happiness. She understood in theory, but had

never experienced that particular form of happiness herself.
That thought led to the next, a dead husband laughing among
his companions, fresh from the hunt. What had she seen in him
when their eyes met? Other than his fleshless skeleton riding a
nightmare horse of bones, of course? Toragana would find out,
but in the meantime Eluneke put the silver charms away and
took down the next feathered nest. Bits of bone, carved in the
shapes of animals. Her teacher would make one for her spe-
cially when she found her totem animal.

In the last nest Toragana kept her hexes and bad luck
charms. She didn't sell them, but said that a good shaman had
to know them anyway. "You cannot cure what you do not recognize," she had explained, taking out with care the tiny silver
ram's horn, and the dagger no bigger than the moon of a child's
smallest fingernail. That one troubled her. The victim of the
hex would cut himself fatally, with his own knife, under the
strongest hex. It would look like an accident or suicide. No one
would suspect murder.

Eluneke put away the hexes and set the case back in its
place on the workbench. She had already learned how to defend against each of the spells in Toragana's box. She could sew
up a wound and she knew how to stop bleeding with spider-
webs, and what molds to press against a cut to prevent the
hard, red swelling that often meant death. To keep her husband
alive, however, she would have to be there when he died.

But what would she do if his enemies didn't use a knife or
a sword? Those counted highest in the eyes of their rivals had
a way of dying by poison. Their own Chimbai-Khan, it was
whispered, had died just so. It seemed a likely place to sharpen
her skills. Toragana had many antidotes on her shelves for accidental poisonings, and the ingredients for more, but their
own small clan lay far out of the eye of politics. Deliberate poisonings, meant to do murder and leave no sign of their presence, didn't come up much.

Bolghai, whose tent lay on the path traveled by gods and
khans, must know about such things, however. She would ask
Toragana to petition him to teach her the arcane knowledge
they would need to keep the handsome young man alive.

As if tracking the movement of her student's thoughts, Toragana popped her head back in through the doorway by which she had lately exited. "Best you should explain it yourself," she said, and waved Eluneke forward.

"Bolghai will doubtless get more out of you than I can." She grinned, twitching her head in a birdlike way, to take the sting out of her words. "He always had more success with me than I would have wished."

That she needed to see Bolghai anyway didn't ease the sour churning in Eluneke's stomach. She put on her coat and started to follow.

"Don't forget your broom!"

As if Toragana would let her forget! What humiliation! With her face flaming red, Eluneke picked up the wretched broom and brought it with her. Somehow this bundle of sticks was supposed to reveal the true totem shape of her traveling spirit. So far it had revealed a quantity of splinters but little else. Sometimes it was no more than an inconvenience. At other times it served as a reminder of her failure to find her true form and she hated it with a passion so great her heart could scarcely contain it. Now was one of those times. Not only would her own clan know that she had not yet learned to fly, but she was about to parade her failure before all the clans of the khan's great ulus, into the heart of the very court itself. What would the khan's own shaman think of an apprentice who had not yet lost the companionship of her broom?

With a sigh, she picked it up with a loathing she was certain the broom shared for her and followed Toragana.

Eluneke knew the reputation of the khan's shaman, so she'd expected the long walk to the little ger-tent off a way from the main camp, close to where the Onga flowed. Bolghai's totem animal was the stoat, so it came as no surprise that his felt tent lay half buried like the burrow of the creature whose coats he wore. She hadn't imagined the smell, though, or the disarray. Her teacher's teacher needed someone to keep house for him.

"Come in! Come in!" Bobbing his head in stoat fashion, Bolghai welcomed them into the little tent. Right away Eluneke noticed the heads of small animals in various states of fleshly decay crowding the tops of the chests. Their skins lined the floor and the walls, making a snug burrow for the shaman. A bit too snug for Eluneke's taste. She preferred the clean order of Toragana's more aerie home, and the sweeter smell. Toragana cured her birds carefully before using them to adorn her costume or her tent, something Bolghai might do better himself.

Still, some things were more usual—a pair of painted chests and a firebox over which he cooked water for tea—and other things Eluneke had grown to expect living in the house of a shaman. Mirrors hung from the lattices of Bolghai's tent to chase away evil spirits just as they did in Toragana's home. Musical instruments lay scattered between the painted chests. Instead of hanging neatly on pegs, Bolghai hung his brooms in profusion from the umbrellalike spokes of the roof, tucked in among the drying herbs.

Brooms. Eluneke ducked her head to avoid them. She'd be happy never to see a broom again in her life. Just to annoy her, one of the things reached with its spindly fingers and grabbed the hair wrapped around the silver combs of her maiden's headdress.

"That's very interesting." Bolghai's stoatlike nose twitched beneath his bright, observant eyes as Toragana patiently untangled Eluneke's hair. "When a broom chooses, what secrets does it reveal?"

Eluneke didn't know what the riddle meant, but Toragana seemed to have more of the story. "Is it the very broom?" she asked.

Bolghai nodded. "A visiting prince when he danced, later a god. Who can say what transformations a broom portends?"

"Well, I'm not a god," Eluneke protested tartly. There were times the whole shaman business seemed too odd even for someone who regularly spoke to spirits. Healing people made her feel good inside, and she'd gotten used to talking to the dead long before Toragana had come for her. But this broom business was beyond embarrassing.

Bolghai looked at her carefully, recognition moving in his eyes. "Two steps in one," he said.

"Greet the dirt," Eluneke answered. She knew what the riddle meant. If you lifted both feet at once, your face would soon be doing their duty on the ground. But it also served as a warning not to reach higher than your station.

In the case her teachers discussed, the student might have seemed to take two steps at once, from prince to king, and then to mortal god. But he had come to Bolghai as an uncrowned king in exile and only slowly accepted his true station. Gradually his rank as a god was revealed to him. Bolghai hinted the broom announced a similar fate for her, but she had no rank of her own. Perhaps it meant her husband's rank. But he was going to die, probably before they ever truly met, which made the prophetic nature of her vision false in one particular or the other.

It was confusing, and she took a breath to tell the teacher as much. Bolghai held up his hand to stop her, however.

"Tea," he said, sweeping the skulls from one of the chests and rummaging through it for a cloth bag that rustled with dried leaves. "More will come clear when you dance with the broom that chose you."

"But . . ."

"First things first. Who are you, when the animal spirit takes hold? Only your totem creature can take you where you must go for your answers."

She needed her totem spirit to carry her to the underworld, he meant, but he didn't yet have all the facts. Talking to the spirits of the dead could be of no help—the young man hadn't died yet. She would have explained all that to him except that he had turned away again, busying himself with the tea. He only poured two cups.

"You have been asked to dance," he told her with a wave of his hand. "It's time you listened to the whisper of the sticks. We will talk when you can fly."

Eluneke took the broom in a huff of temper. At least it would get her out of his noisome tent. The shaman's camp stood a little apart from the city of the khan, protected by the undergrowth and spindly trees that grew along the river. No one would see her dancing with a stupid broom.

Temper set a more forceful pace than she might otherwise have chosen. Her feet beat out the rhythm and she began to dance.

Chapter Seven

WITH A BOW TO THE LADY BORTU, Mergen settled himself on the dais. Looking around the great ger-tent palace, he nodded to a face he knew. Already there were fewer senior chieftains in their places above the firebox. The clans were departing, leaving him his tithe of young men for the army but taking away their wives and daughters and herdsmen, heading back to their everyday lives. Yesugei remained, however, offering his support as adviser to the khan while he stalked Sechule for his second wife. Mergen would have been happier about the one if not for the other.

Tonight, however, he had more pressing matters on his mind. Leaving the general to wander among the courtiers, following the sign of Sechule's passing—her dark hair, and the smell of the herbs she used in her clothes—Mergen turned to his mother with a question on his lips. "Have you seen Bolghai?" His glance roved everywhere in the great ger-tent palace, searching for the shaman in the thinning crowd of courtiers.

"Not today," the lady answered, making room beside her on the heaped furs. Beads of turquoise and coral clacked and rattled on her towering headdress as she returned his seated bow. "Are you ill? Cursed? In need of counsel from the underworld?"

With Bortu, you never knew if she was being serious or secretly laughing at you behind her hand. Chimbai-Khan had never had that problem with her, of course. But Chimbai-Khan had been her first choice as khan. They were alone on the dais now, however. Though she didn't seem exactly serious about the reasons he might want the shaman, he detected a glint of interest—his mother would never show concern—in her eagle-like gaze.

"That fool girl has gone and apprenticed herself to some woman on the outskirts of the camp. Bolghai has to put a stop to it!" He told her the truth. If he couldn't find the shaman, he might need his mother's advice.

"And which fool girl would that be?" she prodded, knowing very well but wanting him to say it. Sechule wasn't the only woman among the clans who had borne him a child.

"Eluneke." He had thought that fostering the girl with a distant family of small holdings and few political aspirations would protect him from those wishing to reach Chimbai-Khan through Mergen's offspring. He hadn't anticipated this.

"Ah. That one." Lady Bortu twitched a shoulder in a gesture that someone watching from the floor might take as adjusting the embroidered cuffs of her blue silk coat. Mergen knew better. "She was a pretty little thing," Bortu mused. "But her mother was nothing special, as I recall, and her people haven't been heard from since disease took their horses. How long has that been? Long enough to have come to our attention if they had any grit at all. I thought you had abandoned her."

"So I wanted it to seem, if anyone discovered her parentage. Her foster family knew better than to allow a poor boy to court her. I gave her no dowry or presents to make certain she would have no suitors from among the better-placed clans. Why they gave her to a shaman escapes my understanding completely."

"It would seem your ruse worked too well. If I'd known you still had an interest, I would have kept my eye open for a likely match. And her foster family might have been more inclined to keep her when her mother died." Which all sounded perfectly innocent, except that Bortu seemed to know an awful lot about a girl in whom she claimed no interest.

Servants were approaching with heavily laden trays. The

delicious smells reminded him of how ravenous he was, but he motioned them away. More important to finish this, now, with his mother.

"Did you know about the shaman business?" he asked her. "Was it your doing?"

"I thought you were the clever son. Don't be a fool if you can help it." Lady Bortu sniffed with a flair of nostrils to show her disdain for his questions. She didn't deny his charge, however.

"But you knew."

"It didn't seem to matter." Gnarled old hands still moved gracefully in a dismissive gesture, just her fingertips showing beneath her deep silk cuffs. "If you do have your eye on her, tell me and I will see what kind of match I can make for her."

"I thought perhaps the Emperor of Shan."

"The Shan Empire is very far away." The Lady Bortu made a sour face. The capital city, she meant, at the heart of the empire: a distance his daughter would cross but once in her lifetime. "And the emperor's affection is fixed elsewhere, or so the whispers say in camp."

Mergen had seen with his own eyes the Emperor Shou's infatuation. Lady SienMa, mortal goddess of war in a foreign religion, held Shou's heart between her sharp red fingernails.

"Not as first wife, of course," he conceded, "but more than a concubine. Maybe even second wife." In the great capital of the Shan Empire, a daughter of the khan might take no slight at being second to a goddess. For the emperor's part, if anyone might find happiness with a woman of shamanistic tendencies it would be one who courted war in a woman's form.

Other options remained to them, of course. "We owe Tinglut a sign of good faith," he reminded his mother. "He's lost a daughter in his dealings with the clans; it seems only fitting to give him a Qubal daughter as wife."

"Ah, yes, I meant to tell you. A messenger from the Tinglut-Khan arrived while you were hunting. Old Tinglut has one of his sons on the march to negotiate a match to bind the continued peace between us. I think they will be unwilling to send us a second princess."

Somewhere on the grassy plain between the Tinglut and the Qubal clans, a bamboo snake-demon had taken the place of the Tinglut princess meant to be Chimbai-Khan's second wife. The princess doubtless lay in some rocky hollow, dead of the fanged tooth of the demon. Tinglut-Khan had come to accept that the snake-demon, and not her Qubal husband, had done away with his daughter. With Chimbai's death at the same poisoned tooth and demons pressing them in the recent war, Tinglut had thrown his troops in with Mergen's, but their truce remained uneasy.

"I sent the messenger to find food and rest in the city, with an invitation for his prince to come at his pleasure." Lady Bortu watched him with a keen eye for how he would react to the news. He was surprised only by the speed with which Tinglut-Khan had moved, however.

"A daughter of the Qubal given as a wife to the Tinglut-Khan might ease those last suspicions," he mused.

"The Tinglut are rich enough," Lady Bortu agreed with a frown that meant she was turning over all the possibilities in her cunning old mind, "but the old khan's looks are lacking and his temper is not sweeter. Eluneke is not so different from other girls that she will thank you for such a match, however many furs and jewels he showers on her. We must ask ourselves, how grateful will the old khan be for an unhappy wife?"

Mergen agreed for reasons of his own. He wasn't ready to throw away Eluneke on a lesser power like the Tinglut. Yesugei had a daughter of marriageable age who might trade a husband's less-than-perfect looks for a rise in rank, however, and Prince Tayy had a sister of seven summers or so fostered among the clans. They might betroth her to the old khan as a promise they might never need to keep.

Lady Bortu had continued down her own track, however. "A son, then," she suggested. "Old Tinglut has sons. The girl is pretty enough, when she bothers to put on decent clothes. We might do well with a handsome Tinglut prince if not the emperor of Shan."

Mergen had no intention of letting her go to the Tinglut, but he was determined on one thing: "She can't be allowed to complete training as a shaman, of course. No sane man wants a shamaness in his bed." Which was another reason Tayy's interest had him worried.

A commotion at the door told him that the younger hunters had returned. His time to speak privately with his mother was running out and he hadn't yet mentioned the most troubling intelligence of the day—Prince Tayyichiut's fascination with a bootless shamaness from a lowly clan. Tayy couldn't know who she was, so what had drawn the boy's attention? And how were they going to put a stop to it? He would have to have a quiet word with Qutula and Bekter. They would join in his loving conspiracy to separate the heir from this inconvenient attraction.

"Have you thought about a match for your brother's heir?" Lady Bortu nodded in the direction of the doorway. Prince Tayyichiut, accompanied by Mergen's own sons, had just entered. His dogs, trying to follow their master, were repelled by the guardsmen at the door, adding to the commotion of the party assembling there with much whispering and jostling of elbows. "If you don't need her for the Tinglut, Yesugei's girl might do," she added. "I can talk to her grandmother."

But Mergen had other plans for Prince Tayy. "The Bithynian Apadisha has a daughter. She's a warrior, so they should get along very well together."

Bortu crossed her hands over the knee tucked under her chin and frowned, not so much displeased, Mergen guessed, as calculating the consequences of such a match. "The clans are so beset by enemies these days that we must have not only a warrior khan, but the same in his khaness?"

She might have planned the conversation to that point, but Mergen thought he'd surprised her with the Bithynian princess. Until recently he would have answered "no" to his mother's question and found Tayy a nice young daughter of a neighboring khan, or even of a chieftain among the Qubal as his mother suggested. The death of his brother and the war for the Cloud Country, however, had taught him otherwise. "Times have changed," he answered. "A prince of the Qubal people must marry for larger politics now."

"And there are no warrior princesses nearer?"

He had added up to something new in her estimation, he thought.

"Find me one," he challenged her. "But not in Yesugei's tent." Mergen didn't want to test the general's loyalty or his friendship too far while Sechule stood between them. "And stop this shaman madness while you're at it. Many moves remain to the game if we are to stay abreast of our neighbors, and we have few enough stones on the board to make them."

"More than you seem willing to use." She gave a pointed look at the young men ordering themselves at the foot of the ger-tent palace, his own blanket-sons among them.

"Later, when my brother's heir has the khanate, I'll advise him, as I expect will you, on how best to use these loyal stones to serve his interests in the world." It should have been obvious to her—"Until that day, I want no accusations of dynastic aspirations."

The Lady Bortu frowned again. He had no time to pursue her displeasure, however. The horde of young warriors descended upon him with much noise and, always a bad sign, a bit too much laughter. He wondered which one of them had nearly gotten himself killed and how they had managed it so near to home.

Ah. Qutula. His companions nudged him forward. The sudden feeling surprised Mergen, like a stubborn horse had just kicked him in the chest. On the long trek back from the high country he'd gotten out of the habit of holding his breath, waiting for the news that battle had taken the bright light of his sons from his life. It wasn't fair, this sneak attack on his unguarded flank. Looked like Qutula had made it home again in one piece, though. He lacked the cocky swagger that surviving a close call usually gave a young man but led the way with his head held firmly erect, his mouth set in a grim line. Perhaps it had been too close a call this time. Or, given it was Qutula, he doubtless hated being rescued even more than he disliked needing the rescue in the first place.

The prince followed behind, trying to look modest, though the excited grin that kept breaking out on his lips ruined the effect. Then Bekter, bursting to tell the story, and two of their companions. One dropped back at the door, but the other trailed his betters with a bundle heavy in his arms. When they reached the foot of the dais, they stopped and made low formal bows.

"Uncle."

When the prince rose from his bow, Qutula was free to do likewise. He considered addressing Mergen as father, but hadn't decided what his next step would be if the khan repudiated him. So, "My lord khan," he said in greeting while in his thoughts he urged his father, *Say it now. Call me your son.* His eyes remained downcast in a respectful manner, showing nothing of the bitterness he felt when the words did not come.

"A trophy in honor of the hunt," Tayy announced with a flourishing wave of his hand.

It was not clear if the prince meant the bear's liver or Qutula himself, returned alive to suffer embarrassment in front of his father's entire court. *I could not love a patricide,* his lady had cautioned him. He would rather have Mergen's blessing anyway; would rather win acknowledgment as a reward for some heroic act of his own. But not like this, cast up at the foot of the dais like a child swept out of danger by a more alert guardian.

Jumal came forward, however, and placed the doeskin bundle in the prince's hands, which in turn he extended to his uncle. "A gift to the khan from his heir and the guardsman Qutula, who killed the beast between them," Tayy explained as Mergen-Khan unwrapped the dripping liver. He was very careful, Qutula noted, to say nothing that would imply any interest that the khan might have in his own son. "It was a very small bear."

It was clear from the great size of the liver that the bear had been huge, at least seven feet tall on its hind legs, which was how Qutula remembered it.

"Here is a tale for the telling." Mergen beamed in pride, though his teeth seemed clenched around some less pleasant emotion that remained unspoken. The khan drew his knife and cut off a sliver of the dripping, raw liver.

"A fine gift," he said, and popped the sliver into his mouth, swallowing it without chewing so that the life of the bear might enter his vitals whole and potent. Blood dripped from the corner of his mouth. With the back of his hand he wiped the smear from his lips and licked away the juices with his tongue. Then he raised his red-stained knife over his head.

"To the cook pots!" he declared, "A portion to all who would be warriors as daring as these young hunters, and a tale of the chase while we eat our weaker porridge in anticipation of that finer fare to come!"

With that he invited his blanket-sons to join him on the dais as Prince Tayy's courtiers. Bekter wasted no time in grabbing a pie from a passing tray, but Qutula accepted no dinner for himself when he claimed his place at the prince's side. As Mergen had done for Chimbai-Khan, he sampled Tayy's dishes before he would allow the prince to eat. His brother fed himself heartily to withstand the exertions of a night of singing, but Qutula took his own nourishment from those bites and fragments he tasted off his prince's plate.

Their own cadre would guess that he served his lord in gratitude for his life. After a time, who would suspect him of dosing the very food he tasted for his prince? A servant filled the kumiss bowls and handed Tayy's to Qutula, who took the first sip before passing it on. The tattoo on his breast warmed under his clothes as his resolve hardened.

"Your guardsman serves you well, Prince." Mergen gave a nod over his own bowl of strong kumiss. He smacked his lips in appreciation for the pungent sour taste of the fermented mare's milk. Unless one knew him very well, he wouldn't notice the tension in the line of his jaw.

"Yes, he does," Tayy agreed around another bite of his pie. They were all too polite—and too superstitious—to mention that Mergen's solicitude hadn't saved Chimbai.

They talked in casual nothings as they ate, but presently Bekter pushed his empty dish away, a signal that he was ready to sing.

"Have you made up a song for us yet about the wondrous

bear and the great battle to defeat it?" Mergen asked, half mock-ingly.

"Not in its finished form," Bekter protested, "But I can play a bit of it for your pleasure, my lord khan."

"Then do so." Mergen gave permission with a nod and a rueful smile. "I suppose I'll never know the real events of this afternoon's adventure, but we'll have the poet's version to en-tertain us, at least."

Prince Tayy made a great show of indignation. "Would you doubt your heir?" he asked. "Or mistrust the truths of your singer of tales?"

"Mistrust? No, never." Mergen-Khan protested in his turn with a sardonic smile. "I trust you all completely—to regale the court with the most outrageous and boastful lies they have heard since your elders told their own tales at your age." Which might have drawn more wide-eyed protests from the prince, but Bekter had wiped his greasy hands on his coats and, with a bow to the court, he settled himself on a low stool in front of the dais.

Bekter had explained to Qutula on other occasions that he preferred to steal the march on those who would criticize his fledgling efforts with the same standards they applied to a ma-ture, completed work. So it didn't surprise him that his brother gave them a warning as he picked up his lute.

"I have only begun to craft this song, so don't expect too much of it," he said, "When I've had more time to polish it, the tale will shine like a fine jewel in the history I propose, to cel-ebrate the heroes of the Qubal people."

Cradling the lute on his bent knee, Bekter offered a last modest word of introduction. "I hope even this poor egg of a tale conveys a little of the excitement of the hunt and the prowess of the hunter. And the terror of the bear, of course, in whose life we will soon share at this feast."

It seemed to Qutula that the bear had shown very little sign of terror, even with Jumal's spear sticking out of its shoulder. But his brother had begun his song, and so he listened for his own part in the saga.

"The prince rode out, whom all men call the Son of Light,
Bright shining in his armor, with silver on his toes,
Strong of arm from fighting many wars."

Bekter may have claimed the song was hastily constructed, but the word he'd used for the Son of Light—Nirun—had more renderings than a riddle. By saying it in the first line, his brother had clearly intended not only to describe Prince Tayyichiut, but to name him so that all the generations who followed would remember him for a hero. The gathered chieftains and clan elders must have known and felt the same shiver that had gone up Qutula's back. They sat, enraptured, as if Bekter's song was a Shannish rocket going off in an eruption of brilliant color before their eyes.

Qutula darted a glance to the place where Bolghai usually sat, wondering what the khan's shaman made of this poetic naming, but the space by the dais remained empty. Half mad as he was, the old man seldom missed a meal. Where was he?

It seemed, to Qutula's dismay, that Bekter sat with his lute making prophecies in the missing shaman's stead. And all the lines of his song rained blessings on the son of the khan who was dead, whose dynasty should have ended there, in favor of Mergen's own sons. Whom the living khan still had not acknowledged. The fire in his breast needed nothing of his lady's pleasure or chastisement for kindling. Where in Bekter's tale was Qutula the brave, who had survived attack by the great black bear? Where, for that matter, were the silver toes of a prince on his own boots? The silver cap of a prince for his head? Caught up in the singing of praises for the false heir, however, Bekter refused to see or sing the worth of his own brother.

"Like an army rode his hunters after the bright shining one
Seeking meat for hungry soldiers and livers for their
*   manhood*
—each had many ladies!"

Bekter had turned the lines from the grave business of naming a prince by his prowess to the ribald humor the court ex-

pected in a heroic song. The prince laughed, breaking the air of
anticipation that had held the gathered company in its grip,
though Qutula could see the court retainers shifting uneasily in
their places. Some of the older courtiers had not yet shaken the
sense of prophecy spoken in the first lines of the song. But here
was the plainer meat of the tale; throughout the great felted
palace, nobles and chieftains settled into the telling. More
verses described the sweep across the grasslands in the lake formation, demonstrating the hunters' mastery of warlike skills.
Then the patient stalking of more common fare. Bekter added
decorative mouth music to signal the approach of the bear.

"Spoor, longer than a hunter's stride marked the trail
Where trees, plucked twiglike by their roots, tumbled.
What monster lay in wait upon that path?"

The tale sounded rough in some parts. Bekter's playing left
much to be desired. But Qutula saw that his brother held the
whole palace—court musicians with perfected skills as well as
the chieftains and warriors—tethered to his words as the
hunters fanned out in search of the monstrous creature. As always, the poet had added an oasis of comedy. Putting himself
in the role of the buffoon, Bekter set his audience at its ease,
only to whip them into a frenzy of anxiety as the hero engaged
once again in life-threatening battle. Already the mythic bear
had grown tall as the towers of the Golden City of legend. When
Qutula threw his spear, it fell in the tale like a splinter pricking
the hairy hide. Then the arrow of the prince, whom the song
named Nirun—Son of Light—plunged through the mad red eye
to bury its iron tip in the beast's brain.

As the great black bear faltered and died, the gathered company gasped a pent-up sigh of relief. All but Qutula, who
ground his teeth in silent frustration. With a bashful grin, Bekter took his bows to uproarious applause from above the firebox
and below. He had made Prince Tayyichiut a hero, dwelling on
the prowess of the heir and galloping right over the little detail
that the bear had nearly killed Mergen's own son. If Mergen-
Khan hadn't been watching him with that narrow-eyed analyt-

ical stare, Qutula might even have believed they'd gotten away with it.

"A bear of legendary stature," Mergen praised the singer when Bekter had put down his lute. "And a hero to stand the test of many singings," he added with a slap to Prince Tayyichiut's shoulder.

"I hope so, my lord." Even his low bow could not hide the blush of pleasure on Bekter's cheeks.

Tayy matched the singer for the deep purple that rose on his cheeks, but he protested the praise lavished on his own part of the tale. "Not so much a hero," he assured his uncle. "You know how tales grow in the telling."

"And yet, this mythical beast out of our singer's imagination has left his liver behind for the strong of heart to enjoy."

Mergen gestured at the servants who had returned with the first crisp slivers of liver for the warriors. As he had with all the other morsels presented to the prince, Qutula took the sliver from Tayy's plate and bit into the rich meat before passing it on.

His father the khan looked like he'd scented prey and was on the trail of the truth missing from the tale the hunting party had agreed upon. Fortunately, the honor of a khan would prevent him from questioning his heir's guardsmen, some of whom might have crumbled under such an interrogation. He didn't think his own peril would distress the khan, but the danger to Prince Tayy had been almost as great, and unnecessary. He might have kept his soldiers around him for protection. A khan as wise as Mergen always did that. Or, he might have crept away again, saving himself while the bear busied himself murdering Qutula. Neither course would have made the prince a hero sung in all the camps of the Qubal, however, and already he heard Bekter's lines murmured among the guardsmen.

Mergen smiled and led the gathered courtiers in their applause. The song would need polishing, of course, and he could not praise his blanket-son's skill on the lute. But already the tale had captured the hearts of the court. Tomorrow the khan's musicians would have mastered the melody and soon he would hear Bekter's words throughout the camp. Mergen looked forward to acknowledging this clever son. He would show the clans that a khan—if only a former khan—could value the talent of a poet in one son every bit as much as he valued the prowess of a warrior in the other. Now, however, it was the warrior son who concerned him. Qutula had a dark and brooding look as he sampled his prince's food and drank from his cup.

At present the service posed no real threat to the safety of either young man. Among his own people, Prince Tayyichiut had no enemies; the Qubal loved their hero-prince. Politically, the clans were at peace with their neighbors and the reputation they had gained in the recent wars would assure they remained so, at least until his young heir had gained enough experience to lead his people. The Tinglut already negotiated a closer relationship with the Qubal. More to the purpose, the Tinglut emissary lodged under the watchful eye of the army for the night. The only other strangers in the camp were prisoners brought back with them from the war. No foreign hand had access to the prince or his food.

Qutula wasn't worried about someone poisoning the prince's dinner. Mergen figured his son still brooded over his near brush with death that afternoon. The bear's liver was large, testifying to a beast that would have towered over his son. Bekter's song had exaggerated some facts and obscured others, but Mergen had stalked game in the woods himself, and could well imagine what had happened. It would have rankled that Qutula couldn't take the bear on his own, and even more that having enraged it with a wound, he needed the help of his companions to avoid murder by claw and tooth. He required something to take his mind off his close call. For that matter, so did his father.

Lady Bortu seemed to feel the same. She drank from her own kumiss bowl and passed it to her grandson the prince with an indulgent smile, far too innocent in its apparent intent to take at face value. Qutula held a bland smile on his face as his grandmother praised her first son's heir through her commentary on the song they had just heard. "An excellent tale," she judged, "And an excellent hero, one who surely earns the loyalty of his followers.

"But," she interposed with one gnarled finger raised before her, almost as if the question were an afterthought, "are the heir's defenders themselves strong enough to stand against the thunder?"

Her words echoed a riddle that had more to do with loyalty than strength of arms. He wondered what she was up to. Qutula's face had suffused with blood at the remark; Mergen had to take the heat out of the moment or risk losing his blanket-sons to blood feud with their own grandmother.

"There's only one way to find out—we must have a competition of games tomorrow!" the khan declared, deliberately misunderstanding his mother's meaning in his reply. He'd had, perhaps, a bit more kumiss than usual and so the gathered courtiers would blame his dulled wits on drunkenness and custom.

In times of peace, the games offered the young warriors a chance to learn each other's skills. Their elders took the opportunity to look over the contestants as prospective husbands for the daughters who cheered their brothers on or, sometimes, wore their brothers' clothes to enter the contests themselves.

In the aftermath of a war as they had lately fought, the games were a chance to celebrate victory and show off some of the very skills that had brought the warriors home. They also gave the horde a way to keep its skills sharp while releasing the tensions that grew between young men still nerved for battle. So the courtiers took up the call for the games while the "shussshh" of swords half raised from scabbards let him know the warriors who lined the walls were eager to demonstrate their worth as guardians of the khan.

Prince Tayyichiut quickly joined in the scheme. "We need two teams to test their strength against each other."

His follower Jumal, who had carried the trophy of the day's hunt, dropped to one knee with his hand to his heart. "I would be honored to serve my prince as first among the Nirun," he said.

Mergen felt the chill of fate run up his spine, raising the hairs on his neck. Others among the prince's followers quickly joined in the chant of "Nirun! Nirun!" The Sons of Light, that was, taking up Bekter's song as they formed their army under the banner of the heir.

Another young soldier strode forward, whom Mergen recognized as Duwa, a childhood friend of his blanket-sons. Duwa had returned with the hunting party but had kept to his place among the lower ranks until now. Dropping to one knee as Jumal had done, he declaimed his own allegiance.

"And to oppose, in honorable mock combat, I put my spear and sword and the muscle of arm and shoulder at the service of the guardsman, Captain Qutula!"

Bekter, who had cozened another pie and a bowl of kumiss from one of the servant girls, looked up from his second dinner with shock and dismay. Mergen thought that Qutula would himself object, offering his sword to defend the heir's honor in the games. Though his son looked surprised, however, the flesh firmed around his eyes and his jaw tightened with a challenge.

"Someone must, I suppose," he said, carefully considering the matter as he spoke. "And what better way to show not only my willingness to serve my prince, but my strength of arms to do so, than by testing them against that very prince."

The Lady Bortu's riddle had clearly smarted. Tayy's grandmother, she was, and Qutula's, too, though like Mergen himself, she had never shown by any public word or action that she recognized his bastard children.

"And if Prince Tayyichiut should lead the Nirun, Sons of Light," Qutula declared, "then we who oppose, even in mock battle, must be Durluken, the Sons of Darkness."

To his son's followers, he thought the name carried no weight to burden the soul. They were just the opposing team— the dark to the prince's light and no more. But Qutula looked like something had settled in his soul; a missing piece of his understanding of himself had found its place, boot to stirrup.

That look slid over Mergen's skin like the earth of a living grave. The clans didn't bury their dead, except as the most dire punishment, to trap their souls with their bodies in the hell of

the living grave. Mergen remembered a time when he'd threatened a man with that worst of all deaths—to slice him open
crotch to gullet and bury him alive with his entrails in his
hands. He felt like that was happening to him now, and didn't
know why, except that his son, whose birth remained buried
from the world, proposed to ride in the morning under the
banner of darkness.

Where was Bolghai when he needed him? Mergen would
have stopped his blanket-son, begged him to change his mind,
to find a name for his team that could not be misconstrued. Led
by Duwa, however, the young warriors who gathered under
Qutula's banner had begun to chant their own name—
"Durluken! Durluken!" as if they might drown out Jumal and
the supporters of the prince.

If he spoke up now, Mergen would draw unwanted specu-
lation to his son, so he kept quiet. But he wished Bolghai were
here. The old shaman would have no qualms damping the enthusiasm of young warriors if he feared they might disturb the
underworld with their games. But Bolghai's place at the side of
the dais remained empty.

Clutching the broom that had once set a god-king on the path
of his destiny, Eluneke danced in the grass. Little moons
Han and Chen had long since chased the sun below the horizon. Great Moon Lun rose and began her descent, casting a
ghostly white light on the grasslands. Still, Eluneke danced.

And still, nothing happened.

After a while, her teacher Toragana came out to watch. Bolghai followed. He tapped his foot to catch the rhythm and set a
fiddle under his chin, playing a tune in time to her dancing.
Toragana added the beat of her drum. Still no change came over
Eluneke.

"Not a large animal," Bolghai said, and Toragana, nodding
in agreement, shifted to a stately rhythm on her drum. Bolghai
added the sweeping rise and fall of a bird's wing to the song of
his fiddle.

Eluneke's stomach growled with hunger. She imagined her feet turning purple from the constant beat of the dance against the grass. But nothing happened.

"Not a hawk, then," Toragana said.

Bolghai agreed. "Perhaps an eagle?"

But she wasn't an eagle either, or a pheasant or a magpie or a lark.

Chapter Eight

IN THE DARKENING shadows of the fading lamplight, Mergen called for more music. Bekter looked up from where he sat with the court musicians, reviewing the new tale one more time as they quietly followed his direction. Although his own play did not match theirs, the musicians would always find a way to include him if he wished, for the sake of his songs. If the light and airy tune clung a bit more tenaciously to the ground, he repaid them with the sure flight of his words.

But tonight he left the second act to the masters. The epic singers came forward to recite the heroic tales of long ago and then, as the lamps began to flicker, the gathered company of the court made their bows and wandered off to their own tents to sleep.

Qutula was among the first to leave. With a smile that hurt his face he waved away another bowl of kumiss. Yawning was easier and, he realized, he didn't have to fake that at all. "If I may be permitted, I would find my rest, the better to acquit myself with honor on the field tomorrow." His bright and hopeful grin gave away more pleasurable plans.

"Rest indeed, but in whose arms?" Mergen guessed, as Qutula had meant him to do. With a laugh the khan warned him, "Don't stray far from camp. You don't want to miss the call to the games."

"Great Sun won't find me sleeping," Qutula promised, and let his smile slide into a knowing smirk.

"Then go," the khan urged him with a wave of his hand, "I'm sure greater rewards await you in the dark!"

Qutula gave a final bow before he made his swaggering exit from the ger-tent palace of his father. He carried himself with the fierce bearing of a warrior as he passed through the chieftains and advisers gathered under the khan's roof. His thoughts, however, already flew to the lady whose mark on his breast burned anticipation in his veins.

L ater, when Bortu and the prince left him to find their respective blankets, the khan quietly bid his general Yesugei to attend him.

"Find out what you can of the life of this girl we saw when we returned from hunting. I don't want her to know she is being watched, but report her actions to me, and in particular if she should meet with the prince."

"As you wish." With a bow Yesugei withdrew to obey his khan's command.

That would have to do for now. Tomorrow, he would talk to Qutula and Bekter about keeping a similar guiding watch on the prince. Which reminded him of Qutula's own boastful withdrawal. When had his son found his way under a friendly blanket? He would have to uncover how serious the connection was, and how suitable the girl to make ties within the palace. At the least he must find a way to warn Sechule against arranging wives of her own choosing for her sons. When Tayy became khan, he would have his own ideas about the alliances he would bind with his cousins' marriage beds.

Like so many of the matters that preyed on Mergen's mind, this one must wait for events to develop. Lying awake fretting like an old woman wouldn't help. A snore off to his left reminded him that not all old women let such cares disturb their sleep. Lady Bortu would have advice of her own—might already have plotted a path for her grandsons through the tents of

their allies. Such decisions were the province of women anyway. Prince Tayyichiut, with his uncle's guidance, might point
in the direction politics would take them, but the grandmothers would decide which young men and women would seal the
treaties with their bodies.

Bortu hadn't approved of Chimbai-Khan's instructions that
Mergen wander through the tents of the Qubal clans, offering
no promises but making the tenuous connections that Chimbai-
Khan required of them all. She would advise Tayy against such
a policy for his cousins as well. Qutula and Bekter must marry,
but carefully. With that last thought for the well-being of his
sons, Mergen rolled over in his blankets and went to sleep.

Qutula found his horse waiting nearby in the care of his followers.

"Company, Captain?" Mangkut, one of his own since childhood, had taken guard duty outside the palace. At his master's
appearance, he came forward into the light.

"I think I can manage on my own." Qutula lifted himself
into his saddle and demonstrated his meaning with a rude
hand gesture that earned him a chuckle.

Mangkut returned the gesture. "Just the kind of duty I
would have asked for! But captains have a habit of reserving for
themselves even the most dangerous missions where women
are concerned!"

"Initiative," Qutula advised in jest. "A man who conquers
the mountains may rest in the valley!"

"But first he must elude the barking dog at the door!"

Qutula laughed at this reference to a potential mother-in-
law. He had seen no signs of such a barking dog complicating
his current interest.

She had not come to him since that one meeting in his war
tent, but the tattoo on his breast tingled promisingly. The memory of her touch drew him like a hawk to its prey, though he
couldn't say how he knew she would be waiting. With a last
farewell to his fellow guardsmen, he turned his horse about,

and headed down the wide allée to the river, far from the tents of watchful aunts and mothers. Sechule would want to hear his plans, but that could wait until tomorrow. His breast burned and he kicked his horse to greater speed.

S echule examined the chains of silver-and-turquoise beads that framed her face in the mirror that hung from the wall of her ger-tent of two lattices. The tent was larger than those of her lesser neighbors but in no way as ostentatious as it should be to shelter the sons of the khan. As she ran an elaborately carved comb made of bone through her long dark hair, she brooded on the unhappy fate that Mergen's fickle attentions had left to her. She still looked younger than her years. Her hair had remained thick and unstreaked by gray, so she had no need to increase its volume with strands pulled from a horse's tail as many women did. No evil surprises for her lovers, she mused, when the headdresses of a matron came off. Not that she had many lovers, of course—she didn't need *that* sort of reputation attached to her sons. Mergen must have no excuse of paternal confusion by which to reject his own offspring.

Since his election to the khanate, Mergen had ceased to visit her tent. With inducements of many presents, however, her resolve against the general, Yesugei, had softened. She had allowed him to crawl under her blankets. The general lacked skill as a lover, but he did have the ear of the khan.

She didn't put her hopes in any romance. Men who craved her blankets had proved inconstant once they had warmed themselves to their satisfaction. Her sons, however, shared the blood of the khan. Bekter seemed content to bask in the reflected glory of the palace, but in Qutula the burning of her own heart for justice found a second home. He would find a way to take his rightful place on the dais and she would be khaness, the mother who ruled a khan. . . .

Through the night Bolghai played his fiddle, taking turns with Toragana on her drum, one playing while the other rested in the grass. Now the tune mimicked the hopping of a jerboa, now the quick, elusive movements of the stoat, now the sinuous slither of the snake. Eluneke danced to them all. The determined rhythm of a mountain ewe didn't call her spirit. Not roedeer nor wolf, not rabbit nor any creature that Bolghai or Toragana could imagine between them brought her totem spirit forth. . . .

By a sharp upthrust of rock Qutula spread his coat and lay in wait for the lady who came to him in the dark. As yet she had given him no name, nor had she let him see her face. This time was no different. Great Moon set, the darkest pit of night descended. In the distance, farther from the camp than he had come himself, he heard the shifting rhythms of music played on the drum and the fiddle. The sound came no closer, however, and he easily put it out of his mind. Slowly his eyes began to droop.

"Aieee!" A slithering pain in his chest brought him suddenly awake. Qutula clutched at the place where the tattoo burned deep into his flesh, but the angry ache suddenly lifted as if it had not existed at all. Breath came easily to him as it had not since the morning he had awakened to find the mark of the coiled serpent on his body. He blinked, staring up into the darkness that blotted out the stars.

"Thank you." He knew she had something to do with the sudden absence of pain, he just didn't know what.

"You're welcome."

Though he still couldn't see her face, he followed the shadow of her movements as they darkened the night sky behind her. The lady of no name slipped her arms out of her coat and spread it to cover him. Then her waistcoat fell. He heard the slide of silk as she stepped out of her caftan, then she was naked between the coats with him, her skin night-cold where it touched him.

Assertive fingers sought out his buckles and the laces on his clothes. As before she did not permit him to undress, but nuzzled him through the openings she made in his shirts and trousers, rubbing her soft face everywhere on his body, as if his scent were the air she breathed.

"I'm starting to think you don't want to know my name," she whispered, and her words crossed his skin like scales, tormenting him with the pleasure of her soft breath.

"I do." He moaned, reaching for her breast with his mouth gaping wide, gasping for the sustenance of her flesh.

"Then prove it." She moved over him, taking him in, between her thighs, and pressing him down into the loamy earth with her round, soft hips. His lips found her breast and he latched on, drinking the sweat that bloomed with their exertions. The perfume of her skin made him dizzy.

"Anything," he said when she pulled away from his mouth. In the small part of his mind left for thinking such thoughts, he mused that her mountains and valleys had conquered him and not the other way around as the riddle suggested.

"The prince." She took his mouth, her lips cool with a liquor that numbed where she licked them and left him light-headed and short of breath. "Not too much." She freed herself from his kiss. "Not yet. You promised me the life of the prince."

"He's too closely watched." He didn't want to tell her that his plan to murder the prince while hunting had fallen to the baser imperative of saving his own life from the maddened bear.

She stopped moving, tilted her head as if trying to comprehend a riddle in a foreign tongue.

"You promised."

Qutula was finding it difficult to breathe. He thought that perhaps he ought to worry. But her fingers toyed with the braids of his hair and he knew that whatever she wanted of him she could have, if she would just move her hips, or let him—he reached up and took her shoulders, began to roll her over, but she slipped away—"Tsk, tsk"—leaving him bereft.

"Next time," she suggested. "Maybe. Bring me a token. A finger bone, perhaps, or a rib of the prince. Then we can take up where we left off—"

"You can't!"

"I have." She had already left him when her final words came back to him. Something slithered across his belly. He went to throw off the coat that had covered them and realized it was gone, as was the mysterious woman who wanted him to be khan. Whatever serpent had crossed his flesh after she left him had disappeared into the grass. In its path it left the smell of moist earth and poisoned meat.

Qutula's heart was beating more steadily, but he struggled for each breath. He couldn't feel his lips. He knew he ought to be afraid of her. He had thought her a woman of the clans wishing to tie a khan to her skirts, but a witch seemed more likely. The tattoo burned more fiercely on his breast since she left him, a reminder of his promise.

It didn't matter. He would do as she asked because it was in his best interest. He would have her then, when he was khan. If she tried to leave him unsatisfied again, he would have his followers hold her down until he had his fill, then he'd kill her. No one would blame him. She was a witch and he would be khan.

Pulling his clothes together, he made his way back to his mother's tent, unwilling to listen to the jokes of his followers at his return. Sechule could have been a problem as well—politically, she wanted much the same from him as his night visitor did. But she was herself occupied under the blankets and didn't notice his return. He crawled into his bed of furs and turned his back on the sounds from the other side of the firebox. Soon enough he fell asleep.

FALSE dawn came, and the light of Great Sun. And still Eluneke danced, leaving bloody footprints in the grass. Her thoughts wandered from the broom in her hand to the tent of her childhood, which had no father in it. As she danced, she wondered about the man who had fathered her. She remembered only the stealthy movements and rumbling voice of the lover who came to call in the middle of the night and disappeared again before dawn. Her mother had loved her, but after one midnight call from the stranger, Eluneke had been sent away for fostering to a minor clan.

Fostering was common among the clans. She had expected to go to the family of one of her mother's brothers. With plenty of time for visiting back and forth, her aunts would have chosen a suitable husband for her. None of that had happened, however.

Eluneke hadn't understood why a distant branch of her mother's family had come to take her far from all she knew, though she thought it must have something to do with the man in the night. She had cried to be torn from her mother. Once she'd settled into her relatives' tent, she'd had few visits home. Her foster family had been kind to her, but she had learned from the experience to hold herself a little aloof. She had promised herself never to give her heart so fully again.

When she heard that her mother had died of a wound in her breast that would not heal, Eluneke made the proper offerings and sacrifices. But she felt that all her ties to the mortal world had been cut. Toragana had come for her shortly after and she left her foster family behind with little regret. She had determined to maintain the same distance with Toragana. Now she wondered. By withholding her heart, even from her broom, did she stand in the way of finding her totem spirit?

She didn't think the question that rose out of her inner self made any difference in what happened next. But she gripped her broom a little more warmly when, in desperation, Toragana began to beat out a hopping jig on her drum. Eluneke hopped, and hopped again. And suddenly the grass was taller than she was.

"Bolghai! What leaps higher than it is tall, yet cannot see over the grass!" Toragana called to her old teacher.

"She's halfway there," Bolghai laughed. He dropped to his belly with his chin to the ground so that he was eye to eye with the toad hopping madly where Eluneke had stood. "Now all she has to do is cross the river."

With that, he turned into a stoat and ran away.

Toragana clicked appreciatively and patted Eluneke's little

toad head. Then she turned into a raven and flew over the Onga.

This, Eluneke figured, was the hard part. The thought amazed her because just moments ago she would have said that finding her totem spirit was the hardest thing she'd ever tried to do. She had rather hoped to be something more stately, like Toragana's raven. Birds knew how to fly already; that must surely give her a head start on crossing the river. She knew her shaman teachers meant more than that, however. She took a hop, another hop, and found herself leaping high over Bolghai's little camp. When she came down again, she was on the other side of the Onga, with no idea how to turn back into a girl.

"Eluneke! Eluneke!" Bolghai shook the water off his sleek fur and turned back into a man, the stoat pelts flying around the neck of his shaman's clothes. Then he realized she wouldn't have understood when he called to her in the language of the stoat, so he tried again. "Eluneke! Let me help you! Show me where you are!"

A hesitant croak brought him to a rock by the side of the water, where a small tree toad sat looking back at him with wide, sad eyes.

"I know," he said as Toragana came to rest on a nearby branch. She didn't return to her human shape right away; the piercing fixed gaze she set on her pupil made him nervous for a moment. Then she shook out her feathers and landed neatly on her feet.

"There we are," she said, settling the folds of her many-feathered dress around her. "Eluneke, you must come back to us. You were looking very snackish even to me, and I knew who you were. Try to remember there are real hawks and ravens about. Snakes, too—"

"Yes, child. It's time to come back to us."

The toad blinked solemnly at him.

"Come on, girl!" Toragana remained a woman standing on her two long legs with her fists resting on her hips, but her head shifted, became a raven's head with a raven's beak. "Snack!" she clacked, and snapped a hair's breadth from gobbling Eluneke right up.

"Think of something close to you," Bolghai added, more helpfully, he thought. It surprised him when her broom took shape beside her—she'd given every indication of hating her partner.

Unfortunately, the rock she had chosen to sit on as a toad was far smaller than her returning human form. She tumbled into the brush and crumbling leaves, dazed for a moment, then hastily brought herself back to order, her first words for her costume.

"How will I catch enough toads to make my ceremonial clothes!" she wailed. "It will take me the rest of my life just to get started!"

"Exactly as it should be," Bolghai grinned and patted her on the back. "Do you think that Toragana or I came to our present level of magnificence overnight? Not at all! Time and travels have brought feathers to one, the skins of stoats to another. To a third, time will bring the hides of toads. But all of that can wait. Breakfast is calling and you have yet to make your first dream journey."

Great Sun rose, lighting the slender trees that huddled close to the riverbank. Its golden glow drifted like a cloak over Eluneke, who gazed wistfully at the sparkling ripples the current stirred in the water. They made a pretty picture, girl and river, but it wasn't getting him any closer to his breakfast. Bolghai waggled his eyebrows encouragingly.

"Breakfast!" he reminded her.

Eluneke sighed. Toragana took up her drum and Bolghai set his fiddle to his chin. Picking up the rhythm of the jig, the girl hopped, hopped, in a fast tight circle. Suddenly, she disappeared.

"I think we've done it," Bolghai complimented his fellow shaman. It seemed unlikely that she would return here to the woods when his little ger-tent, or Toragana's tidier one, must call to her out of the dream lands. With that thought in mind, he turned into a stoat and dove into the river, heading home. He could track her through the dreamscape just as easily after a cup of tea.

Chapter Nine

"MY HUSBAND," Eluneke thought to herself as she entered the world of dreams. "Find my husband." She worried that he had already met his fate and hoped his dreams would give her some clue about who he was or how she was supposed to save him. But . . .

"This can't be him!" Eluneke moaned to herself as she dropped sickeningly into a trough of seawater. Her soon to be dead—but not yet wed—husband rode among Qubal warriors as one of them. He wore a Qubal face over his death's-head skull and dressed in the clothes of a highborn Qubal lord or clan chieftain. No Harnishman—Qubal, Tinglut, or Uulgar madman—would ever go to sea. He would rather fight tigers or demons than cross the Onga River. Even a hero might quake in his boots if he met up with too great a puddle after a rainstorm.

It wasn't that the Harn feared water, exactly. They drank it, after all. But man, woman and child, they preferred it in quantities no greater than a teacupful. The stuff of the universe was at its weakest in bodies of water, even small ones. A man could fall forever into the river, never touching land until his feet brought him to the underworld. In rainstorms lightning might snatch a man's spirit for the sky heaven, leaving his dead body behind with the sign of the tree at the center of the world burned into his chest.

This man whose dream she had invaded feared the water as much as Eluneke did, but it was hard to tell if he had the Qubal belief about standing water or if he feared a simpler death from the storm tossing his little ship like a leaf on the angry foam. Her watery husband wanted to vomit, but his stomach was empty. That could have been either of them, too. Bolghai hadn't allowed her to stop for dinner and now she was missing break-fast as well. But his hunger felt more urgent. She had an image in her head—his head—of hard biscuit and beans, knew she couldn't eat it even as her stomach growled in anticipation. Overhead, birds flew before the storm while in the rocking ship her muscles strained to the breaking while a voice called, "Pull!"

Her bottom felt bruised and she discovered why—with a huge pull on a great tree trunk of an oar, she fell backward onto a wooden bench hard as a paddle with a thin layer of padding on it. "Step, step, pull!" the voice called again, and she moved dizzily to the command once, twice, three times before she broke free. When she became aware of her surroundings again, she lay on the ground by Toragana's feet, exhausted and wet through.

"It seems she's been somewhere." Bolghai spilled a little of his tea on Eluneke as he bent to study her on the ground. She didn't mind; the tea was warmer than the seawater that had lately crashed over her. "Where have you been, girl? And how did you get all wet?"

"I've been on a ship, in a storm," Eluneke answered. She tried to stand up but found she was still too weak from her buf-feting at sea. "I didn't see his face, but bitter despair wrapped clinging fingers around his heart. I might have died of it if I hadn't escaped when I did."

"And is he now dead of this despair, as you describe it?" Bolghai asked, though it seemed to Eluneke that he had already guessed the answer.

She was not so certain. "No. Nooo. Maybe. I tried to find the boy who wore a death's-head beneath his flesh, but I must have lost my way. Who ever heard of a Qubal warrior rowing a ship?"

"Who, indeed!" Bolghai exclaimed, with interest quick as flame in his eyes. "Do you know when in time you traveled— to the past of your young warrior? Or to his future?"

"Past, I think." Eluneke considered the feelings she had experienced in her travels and had to give up with a shrug. "But whether he dreamed a memory or a prophecy I couldn't tell." She would have made excuses, that she had never traveled into someone else's dreams. She had nothing by which to measure the experience.

But Bolghai's thoughts were clearly elsewhere. "I see," he said, and snapped his teeth shut, refusing to say anything but: "Come in and have some tea. My son Chahar has come to visit while you were traveling. The khan has declared a series of games today, to celebrate his recent success in battle and the taking of a bear by his heir in the forest. You won't want to miss it."

Toragana raised her brows, a familiar gesture that marked her surprise that the old shaman had released her pupil for a morning of pleasure at such a critical point in her training. Bolghai didn't seem to notice, however, and more than that she kept to herself.

"Tea," Eluneke agreed. She would have hopped like a toad down the whole length of the Onga for a cup. As it was, she needed only to follow Bolghai and her teacher into the little round tent.

Though loud enough to rouse the spirits of the dead, Bekter's familiar snoring hadn't awakened Qutula; the angry whispers coming from his mother's bed had. Sechule was tossing her lover out by the false dawn of Little Sun again, before the camp had fully cast off sleep around them. Her lover objected, but gathered his things while he made his protests, which mostly had to do with marriage and her own tent in his clans.

That's never going to win her, General Yesugei, Qutula mused cynically to himself. *She's already got a tent of her own. She doesn't have to answer to any first wife to keep it, even if she wanted to forget her schemes to claim a place on the dais of the khan, which she never will.* He opened his eyes a crack, enough to see that his mother hadn't given her lover time to put on his clothes.

"I don't want Qutula or Bekter to see you here," she whispered, and shoved him naked out the door.

"Too late."

When the door closed behind the general, Qutula sat up, scattering the furs that covered his bed. He still wore his clothes of the night before and his nose filled with the musty scent of his lady's strange perfume. The urge to reach out and touch her, even in her absence, was so overpowering that he closed his eyes for a moment, cooling the heat that the memory brought to his blood.

Fortunately, before his mother could call attention to his state, the last heap of bedding stirred. "Can I stop pretending to snore yet?" came Bekter's plaint from beneath the blankets.

"Oh, get up, fools!" Sechule grumbled at them as she put the breakfast pot on the firebox to boil with porridge made fresh yesterday. "I don't know why I put up with either of you!"

Bekter rolled out of bed and stretched, answering through a yawn: "Because a mother will always rule in her son's tent, but a second wife must learn to bow her head to a husband's first, and to his grown children?" Not even this more even-tempered brother deluded himself about his mother's affection.

"Or maybe it's because your beloved children are your only tie to the khan." Qutula followed his brother more slowly to his feet. The hours spent waiting for his dark lady had tired him, but the reminder of her scent on his clothes drove the sleep from his thoughts.

"You do me an injustice!" In protest, Sechule rattled around making more clatter than necessary gathering bowls and spoons. "I want only what is rightfully yours."

"But do you want it for us, or for yourself? If you expect to live in the silver palace of the khan, it will be on the coattails of your sons."

"You are too harsh, Qutula! I don't know what makes you so cruel." Sechule had put on a simple sleeveless shift before throwing her lover out and she hugged it more tightly around her, as if she needed to defend herself against her son's words.

"I've done all I can to put you in front of your father. It should be you beside him on the dais, not the old khan's orphan. But I can't win Mergen's approval for you. You have to do that for yourself if you want to gain your place as heir and take your father's rank when he dies."

She made it seem that it was her sons' fault she had lost the eye of the khan, but Qutula guessed she'd never had his ear. Still, she'd succeeded in placing him close to the khan as she claimed. He only had to find a way to reach Mergen's heart. Then his father's death could come sooner rather than later. His lady had said that she wouldn't love a patricide, but he thought she might be persuaded when he took his place at the head of the clans.

Bekter was frowning over his porridge, however. "The khan is fit and likely to enjoy a good long reign if the spirits favor him. Which, as his son, I devoutly pray they do."

"I know. You are a good son." Sechule petted his brother's head with absent fondness, but Qutula thought she wasn't pleased with Bekter's goodness.

She proved his suspicions when she added, with a wistful sigh, "Life would have been simpler for all of us if the old khan's offspring had fallen with the rest of his line." Died, she meant. "But instead, look at him! Parading around as if he were Mergen's own son, while the true heirs of the khan's body are forced to serve him. Prince Tayyichiut should be serving you!"

Qutula couldn't argue with that. Hadn't, when he'd renewed his promise in the night to kill the prince. Only he hadn't lied about how closely Prince Tayyichiut was watched. It wasn't enough just to kill his cousin; he had to make sure no trail led back to his own tent. Of course, there was a reason that the symbol for two women under the same tent roof represented war. If he were to have any hope for a peaceful life with his dark lady as khaness, it wouldn't hurt to have suspicion fall on his mother. He didn't want to distress Bekter, but he didn't see any other way.

"However we would like our fates to fall, the khan awaits us now," he said, giving nothing away of his plans.

"The games." Bekter set his dish aside and rose to leave, noting with a frown, however, "You need your breakfast. How will you defeat the prince's Nirun if you don't eat?"

"Duty will sustain me in the name of the Durluken!" Qutula smiled for his mother to make a joke of it as he swept his arm in a grand flourish to accompany the words. "Will you attend the games this morning to cheer the team of your sons to victory?"

"Of course I will." Sechule gave Bekter a kiss, first on the right cheek, then on the left. "You are both such dutiful sons. If your father only saw your true worth, he couldn't help but love you."

When it came his turn for a motherly kiss, she looked at Qutula with so intense a gaze that he knew she meant more than the simple duty a son owes his mother. *Kill him for me,* that gaze said, *kill the prince and your father will learn to love you.* He answered her silent command with a little bow and a lift of his chin, agreeing to their silent pact. She didn't know he already planned murder as a gift to his lover, but the snake that coiled in ink upon his breast recognized the vow for her alone, and rewarded him with the now-familiar tingle that stole through his body at her approval.

PART TWO

SONS OF LIGHT

Chapter Ten

"LIKE AN ARMY RODE HIS hunters after the bright shining one—hey! Watch where you're going, there!"

"Excuse me!" Eluneke bounced off the chest of a warrior who parted the crowd like a walking mountain. Flustered, she smoothed the simple day dress of a maiden she wore. The warrior gave her a sharp frown but quickly passed on. Free of his hostile gaze, she rubbed absently at her forehead. He hadn't bothered to ask if she'd been hurt by their sudden collision.

Eluneke had followed the flow of people to the great parade field in front of the ger-tent palace of the khan. Most days it was just an empty patch of churned-up grass where the young played jidu for practice and the warriors took it in turns to hone their own skills under the watchful eye of the khan. For the games, merchants had spread their wares on blankets and sat with their backs against the white felt tents of the high-ranked clans that marked out the dimensions of the playing field. The crowd, hemmed in between the blankets full of wares on the outside of the field and the warriors who paraded within it, buffeted her as she tried to find a spot where she could see the competitions.

"Beads, little one?" an old crone wheedled. "An amulet to attract a young suitor, perhaps?" From her seat on a greasy blue blanket she offered a charm on her upraised palm.

Eluneke dismissed the charm at once; Toragana did much better ones and she was learning the skill herself. But her fingers itched to touch the turquoise bead the size of a nut that nestled in the folds of the blanket.

The old crone followed her gaze and cackled appreciatively at the end of it. "For a richer purse than yours, my girl, but I'll tell your fortune for a copper penny!"

She'd had quite enough of thinking about her future, and each new strand seemed only to tangle the weave even more. Professional courtesy demanded a polite reply, however, so she answered, "Not today, thank you!" before plunging back into the throng.

"I know where you're headed even without the knuckle-bones!" the old crone called after her, laughing.

No mystery there, Eluneke agreed as she made her way toward the games at the center of the field. She turned sideways, trying the childhood trick of sliding through the crowd, but it didn't work anymore. Her breasts got in the way. Womanhood hadn't stolen her best weapon, however; with a last jab of a sharp elbow in an anonymous rib cage she reached the front, where all the girls of marriageable age had gathered. Swaying like butterflies in their bright silk dresses, they had come to watch their potential husbands contest in mock battle.

An orphan and the apprentice to a shaman, Eluneke had no such finery. She didn't mind, though; the leather robes of her office awaited the completion of her initiation. As for her husband, fate or a shaman's calling had seen to that. Fine clothes would little serve her in the difficult task ahead—keeping him alive.

She had come out among strangers, but that was all right, too. The girls from her own clan would have asked her which of the young warriors would be their husbands, how many children they would have, would they be rich. If she answered as they wished, they'd run away laughing, as the company of an apprentice shamaness meant nothing to them. If she told the truth, some would leave weeping and others would leave mad. The rest would just leave, declaring their good mood ruined while they hid their secret smiles at having better luck ahead than their companions. She had more important concerns to worry about today, like finding out who her not-quite-dead-yet husband was.

Luck, or the spirits that drew a young shaman like a child on leading reins, had brought her to a place not far from the gertent palace of the khan. Sunlight flashed off the silver embroidery and Eluneke stared, amazed, at the scrollwork and the patterns of leaves and vines and wildflowers that covered every inch of the white felt. She had never attended a festival so grand, nor ever seen the palace or the khan, though she had heard enough in stories to recognize them now.

Resplendent in silks beneath his ceremonial armor, and with the quilted-silk-and-silver headdress of the khanate upon his head, the khan sat on the back of a sleek white horse caparisoned as richly as her master. On his left hand the mother of the khan and grandmother of the prince his nephew sat astride her own great steed. Adorned in patterned silks of orange and yellow decorated everywhere with chains of silver ornaments and beads, the khaness Lady Bortu viewed the gathered warriors from beneath a massive headdress of silver horns draped everywhere with strings of precious gems. Eluneke didn't see anyone who might be the prince among the dignitaries, clan chieftains, and nobles who gathered to either side. He would, no doubt, participate in the games, but generals flanked the khan and his lady mother on either side, and Bolghai himself sat a cream-colored donkey among the highborn waiting eagerly for the games to begin.

A little apart from the royal party stood an aging warrior in the armor of a strange ulus. Not a prisoner, since he held a post of some honor. Doubtless an emissary of some ally from the war, he pretended not to notice the guardsmen in their blue coats who created a wall of their bodies between him and the royal party. His keen eyes seemed to take in everything around him, however, including the girl watching him from the crowd. Not wishing to draw attention to herself, Eluneke quickly shifted her gaze to the guardsmen.

Only the best young men of highest family would guard the

palace itself. Her soon-to-be-dead husband might hold such rank, so she carefully examined each of the warriors in blue. None of them bore the face drifting like a vapor across the death's-head skull that had ridden past her door. The spirits were making her work for her reward. She would finish her training then, and when she had the skill to save him, they would find each other.

Scuffing the wooden sole of her boot in the turned earth, she couldn't completely suppress her disappointment. Still, the day was clear and the many bright banners of the clans floated proudly on the breeze above the heads of the gathered armies arrayed on the playing field. Harnesses creaked and horses snorted impatiently. Great Sun glinted off shields and helmets and turned the silver embroidery of the ger-tent palace to liquid fire.

The khan nudged his mount with his knee and the mare took two careful steps forward. Next to Eluneke, a woman in brilliant silks and with many amulets in her hair ornaments caught her breath.

"He is . . ." Eluneke began, ready to offer her own praise of the magnificent khan.

The look in the woman's eyes turned the words to stone in her mouth. She couldn't tell how old the woman was, exactly, but her expression left no doubt that her gasp was a very private communication. Hunger and longing, and bitter anger lived uneasily together in that glance. Eluneke had seen pale semblances of the same emotions before, in the faces of men and women both who had come to Toragana looking for love charms, or to be free of love, or for amulets to cause the death of a fickle lover.

Toragana offered them soothing tea and listened quietly to their tales of disappointment and longing. She would send them away with a mild prescription for heart's ease, or a harmless charm and then set Eluneke to scrubbing every cup and airing the cushions, lest the spirits who drove these poor souls should come to rest in the shaman's own tent. So she took a step back, careful to keep her expression open and friendly but giving the woman's spirits the space they needed. The woman didn't notice. Her attention had locked on the khan and she scarcely breathed as he began to speak.

Mergen looked out over the gathered crowd, proud of his people and the youths who had gathered for the contests. Bekter had determined to sit out the matches, preferring to make tales rather than to star in them. Already his song about Prince Tayy and the bear had spread through the camp. Tinglut-Khan's messenger had the tale on his lips when he petitioned the khan for permission to take back to his own camp a report of the games held to celebrate the event. With some misgiving, for the man was no stripling but a seasoned spy, Mergen had granted the request, while setting him under the watchful eye of his general, Yesugei, and the palace guard.

The wrestling matches, in which Qutula and Prince Tayy would compete, would come later in the morning, however. To open the games, Mergen introduced his army. He had strung his bow for the purpose, and he raised it over his head in salute.

"Now we celebrate the glorious moment of your warriors' great return!" he announced. Throughout the crowd his criers repeated his words so that all might hear them. "They have filled the foreign gods and the rightful kings who serve them with wonder while striking terror in the hearts of their demon enemies!"

He would have played down the mystical part of the recent war, but Bolghai had recommended against it. As yet, no one had found the snake-demon who had taken the place of the true Lady Chaiujin in the tent of Chimbai-Khan. The demon-lady had escaped Mergen's effort to have her executed, but the snake's heart would burn with cold fury in her breast until she had taken deadly revenge. Until she was found, Bolghai warned, he must leaven even the sweetest moment of victory with the bitter warning that demons and spirits could strike at the heart of the khanate. Still, the people raised their voices in praise. If the fear of the unnatural shivered in their bones, they had the memory of honor and glory to warm them again.

"Fathers and mothers, honor your sons! Children, honor your fathers!"

A cheer rose up, deep-throated from among the gray-haired in the crowd and lighter-voiced from the children who bounced in their saddles as they waited for the call to race.

"Wives, welcome your husbands back into your tents and give them comfort after their labors!"

Women who had tended the tents of their husbands during the war answered with their own welcoming warmth. Mergen turned his hand and, in acknowledgment of the welcome of their families, the army advanced their horses one step and clapped their spears on their shields, raising an answering din. At a signal unseen by the crowd, but well known to the khan, the rattling of spears ceased, and row by row the warriors rode in dignity from the playing field.

The games proper would start with the children so that the warriors might prepare with no unseemly haste for their own competitions. As the last of them filed out, Mergen let his glance wander over the bright colors of the departing banners and the brilliant silks of the crowd.

At his side, Yesugei held still as a rabbit at the point of the hunter's arrow. Following his general's line of sight, Mergen found himself staring into Sechule's eyes. Once he had thought them beautiful, but now they burned in their orbs with a demon heat. No. If anything possessed Sechule, it was her obsession, not demons. Yesugei stirred in the saddle, his face frozen with the jealousy that he dared not reveal to his khan.

For her part, Sechule seemed not to notice the presence of the general as she held Mergen's gaze with her own. Enough! He turned away, and could not believe what he saw. So close that she might reach out and touch his old mistress stood his daughter, Eluneke, in the plain clothes of the lowest ranks. What relief he might have drawn from the fact that her clothes bore no mark of her shamanic training was completely overturned by the presence at her side of the one woman in the camp who might have both the experience to see the khan's eyes in that lowly face and the motivation to use that knowledge against him.

"Interesting," Lady Bortu whispered at his side.

So, not the only one, though he hoped his mother meant his daughter no harm. Of the two, Sechule showed no interest in the girl fate had put within her grasp. She did not miss the loss of his eyes upon her, however, and began to follow the turn of his head. Mergen continued his sweep of the crowd, leading her gaze to the children waitng on horseback. Boys and girls together, some as young as six summers but none older than eleven, eagerly sat their mounts in a line held back by a silken cord.

Clan custom made no distinction between the sexes at this age, but he saw that some of the older girls carried themselves with a military erectness to their spines. Tales of the women warriors of Pontus had traveled back from the wars with the army. The female warrior Captain Kaydu, servant of Shan's mortal goddess of war, had ridden in their very camp, commanding soldiers both male and female. *Times change*, he thought to himself with hope and sorrow. *Soon, so must we.* He didn't let the crowd see his thoughts, but kept his face grave and kingly as he handed the general his bow in exchange for a pike attached to which fluttered a silk ribbon embroidered in the khan's silver.

"To the victor the khan's ribbon!" As Mergen exhorted the youthful riders, he raised the pike so that the wide ribbon snapped in the breeze above their heads.

With one voice the children cried out, "Victory!" and the crowd cheered its approval.

Sechule's attention had returned to his face, he noted out of the corner of his eye. His daughter had moved a safer distance from the mother of her unknown brothers. He didn't let his glance catch on her again, but turned with a smile to the children waiting with their hands clenched in the manes of their horses.

"Ride!" he cried, and dropped his arm in a grand sweeping motion of the pike with the prize ribbon in his hand. At his signal, guardsmen let go of the silken cord that held back the riders.

Like a whirlwind the horses dashed away in a plume of dust. Their young riders clung to their backs as they thundered down the wide avenue, leaving the white-and-silver palace for the open grassland beyond the camp. They would follow the markers of silk fluttering on stakes that laid out the course; the sun would crest the zenith before the first of them appeared again, returning, on the horizon.

When only the dust they had raised remained to tell of the child riders' passing, the crowd settled for the next call to arms. So many of their youths had achieved their blooding during the recent wars that few remained to play at jidu now. But the number sufficed to make two lines of fifty or so youths holding their mounts at the first yellow stake that marked out the playing field. Too old to ride with the children, they had been too young to travel with the armies whom honor had called to Thebin. Now that he thought about it, there seemed to be more of them than he'd expected. Many had just moved up from the simpler games of childhood and still played with blunted spears, but—

At such a distance, and dressed as they were in training garb, he couldn't be certain. But he guessed the tales out of Pontus had made an impression among this group as well. Many of the new warriors in training were girls. A season ago he would have laughed at the notion. A season ago, his armsmaster would have done the same. Since then, they'd fought side by side with swordswomen and taken orders from a mortal goddess of war. So Mergen-Khan modified his prepared speech.

"Qubal clans, I give you your Qubal young! Judge their skills and welcome them as the warriors of your future!" He'd taken out the word that specified adolescent boys for one that made no distinction by sex and waited to see if the criers would pick up the change. The nearest of them delivered his words correctly; he could only hope that those farther back in the crowd would do the same. His audience responded with jubilation.

Mergen had escaped a reckoning this time, but would speak with his weaponsmaster later about changing customs held by the clans since they first climbed the tree at the center of the universe. With that thought, he exchanged the ribboned pike for a spear which he raised over his head. "To the winner a spear from the khan's own store!" he cried, "Now ride, young warriors, for honor and for glory!"

When he dropped his hand to set the game in motion, the first line of players galloped forward with a roar.

At its heart, jidu trained players in close-order teamwork. Each player worked and trained with a partner who would catch and return the throw of a blunted spear while galloping at high speeds across the playing field. The most skilled of the catchers reached out and snatched a thrown spear out of the air, escaping unharmed. Those who missed the catch, or were unhorsed by a strike, stayed behind with their partners while their more skilled opponents wheeled around in the dust and noise of screamed battle cries and the thunder of horses to repeat the pass.

So it went, until just one team remained. The taller of the two players in the final team might have been a girl. Mergen wasn't exactly surprised. He remembered the ferocity of the women at whose side he had lately fought, and wondered how long his armsmaster had been training girls on the sly before the recent war. The winners came forward, in their pride unmindful of the grime of the competition that covered them. Mergen did not press the girl to identify herself but handed her the spear as the eldest of the team. She stepped forward to touch her forehead to the back of the khan's hand while her younger partner, a brother by the look of him, hung back, unaware that his mouth gaped open.

"Bravely done," he praised them in his most regal voice, keeping his demeanor stern with an effort. They would not appreciate the laughter that struggled to escape. "Keep this spear as a mark of your hard work. When you come of age, I will look for both of you in the armies of the khan."

The girl grinned, her eyes alight with the promise of a warrior's future. Well trained in the courtesies, however, they each made a bow and backed away, the eldest nudging her partner to remind him to close his mouth. That one's face suffused with embarrassment, but he kept his head and didn't turn and run. Someday, when he captained a thousand, he would laugh about the day. He wondered what the girl would say from such a distance, and what a warrior's life would bring her. To say more would unmask her deception, however, so he let them go.

With the games of jidu decided, it was time to return the field to the more serious sport of the blooded warriors. At the farthest end, targets were set up for the archers on horseback while in a protected area out of the range of flying hooves, swordsmen demonstrated their arts. In front of the khan himself, platforms were laid for the wrestlers.

While this was being done, the throngs settled in with lunches they had brought with them in pouches. Servants brought out yogurt and hard cheese and pies of minced meats and the fat tail of a sheep for the khan's party. From his saddle, Mergen washed his mouth with kumiss handed up to him in a bowl by a fresh-faced young girl who blushed and ran away when he looked at her.

"Brazen thing," Bortu muttered around her own meal of yogurt and cheese.

General Yesugei said nothing, but his gaze wandered over the crowd, looking for Sechule with a bitter set to his mouth. Obsessions seemed contagious this season. If only they could have caught it for each other, Mergen would have been well rid of the problem. As it was, he had a sterner cure in mind for his general, though well sweetened as all medicine ought to be. It would mean losing Yesugei's subtle wit in the matter of Prince Tayy and the girl. Better that than lose the man altogether in his madness for Sechule.

Qutula already watched the prince for his father. He might find a way to use Bekter to find out more about the girl. No need to reveal her paternity; he could keep his secret yet. But the platforms were ready. Mergen turned his attention to the wrestlers.

Chapter Eleven

"**E**VERY MATCH COUNTS!" Tayy exhorted his teammates as they waited to the right of the wrestling platform that now covered a broad swath of the playing field. He settled his wrestling leathers more comfortably across his shoulders and slapped Altan on the arm in passing.

"You'll do fine," he assured his friend.

"I'll do my best," Altan dolefully assured him.

The prince moved to the next wrestler with a word of encouragement. He had no worries about Jumal, who strode beside him as he passed up the line with a word of support or a friendly punch for each of his hundred. Altan, however, neither excelled at wrestling nor consented to leave his companions for the more likely competition among the archers. He kept hoping to improve, which never happened.

Tayy had learned enough from the Shannish captain, Kaydu, to know Altan should compete where his skills might shine. Since losing his lifelong friend Yurki in the first of many long battles for the Cloud Country, however, he hadn't the heart to deny their presence at his side to any of his closest companions. In deadly combat he would choose differently, but it seemed pointless to turn Altan away in the friendly contest of a festival. He wasn't the worst wrestler on the team, after all— just not as good as he might be at other games.

But the handlers had completed the platform. Tayy made his way up to the front of his line. He had prepared his team, and his mind, for the bouts to come. Now he watched his uncle attentively for the formal call to the matches.

"Qubal people," Mergen-Khan cried.

The crowd returned his salutation with cheers of "Mergen-Khan! Mergen-Khan!" for their leader.

Mergen waited until an expectant silence descended. "Welcome your sons and brothers as men," he invited them with arms flung wide to take in the hundred young warriors on either side of the platform.

At this signal, the captains led their teams onto the platform. On his right, Prince Tayyichiut marched out with his hundred wrestlers following. From the opposite side Qutula stepped forth, his team of the same number behind him.

Each contestant had earned his blooding during the recent wars. The ceremony accepting them into the ranks of the army as seasoned soldiers had come while the heat of battle was strong in their stink and their blood. But Bolghai had argued that the old and the timid, the weak and the women held by tradition in the rear would yearn to celebrate the rite of passage into adulthood of their youths as well.

As he gave the call for the contestants to stand before him, therefore, the khan invited the gathered throng to join him with their praise. "See how they return to your tents and your camps as warriors, with the blood of your enemies on their hands!"

Mergen's words, traveling back through the crowd on the tongues of his criers, were met by clapping and whistling and stamping of feet. But he was not finished and the crowd, knowing this, quickly settled.

"Grandmothers!" the khan commanded them with a sly smile, "do your work among your granddaughters—your grandsons yearn for the comforts due a new husband!"

The little flocks of silken butterflies scattered through the crowd answered this exhortation with a comely squeal as the teams of wrestlers, two hundred souls to face each other, moved forward in cadenced step on the platform. The ground shook with the appreciation of the clans and the khan added his smile to acknowledge the maidens' eagerness to serve the khanate with their romances. Now, however, it was Yesugei's turn to take the part that Mergen had played so often as Chimbai-Khan's right hand.

Eluneke expected the khan to say something to the wrestlers gathered in two lines before him. Instead, the famed general Yesugei nudged his horse a step closer to the platform, putting himself between the contestants and Mergen-Khan. The crowd, more experienced at royal festivals than she was herself, hushed to hear the general's challenge.

"Who stands before the khan in honorable contest?" Yesugei asked, letting his voice roll deep and sonorous from the bottom of his belly.

"The Nirun, Sons of Light." Their captain stepped forward to speak for his team. "Come to do battle for the glory of the khan!" With that he led his hundred in a deep bow, first to the khan and the khaness, Lady Bortu, then to the crowd, which roared its approval of such courtly manners. When he rose from his bow, the breath caught in Eluneke's throat. She had known her future husband to be highly placed, but a captain among the nobles? It seemed so . . . unlikely. Bolghai must surely know the young captain's history, however, and after today, she would have a name to give him: Nirun. But no, that was a new hero-tale. "The bright shining one." Nirun was the name of his team. She'd heard snatches of the song as she'd wandered through the crowd and now she heard voices around her taking up the refrain, "Sons of Light! Sons of Light!"

The captain puffed his chest out and the leather worked with gold of his wrestling vest stretched open to his waist, revealing well developed muscles slashed by a ragged scar across his belly, still red from recent healing.

"The prince," voices whispered around her. "Prince Tayyichiut."

"The dead khan's son—"

"—Nearly killed in the wars for the Cloud Country—"

The prince? They had to be wrong. How would she win an introduction to the khan's heir, let alone marry him? Little more could she imagine the prince's grandmother arranging such a match. The vision must be wrong. Glancing that way, Eluneke felt herself run through by the Lady Bortu's fearsome gaze. A shaman's eye, that was, though the mother of two khans had never taken training. At least, Eluneke had never heard so. A khaness, however, would have ways of hiding such things from the far-scattered clans.

"And who would best this challenger?" General Yesugei asked, while the criers carried his words to the back of the crowd.

Darkness. The word drifted through her mind a moment before a second youth strode forward to accept the challenge.

"The Durluken, Sons of Darkness, come to do battle for the glory of the khan." When the captain stepped forward, a superstitious shudder ran through the gathered audience. He wore a bit of jade pinned to the open breast of his wrestling costume and, on his back, the markings of a snake worked in green and black seemed to writhe across the leather.

Lady Bortu's intense gaze had fallen on the challenger. Though she hid her thoughts well, Eluneke could see trouble ghosting across her face like the distorted image in a flawed mirror.

"What do you think of that, girl?"

"What . . . ?" The skills of a shaman in training sometimes swept her on their own course without her bidding. So Eluneke was dismayed, but not completely amazed, when the voice of the khaness echoed sternly in her head. Suddenly, her perspective tilted. Eluneke looked down on the young warrior as if from the back of a horse, with the age-dimmed eyes of the Lady Bortu. Terrified, but hoping she could hide it from the old woman riding in her head, Eluneke looked where she was told.

On the challenger's breast, with the jade talisman pinned so that it seemed to rest just within reach of the inky jaws, a tattoo of the emerald-green bamboo snake coiled on oiled muscle. The tattoo would have troubled her enough; such a snake had murdered the former khan and his khaness, the Lady Temulun, after all. A green mist seemed to hover around the young man, however, and in its insubstantial depths, she saw eyes looking back at her. Terrible, deadly obsidian eyes. The murderous spirit of the demon-snake enfolded the young warrior. Qutula, the khaness supplied, regret leaking between their minds. An unacknowledged grandson. There was more to that sorrow, something the lady hid much deeper in her mind than the thoughts she shared by choice, but Eluneke had no intention of pursuing it.

Next to her, in the Lady Bortu's perspective, the khan spoke. "You take this naming of your team too close to the heart," he muttered softly.

Qutula's head snapped back as if he'd been struck. "I serve my khan," he insisted with forced dignity. "I didn't sing the song or choose the names."

"You chose the mark on your breast and on your wrestling clothes."

"To remind me that nothing is certain," Qutula answered with a bow. "I did not mean to offend."

A lie, but covering what, Eluneke couldn't tell. She would have liked to see his eyes—*you're not the only one, girl*, she heard in her head—but he kept his lids downcast in proper demonstration of contrition.

Qutula seemed on the point of saying something more, but with an open palmed gesture to let it go, he led his team in the same formal bows that the prince had given, first to khan and khaness, then to the crowd. It seemed for a moment that his glance lighted on the place where her body remained standing in the crowd. A little frown marred his brow, but he withdrew into the form of the contest with no sign that he had resolved whatever had troubled him.

At her side, Mergen took a beautiful many-layered bow with silver chasings that General Yesugei handed to him and raised it over his head. "To the winner, the honor of the battle and the khan's own bow, a family treasure since the age of the first khan!" No worry that the bow might leave the family, the wry voice of the khaness commented in her mind. It remained a mystery which captain might win the day, but not that one of them would do it. And each shared blood with the khan.

Eluneke suddenly found herself alone, looking up at the wrestling platform from her own place in the crowd. She staggered with the shock and righted herself, aware out of the corner of her eye that the woman she had seen earlier watched her with wary curiosity. Sechule, the woman's name was, though Eluneke hadn't known that before. She didn't have time to think about it, though. The matches were about to begin.

As Mergen raised the prize over his head, the newly tested warriors raised their own competing shouts, some calling, "Nirun! Nirun!" for the Sons of Light and "Prince Tayyichiut!" their captain. From the other end of the platform came the answering cry, "Durluken! Durluken!" And, "Qutula!" his own blanket-son's name, who was captain of the Sons of Darkness.

It was just a game, but watching the referees sort the teams into contesting pairs for the first set of matches, Mergen shivered at that call. His sons had grown to manhood in shadows, unrecognized by their father, but soon he would put an end to their obscurity. When he returned the khanate to his nephew, he could give his name and family to his children, who would serve the clans with their lineage as they had with their skills.

Soothed by his own assurances, Mergen let the bow sweep a glittering curve in the sunlight as he drew his hand down, the signal to begin.

"**Q**utula! Qutula!"

    His heart swelled in his chest as he stood at the head of his team. For many years he had listened to the crowd call for

Tayyichiut, the khan's heir, but now followers called his own name as well. He knew he was a good wrestler, had seldom lost a play-match when they were counted boys together. Qutula did not intend to disgrace himself now that they were men and contended before the khan and the greatest of the Qubal clans. With that thought, he raised his head with princely bearing and glared at his first opponent across the neutral space that separated them, waiting for the sign that would let them begin.

There, like a glittering bird, Mergen's bow carved an arc out of the air. Qutula took a step forward. He didn't know the name of his opponent, but he'd seen him fight and hadn't been impressed. Wasn't now either. Easily done, the fool went down like a sack of dung and blinked up at Qutula in confusion.

"Next!" the referee called up another from the prince's team who had defeated one of Qutula's. Again they matched off. He could hear, from the continued cries, that Prince Tayyichiut had likewise won his round and went on to the next. Half as many left. Fewer now . . .

The last match save one. Tayy gasped for breath, noted Qutula did the same. Altan had made it to the third round, but finally fell to Mangkut, the best of Qutula's Durluken save the captain himself. Knowing the bout the crowd wished to see at the end, the referees were careful about the matches they made for the captains. Jumal had the pleasure of besting Mangkut in the name of the Nirun, however. And so it came down to Tayy and his cousin, facing the khan for the honor of light, or the honor of darkness. Tayy wished that Bekter had come up with some other name in his song. It made him too much the hero, and he wondered what Qutula thought when he adopted the opposite appellation.

Mergen was talking, however, a silver arrow in his hand. The prince squinted against the flash of sunlight, determined to pay attention. "To sweeten the contest as my own ancestors did in ages past, this silver arrow if the loser can draw the bow and hit a target of his opponent's choosing."

Another family heirloom. No question to Tayy the message the khan sent with his choice of tokens. He allowed his opponent a small, conspiratorial smile, but Qutula returned only a flat, calculating stare. Exhausted from his own bouts, no doubt, but his cousin's eyes gleamed hard and unforgiving in a face that seemed carved out of stone. Whatever was troubling him, they would have to have it out sooner or later. Just not now. Mergen called them to the contest and Tayy gave a low bow.

"I dedicate this match to my father, Chimbai-Khan. May his spirit rest quiet in the knowledge that his unworthy son has learned at least this much of the lessons he tried to drum into brain and muscle!"

The clan chieftains and advisers roared their laughter at the joke and their approval for the prince. Though a khan did not compete in public contests such as this, Chimbai had often exercised his skill among his nobles, clearing a space in front of the dais in the ger-tent palace where he might best any man in a throw. Once, in the pretense of a friendly match, he had challenged a traitorous noble whose back he broke in the contest, declaring the game over only when the noble was dead. Tayy hoped never to need that particular lesson and refused to let the memory darken the sunshine of the festival.

The teams had taken their seats encircling the area where the last match would take place. With no sign of Tayy's thoughts to mar their enjoyment, they whispered admiringly among themselves, setting their own bets on the contest. "Nirun," he heard among them, and "Durluken," returned. Even the dogs, held to the outskirts of the playing field, raised their cries as if they wished to encourage their master.

Qutula stepped forward now, his chest running with oil and sweat in Great Sun's yellow glare. "I dedicate this bout," he said, and a shiver of tension went through the gathered courtiers and the closest of their friends on the platform. Would he use his dedication to confront the khan about his parentage?

"To the mother who gave me life. And to the lady of my dreams, whoever she may be!" With a smile he waved a hand in the dizzy motion that signaled a love affair, by which he could have meant to alert the families gathered there that he

was looking for a wife. The slyness of his smile suggested a secret connection already made, however.

"A girl before me! You have won in the contest that counts,
and now you boast of it in front of all the tents of the ulus. But
don't think you have shaken my confidence—I have more to
fight for!" Tayy kept his laughing words just between the two
of them, but Qutula's glance swept the company with a pinched
tightness around his mouth. A lady, perhaps, but it seemed she
brought his cousin as much misery as joy.

No time to question it now, however. Each set his hands to
the shoulders of the other. Tayy had never thought himself
squeamish, but the flesh of his palms crawled to be so near the
emerald green bamboo snake coiled on Qutula's breast. Not an
insult to the dead khan, Qutula had said, but a reminder that
such terrible creatures roamed the Earth. The prince believed
that much. Still, the thing seemed almost alive as it rose and
fell with his cousin's breath. He had little time to consider his
uneasiness, however. Mergen gave the signal, and the match
began.

Each leaned in, pressing any advantage that would send his
opponent to the floor. Qutula's greater reach made it difficult
for Tayy to plant his feet as firmly as he wished, but he had the
greater strength of back and arm. They struggled so with each
other for minutes, neither budging while the chieftains and
court advisers shouted out advice.

"There!"

"His foot moved, he is unsteady!"

"Press him now!"

"The prince will have him!"

"No, it is 'Tula!"

As he set his muscles to press his opponent and overset him,
sweat broke out on Qutula's shoulders and chest. His arms
grew slick, and his hands. He lost a step, forced backward by
the stronger prince. At first, focused on his own efforts, he
scarcely noticed the heat pulsing at his breast. Soon, however,

the sensation of movement crawling down his arm became too powerful to ignore.

"Kill him," the well-remembered voice of his lover whispered in his ear. "Kill him now."

Slowly, his hands slipped inward. Shifting his shoulder to hide his actions, Qutula rested his thumbs on the hollow of Prince Tayyichiut's throat. His hands tightened, thumbs pressed inward.

Tayy tried to catch his eye, but Qutula's gaze had locked on the serpent slithering over his biceps, down over his forearm to join its strength to his squeezing hands.

"**Q**u—Qu!" Tayy scrabbled at the hands around his throat. It was impossible to breathe, impossible to utter the warning that would end the bout. Sparkling lights danced in front of his eyes.

As his head dropped to his cousin's breast, the tattoo shifted and moved. Uncoiling, the creature raised its head. *This is impossible,* he thought. Daylight-sense told him it wasn't real, but the night-sense of his fading consciousness told him otherwise. The design grew fangs and bared them, poised to strike.

"**N**ot now, you fool!" the woman Sechule muttered. Anger seethed in her eyes.

Eluneke hadn't recognized the danger. Her husband-to-be was dying in front of the cheering crowd, his opponent's hands clasped around his throat. Already the flesh-and-blood face that hung like a mask over the death's-head skull was fading.

"Aaah!" she couldn't stop the scream that escaped her lips. The snake that had hovered over the Durluken captain like a mist in the Lady Bortu's eye grew, took on substance in her own as the life went out of the prince. The serpent-demon towered over the struggling warriors, fangs like curved swords poised to strike at the prince.

"No!" she cried, but her voice was lost in the din.

"Nirun!" the crowd shouted around her, unaware that their champion was dying.

"Durluken," cried others, who didn't see that their contender was murdering the prince.

Closing her eyes to focus on the toad that was her totem animal, Eluneke prepared to leap to the wrestling platform. What she could do there she didn't know, but her appearance must at least distract the company enough to stop the match.

Fortunately, Tayy had learned a few tricks of hand-to-hand combat on his travels. The move would give the bout to Qutula, but they'd both survive. He shifted his hands so that he was pulling Qutula closer instead of pushing him away. As his cousin forced him down, Tayy tucked himself into a ball and fell backward, his hands still clasping Qutula's shoulders. When his back hit the floor, he planted his feet in his cousin's middle and lifted. The murderous hands left his throat— Qutula flew through the air and landed on his back at the foot of the dais.

"I win." Qutula was still gasping when he said it, and he hadn't tried to stand up yet. Neither had the prince. He didn't know what Tayy had done to him, but his cousin had certainly taken the first fall in the doing. Mergen agreed. That much, at least, he had won.

"You certainly did," the khan nodded down at him with a laugh, "though by what strategy I am still confounded."

He thought for a moment that Mergen-Khan had seen his thumbs pressed to the heir's throat. The tattoo hadn't really moved. That was impossible, of course, though it had seemed to do so in the uncertain shadows cast by their wrestling arms. But his father wasn't talking about his actions at all. Rather, he looked to his heir with bemused admiration.

"Did you learn to do that on your travels? I can see the use of it, though not in a bout of wrestling. The prize goes to the last man to leave his feet, not the first whose back hits the ground!"

"Qutula bested me." Prince Tayy regained his feet with a reproachful frown at his cousin.

The others might think the prince meant the frown for his own lack of strength or skill in the contest. Standing with some effort himself, Qutula pretended he thought the same. Tayy might suspect the slipping of his hands had been no accident, but nothing in his own demeanor would give his intentions away.

"It was an equal match," he conceded with a bow.

"Almost," Tayy agreed.

Qutula kept his expression open and admiring for the prince's scrutiny. After a moment a little shrug let him know that his unspoken excuse—he hadn't realized what he had done—had been accepted.

"And now, the prize." His father held the bow out in his hands like a sacred offering, his face glowing with the pride of a father.

"Durluken!" His followers were now joined by the clans, celebrating *his* victory. Bekter would make a new song, with a new hero.

"I am honored." Qutula took the bow in his own two hands and gave a deep obeisance of gratitude, as was proper of such a royal offering. His father would say it now—it must be why he had chosen this particular prize, why he seemed so proud that his son had won it. Almost, Qutula wished he hadn't cheated, to make the moment perfect.

"Use it well, in remembrance of this day."

"As the khan commands." With the victory cup, then, it must be.

"The arrow, to he that pulls the bow," Mergen offered the silver arrow to the prince, but he turned with his question to Qutula, the victor in the match. "What target, then, to finish this contest?"

He had intended to set an impossible task, a bead on a lady's headdress or some other challenge that the prince dare not accept. Gracious in victory, however, he offered an honorable challenge. "Hit the center of the target," he said, "from here." A difficult shot, but not unreasonable.

Tayy ran his arm over his brow to wipe the sweat from his eyes and drew the bow. His arms quivered, but he steadied himself and sighted on the target in the distance.

Twang! The arrow flew.

"Center!" came the judgment back through the criers. With it came the cheers of the crowd—"Durluken!" and "Nirun!"—the call and response of victory.

Mergen-Khan turned to a server and gestured to the gathered court. "Kumiss!" he said. "A victory cup to toast the winner!"

When he gives me the cup, Qutula thought, but Mergen left the words unsaid.

Chapter Twelve

EVENTS HAD MOVED on in Bolghai's absence. The prince had killed a bear and the old Tinglut-Khan had sent a messenger sniffing around for a Qubal princess, which complicated things considerably. The messenger had watched the matches from a crowd of lesser notables and then departed with no formal farewells before the feasting that followed the contests of skill and prowess.

The shaman smelled no magic about him, just the skill of a well-traveled spy. The Tinglut could not have seen the trick of light that had raised the serpent over Qutula's head. As Bolghai did his stoat-dance up the aisle of the ger-tent palace to the foot of the dais, he wondered what the Tinglut messenger might have observed that he himself had missed. He had no time to riddle it out, however. The dais lay before him and he made his bows, first to the khan, then to the Lady Bortu, mother of khans, then to the heir.

"And where have you been traveling, while your khan had need of you and could not find you in the night?" Mergen chastised, more gently than he might have done.

"Among the living, on the business of the dead, or maybe among the dead, on business of the living," Bolghai answered with a riddle he wasn't sure he understood himself. While casting his protections over the games that day he had espied the girl Eluneke in the crowd, looking for the young warrior who wore the death's head to her spirit-sight. He hesitated to speak of it to the khan, however—at least until he figured out the meaning of her visions.

She thought she had strayed in her dream travels. What Qubal warrior would find himself half-murdered as a galley slave tossed on a stormy sea? Only one that Bolghai knew of— Mergen's heir. That was the past, however; perhaps the girl's vision remarked a threat already endured and overcome. In his shaman bones and his sharp little stoat teeth, he didn't think so, but until he knew more, he had nothing useful to tell. Certainly nothing the khan would want to hear. As Eluneke's father, however, Mergen-Khan would have to be told about the shamanic powers his daughter wielded with such unthought skill. "It seems we have much to say to each other, when the feasting is done."

"Prophecies from our ancestors?" Mergen's attention sharpened.

"Possibly. Or young hearts only, and the direction they would take." Eluneke hadn't mentioned hearts, but he'd sensed that she'd held back some secret knowledge as troubling to her as that which she'd told him. The riddle was easily solved, of course. She was young and danger always made a young man handsome to women. Romance—and angry fathers—would have to wait, however. It was clear to Bolghai that she exhibited great talent, and that at least for the present, her shamanic abilities would bring her no happiness. Sensible, then, that she had fought them for so long.

She'd found her totem fast enough when confronted with a handsome prince in peril, though he'd swear she hadn't known the boy was Mergen's heir. He didn't think the turn events had taken would please her father. The khan had plans for his daughter, just as he knew the khan's sons fit somewhere into his political strategies. Unfortunately for the khan, the spirits of the dead made their own plans with little regard for the desires of the living.

Mergen-Khan, no fool, grew suspicious. She was his daughter, after all, and he would have his own spies keeping watch on her actions. "We have much to discuss on the topic," he agreed.

With a wave the khan dismissed him, and Bolghai took his place among the closest advisers at the side of the dais. Yesugei was there, solid in his loyalty, though Bolghai wondered if the general's love for Sechule would lead him to betrayal. Bekter, Mergen's blanket-son, sat among the musicians, preparing for the singing to follow the feast. Bolghai looked around but didn't see the prince anywhere.

A stir of jokes and laughter rippling up from the doorway heralded a newcomer, who was indeed the khan's nephew, attended by Qutula, his eldest son. Qutula swaggered to the foot of the dais and gave his father a triumphant bow. Prince Tayyichiut dropped a pace behind to give him the pride of first greeting due the winner of the wrestling matches. The prince watched him with a wary eye, however, and seemed troubled when he gave his own bow.

With a little frown wrinkling between his brows, Bekter reflected the prince's uneasiness, though perhaps no one would notice but the shaman, who was watching his reaction closely. Very interesting. Bolghai sniffed the air for mysteries, found the scent thick above the firebox of the khan.

"Welcome, good warrior," Mergen greeted his son. "Take your place beside us on the dais, first among wrestlers and first among the courtiers to my heir the prince."

"I prostrate myself before the wishes of my khan." Qutula bowed with exaggerated flourishes, as if the khan's offer flattered him beyond his rank. His eyes burned with suppressed longing before he wisely lowered his lashes.

Nearby, Yesugei burned with an equal anxiety that the khan paid such honors to Sechule's son. Sechule still hoped to become khaness through marriage or as the mother of a khan. The general had no place in either plan. Bolghai wondered how Mergen, who showed such cunning in war and such wisdom in statecraft, could be so benighted when it came to those most closely tied to him, his daughter no less than his sons or his generals.

Qutula was smiling when he curled into his place at the

prince's back, but this close, Bolghai could see the muscles
bunching in his jaw. If he could figure out what way that storm
would break, perhaps he could do something to lessen the blow.

The spirits would know, or have a rumor at least. The trick
was getting them to tell him. He thought perhaps Eluneke had
a better chance at that than he did. Her inborn talent far exceeded his own. But her father's wishes might prove an obstacle once he knew what was going on. Bolghai would have to
tell him. Not now, though: tonight was for celebrating victories—in the games, in the recent war. But tomorrow . . .

Qutala sat at his side on the dais, lavishly strewn with furs,
sampling the many dishes that passed before them, but
Tayy ate very few of the morsels his cousin urged on him.

"Eat, my prince, that old shaman is looking this way."
Qutula offered him a broken bit of pie. "If you're not careful,
he'll set the Lady Bortu on you."

It was a joke; the Lady Bortu's interest would include sharp
questions he little wanted to answer. It seemed to Tayy, however, that Bolghai's attention had fallen on his cousin, not himself. He wondered briefly if the shaman had seen Qutula's
hands on his throat that afternoon, but he sensed no urgency in
the gaze which quickly moved to a tray in the hands of a servant girl. Free of scrutiny, at least in this, he shook his head, ignoring his cousin's outstretched hand.

"Kumiss," he suggested

"As you wish." Qutula took the first sip and Tayy accepted
the richly decorated bowl from his hand. Tipping his head
back, he drank a deep gulp that burned like fire going down,
but left his throat numb in its wake. Bekter was watching him,
a troubled frown crinkling his broad forehead. Probably fretting
over a line or the turn of a phrase in a new song.'Tula pressed
a morsel on him, and he took it rather than expend more effort
fending off his cousin. He choked it down with another swallow of the fermented mare's milk and grimaced, not sure which
hurt worse.

"Are you ill, my prince? Is that why the shaman was watching you?"

Qutula seemed wholly unaware that he had nearly murdered the heir to the khanate that afternoon. Rubbing distractedly at the bruises hidden by the high collar of his embroidered silk coat, Tayy wondered if it were possible to strangle someone without realizing where one's hands had fallen. It seemed unlikely, which was a disturbing possibility in one so close to him. He doubted that his cousin could be so thankless as to wish him dead for saving his life the day before, however.

"Just some small injury taken in the bouts." He scarcely recognized the raspy voice, little more than a whisper, as his own.

Qutula was all concern. "You should have the old shaman, then, or my own mother will make you a poultice. She has experience treating wounds."

Thoughts he'd rather not have stirred at the notion of Sechule's hands on his body. *Here*, he imagined, and *it aches here most of all*. But he shook his head, leaving that spiderweb to General Yesugei and his uncle. "I'll be fine in the morning."

"Tell me who did this to you and I will lay my own honor to teaching him a lesson," Qutula fervently volunteered.

"It's nothing. I would have no feud in my uncle's tents." *With you*, he kept to himself. *I would not set my uncle's tents against his own children, no matter that he has not claimed you.* He could never say as much to Qutula, nor could he say what he believed, that Mergen honored his sons with the love of a father even if he did not name them so. But he could drink more kumiss, and he did, gasping as the fiery relief made its way past the swelling in his throat.

With the feast came singing. First one and then another of the court poets stood up to memorialize the events of the day. Prince Tayy leaned on his cousin's shoulder as he settled in to listen with the rest of his uncle's court. The children's race careened from octave to octave as the singer's words followed the rough course until, in triumph, the youthful champion claimed his embroidered ribbon from the khan's own hand.

The game of jidu turned into a comical song, with hand gestures broadly playing out the missed catch, the player unhorsed. No one mentioned the girls who competed, or the champion among them as half the winning team, but pronouns diplomatically shifted to the ambiguous forms.

The archery competition among the seasoned warriors was transformed into a tale of battle so that it was impossible to tell if the winner had claimed victory over his fellow contestants or against the southern Uulgar clans in the recent war. When Bekter's turn came to memorialize the wrestling matches, however, the poet bowed his head in apology.

"I am not happy with my efforts tonight, and would not put my reputation to the test with these poor words. Perhaps this one will do—

"Like an army rode his hunters after the bright shining one Seeking meat for hungry soldiers and livers for their man-hood."

The bear. Prince Tayy listened, politely indifferent to the acclaim the hero's tale heaped in his honor. At his side, Qutula looked as though he'd eaten something unpleasant. Bekter's song should have memorialized his brother's victories in the wrestling matches. Perhaps he had been called away on some urgent matter and hadn't seen them to record in song. Or perhaps he had seen too much. Tayy wondered what he had made of Qutula's thumbs.

But the song in which Prince Tayyichiut killed the bear had already passed from mouth to ear to mouth again. Chieftains and clan Great Mothers, all the nobles gathered in the ger-tent palace of the khan, clapped their hands in time to the music. The newly blooded warriors among Tayy's cadre shouted out their allegiance to the Nirun, the bright shining ones. Duwa, Qutula's follower, answered with the cry, "Durluken!" and his counterparts on the opposing team answered with the same cry, their fists raised to acknowledge their champion's victory, even if the song did not. Qutula modestly lowered his lashes, but his color did not rise. Not embarrassed by the fuss, then, but wishing to seem so. Tayy thought he would surely feel the same in his cousin's position, and gave him a friendly punch on the sleeve.

"Savor the praise while you can, my friend—" He could not call him by any closer name, though he muttered the words for his cousin's ear alone. "—next time, it will be me on the victory stand!"

Qutula turned away his praise. "It was only luck you did not stand there today, my prince," he said

Mergen smiled, and Tayy knew he'd heard the humble words delivered with proper modesty. He didn't see the pride in his blanket-son's eyes, or the hunger, quickly hidden. Tayy hadn't been meant to see it either.

Bekter had reached the part of the song where Prince Tayy struck the bear with his arrow—

> *"An arrow fletched with silver wings,*
> *flew to his mark with deadly sting."*

Suddenly, Jumal left his place along the perimeter to act out the part of his prince, pulling an imaginary bow and letting fly the imaginary arrow. At the applause of the crowd he cut a jubilant caper, beating his chest and leaping in a victory dance before flinging himself at his prince's feet.

To all who watched his comic antics he must have seemed very drunk, and no doubt drink had spurred him to action. So close, however, Tayy saw the tension in his eyes, the drape of his hand carelessly, it might seem, near the hilt of his knife.

"You are the prince's own fool, Jumal!" Acting as drunk as his companion, he leaned over, falling upon Jumal's shoulder almost as a ruse, although the ger-tent palace spun in lazy circles when he moved his head. They had both drunk too much for court intrigues, he suspected, but still he whispered, "What danger?" as he made a mock struggle to right himself.

Jumal drew his knife then, raised above his head in a dramatic sweep that might have sent flying the noses of anyone who drew too close. Half a hundred swords slid from their scabbards.

"Your Nirun will defend you to the death!" he declared for all to hear, still as if drunk, but the words carried the weight of hands around his throat for Tayy.

"I know you will. Now put away your knife before someone gets the wrong idea."

For a long moment, it seemed that no one breathed. Slowly, Jumal lowered his knife until the point rested above his own heart. "My life is yours to spend as you please."

"I am a parsimonious prince," Tayy told him, lifting the knife gently from his fingers. "And would rather save than spend your life. I certainly don't want it stolen by some anxious guardsman of my uncle." He held the knife between his own numb fingers, could feel the blue-coated warriors relaxing in the muscles of his own arms and in his back.

"Nor do I, my prince." With a gentle smile, Jumal spread his hands wide to show that he no longer held a weapon.

"I think it's time you went to bed," Tayy told him. With a gesture he motioned Altan and others of his own cadre to come forward and take their friend away, which they did, scolding him for his foolishness and laughing at his drunkenness. The prince thought he saw something more in their actions, however. He noted that the members of his cadre who had followed Qutula in the Durluken team came forward reluctantly, and only after a gesture from their captain.

Danger, he thought. The Lady Bortu's eyes were bright with calculation she shared with Bolghai. His uncle, lost in his own concerns, had dismissed the scene for no more than Jumal had intended it to appear—a proper devotion made to look foolish from drink.

Mergen watched with strained good humor as Jumal with his helpers passed the firebox. Jumal's clans had pinned their hopes for advancement on the coattails of the young warrior. He ill-served them by playing the buffoon and might have cost them everything if an uncoordinated thrust of his knife had injured the prince. But Tayy seemed to know how to handle him.

The khan had his own political mire to navigate, however, and little thought to spare for a drunken youth. When the commotion that had accompanied Jumal's departure settled, he turned to his generals among the chieftains and nobles. "Tonight we feast our victory over the Uulgar clans and the evil magician who led them," he declared, setting his features in stern lines as the musicians put away their instruments and the singers found their places among the court. "But justice demands answer before we find our sleep. Bring me the chieftains who will speak for the Uulgar in this place."

Chapter Thirteen

A T THE DOOR, GUARDS who had been waiting for the khan's call brought forth the prisoners. Three had named themselves chieftains among the Uulgar when taken prisoner. Others surely marched among those of lesser rank, but they would wait to see what happened to these three before they presented themselves for judgment. A wise choice, Mergen thought, lounging as casually as his tension allowed while he waited for the prisoners to make their way down the long aisle to the dais. Although necessary, he didn't relish the decisions he must now make.

"I would wish for Justice at my right hand today," he muttered under his breath, and meant more than the wisdom of his own judgment. For a while the clans had ridden with a god called Justice among those foreigners who followed the Way of the Goddess. Little more than a boy, on occasion the god had been clumsy as a colt. At other times, of course, he'd shown great powers of compassion and skill, enough to save the Cloud Country from both natural and unnatural foes. But then he'd disappeared into the mountains, leaving the defeated Uulgar clans to Mergen's less exalted disposal.

Old Bortu had not traveled with the army, but she'd met this young god and had heard his story. He knew she had an opinion, and no hesitance to tell it to him.

"You fear to judge, believing that Justice has departed the kingdom of men," she chastised him. "But did the wisdom of the Qubal people follow that young man into the mountains? Did the gates of a foreign heaven lock up the heart of a Qubal khan? Or does justice reside in all of us who see the darkness truly and would find our own path into the light?"

Mergen bowed his head to his mother, recognizing the echo of her words in his own heart. "You humble me with your wisdom."

"Then I would raise you up again," she said with a wry smile. "Look into the soul of a true khan for justice. Look into the minds of your enemies and know what you must do. But you already knew that, or you wouldn't be the true khan of your people."

The mother of two khans could not have a gentle soul. In the crinkle of her eyes, however, he saw pride as he had not since the death of his brother, Chimbai. She had thought him a poor substitute for the great leader they'd lost. It seemed she'd changed her mind. Or something in him had changed it for her.

He wanted to believe that, especially now as three Uulgar with the braids of chieftains strode toward him between the ranks of gathered nobles. Each carried his chains as if they were the most precious ornaments and each ignored the guardsmen in their blue coats who pricked at them with the points of their spears to hurry them toward the khan.

Locks of hair with bits of skin attached swung from the vests of the two grizzled oldest. Brown- and reddish-hued and black as pitch; a braid, a handful still gathered up into a silver clasp as a woman of the Golden City had worn it, dangled from their bits of flesh to adorn the chests of the chieftains. Raiders, then, and no honorable soldiers. He saw no remorse in their eyes, only arrogance and threat. The one with the broadest chest let his eyes rest on the thin switch of gray hair that flowed from Bortu's headdress, as if he measured its worth for his own decoration.

The youngest of the three had been in a training saddle when the raiders had invaded the Golden City. He wore the face of the eldest, though thinner and less well formed, and his soldier's garb bore no tokens ripped from the skulls of his victims. Close up, Mergen saw that much of his arrogance was feigned; the boy's hands shook with fine tremors, making a sound like the tinkling of wind chimes with his chains. He would have released him, but he knew that wasn't possible. By some manner of choosing among the Uulgar themselves, the young man stood side by side with the old. Not for his own crimes, Mergen guessed, but to represent the crimes of all his people for the khan's judgment.

When the prisoners had been brought before the dais, Yesugei left the nobles and advisers to take his place at the head of the royal guardsmen. He stood with his legs a little apart and his arms clasped over his broad chest and waited; he would perform Mergen's justice, whatever he asked. After a moment Qutula followed him, leaving the dais to stand beside the general.

Mergen knew what he had to do. Chimbai would have done it already. But there was a form to justice and this khan was a cautious leader. He turned to the eldest among the Uulgar chieftains, who stood a pace in front of his companions as their spokesman.

"What say you, before the khan decides your fate?" To show that he gave this prisoner no respect, Mergen kept his seat, his tone and glance mild, as though the question of the man's life or death held no great interest for him.

If he had claimed compulsion from afar by the mad magician for his deeds, or demonstrated remorse and pledged to live in peace with his neighbors, Mergen-Khan might have sentenced him to hard labor as a slave. After a proper time he could have freed the chieftain to make amends for his actions as he might.

Instead, the chieftain laughed. "The Uulgar have done no harm to the Qubal people! What does it matter to a Harnishman if the prayer-mad traders of the Golden City die?"

He used the Tashek word for the people of the grasslands, Harnish, meaning the movement of the wind in the grass. "If you want a share in the loot, you will have to wait until the fools rebuild the Golden City, but something can be arranged, I'm sure."

As the chieftain's breast rose and fell with his words, the blood-crusted hair of a long-dead woman swayed on the silver clasp pinned to his vest. Mergen found himself fascinated by that rich red hair. He wanted to reach out and touch the clasp. Was it warm to the hand, or cold as the grave of the woman who had worn it? He couldn't find out without losing his dignity, but its presence told him enough about the man who bargained for the lives of his people with carefully veiled threats. He had wondered who among the clans who roamed the grasslands could build a wall around a city. Now he knew.

"No harm to the Qubal?" He said it so softly that the Uulgar chieftain seemed to think for a moment that Mergen spoke to him alone, and in secret agreement. Gradually, however, his voice rose so that all the gathered court might hear each word as it vibrated with indignation.

"Otchigin, my anda, fell in the battle against the stone monsters raised by your master. Our shaman Bolghai lost a son, and many others died in the battle to free the people of the Golden City. And you come before this court with the ignoble badges of your treachery emblazoned on your chest!

"To conquer one's enemy in battle brings a soldier honor. To fall upon an unsuspecting people and murder the weeping innocent with no declaration of war is the work of a craven. It brings shame upon his people."

As the khan of all the Qubal ulus spoke, the youngest of the prisoners hung his head in shame. The second of the elder chieftains cuffed him sharply for his remorse. Their spokesman clamped his lips tight against a hasty retort, but the color rose from his throat. He held Mergen's gaze with threat carved into every tensed muscle of his body until Yesugei stepped forward to chastise him.

Mergen stopped him with a hand sign. "Shame, and no honorable death. For the injustice the raiders of the Uulgar clans meted on our allies of the Cloud Country, I sentence you to death. For allying with the evil magician who raised up the stone monsters to murder the khan's own anda, Otchigin, I sentence you to death. For the destruction your actions would have brought down upon all the living and dead and the gods in their heaven if our war had not put a stop to them, I sentence you to death."

Moving like lightning he rose from his place on the dais and seized the prisoner. Then he dropped to one knee and bent the man backward with a sharp twist. The snap of the chieftain's spine rang sickeningly through the tent. Surprise came first into the dying eyes, then slowly the light went out of them.

Silence followed, as if winter had blown through the gertent palace, freezing the moment in time. Of Chimbai the Qubal had expected such swift justice. At Mergen's hand it sent a message to more than the defeated Uulgar; his own chieftains with a mind to seek the khanate for their sons shifted in their places.

General Yesugei recovered first, or perhaps had guessed even before Mergen what his khan intended. "Take him," the general instructed a handful of his troops, breaking the moment with his voice. "See that no drop of blood taints this place."

Mergen heard breathing again, the rustle of warm bodies. With a nod he acknowledged the service. He wanted no part of the raider's spirit to touch the palace of his ancestors.

When they had taken up the body by its hands and feet, the second of the two old raiders barked a protest, "You can have the loot, all of it! Take the cub if you want him. Only spare my life and I will give you the Uulgar people!"

The young chieftain quaked where he stood, very pale as he watched the guardsman carry out his relative. He showed no surprise to hear himself offered up as a sacrifice to Qubal vengeance, nor did he speak either to confirm his guilt or to separate himself from the raider who blustered at his side. He could be no older than his own son Qutula, Mergen realized, a fact which must not influence his judgment. He set the thought aside, unwilling to consider the boy's fate sooner than he must and focused on the more pertinent of the chieftain's bribes.

"As you can see, I already hold the Uulgar in my palm. The question remains only, do I clasp it lightly?" He extended his hand to show the fingers curved gently, as if they held something both fragile and precious. "Or crush it, as the Uulgar would have done to the Qubal, squeezing the life out of the clans to fill your coffers by the blood of our dead? As he spoke, he tightened his fist until the knuckles whitened.

Sweat bloomed on the old chieftain's lip as desperation replaced arrogance in his eyes. He would have fallen to his knees, but Mergen's guardsmen held him up by his arms.

"I can make you rich beyond your dreams!"

"Perhaps," Mergen agreed. "But I can send you to a place beyond wealth or dreams."

It took only a glance at the guardsmen who stood behind the prisoner, but he hadn't expected his own blanket-son to step forward.

Qutula seized the hair of the Uulgar chieftain "How, my lord khan?" he asked, readying himself to strike. It troubled Mergen that his son chose to honor him with this grim service, but he would not shame him by hesitating.

"Quickly," he answered. At need, to extract information or to serve as a lesson, he could draw out the death of a prisoner for days of screaming torment. But he took no pleasure in such punishments and hoped Qutula understood.

Like a serpent striking, Qutula's arm curled around the man's throat. The man struggled, but the khan's guardsmen grasped him firmly. Muscles stood out in carved relief as his son's arm crushed the wind out of his prisoner with iron strength. Mergen held his eye, refusing to flinch away from the act as the dying man's thrashing slowed, then stopped. Someone had to do it, certainly. Death was the work of a soldier and he appreciated how promptly his son obeyed him. Some hesitance in the matter of cold-blooded killing would have pleased him more, though he wasn't certain why he felt that way.

"How do your stolen riches serve you now?" Mergen asked the dead man as Qutula released his hold and stepped back, letting the body fall into the arms of the waiting guardsmen.

Unruffled, Yesugei watched him over the body between them. Mergen saw well into the soul of his friend, however; saw the furtive, troubled glance he cast at the youngest warrior brought before them as a chieftain. The sacrificial goat, he figured, meant to be the one to pay for all their crimes, while his elders haggled with the khan over the spoils of the recent war.

The general would take it on himself to execute the boy if it were demanded of him, but he questioned the justice of such an act. As he turned his attention to the young man, a son perhaps, or a nephew of the old chieftain, so did Mergen.

Guardsmen in blue had laid hold of the younger prisoner, but he made no move to defend his relative or to take vengeance for his death. Rather, he raised his head with the pride of one who has seen too much and looks only to finish the job as bravely as he began it.

"We have lost our khan to an evil sorcerer," he said, "the sorcerer to battle, and yet a third khan to your vengeance, my lord." The young warrior's voice drifted off, his eyes lost to a private grief that went far to explain his place among the chieftains. Mergen winced, imagining his own sons, his nephew and heir, standing in the youth's place in front of an unfriendly khan.

"I have seen the futility of trying to strike a bargain with the Qubal-Khan," he went on with less bitterness than despair. "But I beg mercy—" He dropped to his knees then, almost ending his life at the hands of battle-nerved guardsmen. But he stayed where he was, arms out in supplication, "—for my people only, the ten thousand you hold prisoner here and the tens of ten thousand, peaceful herders and their wives and flocks who await their return. What will become of them?"

Not "us," Mergen noted. He expected to die as his elders had, but still he pleaded for his people. "You wear no badges on your chest," he persisted, wanting an answer to this riddle before he handed down judgment. He had a nephew watching him, learning how to lead, and sons who understood from his actions the value of following a just khan.

"Not all the Uulgar take such trophies. We have come to know, at great cost, the price of honor."

"Master Markko was good at teaching such lessons, I understand." Mergen goaded him. The magician had left a path of death and destruction across thousands of li. Accepting the hospitality of the raider clans within sight of his goal, Markko had poisoned the Uulgar-Khan and seized his tents and armies as a weapon he used to lay siege to heaven. He'd lost that final battle, but the Uulgar had a head start on conquest and tyranny well before the magician had shown up to give them a touch of their own lash.

"He certainly taught us the cost of losing," the boy agreed. "I don't need another such lesson. The Uulgar are yours. If you plan to kill me, I wish you would do so now and save me the humiliation of abasing myself any further for nothing. If you would ransom me, I must in conscience tell you that the only person who would have paid for me now lies dead at the khan's own hand."

Well spoken. With better teachers than a mad magician and a raider for a parent, the boy might have made a worthy khan, perhaps even a husband for Eluneke to seal a treaty of friendship between their people. Mergen gave no sign by any softening of eye or quirk of lip where his judgment might lead, but he wanted to test the young man further. "And what would you do with one such as yourself, were you on the dais and I at your feet?" he asked.

The young man who would have been khan of the Uulgar people sat back on his heels, considering the question. He answered with one of his own. "If I said that in your place I would return your flocks and herds and send you intact to reclaim your lands and tents, would you take my advice and free me to lead my Uulgar clansmen home?"

"No," Mergen conceded. The court murmured with laughter. A chuckle escaped even the Lady Bortu, though she might have drawn blood with the sharpness of her gaze on the prisoner. Next to him, Mergen felt the presence of his heir, tense and waiting, absorbing every word. *That's right,* he thought. *Pay attention. If things had gone differently, you would be kneeling in this young khan's place, begging for the lives of the Qubal clans.*

"That isn't really an option."

"I didn't think it was." The young man gave a bitter laugh. "I won't bandy words with you. I'm not a diplomat and I'd rather not make a fool of myself before I die. But if you would grant me one boon, I ask only to accompany your army as a hostage. With my words and actions I would persuade your emissary that a whole people should not be judged by the actions of a few." He gave a little shrug, a rueful half smile. "Even if those few are their leaders. By my example as our dead khan's heir, the Uulgar will learn to love the Qubal-Khan as their own."

The boy had offered him a gift in the loyalty of the Uulgar, but too much mercy would make the Qubal look weak. A price had to be paid. But, "Not a hostage," Mergen-Khan judged, "since by your own word there is none to pay your ransom. But a slave, bound to serve for a full cycle of the seasons, or more if your master should deem your freedom to be a danger to the Qubal ulus. As for what is to be done with such a slave, that is a decision best made by he who will hold your bond. My emissary, indeed. General Yesugei, what would you do with this young warrior who will not, it seems, be a khan today?"

Yesugei's gaze searched the khan's face as if he might find some other meaning there, but Mergen didn't soften in his resolve. "In the morning, good Yesugei, allow the women who lost husbands in the war to choose from among the most presentable of the prisoners. Then I would have you ride out with an army of our best warriors and the ten thousand of prisoners to lay claim to the Uulgar lands and rule there in my name."

"If my own wishes carry any weight in the decision, I would not leave your side." The general bowed low to his khan while his eyes accused a friend of many complex things. Banishment for one. Standing in the way of his suit for Sechule's attentions for another. His words, however, offered perfect solicitude. "Who knows better the enemies closest to your tents than one who has fought at your side and at your command to the very gates of a foreign heaven?"

The Lady Chaiujin, he meant, who had murdered Mergen's brother and his brother's wife. They had seen or heard no sign of the lady-serpent since their return from war, however. Given the politics of a living court and his knowledge of both ladies, Mergen believed Sechule the more dangerous of the two. The false Lady Chaiujin had no claim on him.

To make certain the general understood the full import of the honor bestowed on him, Mergen countered the question with one of his own, spoken loud enough for all to hear. "Who would I send to be khan in my place but my best right hand?"

A murmur passed through the great ger-tent palace like a wave through grass. The general would be a khan in his own right. Not over the Qubal ulus and still answering to Mergen as his gur-khan—-khan of khans—but a khan with a ger-tent palace and five hundred retainers and an army of his own. Perhaps that would be enough for Sechule. If not, Yesugei might choose from among the noble ladies of the Uulgar as many wives as he wanted to warm his tents.

A light had ignited in General Yesugei's eye as he came to understand the full import of his new position. "As the gur-khan wishes," he agreed, the first to address Mergen by the new title he had claimed, and held himself a little taller, as befitted a khan.

"Now about this noble slave—" Mergen's conscience would let him sleep peacefully enough over the death of the old raider who had worn the trophies of his murders on his chest. He counted on his general's humanity to spare an innocent boy, however.

"I will need captains to ride at my side," Yesugei said. "And a figure known to the prisoners to treat with his master on their behalf." He turned to the young man, who balanced on the knife point of his words, knowing that his life or death depended on the outcome. Mergen watched with admiration as he drew himself up, waiting for reprieve or the blow that would end his life.

"Do you pledge fealty to the gur-khan Mergen of the Qubal ulus?" Yesugei asked him. "Do you declare that all the lands and clans of the Uulgar-who-were now belong to the Qubal-who-are?"

The mouthful was hard to swallow. The boy had pledged the loyalty of the Uulgar, but had not surrendered their name. Tears he had not shed at the death of his father now gathered in the corners of the young man's eyes. But he bowed to the dais, so low that his head knocked on the carpets. Still bent over his knees, he touched his forehead to Yesugei's booted foot.

"All that the Uulgar were has been destroyed," he said.

"Only the Qubal remain, stronger now by ten thousand of army and many tens of thousands of herders who call the South their home. This I pledge with my life."

"You do that a lot, boy," Mergen commented wryly as the boy climbed to his feet. "Are you so anxious to throw away your existence on this plane?" The question was a test of sorts. In less than a season he'd lost a war, his father, and now his home. Perhaps he offered his life so glibly in the hope that someone would take it and spare him any further losses. If that were so, better to give him what he wanted now than after he'd committed some costly mischief to earn it.

"I'm more anxious to keep my skin intact than you could know, Mergen-Gur-Khan. But I've seen what happens when a soldier trades his honor for gain. I would not ride down that road."

"Spoken like a true Qubal warrior."

"Thank you, gur-khan."

Mergen saw him flinch at the reminder of his losses, but the boy bowed deeply to accept the compliment. Taking a breath to gird himself against the shame, he turned next to Yesugei. "What would you have me do, master?"

"If I have your parole, you are free to go. Find your people and prepare them for the morning." Yesugei-Khan gave no sign of softness that might have humbled the boy further, but waved a dismissal.

With a bow, the young slave backed away from the dais but Mergen stopped him with one last question. "Do you have a name, boy?"

"I did." He turned and bowed again, offering Mergen a level gaze filled with meaning. "That name, like the people who gave it to me, no longer exists."

Mergen nodded, understanding. Shame demanded one more loss. In this, at least, he could reward the sacrifice. "Then I will give you the name of my anda, Otchigin, who died in the wars brought on us all by the magician-usurper."

Again the nobles and chieftains put their heads together; the buzz of their whispered conversation reaching even to the dais. All the court knew of the love he had borne for his blood brother. But Otchigin the elder would not be coming back from the dead. It was time to move on. The young warrior read more in Mergen's silence than he felt comfortable sharing, but he accepted the gift as the challenge it was.

"If my fame should rise in the service of my khan, I share it gladly with my namesake." With that, the new Otchigin turned and walked down the aisle, his back tensed as if he expected a spear between his shoulders with each step.

Mergen waited until the boy had passed the firebox, then he yawned and stretched. "Great Sun rises early after feasting," he said, giving his general and all the court permission to find their own beds.

"We march at break of day, but now I must find sleep," Yesugei agreed. He gave his bow and followed the new Otchigin from the ger-tent palace, trailed by the chieftains and many of the nobles. They would whisper of this day's work in their own tents, and make their own judgments about their new khan.

Bolghai, who had waited until Mergen-Gur-Khan had made this latest pronouncement to speed the spirits of the Uulgar dead on their way to the underworld, settled a stoatlike gaze on him. Slowly the lashes lowered over the shaman's glittering eyes and slowly they lifted again. What thoughts he hid behind them as he began to beat his drum, Mergen chose not to ask.

Mergen likewise refused to wonder what bed Yesugei would find that night. Casting about for something to occupy his mind before the feel of a man dying in his hands robbed him of all sleep, he remembered Jumal's strange behavior during Bekter's hero-tale about Prince Tayy and the bear. What had Jumal meant by it? So far, the boy had held Prince Tayy's friendship, second only to Mergen's blanket-son. Did he chafe to take Qutula's place on the dais? To offer gifts of blood brotherhood? That would be impossible. Qutula rose above his rank on the unspoken promise of his father's favor. Jumal had no such claims to lift him to a higher saddle.

One drunken night did not conspiracy make. Jumal seemed more likely to throw his life away in some extravagantly heroic act to win favor than to harm the prince in some rage at his own lot in life. He didn't want to cause dissension in the ranks of his nephew's guardsmen with suspicions if the young warrior's intentions were pure, and he wouldn't trust an inexperienced watch to know if they were not. With Yesugei gone in the morning, who would he trust with such a duty?

None. But Yesugei might still serve in this if not in matters closer to home. He would send Jumal as one of the young captains in the new khan's personal guard. The fortunes of Jumal's clans would rise in the South and Mergen would remove the risk that some rash act might drive the Qubal clans into grief and disaster again, so soon after Chimbai's death.

Satisfied that he had resolved the most pressing problems of his court, Mergen rolled over in the furs of his bed and tried to sleep. It was a lonely bed, however, and he allowed himself to dream of the day that he might step down from the khanate and take a wife. Until then, he resolved to sleep alone; Sechule had taught him well enough the dangers of a casual bed.

Qutula sat astride his horse at Prince Tayyichiut's right hand, and watched General Yesugei—now Yesugei-Khan—lead the army of ten thousand prisoners south to lay claim to the Uulgar lands in the name of Mergen-Gur-Khan. On either side of the broad central avenue crowds had gathered to cheer the army on its way. Prayers followed like the dogs who ran beside them, baying with their own mournful greeting. All but the prince's hounds, of course. They flanked his mare, alert to every movement in the crowd but never leaving his side. Occasionally the red bitch snapped at the heels of Qutula's mount, but she made no other protest at his presence this morning. Court manners, even in his dogs.

He didn't let the bitch's dislike bother him but held his head up proudly as befit one who stood among the highest members of his father's court. All might see who looked upon them that he ranked second only to the prince and the Lady Bortu themselves in closeness to the khan.

Pride wasn't enough to keep his mind on the rank of scruffy

prisoners filing by. Memories of the night before, however, had offered sufficient entertainment to hold him quietly to his seat this morning. His lady of mystery hadn't come to him in their place by the river. He finally wandered home to his mother's tent to find the general there, hidden under his mother's blankets as if no one would notice who lay there. Qutula had politely muttered a singular greeting on his way to his own bed, pretending to ignore the pair who quickly resumed their argument in hushed tones under Sechule's blankets.

"I *am* a khan!" Yesugei had whispered himself hoarse in his impossible quest. Sechule had been adamant: she would not follow him south.

"I don't stay for myself, but for my sons," she insisted.

True enough as far as it went, Qutula thought. She planned to ride her son's coattails into Mergen's tents.

"You see how close my son sits to the khan, who now calls himself gur-khan, ruler over khans as well as clans."

That would appeal to her more than traveling as a camp follower and second wife to a minor khan who still set his hand beneath Mergen's foot, however great his title. But Yesugei refused to take "no" for an answer, and Sechule somehow managed to reject him without ever quite saying "no" in the first place. It had all grown so boring and useless that at one point Qutula had risen up in his bed and muttered, "Who's there?" as if he'd just awakened to their noise.

The poor general had fallen silent, as if he hadn't meant to be caught in a mother's bed, arguing for her to leave her sons behind for an uncertain future among people who had, until this night, been the enemy. Finally he had departed with his trousers in his hands instead of promises and they'd all gotten some sleep. He'd still be annoyed about the whole thing except that there in the front, next to Yesugei and looking about as happy to be going as the general, rode Jumal. The spirits were smiling on Qutula today, and about time, too. He didn't let his elation show, but sat firm and proud in his saddle, imagining Prince Tayyichiut dead and his own horse one step closer to the heart of the khan.

Mergen's voice, full-throated to reach the crowd, brought

him out of his reverie. "Salute your victors!" he cried, meaning the soldiers of his army who filled the grand avenue. Half would go with General Yesugei to subdue the Uulgar while the remainder would stay behind to serve the khan at home. And then he gave the word to break camp. "We move before Little Sun reaches the horizon!" he declared. Enough time to fold the tents and pack them on the carts, not longer. Great Sun would still be on the rise. Some would head out in their own directions, but the army and those who supplied it would follow the khan to the court's next camp, farther up the river. And with Jumal gone, Prince Tayy would need his company all the more.

With a smile that might have been joy that the camp was moving again, Qutula asked permission to help his mother fold her tent. When it was given, he bowed his thanks and turned his horse down the avenue where a conquered army had just passed. The crowd had not yet dispersed and would have seen him speaking familiarly with the gur-khan. He rode with his head high, therefore, and with a stern and courtly expression on his face, so that all who saw him would wonder at his heroic profile and remember him when he had passed.

Chapter Fourteen

BEKTER LEFT HIS HORSE to crop the wet grass by the shamaness' tent. The rains of late summer had begun soon after they'd made camp, and he cursed his luck at having to be out in the wet. He had songs to write and music to work out on nice dry instruments in the comfort of the ger-tent palace. Instead, he was out on the ragged edges of the tent city, following the gur-khan's secret instructions.

"Find out what you can about this girl," his father had charged him, "but don't tell anyone—especially Prince Tayyichiut."

He hadn't understood at first. Then it was clear that Mergen had seen Tayy looking at the girl on their way home from the hunt for Nogai's Bear, as it had become known. He'd protested the gur-khan's concern.

"It was nothing, a chance encounter with a stranger. Neither of them spoke a word. I'm sure the prince hasn't seen her since the hunt." Tayy knew better than to look at a lowborn girl for a wife, and he knew better than to take on a shamaness as a mistress. Lady Chaiujin had taught them all a bitter lesson about the power of potions in a royal bed. But something in the way Mergen-Gur-Khan had looked at him cautioned Bekter against saying any of that to his father.

So here he was, out in the rain and the mud, tracking down

an apprentice shaman in a clan that didn't have two sheep to warm a pen together while his brother got the easy task, keeping an eye on the prince. Qutula already sat at Prince Tayyichiut's right hand, tasted his food, and rode with him in the hunt, all of which gave him every opportunity to serve the khan in his request. How was Bekter to explain his presence in the tent of a lowly shamaness who served a nameless clan?

Above the lintel the shamaness' totem—a stuffed raven—watched him with a penetrating glassy gaze. "What are you looking at?" he mumbled at the bird. Shaking the water off of his oiled coat he reached out to open the door and halted, frozen where he stood. He could hear the shuffle of bodies on the other side, more than seemed reasonable for a tent of just two lattices. A religious ceremony? When the visitors settled, a woman began to tell a story familiar to Bekter. He would have thought to no one else, however. Had Mergen been right about the political danger all along?

"This is the story of two kings, and two wars, and a princess of the Qubal people whose name was Alaghai the Beautiful."

Toragana sat on the stool normally reserved for patients, the hem of her feathered robes puddling around her feet. On her head the raven headdress gazed down on the children who huddled together on the floor in rapt attention as she began the seldom-told tale of the Unfaithful Brothers. Until the coming of the god-king, few among the Qubal even remembered that such a tale existed, or that a foreign king had ever held the reins in the grasslands. Now people wanted to know why their khan had taken the Qubal to war for the Cloud Country in the god-king's name. And so the story had come full circle. The shameful tale of betrayal by the Unfaithful Brothers had become the tale of Two Kings and honor restored.

"In that long-ago time, the Qubal-Khan had two warrior sons renowned for their cunning in battle and a daughter, Alaghai, known for her wisdom and beauty. Swift as the move-

ment of caravans over the grass, reports of the princess had
traveled, from the Shan Empire to the Cloud Country on the
roof of the world."

The eyes of the children grew wide with awe. A thousand
li of grasslands lay between those two great powers, and a thousand more. She might have said heaven for all they compre-
hended such distances. They understood the next part easily
enough, though—

"She had eyes warm and deep as a doe, the poets said, and
a figure graceful as the summer wind in the grass. All the nobles and the princes from afar came to win the hand of Princess
Alaghai the Beautiful, but she loved the Qubal people dearly
and honored her father above all men."

The children applauded Alaghai's loyalty. "Loved us best of
all!" they crowed. "I love my papa best, too!"

Toragana took up the story firmly, and her audience fell still
again, listening as she set her hands to her heart and recited
Alaghai's challenge: " 'Find me a husband as brave, as true as
our own khan. Let him set up his tents among the Qubal. Then
perhaps I will choose differently,' she told the old grandmothers who came to the ger-tent palace with suitable young men for
the princess to wed. They went away again shaking their heads,
for who could find a man of more regal bearing, of greater
strength of arm or spirit than the great khan of the Qubal people?"

A stirring at the door brought Toragana's head up. The
young man who stood there made her smile in spite of herself.
He had opened his oiled coat to reveal rich clothes of embroidered silk he wore thoughtlessly, as if they meant nothing to
him. And yet this was no handsome hero to sway a princess out
of tales. He stood no more than middling height, but with a
girth to make up for his lack in length. His face was soft and
welcoming, though caution warred with a natural lively curiosity in his eyes.

"How may I help you?" she asked him, while a suggestion
or two passed wistfully through her mind. She might have
shared at least the offer with him if not for the children gathered at her feet. Too young, she amended her own unspoken

thoughts; her visitor had seen barely nineteen summers, she guessed. Not much older than her apprentice, and the wary expression he'd worn on entering had turned to confusion. He might have come for the answer to one riddle only to discover suddenly that his questions had become irrelevant. She didn't see how the story of Alaghai the Beautiful could have troubled him so. It ended sadly, of course, but that all happened long ago.

With a wave of his fingers he set aside his own errand, however. "I can wait. The story is more important."

Any well-mannered Qubal would withdraw with some polite phrase until the lessons were done. But the young man in clothes more suited to the ger-tent palace of a khan than the poor tent of a shamaness didn't excuse himself. Instead, he curled one leg under him, propped his chin on his other knee, and prepared to listen. The children made room for him with their own solemn courtesy and together they turned their watchful eyes to her, willing her to continue.

There seemed no way to budge him short of rudeness or some spell of magic, extreme measures and uncalled for given his benign regard. With a little shrug to settle her robes more comfortably about her, therefore, Toragana picked up the tale where she had left it.

"Like our own times, the days of Alaghai the Beautiful were filled with war and suffering until a king came down from the Cloud Country with his tents and armies, bearing peace in his right hand and demanding tribute with his left. At the great feast of his goddess the clans must come forward with their offerings, from each a horse or sheep as they might spare. In the peace he brought, the sheep grew fat and the herds thundered over the grass like a great dark storm sweeping the land. No Qubal would lack, and some called the king from the Cloud Country Llesho the Great. But some chafed at a foreign ruler and some took insult at foreign gods. And some burned with jealousy for the love of Alaghai the Beautiful."

Bekter smiled in spite of himself as the shamaness acted out the tale, puffing out her cheeks like a fat sheep and swaying her arm in elegant waves to mimic clouds of horses running on the plains. He hadn't found the girl he'd been sent to investigate, or a conspiracy. Rather, ten small children—he counted them for his report—stared up at the shamaness with shining eyes as she told the story of the Qubal debt of honor.

The old tale drew him in and, against his better judgment, so did the subtle power of the teller. When she smiled at the children, they followed her every move like flowers to sunshine. Bekter found himself doing the same. Bolghai didn't have that effect on his audiences, so he figured it wasn't the dangerous influence of a shaman's knowledge. She wasn't beautiful in the usual way either. He knew the pitfalls of a beautiful woman; Sechule had raised him, after all. She was too tall, for one thing, her features sharp and alert like her totem animal.

And she was too old, nearly as old as his mother, he guessed. He'd looked at girls his own age before, even visited a tent or two, though he'd never exposed his own timid experiences to his brother's ridicule. He didn't feel that way about the shamaness, though. Modesty and his own taste had turned his eye from the matrons and widows and that hadn't changed suddenly.

But the shamaness loved the tale and the children. He felt a stern and demanding affection for all things in the living world and the dead rolling from her robes like a summer breeze, warming each heart she touched. When she smiled, he wanted to smile. And if she walked, he thought, his feet would carry him along behind her.

"Was he handsome?" a little girl at her knee asked. It took Bekter a minute to realize that she was talking about King Llesho in the story.

"Was he brave?" a boy's voice demanded.

Bekter remembered the story as Chimbai-Khan had told it, before he died and Mergen took his place to lead them against the mad magician for the Cloud Country. *Was love worth the price he paid for it?* The thought left a bitter taste in his mouth. But the ending wasn't always the point of the tale. . . .

"**W**as he a good king?" the young man asked with a bitter-sweet smile, secret knowledge curled at the corner of his upturned lip. In his eyes, Toragana saw layers to his question, none of them simple enough to reassure children.

"Brave, surely," she answered the easiest question first. "King Llesho drove the Tinglut from the western grasslands and set the Uulgar lands under his own watch in the South. By strength of his arms and the might of his sons he brought peace to all the grasslands.

"As for handsome, his hair was streaked with gray and his face lined with the cares of a king and a father. Alaghai the Beautiful could have chosen a prince of Shan, or a khan's son. The king of the Cloud Country himself had many sons, all swift and strong and handsome and some in need of a first wife. In the king's eyes, however, she saw understanding, like sunlight glinting off the mountains, and a yearning kindness that belied his prowess in battle. So I would say that Princess Alaghai thought him good, and that his goodness made him handsome in her eyes."

The children giggled. Behind them, the young man smiled. *I know how that girl felt,* she realized, though he was too young instead of too old, and not a king. One never knew what the winds of fate would blow up against one's tent, of course. He wouldn't be the first king to sweep into the city of the khan, but it didn't seem likely in spite of the casual wealth he wore about him. Toragana trusted her shaman's instincts, but they were confused today, except for the absolute clarity of the young man's goodness.

Foolishness. A woman her age had better things to do than contemplate the virtues of young men. She would finish her story, give him the charm or potion he'd come for, and be done with it.

"Now it happened that King Llesho's first wife had died. He had his second wife and his concubines to keep him company, but his heart wept for what he had lost, a true companion his equal in wisdom and charity."

"Alaghai the Beautiful," the children whispered among themselves, for who would better suit this wise king out of the clouds.

"Alaghai the Beautiful," she agreed. "The great king came down from the Cloud Country to accept the tribute of the Qubal people. At her father's side, he saw the princess so renowned for her beauty and instantly he fell in love. When he returned home, he sent many gifts to her father the khan, and asked for his daughter in marriage.

"At first, Alaghai saw only the sorrow that wrapped the king like a cloak. Gradually, her pity turned to admiration, then to love as well.

"The swan drank deeply from the rivers between them . . ." Love letters. An old riddle, even the children knew the answer to that one and giggled behind their hands at an old king behaving like a young lover.

Toragana nodded, accepting their judgment of their elders. "Yes, it seems foolish now. But the king yearned for love, and Alaghai called to his heart.

"Her father refused him, unwilling to give the greatest gift of the Qubal people to a far country. King Llesho would not be denied, however. Disguised to hide his kingly state, he traveled by caravan to the ger-tent palace itself, and it seemed that no one recognized him except for Alaghai."

As she spoke, Bekter fell more deeply under the spell of the tale until it seemed that he lived it. Taking the part of neither lover, he saw out of the eyes of the khan, first of his line on a dais so like the one he knew that it might have been the palace of Chimbai-Khan and not his ancestor. He knew the look of that old king as well; the bust he'd sent as a bride's gift had stood on a chest in Chimbai's court for all the generations his line had ruled. The god-king Llesho had worn the same face when he crossed the grasslands, asking Chimbai for soldiers to reclaim his throne.

Half in a dream he saw the old king hidden among strangers

come to pay their respects below the firebox. He saw Alaghai's eyes turn toward him and hold like a doe caught in the gaze of a tiger. Not prey, though. Color darkened his imaginary daughter's cheeks, then she cast her eyes down modestly. When she left her blankets late at night to meet her lover in some traveler's tent, the khan wept, for he had heard his sons plotting murder if the foreign king should return. For the honor of their sister, they muttered among their guardsmen. For the honor of the Qubal people they would take back the grasslands from the Cloud Country and lay waste to their oppressors.

"The khan feared there would be a child come of this late meeting," the shamaness recited. "If he refused the king his daughter in marriage, Alaghai's honor would lie in ruin. Her brothers would avenge the insult to their line with murder. They would kill their sister and her lover, bringing war again to a weary land, and the khan would lose the brightest jewel of the Qubal clans—Alaghai the Beautiful.

"But if that long-ago khan acquiesced, gave in to the demands of the importunate lovers and let his daughter marry the king, what would his sons do then? What would the sons of Llesho the Great do, seeing a new wife put above their mothers? Seeing a new heir to supplant them at home? As bitter as any war of conquest, more so is a war between those who count themselves cast aside by a father's love."

And so the king wept in the tale, and so Bekter wept to be that king, as if ensorcelled by the steady rhythm of the words.

"The day was set when the two lovers would wed." The shamaness drew the story to its early conclusion, before treachery and murder entered it. "King Llesho the Great went out to meet his sons as they came down from the mountains and rode with them in his own true form to greet the khan who waited, surrounded by his own sons and his daughter and the nobles of the Qubal people."

Bekter met her eye and it seemed the world turned in that meeting. *This is the center of the storm.* The certainty welled up in him as though his heart was too full; dread chilled the sweat that trickled down his back under his clothes. *We thought the worst was over, but this is just the calm before the arms of chaos embrace us again.* The notion tied his guts in a queasy knot. Whatever was going to happen, the shamaness was part of it. And her apprentice, no doubt. If he were a different kind of man, he would have recommended that his father kill them both to protect the ulus. But he wasn't, so he added a last coda to the story as a warning.

"At the wedding, Alaghai danced with her husband and her husband's sons," he said. "Each son kissed her on the cheek and called her 'mother.' But her brothers gave no blessings and her father wept."

The children wouldn't understand, hearing only the part of the story she had just told them. But the shamaness would know how history ended the tale. Warned that her plots had been found out, if such they were, he hoped that she might set aside the whirlwind.

"We're finished here," she told the children, rising and flapping her feathered sleeves at them. "I have work to do. Potions to mix, patients to see. This young man has waited long enough to have his needs tended."

She waited until they had all run squealing with energy out into the rain. Then, settling the ruffled feathers of her robes, she turned her inquisitive, birdlike gaze on him.

"So, then, good sir. What can I do for you that the shaman who serves your own clan cannot give you?"

Poison, he thought to ask, *an unfaithful lover* to probe the areas of her complicity against the khan. But he saw no guilt in the birdlike eyes that watched him, only a wry amusement. Young men wishing to keep their affairs secret had crept into her tent more than once, he figured, and from her expression guessed that they went away again no more satisfied than when they had come. Or at least, in the matter that had brought them. He'd seen that look on women's faces when they gazed at the prince or even Qutula, but he'd never seen it turned on himself before. Not even in the beds he'd found his way to in his own sooty nights.

She made no offer, not that he would have accepted, but she left him rather at a loss for a moment.

"My name is Bekter."

"The khan's great poet! 'The prince rode out, who all men call the Son of Light, Bright shining in his armor,' " she recited with a slight bow. "Your songs carry your reputation before you. I am Toragana, of little repute, but you must know that already."

He blushed to hear his songs returning to him from this unlikely place, sufficiently flustered that the shamaness didn't look too closely when he made no comment about her own identity. Mergen-Gur-Khan had charged him to find the girl, and he'd asked around for what he remembered—a tent with the sign of the raven above the door. In a more peaceful age those of whom he asked directions would have nodded amiably and given him her name and a story or two to go with it. But these were less trusting times; strangers had brought death into the Qubal city even before the gur-khan's army had marched to war. So he had found her tent, but only now her name. Knowing that would give her the high ground between them, he was still trying to figure out what precarious ground they stood upon, so he let his expression answer while he posed his own excuse for being there.

"The gur-khan has charged me to make a history of the Qubal people. With your permission, I would listen to your stories and make them into songs for the court." He hadn't planned it but, being mostly true, it seemed as good a reason as any for spending time in the shamaness' tent.

She looked at him as if he'd sprouted a second head. "I am familiar with Bolghai, who serves as shaman to the court," she said. "He knows the story at least as well as I do. Better, I have no doubt. Why search out one as insignificant as I, when better is right at hand?"

"If you're familiar with Bolghai, you shouldn't need to ask!" He answered her wry smile with an effort at the sexy grin Qutula seemed to manage so easily. "His face is far less fair, his form less interesting, and—"

"His smell is certainly not appealing," she said with a laugh. She didn't take his foolishness seriously, but it had distracted her from his deception.

"May I come again? Tomorrow, if it wouldn't be too much trouble?"

"The day after," she suggested instead. "I have heard that we move camp again tomorrow."

He opened his mouth to offer his help in packing but closed it again. He had Sechule to consider, and when the court moved every hand took guard duty, even Bekter. "The day after, then," he agreed with the slight bow proper when asking a favor from one of ambiguous status. Her position as shamaness gave her rank that her lowly clan took away again.

"Ask for Toragana," she told him. "Anyone in these parts will know where to find me."

She watched him as he bowed himself out, imagining his strong, sure fingers playing the lute for the khan's court. Other uses for those fingers came to her, but she put those thoughts aside. She had no question that Bekter's sudden appearance bore more on Eluneke's visions than her own personal charms or storytelling ability. " 'Bright shining one' indeed," she mused. "I wonder if you realize all that you have done with your song?"

But he was gone, and until she knew more about him, she wouldn't have asked it anyway.

Chapter Fifteen

SOMETHING WAS GOING ON between General Yesugei and his uncle. He'd been thinking about the problem ever since Mergen sent the general to hold the grasslands of the Uulgar clans in his name. Tayy figured it wasn't exactly an argument yet, but it was enough to put him on his guard. From the dais he took a quick look around him. Yesugei's absence left a gap in the gur-khan's defenses not easily filled. Politics had a part in it, for one thing. Mergen had named Yesugei khan in his place among the Uulgar and had taken the title of gur-khan— khan of khans—for himself.

That the general wasn't happier about his sweeping change in fortunes had a lot to do with Sechule, Mergen's poorly-kept secret since before the prince or his cousins were born. If wealth and distance didn't mend the breach, Tayy feared the gur-khan might be compelled to end it more permanently—and to his sorrow—with an execution. Before the war he would not have credited it, but Mergen had lately proved himself in delivering swift and deadly justice against his enemies. He hoped General Yesugei saw as much and tempered his love with caution.

Beside him on the dais, Qutula handed Tayy a meat pie with one bite missing. He accepted absently, grown used to his cousin tasting his food. When he bit into the pie, the richness of sheep fat exploded pleasantly in his mouth. He took a moment to savor it as thoughts about his elders tumbled in his head.

For Mergen's sake, and because her sons Qutula and Bekter had been among his first childhood companions, he tried to like his uncle's former—probably—mistress. She was pretty enough for somebody that old, but she had a way of watching him when she thought he didn't see it that unnerved him. Sechule always seemed to be counting up the pebbles on the board and she was never happy about the sum. He figured to stay out of her way. Licking his fingers, he decided that if his elders didn't have the sense to do the same they deserved their broken hearts. They were too old to be chasing women anyway.

Sechule wasn't the only bad match on his mind, however. The khan's tent city, much reduced from the size it had grown to during the war, had set up on the plains. As always, the khan's city followed the Onga, but here the river disappeared into a little dell. When last they had set up camp in this place, the emerald green bamboo snake-demon, masquerading as his father's second wife, had murdered Chimbai-Khan in his bed. Tayy planned to visit the shrine where his father's pyre had burned and make an offering of his own to the ancestral spirit. He thought he'd kept his intentions to himself, but his grandmother had been reading his heart since he was on leading reins. It didn't surprise him that she anticipated him now.

"Give this to my son among the spirits for me," Bortu told him, and put a pie into his hands.

"I will." He wrapped the gift in a clean bit of red silk, his own offering, and tucked it in the pocket of his lightweight yellow court coat embroidered from the upturned silver toes of his boots to his throat with the symbols of earth and sky and water. "If I have your permission?" He bowed deeply to his uncle the gur-khan, who gave it with a nod, his own sorrowful memories clear in his eyes.

"Give my brother a good account of me," Mergen asked, to which Tayy gave a second bow.

"Always," he promised. Then he kissed his grandmother respectfully first on one cheek and then on the other.

Qutula followed him from the dais. On the way past the firebox they picked up Bekter and Mangkut and others of his cadre on duty in the ger-tent palace. Together they headed for the door, where Altan waited with the dogs and the horses. Jumal had gone south as a captain in Yesugei-Khan's army to claim the Uulgar clans in the name of the gur-khan. The tents of his clans had gone with him, counting the young captain's rise in fortunes as their own.

They were gone, and Altan was already having trouble with the dogs. Tayy gave his friend a companionable nod over the heads of the hounds who snugged their bodies up close on either side of him and snarled to remind Qutula of their dislike. The dogs made his mare nervous and she kept her distance, stamping her foot and shaking the bristles of her mane in her impatience to be going.

"Enough, both of you!" With a vigorous rub to remind them of his affection, Tayy settled the dogs with a sharp command and whistled for the mare. When his guardsmen would have mounted their own horses to join him, he put a hand on Qutula's shoulder, to keep him on his feet. His cousin flared his nostrils, perhaps seeing in the gesture too much of the same command that had put the dogs in their place. He didn't mean it that way.

"Not today," he said, and gave Qutula's shoulder a companionable squeeze to show that there was no rift between them. "This is something I have to do alone."

"Your uncle won't approve," Bekter objected, though Tayy knew this cousin would rather compose songs with the court musicians than ride with the warriors. "We have the khan's orders to protect you."

"Protect me from what? We are in our own lands, our enemies to the north have become our allies and our enemies to the south answer to the khan through his general."

"Accidents—" In Duwa's mouth, it sounded like a suggestion more than a warning, but Tayy dismissed this excuse as well.

"Which you can't prevent if they are to happen."

"There may be poisonous snakes in the grass," Qutula suggested, a painful reminder of how Chimbai-Khan had died. He seemed unaware that his hand rubbed at his breast in the very place where Tayy had seen the emerald-green tattoo come to snaky life.

The gesture troubled the prince. His cousin had called the mark a reminder, but Tayy had felt the bruises of Qutula's thumbs for days after they wrestled for the khan. Try as he might to believe in his guardsman, suspicion, like a worm, had crawled into his heart and slowly ate away at his trust.

"I'll make plenty of noise to warn away the natural vipers," he said. "As for the unnatural kind, the one I am thinking of had too much love of luxury to remain long in the grass. The Lady Chaiujin is long gone, off to steal the life of some less suspicious victim, I am sure."

At the mention of the serpent-demon the dogs took up their baying, demonstrating with their voices a will to defend their master.

"Of course." Qutula stepped away from the snarling dogs. He let his hand fall, but it seemed to take some effort to keep it at his side.

Tayy guided his mount toward the open grass. "If I don't come back, you'll know where to look—" The last time he'd ridden off on his own, he'd been kidnapped by pirates and set to the oar as a slave. The Marmer Sea was far from here, however, and the Qubal tent city well guarded by the khan's army.

"But nothing is going to happen. I expect to find you waiting here for me when I get back—we'll want a full accounting of this woman of yours. What we don't have ourselves, we must enjoy at secondhand!"

He had thought to lighten the tension with his gentle teasing but a furtive glance passed over Qutula's face, quickly gone again for a bland smile.

"And how long would I find myself welcome in any lady's bed if word of my visits should find their way into the camp?" A lifted eyebrow promised voluptuous secrets remaining unspoken.

Qutula hadn't mentioned her in days, and Tayy wondered if that promise was all bluff. Perhaps his cousin no longer sneaked under the tent cloths of his mystery lady. Having a few secrets of his own he felt uncomfortable pressing the point so publicly. But secrets made excellent trade goods in private. "I think you're afraid that one of us will steal her away from you," he countered. "When I return, perhaps we can find something more interesting to wager on than 'Tula's love life."

Urging his horse to a trot, he laughed at his companion's suggestions for their wagers. "Races!" Altan cried out. He had the fastest horse.

"Music!" Bekter called after him to the noisy objections of his companions. Bekter would doubtless require original songs as part of the competition, which guaranteed him the win.

"Hunting," Qutula's voice whispered in his ear, though Tayy had already ridden a distance and could scarcely hear the shouted suggestions of the others. A chill wind raised the hackles on his neck; he wondered what his cousin planned to hunt.

But the sky was clear, the tents had fallen behind with his companions, and out ahead the dogs leaped in the grass that rolled in long waves rising to the south. Outcrops of flinty rock sparkled in the afternoon light, promising mountains that were just a smudge of smoky blue in the distance. Herds of horses ran ahead of him, scattering the sheep grazing on the wildflowers that raised their heads in bunches of blue and pink and yellow and white. Tayy could feel the joy of the day surging in the horse beneath him.

"Go, girl." He gave her her head and she ran.

It wasn't until they had tired each other out and he had turned back toward camp that he saw the circle of beaten ground. The fire had reduced Chimbai-Khan's pyre to ash that had fallen in upon itself. Hooves of animals had driven the dust into the ground until nothing remained to show that a khan had gone to the ancestors but a smudge of gray, slowly losing its battle with the hardy grasses of the plains.

The beginning of a low stone shrine had formed at its center, however. Tayy slowed his horse to a walk and gave her the signal with his knees to turn toward the circle. He brought her to a halt a little distance away and dismounted, leaving her to lunch on the sweet grass. He saw no vipers, nor did any lady snake-demons dressed in green come across the grass to lure him to his death. Others had been there before him, leaving their own small gifts of food and drink and ornaments. A small bunch of wildflowers lay beside a dish of kumiss.

Stones, of course, to mark the place, rose in a small heap growing larger with each offering. Stuck into the crack between two sun-flecked rocks at the top, a ribbon with a prayer on it fluttered in the breeze. Tayy found a smooth, flat stone and placed it on the others, adding to the shrine.

"Bortu sent this pie," he squatted in the ashes of his father's pyre and unwrapped the offering, set it next to the kumiss. They would make a good meal together. Then he laid the red silk on the stones at the top of the shrine.

"The cloth is my gift, Father. The seamstresses in the underworld can make you a coat suited to your rank among the dead. Or perhaps you will want to give it as a gift to your first wife, my mother, to keep her spirit in good temper. She always loved the things you gave her."

He stayed like that a little while, in the posture of a supplicant. The red cloth caught on the sharp edge of a stone and he watched it ripple like a banner in the breeze until invisible fingers—a doubter might have said the wind—plucked it up and carried it aloft. When it disappeared into the sun, he bowed his head. "Father, I miss you. The world has changed since you left it."

As if in answer, his own black hound howled mournfully. The dogs had circled in, closing around him as they did when they sensed a disturbance. This time it didn't mean earthly danger. The hair on Tayy's neck stood up. Spirits, he thought, brushing his sleeve as they passed in the grass. When the red bitch batted his hand with the top of her head, he admitted to himself that he was glad for their company. He sat with his back against the stones, the dogs settling around him.

When he'd spoken about change, he'd meant politics. The Tinglut once again desired to negotiate marriages between their peoples in friendship. The conquered clans of the Uulgar no longer posed a threat to the Qubal or their neighbors far to the south. He didn't consider himself a hero but hoped he had grown into the man his father would be proud to see as khan.

The black hound stared up at him with such warm understanding in his eyes that Tayy felt the weight on his heart ease.
The words that came to him were of more private matters.
"Jumal is gone," he said. Rubbing the dog's neck seemed to
comfort him as much as it did the dog. "Someday, when I am
khan, I'll call him back. But what can an orphan offer him now
to match the advancement he'll earn bringing the Uulgar under
Mergen's sway?"

The black dog raised his head and uttered a high-pitched
whine of sympathy, as if he shared Tayy's pain. "I wish you'd
explain it to me," the prince muttered with his arm buried in
the dark and bristly ruff. "He thinks I'm in danger, but Mergen
sent him away before we could talk—"

The dog lifted his head so abruptly that Tayy's arm slipped
from his neck. The keenly suspicious squint in the doggy eye,
so like the thoughtful glare of Tayy's own father, made him
wonder if the creature understood more than a beast's mind
rightly ought. He knew better, of course, but it helped to pretend even for a little while that his father could hear and re-
spond through the hound. To play the game properly, he first
corrected the misperception his words might have given.

"Not Mergen. He is faithful as Great Sun, and has lost none
of his subtlety of thought while gaining your own powers of direct action." He didn't mention the deaths of the Uulgar chieftains, but the dog seemed to follow his meaning well enough.

"The danger remains unclear and Jumal, if he knew more,
didn't offer his intelligence to my uncle's general before they
set out for the south. So I am left with a warning, but with no
clue what it means."

The dog howled his anxious agreement while the red nuzzled them both like a worried mother. But no spirits spoke to
him out of their mouths and Great Sun had risen almost to the
zenith. His uncle would worry if he stayed too long at his
mourning.

"I'll figure it out," he promised himself as he regained his
feet. "In the meantime, I trust only the people who have proved
their loyalty by their actions." Mergen, surely, and Lady Bortu.
Qutula and Bekter, for his uncle's sake, though his cousin's

lapse during their wrestling match still troubled him. Altan as well, perhaps, but only Jumal and Yesugei had his complete confidence. He said none of this last aloud and the dog whined his objection.

"It's the best I can do for now." Whatever the dog or the spirits wanted, if indeed they did inhabit the hound, they hadn't made it clear enough for him to act on. They'd just have to settle for what he could manage on his own.

The mare had strayed only a little way. As he gathered up her reins, the matter of Qutula's woman came back to devil him. Or, not the woman herself, but women in general and his own hopes for a marriage to be arranged by his uncle.

Except that every time he thought of marrying, his mind supplied the face and form of the girl standing in the doorway of a tent far from the centers of power in the palace of the khan. He'd only seen her once, though he'd ridden with an eye to finding her almost every day since. Her family might have gone their own way as so many others had, taking their herds and flocks in search of fresh pasture. But he hoped not.

Just curiosity. Mergen would find him a first wife to bind the clans, and he would learn to love her as his father had loved the Lady Temulun, his mother. Perhaps some day, when he had the age and experience of a khan, he might take a second wife of his own choosing. But even then she must be of a proper family. He couldn't debase his father's blood by reaching too far beneath him, and he wouldn't dishonor the girl by sneaking into her tent at night and pretending not to know her in the day.

"I won't bring any shame to your name," he promised his father. No matter what happened, he'd never dishonor the khanate. He thought he knew that much about himself. But he longed for his father's arm around his shoulder and his gentle chiding as he explained how it must be for a young prince of royal blood.

He tried to let thoughts of the girl slide off his shoulders like rain off an oily woolen cloak, but it didn't work. In his imagination Qutula writhed in a tangle of limbs with his mystery lady. His blood leaped as he imagined himself in the scene. Setting his cousin aside, he took his place under the seductive heaps of blankets, finding there his own lady of mystery, the girl with the wide dark eyes who had entranced him with no more than a glance.

He couldn't face his guardsmen like this, so he headed away from the camp, to the place where the grasslands fell away to meet the river at the bottom of the dell.

T he Lady Bortu, who had slit a throat or two in her day and knew the ways of a spy, had grown old on the path of politics. She had seen the love her sons bore each other ease the conflicts both necessary and inadvertent that often came between two headstrong men. Then she'd seen one die and the second take his place in honorable stewardship.

Chimbai had made mistakes. His mother thanked the gods and all the spirits that his own errors hadn't killed him. That had taken treachery from outside the Qubal ulus. But they still had the aftermath of bad decisions to deal with. Mergen would recognize his sons, or not, as his conscience led him. A girl, however, was the responsibility of her grandmother. And one who set herself upon the shaman's path required more than the usual tasks of matchmaking.

Which presupposed she was the offspring of the khan and that she had the skills to take her to the underworld and back again in the rites of initiation. Many years ago Bortu herself had traveled far on that path. She had danced with the broom and in the shape of her totem had journeyed in dreams. When faced with the tree at the center of the world, however, she had turned back, choosing khan-maker over healer as her fate. She had not sought her totem form again.

How many times had she regretted that decision? When her husband died? Her daughter-in-law? Her son? The children dead in her womb before she ever bore them?

Wind in the grass, the past. Impossible to catch it or change its flight. But she would have some say in the fate of this girl. First, however, to test the truth. Did she have the shaman's gift? Was she Mergen's daughter?

Lady Bortu had to know, to have her persuasions ready before Mergen turned his eye on her. So she had outfitted both herself and her horse as drably as she might, and left at home the better part of the decorations that usually hung from the silver horns of her headdress—the fine wires laden with a curtain of beads that dangled from her lobes at court—to pass unnoticed as any old grandmother through the camp.

She asked no questions of the ranks that surrounded the ger-tent palace, who would look to Bolghai for their healing and scorn the gifts of a minor seeress of no rank at all. As she expected, however, many of the lesser folk who made their camps out of sight of the silver palace knew the tent of this shamaness, Toragana. With a weary sigh and a suggestion of the true pain in her joints she had no trouble drawing out the direction.

Leaving her mount behind the little tent, she made her way to the door at the front. Above the door the gleaming eyes of a raven greeted her, sharp and wise even in death. She knocked once, to announce herself, and entered. The tent surprised her. For one thing, it smelled of herbs and fresh things. The shamaness preserved her totem animals more carefully than Bolghai did, it seemed, using sweet herbs and scented smoke as well as other things. For another she maintained a level of tidiness that Bolghai had never imagined. The tent reminded her of her own girlhood studies and a shaman dead in battle before her grandchildren were born. There was no sign of Eluneke, however.

"You're the shamaness Toragana, then?" Lady Bortu inquired as a new patient might, cranky with her age. It disturbed her that the part came so easily to her.

"Yes, that's me. Come in." The shamaness looked up from the scrubbed workbench where she was crushing fragrant spices with a mortar and pestle. "Here, sit down." The woman gestured to a low stool by the door for the khaness to sit and reached into a small chest, painted with elaborate designs and polished until it gleamed. The corners of her gray eyes lifted in her open, friendly face, ready to sympathize with her patient. She didn't smile, which would have been improper when addressing one who needed her services, but the lines around her mouth gave her away.

The Lady Bortu declined the stool. Stealing a glance around the little tent, however, she noted that Toragana kept her rugs tidy, her brooms neatly tucked away on strings of sinew hung from pegs on the lattices. The furs of the beds were neatly stacked on the far side of the firebox, well away from the stool that marked the space by the door where the shamaness saw her clients.

"May I give you something for that toe? I have an ointment that often helps in such cases." The woman held out a small stone pot. "Apply it with a clean soft cloth on rising and before you go to sleep. The pain will come back if you stop using the ointment, but I've had no complaints of those who are faithful in its use."

Bortu turned up her nose, though it took an effort of will. "I didn't come about feet." The second joint of her right big toe certainly ached, but she thought she kept the pain reasonably hidden from the interest of strangers. Certainly she wanted to show no weakness in front of one who might prove to be a potential enemy.

"I understand." The woman's expression subtly sharpened and she put off her apron with birdlike movements. Hanging the discarded garment on a peg beside a mirror on the wall, she moved to her robes, soft deerskin covered with the feathers of ravens.

"My apprentice isn't here at the moment. I can't leave until she returns, but we can have a cup of tea while we wait. Or you can give me directions to the patient and I will follow when I can. If it's someone I've treated before, a name should suffice. We don't often see strangers here." The shamaness combined both interest and concern in her request for directions, something Bolghai had never succeeded in suggesting even under the most dire circumstances.

The Lady Bortu stopped her with a raised hand, however, as if she would physically restrain the shamaness with the gesture. For the first time since she had entered the tent, this Toragana looked uncomfortable, which was just the way Bortu wanted her. Now that she had the upper hand, she allowed herself to sit on the little stool. "I didn't come about a patient. I am here about my granddaughter."

But not a patient. The woman drew almost the right conclusion quickly enough. "As I said, I have an apprentice right now. If your granddaughter truly shows promise, you would first want to talk to the shaman who tends to your clans about taking her on."

"It seems that he has spoken to her already," Bortu answered dryly. "But you misunderstand me. Do you have no idea who I am?"

"I'm sorry, my lady, but I don't believe we have ever met."

"No," Bortu agreed, "but you have met my granddaughter."

"Eluneke?" The shaman was clearly bewildered. "Eluneke's grandmother is dead."

"One of them, perhaps."

That got the bones rolling in the woman's head. Click, click, click, it came together. A father, not unknown, but one who had chosen to stay out of Eluneke's life. Who, for some reason, had sent his mother to check on the daughter after all these years. But if the old woman was indeed Eluneke's grandmother, and her own shaman was involved in her training—Bortu saw in Toragana's eyes the moment when she realized they were talking about Bolghai, who was giving the girl a lesson this very minute. Bolghai, who served the royal court.

"Oh, my!" Eyes satisfyingly wide, hands covering her gaping mouth, the shamaness Toragana sank to the carpets as the answer to the riddle came together. "My lady khaness!"

The Lady Bortu held out her hand to be kissed, which the shamaness did, bowing her head low over Bortu's aged knuckles.

"But," the woman continued, confusion wrinkling her brow, "Bolghai must have known."

"Indeed," Bortu agreed. "He will have much to answer for on that score. But I am an old woman, and prone to seeing spirits in the wind. Perhaps my presence here means nothing and the girl can go back to all this—" She waved a dismissive hand taking in the little tent. "As if I had never been."

"If that were so, you would not have come," the shamaness countered.

Bortu didn't like the way this Toragana was gathering her cunning around her. She was right, though she couldn't know why. The khan would need young bodies to seal the compacts he made with the clans, with the Tinglut and even the Uulgar. Yesugei would need to be placated for his failure with Mergen's mistress, and the general had sons.

"Your spies have already been here—"

Spies?

"The court historian, Bekter the poet. I knew he could have no use for the tales of one like me. But if he said nothing of this, why are you telling me now?"

"Ah, Bekter. I doubt he knows, nor would he be competent to judge, though at tales no one can best him. He never lies about stories. If he said he was interested, he was, though you're likely right he didn't come to hear them in the first place.

"But this is a matter for grandmothers. I can pay you for your teaching to this point, and cover any losses you may incur from her absence. There are always girls, or boys, with the gift to replace her—"

Bortu had said too much. She saw the flicker of calculation in the woman's eyes. Not avarice, the shamaness had scented something more valuable to her kind than money or jewels. A final piece of the riddle had fallen into place, or so the woman guessed. Which was, Bortu thought, more dangerous yet.

"Your granddaughter, if so she should be, has extraordinary gifts."

"Bolghai has said so," Bortu agreed. The woman carefully had not mentioned that the khaness' granddaughter was also the daughter of the khan, and a princess, if her father chose to make her so.

"She has foreseen a grave danger."

Bortu rolled her eyes. "Why am I not surprised?" Nothing, it seemed, was ever easy.

The woman took a breath to answer, but Bortu stopped her with a freezing glance. "First I will see her. When do you expect her back?"

"That's hard to say, my lady khaness."

Bortu understood her well enough. Spirit quests seldom followed a schedule. "Then I suppose we go to her."

"I was preparing to do just that, my lady." With a deep bow, the shamaness returned to her workbench. She gathered crushed herbs into a loosely woven little sack which she threaded onto a string. Putting on her robes and her headdress, Toragana faced the khaness with eyes grown dark as the raven that watched with the wisdom of the dead from atop the shamaness' head. "I had planned to fly, but if your horse doesn't mind, I will travel with you to show you the way."

"I think he can manage," Bortu agreed, her answer laced with irony. She hoisted herself from the stool with her head held very high as befitted the mother of khans, though she wished she'd taken the ointment for her toe. Too late for that now. She led the way from the tent.

Toragana didn't follow immediately. Lady Bortu mounted and brought her horse around the front, considering a suitable punishment for a shamaness who made the mother of khans wait like a beggar at her front door. None, she concluded ruefully. With the gifts came a certain disregard for the world of living men—or women. Bolghai did it all the time. Even khans knew better than to challenge the spirits for dominion over their own. She considered leaving without the woman, could have found Bolghai's tent on her own with little trouble. That didn't guarantee she'd find Eluneke.

While she was brooding on such thoughts, a raven flew out the smoke hole in the roof of the tent and circled the khaness' head. Bortu shook her off when the creature settled on her shoulder. There were limits even for the spirit world. The creature rustled her wings as if miffed, but she never flew out of sight. Bortu followed with little more than a press of her knees against the flanks of her horse to keep the gelding on the course set by the raven. As she had guessed, they traveled away from Bolghai's little camp, heading for the river.

Chapter Sixteen

SLIDING OFF HIS HORSE, Prince Tayyichiut followed the downward path to the river on foot, drawn back to the place where his life had changed so completely. His dogs followed close on his heels, as if they feared for his safety in this place even now. He'd fought in his first real battle in this little dell and, among the dead, lost Yurki, who would in time have been his anda—the sworn friend of the heart. Here had begun his adventure with the god-king. The Lady Chaiujin had nearly killed the king-in-exile of the Cloud Country here and Llesho had nearly let her do it, or so he'd heard. And from here Tayy had taken off on an adventure that had plunged him into slavery and almost killed him.

Nothing about this place should have called to him, but it did. Nothing should have impelled him to follow that call, but he followed anyway, into the tangle of spindly hazel and scrub oak and undergrowth that lined the riverbank at its lowest point. And there, by the Onga, he found the girl who plagued his dreams. She was dressed much the same as the last time he'd seen her—the simple, dull-colored clothes of a less-than-prosperous clan and the headdress of a maiden, with none of the exaggerated curve of silver horns and cascading beads and jewels that the married women wore. In her hand she grasped a long pole with a net woven of grass at one end that she poked haphazardly at a thin, high branch.

"Hello," he said, and cursed himself for sounding like an idiot. "Do you need some help with that? What are you trying to do, by the way—"

"I'm trying to catch that toad—" She didn't look at him but kept her eyes sharply on something hiding among the leaves that shook violently when she jabbed at the branch. The dogs chose that moment to greet her with their cheerful baying.

"Oh!" she slapped down on something with the net, but her prey eluded her. "Damn! He got away." With a glare at the dogs who had joined her at the tree, she added, "If these mongrel curs are yours, you owe me one large toad."

Tayy didn't know quite what to make of her. In front of the shaman's tent he had felt both a connection to her and a sense of remote study, as if she read his soul and knew something he didn't about his own spirit-life. He'd expected neither her sharp tongue nor her interest in tree toads. Lady Chaiujin had kept a tree toad in a cage in her tent. He thought perhaps she had used the exudations of its skin for her evil potions.

"Aren't toads dangerous?" he asked, giving her the benefit of the doubt for reasons that didn't bear too close examination. "I thought they poisoned their victims with their skins."

"If you were a fly, you'd be in a sad way," the girl agreed absently. "Since you are a human being, you'd feel slightly numb where you touched one, but even that wears off quickly. It would be unwise to eat one, of course. That might prove nasty in the extreme."

Only when she had given up on the tree toad did she turn around to look at him. When she did, her mouth fell open in a round "Oh!" of surprise. "You!" she said. The dogs joined the conversation, butting her in the hip. Her net flew out of her hand as she lost her footing on the slope

There wasn't time to think. The prince reached for her hand to keep her from falling into the river and she reached back. When their fingers met, he felt a bolt of lightning run up his arm and explode in his heart. He knew the many-branched pattern lightning made when it struck flesh and expected to find the sign of the tree burned into his breast when he looked inside his shirt. The shock so overwhelmed him that he almost pulled his hand away. That would have sent her pitching head-long into the Onga.

I'd rather plunge into the current with the capstone of my father's shrine in my arms than let her fall, he thought. His hand spasmed closed around her smaller one and he tugged. The girl tipped forward into his arms to the exuberant approval of the dogs.

"Excuse me." Her voice was firm, but he felt her tremble as she carefully put him at arm's length. "Thank you for saving me from the river, though I wouldn't have needed saving if you hadn't startled me like that!"

Trying desperately to cover his confusion he stammered out an answer. "We've met before, sort of, though we were never introduced."

"I know." She primly brushed her palms off on her apron.

"I'm not that dirty," he objected to the gesture. And then he wiped his own hands on the skirts of his coat, which made him feel even more foolish.

The maiden's headdress she wore hid almost none of her thick, dark hair and he found himself staring at it. She, on the other hand, seemed to be waiting for him to burst into flames or turn into a demon or something equally as unlikely. "Who *are* you?"

He had a feeling she wouldn't take the truth—"I'm the heir to the khanate"—any better than the things she was imagining behind her frown. So he didn't exactly lie when he said, "I'm a soldier; I fought with the khan to free the Cloud Country."

It was a selective truth, but she accepted it with a little nod, as if his sudden appearance had posed a riddle and the answer was starting to make sense. "And the prince," she added, as if he didn't know, which confused him even more. "I saw you wrestle for the khan."

"That, too. Prince Tayyichiut, at your service." He bowed, low enough to make a joke of it, but wondered. If she knew who he was, why did she ask? She was looking past his face again, like she had the first time he'd seen her, and he figured she must have understood from his answer more than: "I'm the khan's nephew."

The toad thing urged him to caution, however. He decided that he wouldn't love her, no matter the fantasies that had plagued him. At least, not yet. "What else should I be that you didn't know, then?" He dug the toe of his boot into the dirt, unwilling to meet her dark and knowing eyes. But that had been the god-king's habit and he stopped himself, refusing to follow too closely in the footsteps of his friend.

"I don't know yet, but I'll figure it out." She sounded determined to unravel all his secrets, but had turned her studious gaze away from him, to the river. Tayy was grateful. He felt a little less exposed that way.

"I think there was a battle here." Her head moved as if she tracked the fighting even now.

"I was there," he agreed. She would know that, of course, having recognized him for the prince, but she nodded gravely anyway, as if his words confirmed something she had only guessed.

"The wild creatures still haven't settled. That's why I'm having so much trouble catching toads."

He knew nothing of toads or their habits, but figured he hadn't yet settled himself. "I lost a good friend on this spot," he offered, an exchange of intelligence. "The Uulgar forces drove our troops into the river, and he drowned."

"I'm sorry."

"Thank you. But why are you trying to catch toads anyway?" He flung himself onto the carpet of soft earth and rotting leaves, prepared to listen to her story. His black dog settled beside him and Tayy flung a careless arm around the beast's neck, a gesture grown familiar since he'd come home.

The girl tapped her foot, but in spite of herself, he thought, a little smile sneaked onto the corners of her mouth. "If I told you, you would laugh at me, or recount your ills for me to diagnose, so perhaps I will not tell you after all."

"I could never laugh at you! I swear it!" It took all the discipline of a warrior not to wrap his arms around her where she stood, so he figured that was as safe a promise as he'd ever made. He was far too diplomatic to mention that if he was still talking to her, in spite of the difference in their rank, then he wasn't likely to be chased away by any other secrets she might be harboring.

"Are you daring me to reveal all my mysteries?" She was smiling openly now. In fact, he thought she might be laughing at him rather than the other way around, but that was all right as long as he got to look at her eyes and imagine his hands on her hair and her lips—*Don't think about her lips,* he warned himself. *Don't fall in love; she's dangerous.* Duty demanded that he make his matches for peace and politics, outside the clans. But it was too late, and his face flamed red at the thought of touching his mouth to hers.

"They're not that kind of secrets!"

What did she think of him? Whatever, she was wrong. "I didn't imagine they were!"

"Oh." Mollified, she sat beside him. The red bitch whined and put her head in the girl's lap. She didn't look at him, studying the curled toes on her boots instead, while her fingers absently stroked the soft red fur.

T he death's-head hadn't obscured his face this time. When Eluneke turned to look at him, she saw that the prince was very handsome, with thick braids tightly bound and high cheekbones sharp enough to cut thread on. His clear deep eyes saw more than they said and probably were saying more than he meant to reveal about himself on such a short acquaintance. He hadn't touched her in the way of a boy who wanted a tumble in the grass, but she could tell he was interested enough.

That might change when he knew what she was, of course; it often did. But the spirits of the dead had given him to her, so she had no worry that they would eventually choose one another. Keeping him alive to enjoy his marriage bed, now that would be the challenge.

"I'm Eluneke, apprentice to Toragana the shamaness and lately a student of Bolghai as well, it seems."

He took her explanation a lot more casually than she expected. "You don't smell like Bolghai. Which is a good thing, by the way."

He startled a laugh out of her with that. "Neither does Toragana," she assured him. "I wonder sometimes if it is because he is a man, or because he is a stoat in his spirit form, or just because he is Bolghai."

"Until now, I hadn't thought about other shaman at all," he admitted. "I suppose I assumed they were all like Bolghai."

"Nope. We're all different."

Bolghai was shaman to the khan's court. Eluneke hadn't met him herself until her vision about this very soldier-prince had compelled Toragana to seek assistance in her training. She had never been very interested in clothes or ornaments, but now that she thought about it, she felt herself lacking in all of the graces a matchmaker looked for in a royal wife. She owned neither elegant silks nor embroidery, for one thing, nor had she beads for her hair. She perched ungainly as her totem animal in the mud of the riverbank with, she feared, a smudge on her cheek like a truant child.

Worst of all for a royal bride, Eluneke knew, she had no name, no powerful clan to bring to a prince in marriage. She had a father somewhere in the clans, but her mother had never revealed his family. Now her mother was dead. She thought her relatives must know, but they had refused to say anything about him. From their glares and muttered curses she had guessed that he must be of high rank, and that their expectations of gifts and rewards for her care had been disappointed. She could look for no help there to make her an acceptable match. Her calling set her apart from any position she might have claimed through her father anyway.

If the prince had been the simple soldier he had claimed at first, their union might have met with approval from both their families. Approval from hers, at least. His might not have liked the idea of a shaman added to even a humble bloodline, but there would have been nothing to stop a marriage between them. Well, except for the little matter of his death, of course. But if he had a dangerous fate in store, he could ask for no better wife than a shaman, who could negotiate with the ancestors for his spirit.

A prince of the royal blood, however, was so far above her reach that it didn't bear thinking of. He must look at girls like her for entertainment until his uncle the khan made the matches that would bind clan to clan, ulus to ulus—something she could never do. If not for the visions she would have fled, refusing to allow this confusion he stirred in her to continue.

But he was hers, a gift of the spirits no matter that their ranks might say otherwise. Convincing him of that, however, required skills of persuasion well beyond her talents. Even the most general of conversation failed her; it seemed easier suddenly to study the upturned toes of her shoes than to make small talk. Silence fell between them comfortable as an old coat and painful as a knife to the heart. Even the dogs had fallen quiet, content with the slow stroking of their fur. Finally, when she thought she might scream just to remind herself that she was really there, with him, the prince spoke.

"You're a healer, though, right? You aren't interested in poisons or spells or anything like that, are you?"

The idea of it offended her. But he knew only one other shaman from whom he might have drawn such a conclusion.

"No. Never. Of course not," she insisted, while a cold weight settled in her stomach. She'd thought Bolghai a bit strange but a good man who honored the spirits of his calling. Toragana wouldn't have taken her to see him if she knew he practiced the darker side of a shaman's trade. Would she? Would the khan they all followed require assassinations from his shaman? The very thought made her ill. So did her second thought, a reminder that a shaman with a knowledge of poisons might be the very one she needed to keep her prince alive.

"One must, of course, learn a bit about such things in order to treat them in a client. I hope to acquire that knowledge along with other healing arts from my teachers."

"That's good," he said, which relieved her mind a little. If Bolghai did commit murders for the khan, her future husband seemed not to approve. They had that much common ground.

His next words, however, chilled her like the winter wind off the mountains:

"My stepmother was a poisoner. At first we thought my mother had died of a sudden illness. By the time our suspicions had turned to the Lady Chaiujin, she had murdered my father as well. She kept a toad in a cage in her tent. I think she used the poisons from its skin in her potions. Perhaps, if we had known in time, we could have saved my mother."

"But not your father?" If Bolghai knew the antidote for ingesting the poison from a toad, perhaps he could teach her enough to save the prince. But she wondered what had happened to his father that even the royal shaman could not help him.

Prince Tayyichiut shook his head, his eyes focused on that distant memory. "Even Bolghai has no cure for the venom of a bamboo snake-demon."

"Demons are difficult in the best of circumstances," she mused while her heart sank.

"Worse than you can imagine," he agreed, almost in a whisper.

The prince had already faced demons and knew their terrors. He could teach her a lot as well. "If the demon chooses to kill with the fangs of a viper, the victim's body is ruined almost immediately. No honorable shaman would attempt to hold the unlucky spirit in such putrid flesh."

Eluneke's thoughts were torn between the technical problems of the case and her own terror that a fate like his father's might await the prince. How would she keep him safe from such a creature? She almost missed the shiver he gave at her cool analysis, but the red bitch leaned into her side and whined a high-pitched note of distress. Looking about her for the cause of the animal's discomfort, she saw the prince, his hand buried up to the clenched white knuckles in the black dog's fur. His features, set in lines of bleak desperation, took her breath away.

"I beg your pardon, my lord. Toragana has cautioned me about speaking my unguarded thoughts in public. I'm not so unfeeling as I seem: it's the way shaman are trained to think, that's all. We hold our own terrors at bay with the knowledge of our calling."

"I know about terrors," he agreed, making it sound casual,

though his eyes reflected a spirit struggling against crushing memories. For politeness, he tried to shake them off. "So, I can understand if you were afraid I'd burden you with my sad tale of painful old war wounds, but why did you think I would laugh at you? You never did tell me why you were chasing that tree toad."

"Are you in pain?" He'd tried to pass off the suggestion as an exaggeration, but Eluneke caught a quaver in his voice when he mentioned old wounds. Instantly her professional concerns set aside more personal considerations. He was a patient in pain, and she could help him. All he had to do was, "Describe it for me."

"It's nothing. I meant only to ask what kind of shaman you were, not to do the very thing you accused me of."

His head reared back like a horse with a twitch in its nose. She thought the pain must be very bad, then. Or the memory of how he received the wound must still prey on his mind. But he didn't want to share it with her now and he wouldn't be diverted from his questions by his own concerns. "I could use a good tale to take my mind off myself. Perhaps you'd better tell me the worst and get it over with."

It seemed that the spirits were determined to humiliate her. As her future husband, however, he would have to find out sometime. Now was as good as any. Eluneke huffed a sigh and relented. "To become a shaman you first have to find your totem animal."

"I know about that," the young man said. "I have a friend who used to turn into a roebuck and fly away whenever the mood took him." Picking up a pebble from the littered ground he tossed it into the river and watched the rings it made as they moved outward toward the shore. He seemed in that moment to have forgotten her.

"What happened to him?"

"Nothing bad for a change." The prince shrugged. It amazed her that so expressive a gesture could leave her wondering what he meant by it. "He missed his wife, so he went home to her. Master Den says he'll come back, but he needs to rest a while."

"And you miss him," she said of his friend.

Though he didn't look at her, his eyes sharpened as if he hadn't thought of that most obvious of facts before. "Yes, I guess I do."

Complicated things passed behind his eyes. Not an easy relationship, then, but important to him. She didn't know who Master Den was, but the prince seemed torn between belief and caution. So he worried that all was not as he had been told.

"But this was supposed to be about you, not about me." He did look at her then, and smiled.

Eluneke's heart turned over in her breast. "What?" she asked, too caught up in his eyes to remember the question.

"You were explaining how Bolghai helped you find your totem animal, I think."

"Um, yes. Well, um, I had to dance with this awful broom—" She wondered for a moment about the story Bolghai had told, of a young man who discovered his totem and became a god. It seemed far-fetched, however, and she tried to put the idea out of her head, while wondering if a prince so elegantly dressed as the one in front of her could be in any way inferior to a god.

"Anyway, the broom. I danced and danced, and when I thought I couldn't stand the pain of the blisters another moment, I turned into a tree toad. Now I have to catch enough tree toads to decorate my shaman's robes before I can take the last steps on the road to becoming a shaman."

"Your dream travels."

He struggled to keep a smile from his face, but Eluneke could see his imagination at work as he looked her over. "You don't look like a tree toad."

"I thought it unlikely myself, but there you are. A tree toad. For my next lesson in dream travel I must have at least the beginning of a shaman's costume, which requires that I catch some toads." The stages of a shaman's dream travel remained a secret of the calling, so she didn't explain where she must travel next in her dreams. Prince Tayyichiut—she'd known the name as well as her own, of course, though she'd been surprised to discover that the face of her own hero went with it—

seemed to enjoy her tale of woe, however, reaching out to her for strength of spirit. She felt a warm glow of satisfaction at performing a healing service for him, even if only with her sorry history.

"I see the problem," the prince agreed. "But perhaps I can help."

"How?" She didn't trust that grin one bit, but it tangled her in delicious tendrils of feeling and she shivered in spite of the flush that burned her cheeks. Toragana would know for sure, but she didn't think this particular effect he had on her had any basis in her shamanic training.

"You must, in your toad form, be as beautiful to the toads as in your present form you are to . . . humans," he began.

Eluneke accepted the compliment with a gracious bow. She caught the hesitation, however, and wondered what he started to say before he changed his mind. She didn't think it far-fetched that he might return her interest. At least, until he saw her as her totem animal. But she didn't see how it helped her catch toads for her robes, and she told him so.

"This helps me how?"

"It's simple. Sit here beside me as you do now, but in your totem form. When they see how beautiful you are, the lovesick toads will come a wooing. While you pretend to have a hard time making up your mind which of them you will choose for your mate, I'll drop the net over you all. Then I'll pluck you out and you can return to your human shape again."

"I think I'll stay on the outside of the net, if you don't mind. Besides," she added ruefully, "I don't think I can kill them even if I do catch them."

He'd managed to keep the smile down to an occasional smirk until then, but now he laughed out loud, wrapping both arms around his belly as if it hurt him and fell laughing onto his back in the leaves. Eluneke bristled, ready to take him to task for offending her with his ridicule. But it didn't sound like he was making fun of her. She wasn't sure why he was laughing, except that he seemed happy to have discovered her weakness when it came to killing toads.

"There must be another way," he suggested when he had

calmed himself and wiped the tears of laughter from his eyes. "Bolghai will know."

"Bolghai has a burrow full of stoat pelts. I doubt his sympathy in the matter."

When they began to talk about the toads, Eluneke noticed a rustling in the leaves above their heads. Sunlight flashed off the secretive eye of a tree toad as big as her own head. He sat well under cover of the branches of a willow. The leaves, where they fell about his head, gave the illusion of a crown and she half expected him to climb down and address the prince as one ruler to another. The king of toads seemed to read the fanciful thoughts in her eyes, but withheld his counsel, withdrawing more deeply under his cover of leaves and limbs. When the prince turned to see what she was looking at so intently, there was not even a twitch of a leaf to give old King Toad away.

But something about the day or the moment had carried their minds along on the same breeze. "If you don't want to kill the toads you need for your costume, and you can't catch them anyway, perhaps you can make a treaty with them."

"A treaty?" Eluneke glanced up and indeed, the king of the toads had crept out on his branch again, listening keenly, she thought.

The prince must have known something was going on behind his back, but this time he refrained from following the direction of her gaze. "Lady Chaiujin kept a toad captive in a cage in her tent—"

She didn't think he meant for her to follow in the footsteps of the lady who had murdered his mother. King Toad, however, bent a baleful look in his direction, reminding Eluneke that he was not only very large but poisonous as well. A casual or therapeutic touch of skin against skin should do no harm. She was uncertain of the damage if the toad aimed an attack at eye or nose or mouth and hastened to set the creature's mind at ease.

"I could no more keep my totem caged against its will than I could wage war against the toads for their dead skins to decorate my costume. But—" She caught the gleam in his eye, knew when their minds found harmony. "—I might, I suppose, make a treaty with the king of toads, as a traveler in his domain."

King Toad had started down out of his tree. He was larger even than she had thought, and the leaves that had seemed a fanciful accident remained in a crown about his head.

"Exactly." Prince Tayyichiut kept his eyes on her, but he spoke a little louder than necessary, cocking his head as though he meant the authority behind him to hear as well. "Lady Chaiujin forced the attendance of her toad by locking her cage on the outside. But if you made comfortable little baskets in which the toads might join you at will on your healing journeys, and if you promised to leave them in peace except at need, killing none of their number to pin their hides on your clothes, you might strike a bargain very nicely."

"The latch should be on the inside," Eluneke agreed. "We wouldn't want anyone falling out and getting hurt. But they must be able to unlatch the baskets whenever they want."

Chapter Seventeen

WHEN THEY REACHED the very edge of the dell that fell away to the river below, the shamaness Toragana continued flying, into the tops of the spindly trees that crowded close to the river. Lady Bortu stopped. She had sat astride her first horse in her second summer and could take her mount down the steep incline as well as any of the khan's soldiers. The clatter of hooves breaking through the undergrowth would make it difficult to study the girl Eluneke unobserved, however, so she waited until the raven returned with news from her reconnoiter.

Fluttering to the ground, Toragana took human form, straightening her feathered robes around her as she settled. "This way," she said. Her sleeve fell back to the elbow as she pointed. "Bolghai's gone. They're sitting by the river."

"They?" If not her teacher, then who?

The shamaness lowered her lashes and said only, "Back to back, or front to front? Who knows?"

Bortu understood the riddle: the girl had met someone at the river. But did the two join together for love or had her companion come upon her as a chance encounter? She would only find the answer at the bottom of the dell, so she followed as Toragana led the way off the high plain, into the little valley below.

Taking the slope on her own feet proved more difficult than

riding for the Lady Bortu. The shamaness took her arm, however, and helped her over the rough places with a professional ease the khaness found comfortable to accept where even a single word of sympathy would have driven her to reject any aid. In the shelter of a spruce tree above the river, Toragana halted with light pressure on Bortu's arm to signal their stop.

"There," she whispered.

Lady Bortu saw, and her eyes grew wide with the shock of her discovery. "The prince!" she hissed. "What is this?"

"Fate," Toragana answered.

"But what fate?" The khaness pressed. "They are no use to the khan together!" She felt spirits moving in the little dell, the boy's dead father and others both benign and deadly.

"The girl has visions." Toragana didn't speak aloud, but Lady Bortu heard her voice, a whisper in her ear. "Since childhood, or so her guardian informed me when I took her in. Lately, they have all centered on the prince."

"Many young girls dream of princes. That's the way of a girl's heart, not magic or fate. Am I to believe these visions brought them together, and not the ambitions of a raven who would install her apprentice as a shaman-khaness in the highest tent?"

"She did not know his name until the day of the matches." Toragana answered. "I was uncertain of his identity myself until this moment. But prince or slave, it little matters when the maggots are crawling out his eyes."

Easy enough to solve that riddle, Bortu thought. Not so easy to hear it, however. "She sees him dead, then." If true, the girl had a rare talent. The calling required that a shaman intercede with the spirits of the dead on behalf of the living. Few saw into the future, to speak to the dead while they still lived.

"How old?" Death didn't always mean tragedy, after all. If he had died old—

"Young," Toragana whispered. "Very young, as their elders see such things. She believes it will be soon. But even when she thought him no more than a simple soldier, she felt herself drawn to him by fate, to save him."

"At one time, perhaps, the girl thought only of her duty."

Bortu conceded that much. Seeing them together, however, she knew that time had long past.

"They are deep in conversation," Toragana agreed, "I can get closer, and hear them in my totem form—"

"It hardly matters what they say." The khaness dismissed the suggestion with a wave of her hand. "Love words or recipes, their hearts fill their eyes. See how she follows every change in his expression as if the wrinkling of his nose or the curve of his mouth hides the secrets of the universe."

"I never intended . . ."

Somewhere in the back of her mind, the Lady Bortu knew that the shamaness made her apologies: for not having the talent to foresee this outcome, for not having the answer to saving the prince herself, for whatever. Bortu didn't hear; she had come out to discover for herself what she must about the girl, and now her mind spun with revelations that froze her heart in her breast.

Mergen's daughter, with visions of her beautiful, precious Prince Tayy dead. She wanted to curse the shamaness for a liar but knew that to save the prince she must believe it, and act. The moment seemed ripe for the Lady Chaiujin's deadly interference. Reflexively, Lady Bortu scanned the branches of the trees for an emerald green bamboo snake but saw instead a giant toad, creeping down from the very tree against which Prince Tayyichiut rested his back.

"Look there, a poison toad!" She clutched at the shamaness' arm, shaking it in her terror. "You must fly, warn them of their danger!"

Toragana's head twitched like her totem as she turned an eye grown suddenly more beady and sharp on the pair. "Eluneke's totem," she muttered. "What can it mean?"

"Is she his salvation, or his doom?" The Lady Bortu asked, but there was no one to answer. The shamaness had turned into a raven and flown away.

" **. . . P**in their hides on your clothes, you might strike a bargain very nicely."

Not an option, King Toad agreed. The thought of his people dead and dangling like so many beads for the pleasure of the toad girl set the poison glands in his skin to quivering. Caged in little baskets seemed no alternative at all. But she had said she wanted to bring them no harm, so he listened, creeping down the trunk of the tree.

". . . they must be able to unlatch the basket whenever they want." Better no baskets at all, but they had come, at least, to a talking place.

"RRRRibbbit!" he added his own voice to the negotiation. He'd been listening from the beginning and had opinions on all of it, including the lady's appearance. She might, he thought, be beautiful enough to a human. He'd seen her in her toad form, however, and she would not have made it past the lowest ranks of his harem. An air clung to her, ineffably human even in her toad shape, that he found vaguely unnerving.

As a veteran of the eagle war debates he had enough diplomatic sense not to mention that though it didn't seem to matter. The human shaman and her prince were staring at him eagerly, as if they expected him to break into a speech on the rights of toads in the Harnish tongue at any moment. As king of the toads, it would be beneath his dignity to do so even if he had the skill in the language or the physical ability to form its sounds. Which he didn't. The girl could take her totem form, however, and they could talk as toad to toad if she had the sense to think of it.

"Ribit," he repeated with as inviting a little hop as he could manage without admitting her into his harem.

The prince looked at him dolefully. "I don't think it speaks Harnish," he volunteered.

What gave you the first clue? That I'm a toad, maybe? King Toad observed him with a sardonic eye. *Aren't you the master of the obvious.*

Not quite, though. "Ribit," he corrected the prince. " 'He.' I'm not an 'it.' "

"Do you speak Toad?"

No, I'm a foreign toad. I speak salamander. Abashed, the king of toads realized the prince had addressed the shamaness and not himself. Fortunately, he hadn't spoken aloud. The humans might not understand the language of toads, but other creatures did. He'd have been the laughingstock of the forest.

For her part, the human female answered her male with a noncommittal shrug. "Not in my human form."

Figure it out, girl.

She finally did, shaking herself all over to loosen sinew and bone. "I haven't done this without Toragana or Bolghai to watch over me," she warned the prince, whose face shone with new purpose.

"I'll watch for you!" he promised.

Shifting her determined grip from one branch to the next, Lady Bortu edged her way down the steep slope. Still too far away to save the young folks—or the prince, if the girl had called the toad to murder him—she searched the sky overhead, saw the arrow dive of the raven which was Toragana. If she attacked it in her totem form, the toad's skin would surely kill the shamaness. But Bortu couldn't reach them to warn them, or to stop terrible murder. She braced herself for a skittering run down the slope.

As she took her first running step, however, the girl Eluneke began to transform before her eyes. Not as fast as her mentor or Bolghai could do, but slowly, surely, the girl shrank, bent, and colored until she sat on a rock, face to face with the toad that seemed to threaten her.

The khaness saw through the eyes of the raven, heard through her ears. Toragana had seen her pupil's transformation and aborted her suicidal attack. She lighted on the lowest branch as if she had meant to do so all along and cocked an eye at the two leaf-colored diplomats. For so, it seemed, they were. Though the girl and the toad—king of toads, she discovered— spoke the language of their species, the raven understood and so did Lady Bortu.

Eluneke was much smaller in her true totem form than the king of toads, and her skin possessed no poison glands at all. She wanted to give him no such obvious advantages, so she wove a glamour around herself as she drew her body tighter. She would appear to be a much larger toad to anyone who didn't know to look beneath the surface. If the prince were worth the struggle she expected in his future, he would see her for what she was, but she hoped her toady adversary would give her the dignity of her chosen image.

He croaked a greeting and bobbed his head in a way that neither submitted to her dominance nor demanded that she submit to his. *Very nicely done,* she thought, and he was looking into her glamour eyes, not down into her true face. She answered the bobbing of his head and, since she had opened the negotiations, began with an explanation that she hoped would make her offer palatable to the toads.

"As you can see, I share a common soul with the toad people." Great Sun had chased Little Sun nearly to the end of the sky. The air grew cooler, the signal for the mosquitoes and flies to make their presence felt. Eluneke smelled them on the air and realized she was hungry. As she spoke, it seemed natural to flick out her tongue and snap a fly out of the air. Almost before she knew what she had done the thing was sliding down her gullet.

"So I see," King Toad agreed, with—if such were possible—a smirk upon his lipless mouth. He followed her lead, snatching up insects on his sticky tongue and swallowing with a great show of exercising his throat.

The two sides of Eluneke's nature strove for control. She allowed none of that to show in the way she dipped and nodded at the king of toads, however. She had just made a claim to a relationship and proved it with her dinner. Now was not the time to let her human taste exert itself. "As I was saying," she continued when she had regained her composure, "I am a shaman among the humans. My totem spirit is in the toad family.

"It is the practice of our craft to secure the skins of the totem animal to our sacred robes and by their presence assume their character. The shaman Bolghai wears the pelts of stoats about his neck and lines his burrow with them. Toragana bears within her the spirit of a raven. Though she has collected most of her costume from the fallen feathers of birds in flight, she has taken

the lives of that people at need for the more limited require-
ments of her headdress and her tent."

"And you wish to take the lives of the toads for this purpose—" The king of the toads puffed himself up, his poison
glands swelling threateningly.

Eluneke's toad nature lacked the instinct to spit venom at
her foes. She held herself erect against the threat but had no
way to counter it. The human prince, however, had kept his
promise to guard her. From above, as if the gods of the heavens
had set their protection on her, the point of an arrow appeared.
It came to rest on the head of the king of toads.

"You may kill her," Prince Tayy conceded levelly. "But it
will be your dying act."

"You heard me refuse that option," Eluneke reminded him,
"I am trying to find my way to the best solution for both of us.
Right now, we are facing the worst."

"I see your point," King Toad agreed. "It's poking me in the
head. Call off your male, please."

"I can't. He doesn't speak toad. You will have to show him
it is safe to unbend his bow."

"All right." King Toad flopped down into a submissive
pose. "Can you send him away now?"

Eluneke didn't know why, but she had the sense that King
Toad was laughing at her in spite of the danger he faced at the
prince's hand. She took two short steps back and forward again,
settled her leaf-colored arms in a toad shrug. "I will certainly
do that as soon as I return to my mortal form. We'll all be safest
if we finish quickly, I think."

"Very well." The king of the toads relaxed over his arms,
eyeing Eluneke with a baleful gleam. "State your case."

"The toads will agree to attend me in their baskets as needed
for healing the sick, or for easing the way for the dead. In return,
I will allow each the freedom to leave when the need has passed,
and I vow to harm no living toad to make my shaman's robes."

"You're talking about a serious inconvenience to the toad
people, for no return other than your promise not to commit
mortal crimes against them," King Toad pointed out. "It doesn't
exactly work as a long-term arrangement."

Eluneke had to agree the king of the toads had a point. The empty skins of a shaman's totem animal didn't complain about the hours. A powerful shaman might fill the dead husks with his or her own presence, so that the robes of office bore the stamp of the one who wore it into the next generation. But if she didn't kill the toads—

"How do the toad people feel about their dead?"

"Glad not to be among them," King Toad responded. Then he seemed to catch her meaning. "There is a place where my people go when they know they are dying. The branches of the trees hang low and golden drops of sunlight dapple the leaves. It is a sacred place of peaceful endings. But once the spirit has passed, a toad has no use for what is left behind.

"There are no heaps of bones and skin," he warned her. "Few enough of our number make it to the final home and few remain there long when dead—nature turns us all back into dirt soon enough."

"I understand." Eluneke bobbed her head in a human nod that she realized belatedly made an offer she hadn't intended in toad language. "If you show me this place, I can slowly begin to gather the hides I need for my robes."

King Toad pretended not to notice the awkward suggestion about fathering her tadpoles. "Promise only to pin the dead out of sight of the living and I will do so," he agreed. "Now, how do you plan to return to your human form without startling that young male into putting an arrow through my head?"

"I think you ought to back away first, so he doesn't think you are a threat."

The toad moved away in a submissive posture, but with an ironic gleam in his eye. "Come alone at this time tomorrow and I will show you what you want. But leave your male at home. And if you should like a toad husband . . ."

King Toad's intentions were lost in the croaking of his kind. Eluneke stood next to the prince and gave him a triumphant smile. "We have a deal."

Chapter Eighteen

"**W**HAT DID HE SAY?" Prince Tayy had seen many wonders in his travels. A galley slave who turned into a dragon and a boy who turned into a roebuck, then a king, and then a god came immediately to mind. So he controlled his instinctive jump back when Eluneke stood before him as a girl again. He didn't make a habit of kissing toads and the great desire to kiss her that he'd felt when he first stumbled into the dell was considerably dampened. An edge of curiosity remained, however; it seemed he had an affinity for magical creatures, including the shamaness in training. He wondered about his children if such beings were his fate.

"King Toad has agreed to our bargain for the time being." She dusted her hands on the sides of her dress, looking as disconcerted as he felt himself, which raised the prince's confidence. She was no more accustomed to making treaties with her totem animal than he was to watching her do it. He thought he ought to say something useful, but an explosion of feathery flight brought both their heads up, searching out the sudden threat. Just a bird. Her eyes narrowing with a tension he recognized, Eluneke followed its skittery flight into the higher trees.

"I'm fine!" she shouted after it. "You can go home now!

"My teacher, Toragana," she apologized, rolling her eyes. "Checking up on me. I'd have been a lot less nervous if I'd known she was keeping watch, but the danger is over now. I don't know why she hasn't gone home."

The dogs seemed to agree with her, adding their own baying commentary on the matter of privacy and spying shamanesses. The bird merely pranced on her branch, settled on the other side of a knot, and groomed under her wing until some more interesting scent caught the fickle attention of the hounds, who abandoned their prince and the threat of the raven to mill about among the trees. Searching with a hunter's eye the area around the tree where the shamaness perched, he found her answer in a flash of blue just visible through the spiny fingers of a spruce tree. "Someone is up there," he said.

"An enemy?"

"No, an ally, I suspect. Your teacher would show more agitation if you were in danger."

"Or you," Eluneke agreed in principle. "The dogs don't seem upset either." She leaned closer to him, hoping perhaps to gain a clearer angle to their observer. "Who is it, can you tell?"

Tayy couldn't see that much himself. He knew he ought to tell her that, but when she stood with her hair so close to his mouth and his nose he found it difficult to remember she had so recently been a toad. Would she let him touch the sleek strands hiding the side of her face like a curtain? Not with an audience that included her teacher, surely. His hand had started its own journey of exploration when the dogs raised a cry and bounded from the woods behind him. He turned quickly, reaching for his bow.

"They're over here, by the river!" Qutula stepped from among the trees, brotherly exasperation fixed in the vee of his brows and the downturn of his mouth, which he caused to twitch as if a smirk were trying to escape. "Would you call off your dogs? We've been looking all over for you."

The blood rose dark in the prince's cheeks, but he called his dogs to him and settled them with a hand at their necks. "Has something happened?"

"Only that you disappeared without your guardsmen this morning and no one has seen you since. The gur-khan is beside himself with worry and here you are propped up against a tree with a strange woman falling into your arms."

As Qutula spoke, the young warriors who made up the prince's personal guard gathered behind him, their approach ghostly silent on the rain-softened ground. His own followers Duwa and Mangkut came first, with others who counted themselves Durluken. The prince's Nirun came after; they did not stop with Qutula but formed up like the dogs around their own master.

Jumal was gone and no longer a threat, thank the spirits. Altan, who lacked the other's intelligence and skill, remained with a handful of young hopefuls of no importance who gathered at the heir's side for politics rather than love.

Once over the shock of the interruption, the girl showed no surprise at his mention of the gur-khan. Prince Tayy had been about to kiss her when he'd broken in on their little tryst. She'd been about to let him, if Qutula was any judge of women. His own lover sometimes gave him cause to doubt that, but he had this one figured out well enough. She wouldn't say no to a royal ride, he thought, as long as she held a prince's reins. The idiot had given her his true name.

Mergen was right to be worried. The girl was a nobody; he could tell that from the poor and threadbare quality of the clothes she wore, bad enough even if she weren't an apprentice shaman. As for Tayyichiut the hero, his abject guilt in the face of his cousin's gentle chiding made him look more like a repentant pup than a doughty warrior.

If he'd come alone, Qutula could have apologized for interrupting the tryst and left the girl to set her talons in tight. See then who would be heir, with Prince Tayyichiut making alliances in disastrously wrong tents. But he had witnesses for whom he must act the dutiful servant of the gur-khan's wishes.

"Sorry," he said and smiled contritely at the prince, that much at least. "I didn't realize you were busy. But the gur-khan really is getting worried. He'll want to see you with his own eyes before he'll believe you haven't drowned yourself in the river, or that your horse hasn't broken a leg in a rabbit hole and fallen on top of you."

"I'm the one who should apologize. We were talking, and I completely forgot." Tayy held out his hand to the girl, but his guardsmen had surrounded him, effectively separating them.

"Go, then, before he sends his own guard to find you."

Altan gave a dramatic shudder. "Qutula's right," he said. "I don't want to be dragged home by my father in front of the whole camp." Jochi, his father, had taken Yesugei's place as general of the gur-khan's armies and captain of his private guard.

The younger guardsmen all laughed in sympathy for their companion. Most of them had a parent or older brother in the gur-khan's service and none wanted to be dragged home like an unblooded boy by their elders. The prince conceded with chagrin when Qutula motioned the Nirun to take him home. He allowed no expression of triumph to show on his features as they quickly obeyed him. They all knew he carried out Mergen-Gur-Khan's instructions, but still Qutula felt his power among them grow. Soon they would take it for granted that he was the greater of the two. When the prince met his all-too-timely end, they would look to Qutula to lead them.

"I'll make sure the lady gets home safely," he managed a courtly bow almost hiding the contempt in his eyes.

The prince didn't notice, though his "lady" gave an indignant snort. "I can find my own way, thank you."

"Please—" the prince turned back. He reached hesitantly for her hand and Qutula saw the doubt cross his eyes as he aborted the gesture before she could refuse him. "I have to go now. Will I see you again?"

"Of course!"

"When?"

Qutula had expected her to smile seductively as he had seen his mother do to entice her lovers. Instead she frowned as if she didn't see him clearly, though he had gone only a few paces into the trees with his Nirun. "I don't know. I have to think—"

"What have I done?" The prince would have returned to her

side, but Altan took him by the shoulder and whispered in his ear, a reminder, no doubt, that the gur-khan awaited him.

"Nothing. It's not you. You're perfect—" She smiled so sweetly that Qutula wanted to gag.

It cheered Tayy right up, though. With a bow completely inappropriate from one of his rank to a girl of her low status, he left her in his cousin's tender care.

When the prince had passed out of sight among the trees, Qutula signaled his Durluken to draw closer while he mockingly applauded her performance. "Innocence and adoration. How could he possibly resist? You did that very well." Clap. Clap. Clap. He had to hand it to her: she had perfected the moves of a seductress after all, though her person left much to be desired.

"I have to go home—" She shook off his followers and tried to move past him, but Qutula was faster. Quick as the snake that coiled around his heart he snatched at her throat, so slim that his fingers almost met in a perfect ring around her neck. "You will leave when I say 'go.' " He pinned her against the tree where lately she had stood making love with his cousin. Or not. She hadn't the stink of it on her, but there was something between them.

"First, you will listen. You may think a roll in the summer leaves will make you a khaness, but don't fool yourself. His uncle has other plans for the prince. Cross the gur-khan again and you may not live to contemplate the consequences. I have orders to protect the prince from your wiles, and if I have to snap your neck to do it, I will. I might even like it, so don't push me."

An impoverished charm-seller held no interest for him, but Qutula knew the terror men's bodies could bring to women. He leaned in, pressing her back against the tree. Under her poor clothes, he felt her trembling against his flesh.

His Durluken snickered rudely, not even hiding their sneers behind their hands. "Teach her a lesson!" He heard the tension in Duwa's voice, smelled the excitement rising from his followers like a mist. "Show her who's boss!"

His own lady demanded constancy only in his resolve to

the dais. He felt her watching through his eyes, felt her mark stir against his skin as she scented prey.

"You must have hidden depths beneath your skirts, to have ensnared a prince against his gur-khan's will." He ground his hips against the girl, licked the curve of her jaw with a wide, lascivious tongue. The tattoo over his heart grew heated. His breath came deeply, impassioned as he felt the serpent slither down his belly.

Among the trees, the Lady Bortu waited and watched. "What have we done, that you come to this?" she muttered, seeing her grandson threaten his own half sister. Toragana flew off the moment Qutula's hand pinned the girl's throat. The khaness struggled another step down the steep incline but was forced to grab hold of a branch to stop a tumble that doubtless would have broken her old bones. She could do nothing to help Eluneke but bear witness to the gur-khan after the worst had been done.

That she could do well, however. She directed her gaze on the unhappy pair so forcefully that she almost missed the plunge of the raven, spinning out of the shadows to peck at Qutula's head. Images spun behind her eyes then. She looked through the shaman gaze of the raven, saw when Qutula ground his hips against the girl, Eluneke. The green shadow of the bamboo snake that had enfolded him during the wrestling match again obscured his true form from her eyes. Through that grassy dusk glinted a shard of green jade gleaming at his breast.

Had the false Lady Chaiujin taken another victim in her grandson? If not the lady, had he fallen under the spell of some other demon of her kind? Or was her unacknowledged grandson a willing accomplice in some plot of demons to overthrow the khanate? It seemed clear that however the thing had arranged itself, the green talisman reflected the power of its serpent master over Mergen's blanket-son.

Qutula dropped his mouth to the girl's ear. With the sharp ears of the raven Lady Bortu heard his whisper, "Show me what would drive a prince to set his own desires above the will of his gur-khan."

"Prince Tayyichiut has done no such thing," she answered him. Her breath came in shallow, frightened gasps beneath his fingers as he tore at her clothes.

"I think my father would see it differently."

At court he dare not declare his relationship to the gur-khan. Patience had never been his strength; his grandmother had known the truth of his birth festered like a canker in his heart. She had not expected the pride and anguish that flavored the words on his tongue. "Show me what you give my cousin—"

Toragana attacked, tugging at his hair and pecking at his head.

"Stop!" Lady Bortu commanded in their silent communication. A little smile had touched the girl-shaman's lips. "If fate is at work here, let the girl prove her good faith. If not fate but simple villainy, we will still have time to chastise my overeager young warrior." Mergen would have to know, and Bolghai, but first she must have the facts to tell them.

Toragana cawed her agreement. Allowing the young men below to think they had chased her into the trees, she perched within easy reach to watch and listen.

"You want to see what he sees when he looks at me?" Her gaze drifted off, as if she had gone somewhere Qutula couldn't follow in her mind. Fortunately, she wasn't very good at her craft yet. He'd heard tales enough of shaman and other dream travelers disappearing from the midst of crowds. Even the gur-khan had told such tales as one who had seen them. If she'd been able to escape him, Qutula felt sure she would have.

Suddenly, however, he was looking into the eyes of a toad, huge and malevolent and as poisonous as the snake that now coiled herself at the bottom of his belly. The toad tongue flicked out, testing the air between them, and he pulled his hand away, his fingers grown numb from contact with her poison touch.

"Tell your lady I am ready for her." Somehow, words the grinning toad face could not form found their way into his mind.

Qutula knew better than to show the sick dread he felt—his Durluken would abandon any leader with less than heroic resolve in the face of such a foe. If he lived, he would go home before presenting himself at the ger-tent palace. His mother would have a simple to cure him of the toad-girl's touch. As for his mind, he must speak to his lady. Could the girl read his intentions as well as speak inside his head? Did his own lady know his thoughts? The possibilities turned him cold inside. Or perhaps it was the girl's poison, chilling him through his skin.

"Go," he said, as if it were his choice to release the girl. "But keep in mind that an arrow or a knife can kill even a shaman. There will be no tainted blood running in the veins of the khanate."

It seemed she would say something in answer, but she only rubbed at the bruises on her throat, staring at the jade that hung over his breast as if it were a clue to some riddle she must solve about him.

"Don't forget our little conversation. Don't think I will forget it either." With a final baleful glare Qutula turned and walked away. It was a calculated gamble, but the poisons of her kind worked best on contact with eyes or skin, an open wound to act like an open door to his vitals. With his back to her, he presented no vulnerable targets. But he tensed for the numbing effect of the toxin until he made it to the clearing at the center of the dell. He did not feel completely free of her until he had climbed the steep sides to the horses waiting above them on the plains.

The raven allowed Lady Bortu to see what Toragana saw with her shaman's vision. The giant toad with toxins glistening on her skin was an illusion. At its center stood the girl who carried within her the spirit of her totem, a harmless toad small enough to sit at the center of Bortu's palm. Qutula, who had never enjoyed a deep insight, had recoiled from her as if touching her skin had indeed poisoned him.

Through the shamaness she heard him tell the girl. "Go." And then he left her there as if he weren't running away. When he had gone, taking his followers with him, the shamaness fluttered down from her tree and turned again into the tall and lanky woman Bortu had confronted in the raven tent. She was too late, however, Eluneke had vanished.

Lady Bortu stepped out from behind the tree from where she had watched both the lovers and the rivals. "Follow her," she said.

Toragana looked up at her, torn between her duty to her apprentice and to the khaness she had left watching on the shoulder of the dell. It was easier to climb up than down, however.

"I'll be fine," the khaness assured her, "Come back, if you wish, when you have found your apprentice." *My granddaughter,* she didn't say, *my grandson's salvation.*

"Thank you." Toragana's voice echoed softly in her head. "I'll come back for you."

"I know you will." She began the slow and painful trip back to her own horse, certain that Toragana would honor her word, no doubt with her apprentice in tow. She wasn't ready for that meeting yet, though she'd thought to be when she came out that day. It was one thing to take the measure of a simple shamaness in training, no matter her blood. Quite another, she discovered, to find that same girl holding off the threats of her own half brother, and that for love of her cousin the prince.

If the story Toragana had told was true, the young shamaness would need that love to save the prince's life. If it were true, Qutula might be the threat that rumbled like a storm on the horizon. Or he might have taken his father's instructions to mean the girl was a threat and acted against that danger. The matter required deeper contemplation than she had yet given it. But later. Toragana knew where to find her now. And Bolghai would see that she did.

Chapter Nineteen

ELUNEKE TREMBLED under the warrior's touch. She recognized him from the wrestling matches. The shard pinned to his leathers that had seemed to rest between the serpent's fangs now hung from a golden thread over his breast. Through the eyes of the old witch who sat at the left hand of the gur-khan, she had watched the same green demon mist rise up to envelope him in the form of the emerald green bamboo snake. No question about the meaning of that warning. Though he followed the prince and acted his friend, he was at the heart of the danger that threatened not only the heir but the whole ulus as well. And he had help, whispering in his ear and resting over his heart.

Toragana waited on a branch above her, so she wasn't really worried about the immediate threat he posed her. But what serpent had he brought into the ger-tent palace? How could she stop him if he wielded a sinister magic more powerfully than a shaman?

". . . an arrow or a knife can kill even a shaman . . ." His power didn't have to be stronger; a resolve to evil might destroy the purest unguarded magic. The bark from the tree pressed into her back while his hand around her throat demonstrated his threat. He could kill her now if he chose; only the image of her totem she wore like a shield kept her alive. In his eyes she saw anger building against the fear that stayed his hand.

Her strongest instinct urged her to run, to turn into her totem animal and travel the secret paths of shaman as her teachers had shown her. If she were the dangerous creature she pretended to be, she might have tried it. But Qutula wouldn't need magic to kill her if he caught her before she disappeared. All he had to do was step on her, sealing the prince's fate and her own with one messy boot.

She waited, therefore, until he turned away. "Go," he said, and she did, faster than she had thought her skills would take her. She couldn't do this alone. Toragana had the skills to lead her to the gods, but only the court shaman understood palace intrigues. Bolghai had lost a khan to treachery, after all. He wouldn't let it happen again if he could help it. She knew where she had to go.

Sechule banked the fire in the firebox. The day's chores were done—bedding stacked against the lattices, mirrors polished to keep away evil spirits, a hole in the felted tent cover mended. The pies rested in the cooling chest and the millet stew that Qutula liked would simmer gently in its pot on the firebox until her sons returned wanting to be fed. She didn't expect them until late, but a racket at her door set her plans aside.

"The bitch poisoned me!" Qutula raised his voice in outrage. "I can't feel my fingers!"

"What did she do?" Bekter, as always, tried to sound conciliatory while the voracity of his hunger for a good story urged his brother to greater heights of expression.

"What do you mean, 'do'? Didn't you see her? The very skin on her horrible body was poison to the touch!"

"I arrived late, remember? But she didn't look ugly to me."

"No wonder your bed is always empty. Where do you meet your lovers if you have such a taste for giant poison toads?"

Her sons had burst through the door, still engaged in the thrust and parry of their conversation. Bekter, as she might have expected, blushed purple to the roots of his hair at his brother's suggestion.

"I have no such interest and I don't know why you would say such a thing," he huffed indignantly.

"Because that's what she was. A giant, poisonous toad!" Qutula held his hand out to his mother.

Sechule noted that, as his argument with Bekter heated up, Qutula's panic seemed to recede. "Symptoms?" she asked him. And, "How much contact did you have with her?"

"Just my hand around her throat. It's numb. I can't feel it."

She had taught her sons that distinction early—between a heavy numbness and the absence of feeling. The poison from a toad should have had the other effect, however; he should have felt his hand, through a separation that clouded the brain with a fog of waking dreams. But his eyes remained clear of all but his rage. Only one way to find out. She turned his hand over and licked it. Salt from the girl's throat still clung to his skin but she tasted no toxic bitterness on her tongue. Waiting, she felt no effect of residual contact—her mouth should feel puffy and separate from her body, dizziness should have shortened her breath. Colors should have sharpened. Nothing.

"Who is this girl?" she asked.

"No one," he answered, "A shamaness in training that the prince has tangled his ankles over."

She was starting to make him suspicious. It wouldn't do to show her eldest son for a fool in front of his brother. Rummaging through her simples for a salve she used for rashes, Sechule nodded as if this answered the question of his symptoms and not why his hand went around the girl's throat in the first place.

"Rub this on both your hands—you may have touched her in passing with the other as well. Don't skimp on your fingers; any little cuts will give the toxin entry."

Mollified, Qutula took the jar from her with a grunt and threw himself down on the furs piled against the side of the tent. As he rubbed the salve carefully into the cracks around his fingernails, Sechule thought she saw a shadow gliding from the deep cuff of his summer coat and into the bedding. A vision brought on by the toxin Qutula claimed for the girl? Perhaps she should have paid more attention to his complaint. Her son was looking at his hand as though she had created a miracle, however, waggling his fingers with satisfaction.

"Better," he said. "I knew you would be more powerful than the little shamaness."

No normal toxin, then, but one with a short life. In answer to Qutula's praise she offered only a mysterious smile. She knew when speech would lessen the impact of her power over her sons and she kept silent now.

"Who is watching the prince in your absence?" she asked them, her brow arched to take the sting out of the reminder.

"Nirun," Qutula answered with a sour twist of his mouth. His frown pointed at his brother for so naming those who followed the prince as their captain in their warrior games.

"Then you must set the Durluken in their place, my son." She left it so that anyone who heard—including her fool of a son Bekter—might think she meant to protect the prince with their superior service. A glance assured that her more ambitious child understood her perfectly. His Durluken would truly stand at the side of their prince when Qutula had taken both the position and the title his father owed him by right of blood.

"Take this—" She reached into the cabinet and opened a secret door, took from the shelf within a sealed vial no bigger than her thumb. "For the poison."

He knew the value of silence as well, and bowed over her hand with a smile between them before slipping the vial into his sleeve. Then he gathered his brother up before him and shepherded him to the door. "Come on, Bek. The gur-khan will wonder if we've lost our way."

She smiled until the sound of their voices faded in the distance. When she felt certain they would not quickly return, she sank down in front of her herb chest with a frustrated moan. A toad-girl with no poison Sechule knew? Had she bewitched the prince? What else would he be doing with her? Who was she, and where had she come from? Did Mergen want to protect his nephew from a politically disastrous marriage, or did he want the girl for himself? She was, it seemed, very young, but men were prone to such fancies in their middle years.

Sechule had accepted that after so many years in which

marriage had been forbidden him, Mergen would want to wed. She had expected him to make a political marriage for the clans and had considered potions that her sons might slip into his food that would draw him back to her. Second wife to a khan would do. A first wife untimely dead would raise too many suspicions—Lady Chaiujin had already used that trick on Chimbai's khaness—but it would be easy enough to ensure that Mergen's political union bore no fruit. Her plans had all assumed a horse-faced foreigner of high birth; the thought that Mergen might have cast her aside only to take a lowborn slip of a girl as a lover rankled.

Fortunately, the girl had her eyes on the heir. It seemed unlikely that anyone at court would ask her preferences, though how an apprentice shaman managed to catch the prince in her spells remained a mystery. If Mergen had any sense, he'd ride around that one like she were quicksand. Wasn't anybody paying attention? That might work in their favor.

Eluneke landed lightly on the smoke hole cover of Bolghai's tent-burrow. In her form as a small toad, she crawled to the center of the roof where the flap had been turned back and carefully let herself down onto one of the arched spokes that made up the tent's ceiling. From there she made her way to one of the many brooms hanging from the spokes. She thought the crawl to the floor might be arduous, but Bolghai himself was standing there with his hand out, just a short hop from where she sat on a broom made of sticks.

"Who comes calling over the sill of the door?" He gently set her down on the floor and stood back so that she could turn into a girl again.

"The wind," she answered him and pressed down her skirts, which had gotten badly mussed by the river.

"Just so. Sometimes," he agreed. "What does the wind blow in today?"

"Trouble." Almost a shaman, she had given him almost a riddle, which seemed to please him.

"Would you like some tea?"

She couldn't figure out the riddle in that, but it came clear enough when he wiped a dirty finger around the inside of a cup and offered it to her. "No, thank you." Events were moving, she had no time for tea.

A raven flew through the smoke hole and landed on his shoulder, but Bolghai waited patiently, the cup in his outstretched hand until she figured it out for herself. "Yes, please. And your help, if you will. And Toragana's help too, of course." She deferred to her teacher, who watched her with dark, expressionless raven eyes while the shaman swept the skulls of his totem animal, the stoat, from a chest and pulled out a cloth sack half full of rolled tea leaves.

"Now tell me what has happened." Bolghai looked up from the firebox where he had set about steeping the tea. "How can I help?"

That was the riddle, sure enough. Toragana flapped her wings and disappeared out the smoke hole, as if she had joined them only to put her pupil in safe hands before heading off on some errand of her own. Eluneke let Bolghai fill her cup and accepted a pat of butter in her tea. As quickly as she could, she told him what she knew, about Qutula's threats and the shadow-image of the serpent that seemed to envelop him when she looked at him.

"What serpent is it?" he asked, focusing his disconcertingly bright gaze on her.

"I'm not sure." Eluneke remembered hearing that the previous khan had died of snakebite. She wondered what the connection was.

"Not one local to the grasslands, though it's hard to tell, in the presence of magic, what is real and what is not. Surely the true serpent couldn't be so large—it's taller than the warrior who carries it and almost as transparent as air. It seems to have some connection to the jade talisman he wears. If the Great Mother hadn't shown it to me that first time, I wouldn't have noticed it at all."

"Great Mother?" Bolghai sipped his tea, his eyes wide and shining as the brother moons Han and Chen. "Talismans and serpents and Great Mothers. Surely we have the making of a fine riddle here."

"Not so much of one," Eluneke admitted. "I saw her once before, at the festival to celebrate the army's return from the Cloud Country. She sat a great broad horse at the khan's side so she must be Great Mother the khaness."

"Doubtless you are correct, but what has this to do with me?"

He meant it as a question, she saw; not a dismissal but a challenge to find her own answers in him. She thought past the obvious, that she was a student and he a teacher. Her eyes looked on far distances and she almost missed the change in Bolghai's regard. Toragana had trained her well in the basics, however; she kept one toe in the here-and-now even as her mind wandered in the might-bes and the happens-nexts.

"Powers are moving in the grass," she gave him riddle for riddle: not just the serpent or the two young men who faced each other in love and envy. The answer to this one lay out beyond the ulus.

Forces were moving. The thunder of horses set up a fine vibration in her bones and she heard the flight of arrows in the wind.

"Then I suppose it is time you became one of those powers," Bolghai agreed and she knew he felt the coming storm in his marrow as well. "I expect the gods will have something to say on the matter. It's time you climbed the tree at the center of the world."

To become a shaman the apprentice, in the shape of the totem animal, traveled first in the dreamscape to learn about the living, second to the heavens to learn about healing from the gods, and third to the underworld to learn about death and the spirit world from the ancestors. Eluneke had already visited a young man's terrifying dreams. Now she must climb the great tree at the center of the world and bring back from the sky god's daughters the secret knowledge of healing.

No shaman learned the same mysteries, Toragana had explained to her. No shaman could speak in human language the secrets they brought back from the heavens. An apprentice had many teachers, but becoming a shaman was a solitary climb to the top of the tree. Eluneke had fully expected to make this great trek. Just, not so soon after treating with the king of the toads.

Bolghai made a chittering sound in response to her look of dismay. "You should be fasting," Bolghai chided her and took away her teacup. "We have little time for the niceties."

He paused, took in her ragged appearance and the mud on her nose. "But time for a nap, I think, and to wait for Toragana to bring your robes."

He took her cup and passed a hand over her eyes. Suddenly she was falling into the furs that covered the floor of his little burrow-tent. "Sleep," she heard him say as she drifted on soft clouds of fur. "It will keep until tomorrow."

Sechule was neither a witch nor a healer in the usual way, but she had learned as all mothers must the ways to keep her children alive. When they were small, fatherless, and alone, that had meant tree bark to cool a fever and the mosses to stop the bleeding of a wound, the teas that soothed an angry belly and those which calmed a moody temperament. As her sons took their places in the court of their father the khan, the love of a mother demanded more.

She thought she knew who had slithered from her son's cuff into her blankets. But how had the bamboo snake-demon found her way up Qutula's sleeve? And what did the serpent want with him? Yesugei, her only regular visitor these days, had departed on the khan's business with the defeated Uulgar captives. Her tent was empty and she expected it to remain so until her sons wandered home from the palace late in the night to find their dinner and their beds. Perhaps it was time for Sechule to confront the lady on her own ground. Carefully she turned the mirrors, lest the lady's demon reflection scare her away. The precaution of mirrors hadn't saved Chimbai-Khan or his insipid first wife, the Lady Temulun, but one wanted to appear hospitable when treating with demons.

She had shared with the Lady Chaiujin an interest in herbs,

so while she waited for the serpent to reveal herself, she sat before a painted chest and opened first one door and then another.
Picking up in turn each of the thick stoneware jars lined up on
their shelves, she made note of which herbs she had in full supply and which rattled forlornly at the bottom of their jar.

Quickly finished with the beneficial medicines, she turned
once again to the secret door which she opened with a manip-
ulation of the design on the front of the chest. Here she kept a
small supply of various doses that might produce the very ills
the others cured. Though she knew the uses for each, until
tonight she'd had few calls for most. The jars offered ample options, though one larger than the rest, that held the death's-head
mushroom, was almost empty. In great enough amounts the
mushroom could drive one mad, or even kill. But Sechule did
a tidy trade in small doses which jealous lovers used to summon dreams of the misdeeds of their beloved. She made a note
to replenish her stock from the nearby wood.

She wasn't a witch, but her grandmother had taught her
much before the clan had stoned her to death after the fatal illness of a rival. Among her lessons, Sechule had learned not to
show surprise to her disadvantage. So when a woman's voice
said, "Good afternoon, O mother of khans," she first stilled the
sudden speeding of her heart. This was, after all, the reason
she was sitting here making an inventory of her poisons. When
she was better able to control her reactions, she set the jar
down with careful deliberation and rose to her feet. Pretending to a shock she no longer felt, she turned on her visitor with
an imperious scowl as if she did not expect the intruder.
"What are you doing in my tent?"

"Visiting an old friend, of course." The woman smiled conspiratorially, sharing the sort of secrets that had gotten
Sechule's grandmother murdered.

"I don't know you." Sechule made a warding sign behind
her skirts. This creature spoke as if she were the Lady Chaiujin,
but she wore a different face.

"Come now. We were friends once." The air around the
woman swirled in a thickening mist, in which her face ran like
water, changing.

"Lady khaness!" Sechule bowed deeply, as subject to ruler, burning to know what the demon wanted of her, and her son. She had met the Lady Chaiujin from time to time when gathering herbs of the kind neither wanted known about them. But Chimbai's second wife had never declared herself a friend to anyone.

The lady held out her hands to be kissed. Sechule hesitated only a moment before she brushed her lips upon the backs of the lady's fingers. In the form of an emerald green bamboo snake the lady had sunk her venomous fangs into her husband's breast, murdering Chimbai-khan in their bed. Her fingers seemed perfectly normal, but beneath her sleeves the skin shone a pale green, with a faint tracing of what might be the reflection of the pattern of her green dress, or might be scales sheathing her arms above her wrists. Sechule wished briefly that she hadn't turned the mirrors, but the khan's palace had many such and they hadn't stopped the lady's magic. But today, perhaps, she meant no harm.

"Do you mind?" With a graceful gesture in the air, the mist returned. When it had lifted again, the lady wore a stranger's face, spoke with a stranger's voice.

Sechule wiped her hands nervously on the apron she wore. She had never liked it. Mergen had given it to her when she still had hopes of him. When she promised to put it safely in her marriage chest, he had chastised her, saying that could never happen between them. After so many years, stains splashed the embroidered birds nesting on vines curling sensually at her breast and she wished she had put on something more fitting a visit from a khaness, even if she were a murderess.

"Be at peace," the lady encouraged her, "We share the same hope for your son, Qutula."

"My son? I don't understand . . ."

"Of course you do. You saw me leave his sleeve and invited my presence with your turned back. We both want the best for your son. Mergen's son. The rightful heir."

The lady smiled, as if this must be the most obvious thing in the world, that she should take an interest in Sechule's blanket-sons. "I cannot say I know him well. But . . . intimately . . . He knows of my interest in him. The spirits will approve, once it is done; his father sits on the dais as khan, after all. What could be more natural than that a son follow his father's path?"

Sechule blinked, but otherwise showed little of the feelings that bubbled inside her like the stewpot on the firebox. Qutula, khan. She had dreamed it, but to know that others felt the same, that her son had attracted the support of supernatural forces to his claim—

"His father has not acknowledged him." The most bitter reminder of Mergen's treachery burned in her heart. Until his father claimed him, Qutula—and Bekter, for that matter—would be heir to nothing.

"An obstacle, I know, but one I trust him to overcome."

Not all the years of his young life had taught his father how to love him enough to name him son. That left little, in Sechule's estimation, but murder. Not the khan, of course, since that would put Chimbai's heir on the dais. But if some accident were to befall Prince Tayyichiut, to whom else would Mergen turn?

The lady followed all Sechule's thoughts with a smile on her lips. "You see it, too," she said, though neither spoke aloud the words that would seal the pact between them.

Many questions remained unanswered, but of them all one troubled Sechule most: "Surely Qutula must value the support of the spirit world, but how does his place at his father's side help you?"

"His father will not live forever."

Sechule guessed that the lady would make certain of that.

"As his gift to me, Qutula has promised to return me to my rightful place on the dais, as his wife. I have come to assure you that I welcome your presence at my side there, as the mother of the khan."

"But how . . ." She didn't mention the potion she had given her son to feed the prince. It would begin the process, but not end it. They needed illness over time, she thought, not another suspicious sudden death. The lady seemed to know all that, however, and set it aside with an undulating wave of her hand.

"That is for Qutula to decide. We are only women, after all. We may advise, but men must wield the sword and the spear in our names."

War? Qutula had ambition, surely, and followers, but she had hoped to limit the conflict to a few judicious murders. Sechule shrugged a languid shoulder. "We women don't wear the stag's horns, but we have our own quieter ways to set things right again."

"Exactly." With a pointed look at the empty jar that had lately held the death's-head mushrooms, the lady added, "I can teach you more."

It seemed pointless to dissemble with an ally. "Yes," Sechule said, and returned her guest's smile. "Would you like some tea? From the other chest, of course."

"That would be very nice—" The lady sat in a place of honor while Sechule pulled out cups and offered honey or butter for the tea.

Eluneke slept, and in her dreams the king of the toads came to her with all his followers behind him. "Queen of the humans," he said. "Queen of the toads," and bowed to her. When she tried to raise him up, he turned into the prince and kissed her, but his kiss was deadly and she swooned. He reached to catch her, but she passed through his arms, falling as if from out of the sky, and above her she heard the gods thunder their anger that she had disturbed them at their rest.

When she struggled out of dreams, Bolghai was there to pat her shoulder and tell her, "Sleep." It seemed much easier than waking, so she did as she was told.

"Butter," the false Lady Chaiujin chose, while snaky thoughts of juicy rodents and her hostess' beating blood slithered through her mind.

Sechule poured. "You know my son Qutula has ambitions,"

she said as they sat to drink. "Bekter worries me, however. He hesitates; that's his way. He needs persuasions that a mother can't apply."

The emerald green bamboo serpent demon drank, though she had no taste for tea. "I suppose I could whisper inducements in his ear."

And if he remained unmoved? Did Sechule intend for him the fate of the serpent's late husband, Chimbai-Khan? A mother in the demon realm had many young, and ate them to sustain her when other prey was scarce. She hadn't noticed such behavior in humans, though they seemed quick enough to send their young to be slaughtered by others.

"We think alike," Sechule agreed. "I knew I could depend on you."

"Of course." Lady Chaiujin nodded, though she suspected the woman was very wrong in her certainty

"For myself," Sechule continued, offering an opportunity. "I think I will make a brief visit to the ger-tent palace. My son will be singing a new song he wrote for the khan."

"I suspect the khan will grow tired very soon thereafter." The lady gave a smile a bit too mocking.

As is the way of allies who need but do not necessarily like each other, Sechule kept her objection to herself. Only the brief flicker of anger in her eyes gave her away. "You will have only my sons to attend you tonight, whichever bed you choose. The palace is full of fine young men with strong arms and an appreciative eye. I'm sure I can find one with a warm bed as well."

"Enjoy your young man, then, as I shall enjoy mine." Bekter was not as handsome as his brother, nor as sharp of wit. Qutula had come to the desired conclusion about his cousin the prince on his own. All she had to do was encourage him. Bekter, like a dumb beast who adored his master while that master sharpened his butchering tools, still hoped that a steadfast nature would win for him his father's love. She anticipated no great pleasure from the encounter, but trusted the young man to be quick.

The boy's mother must have picked up some of the lady's

hesitation, because she stopped in the doorway with a warning. "Don't hurt him. He is not, perhaps, the hero a lady dreams about when she sleeps alone, but he has a good and willing heart. And whatever you may have thought you understood of them, remember this about mortals. They mourn each other more in the loss than they may love each other while living. If you wish to bind Qutula to your will, you would not hurt his brother."

So, she didn't mean for her demon conspirator to eat him after all. "You worry too much," the stranger who had once been the Lady Chaiujin assured her. "I value my alliances. But if it makes you feel better, I promise to be kind to your son." She wondered what other reassurances the woman needed, but that seemed enough. With a final bow to acknowledge their pact, Sechule departed.

Alone in the unfamiliar tent, the lady poked among the herbs and poisons and examined Sechule's clothes with a sneer. Finally, she returned to her serpent form, coiled in a nest she made of Sechule's best silk coat. Deep within her slumber, she felt the promise of a snaky egg slowly taking shape. Soon she would need to find a father. But not Bekter. Her child must be the heir to a khan.

Mergen wouldn't do. Another man in his place might have been grateful for the opportunity she had given him. But he hadn't wanted to be khan and he'd been a lot angrier about Chimbai's death than she'd expected. Sechule must be right about brothers.

Prince Tayy was just as useless to her. The boy saw more than skin-deep and he had never forgiven her for his mother, let alone his father. So that left Qutula, who had a mind for strategy and a heart for conspiracy. And later, when her place at his side as the mother of the heir was secure, she would make it seem that Sechule had committed his murder.

Thinking such thoughts, she slept.

Chapter Twenty

THE GER-TENT PALACE was lit with many lamps reflecting off the mirrors on the lattices. It looked like the hunters of the Qubal had captured little moons Han and Chen and put them in cages to reflect their holy light upon the khan. Sechule slipped in at the back, where the light was dimmest, and gradually worked her way toward the brightest glow around the dais. There were those among the nobles and Mergen's advisers who eyed her with a speculative gleam, wondering if she planned to entertain them with a scandal tonight. Would she confront the khan, spitting curses like a deserted wife? What would the khan do when he saw her? Bekter had begun to play, however—she recognized his playing by the slightly off-key G—and his presence in front of the khan gave her reason to be there.

"Sechule." A hand reached out, stroked down her arm as she passed. Altan, that was, a friend of the prince in Qutula's age group. He had graced her bed on a few occasions, but neither had sustained the other's interest for long. She heard his family had chosen him a young wife from a wealthy clan. Still, if nothing else presented itself, he seemed willing to take a walk to the river. She returned the caress with a warning tap of her finger against the back of his hand. Discretion, that warned, and promised, "Maybe." He smiled, and drifted away to take his place among the prince's guard. Later, she knew, he would look for her in the half-light below the firebox.

There were other men. Powerful men, who stood almost as close to the ear of the khan as Yesugei had, would bed her for her looks and perhaps to challenge the khan, if he still cared. Young men who believed that sleeping with the khan's mistress—even an old one—put them closer to the khan himself would pretend to an attraction they didn't feel. In the dark, they would doubtless manage. The sheep never suffered for lack of company, after all.

No one hindered her passage through the crowd of followers and hangers-on, past the guardsmen with their blue coats and their backs to the lattices. They should, perhaps, have stopped her as she neared the dais. She had exceeded the limits of her rank. But Bekter was her son, and the whole court appreciated his songs, if not his playing.

The usurper, Prince Tayyichiut, was there, trying to pay attention, though his gaze seemed distant and given to restless sweeps over the crowd. Mergen seemed to be doing a better job of listening to his blanket-son, though sometimes a smile threatened to break over his face at inopportune moments in the song. Bortu was watching the khan with her own secrets simmering in her eyes. Sechule wondered what that was about. Then Mergen caught her gaze. He didn't turn away.

The ger-tent palace was hot tonight, almost crowded, especially nearest the dais of the khan. Farther back, the crowd was thinning as it did late at night. Those below the firebox had less to lose at his displeasure, as if he wouldn't have done the same in their places. Mergen took it all in with an ironic eye. *All this belongs to me*, he thought. A little bit of pride touched his lips. He'd kept the Qubal alive, after all, and together as an ulus in spite of murder and war. For the rest, he wondered what fate had put him here when he knew himself to be singularly unsuited to rule.

Fortunately, the assembled nobles and clan chieftains

hadn't figured that out yet. With a bit of work, he hoped they wouldn't catch on until he had passed the khanate to his nephew, who should have had it by right of birth. He hoped the young man would take the reins of power among the clans more easily than his uncle had. He hoped they could do it with celebrations and ceremonies, with none of the death and anguish that usually accompanied the passing of power from one khan to another.

This time, however, the passing khan was ready neither for his dotage nor for his pyre. The new khan had neither to wrest the dais from his predecessor nor to convince the ulus of his fitness to rule. Any khan might step aside for a hero who had talked with dragons and lived to tell of it. An uncle who preferred a quiet life could do no less. *This is all mine,* he thought, *but soon it will be his.*

Bekter was singing a new song involving crashing swords and the king of the toads. A fond smile came of its own accord.

Tayy held his breath, but Bekter's song put the hero-prince of the Nirun in the place of the shamaness in training, fighting rather than negotiating with the king of the toads in single combat. To the laughter of the court, the creature admitted defeat in the croaks and belches of Bekter's own version of the language of the toads.

"The king of the toads indeed!" Laughing with the rest, Mergen took a sip of his kumiss. "What gave you such a notion?"

"As to that, you must ask the prince!" Putting his instrument aside, Bekter answered the khan with an easy jest as the tellers of tall tales were wont to do.

Tayy knew there would be talk. He might have sworn the Nirun to secrecy, but the Durluken would put this to a contest as they did everything, it seemed, between the captains. Who had the more beautiful woman to warm his blankets—Qutula or Prince Tayy? No one had seen 'Tula's lover. Tayy hadn't ever bedded the girl at the river—they'd spoken for the first time today—so the whole exercise seemed as pointless as a practice stick at jidu.

Declaring herself too exhausted from a day of visiting to partake in the gossip, the Lady Bortu had gone to her bed leaving more whispers behind her. Had she been out among the clans, sounding out political matches? Were the prince's exploits at the river the first steps in a dance that would lead to a royal wedding? As the kumiss flowed and the roasted meats disappeared, the wagers grew more outrageous.

The tale of the king of the toads didn't help. Bekter didn't know the part about the shamaness in training making a treaty with the toad people, but like the Nirun and Qutula's Durluken, he'd seen the girl. Tayy needed something to take their minds off what they had seen and at the moment King Toad seemed to be it.

"He was the biggest toad I've ever seen," he said, "and he had a crown of leaves on his head. He walked up to us bold as a warrior of the khan and croaked his royal command."

Qutula handed him a bowl and he drank, gasping at the bitter fire of the kumiss. After only a few mouthfuls of the fermented mare's milk, he had enough and set the bowl down next to him.

"Such creatures are dangerous when cornered," Mergen reminded him, and then turned to the gossip that Bekter had discreetly left out of the song. "And yet, all I hear in whispers badly hidden behind the hands of your guardsmen is about this girl—" Mergen kept a smile on his face, but the prince felt his anger through the mask of good humor. "Or was she a toad as well?"

The Nirun laughed; they had seen her and assured their khan that the girl was no toad. "Beautiful," Altan declared her, "with eyes to drive a man to deeds worthy of Bekter's songs."

Jochi, Mergen Gur-Khan's new general, glared at his son. They had, no doubt, each drunk more than was sensible. Tayy knew he ought to silence his guardsman. He was occupied with a strange attack of dizziness, however, and failed to warn him when, in defense of his opinion, Altan grew more emphatic in his praise.

"Her lips were plump and other parts more so—" he held his hands in front of him in a pretense of holding up breasts.

"Enough!" Jochi struck out with the back of his hand, leaving the mark of his knuckles on Altan's cheek.

As if one body, the whole court sucked in a great breath and waited for the khan to answer the quarrel on his very dais. Mergen, however, waved an indulgent hand. "Fathers and sons," he said. "Who would stand between the molding of the young by their elders?"

At Jochi's bow, the khan added, "You have my permission to continue his education later, in your own tents." Few beyond the dais saw the blood flare in the khan's eyes. It would have surprised no one. Altan had addressed the khan too familiarly, on a matter of great sensitivity. The general muttered something into his son's ear and Altan dropped his head, obedience and shame in the dejected curve of his shoulders.

"My apologies, lord khan," he begged with an abject bow. Mergen Gur-Khan gave a stern nod, accepting the apology but not forgiving the young man. "Go," he said. "Guard the horses until you learn to guard your tongue."

Altan's face burned dark with blood, but he kept his head low and bowed his way down the aisle between the nobles and chieftains who watched him go with pity or jeers as they felt themselves in sympathy with the Durluken or the Nirun. When he reached the firebox, he turned and ran. They all knew he took the blame for Tayy's indiscretion.

"So tell me more about this princess of the toads," Mergen asked him sharply, when Altan had gone. But Tayy found himself overwhelmed by dizziness again and unable to answer.

Someone covered him—he felt the warmth of his blanket over him—but his eyes refused to open to discover who had done him the service. Qutula, no doubt. His guardsman spoke softly from somewhere high above him: "He sleeps my lord khan. Tomorrow—"

"Is he ill? What are you doing?"

Tayy's body tried to tense, his eyes to open at the sound of alarm in Mergen Gur-Khan's voice. His cousin had nearly strangled him during the wrestling matches and he didn't want

to be at a disadvantage if Qutula had one of his convenient accidents again. He couldn't move, however, when someone took
his hands and rubbed them with a salve that smelled like
moldy herbs.

"I don't think so, or at least not badly ill," Qutula answered.
"My mother gave me something for protection against the toxins of the king of the toads, though, and I thought it couldn't
hurt."

He hadn't touched King Toad and Eluneke wouldn't have
poisoned him even if she could, which he doubted. But he felt
heavier than a normal sleep should make him, and the gentle
ministrations felt good even if they smelled bad. The salve itself might be poisoned. But Qutula laid it on with his bare
hands; he couldn't do Tayy harm that way without hurting
himself.

As if reading his mind, a woman's voice spoke up from
below the dais. "A harmless comfort, my khan. I would do no
harm to your own—"

What was Sechule doing there?

"I know you wouldn't," Mergen answered her. "If it will
give him comfort—"

"I think he only needs to sleep, my lord khan," Qutula had
finished rubbing the salve into his fingers and settled down beside him to guard his rest.

"As well should you all," Lady Bortu muttered from under
a pile of her own bedding. Soon her snores filled the quieting
hall. It sounded like a good idea, So Tayy let the sleep take him.

S echule. His breath came rapidly in spite of the fact that good
sense told him to have her sent away. How had she gotten
past his guards? Her sons, no doubt. She wasn't looking at
Qutula, however. She was looking at Mergen, her eyes as dark
and mysterious as they had ever been. Her coats hid the curves
of her body, but her round, soft lips made promises he knew
her body would keep. The light gilded her hair and turned her
face to molten bronze. He might have said once that she looked

like a goddess, but he had seen goddesses since then, and none of them had her sensual beauty. He could no more imagine bedding the Lady SienMa, Shan's goddess of war, than he would make love to his sword. Sechule offered more earthly hills, and a welcoming valley between her thighs.

He remembered the yielding lushness of her body and the ger-tent palace was suddenly too warm. He couldn't look away.

Jochi, the captain of his personal guard, stepped closer to the dais, guessing what his khan's instructions must be. The whole court must know—Mergen shifted in his stiffly embroidered coats, wishing they would all go away. His blanket-sons turned from one to the other of their parents; Sechule looked a challenge back at him as she made her bow and withdrew to a more proper distance from the dais.

"Tell her to stay—discreetly," he muttered, though he might as well be wearing the stag's horns for all the discretion he was exercising with his eyes or the flush of his skin.

Jochi was Altan's father. The son—perhaps the father as well, though Mergen doubted it—had slept with Sechule at one time or another. He bowed without comment, however, and disappeared into the crowd, making his roundabout way to the woman the khan would take to his bed that night.

A "Tsk" from beneath the nearby covers told him all that he had to know about his mother's opinion of his choice. Prince Tayy, at least, seemed really to be sleeping but Bekter flicked him a quick, fretful glance, expecting trouble. He half expected it himself, though Sechule had never given him anything he couldn't handle, and then only to further the cause of his children. Mergen looked forward to the day when he could invite his sons to call him father. Soon. When Prince Tayyichiut was khan.

But Jochi had found his way to Sechule's side, resting his hand on her arm while he put his lips to her ear. Mergen forgot what he was thinking. In that distant way that happened sometimes in moments of intense desire, he felt the smooth, warm skin under Jochi's hand, felt his own mouth so close to her skin and her hair that the moisture rising off her heated body left a fine dew clinging to his lips.

"I'm tired now," he said, "and the day is long tomorrow," a signal for his court to find their own beds. As he expected, Qutula didn't leave the prince's side. Flustered, Bekter gave him a proper bow, but Mergen only dimly noticed the distress that crossed his face.

This is a mistake. Mergen knew it as well as Jochi or his mother or his sons. Or the rest of his court for that matter. In affairs that touched the heart and the ulus he would agree. But Sechule's attraction fell rather farther south than that, taking the body as a map of the world. Which it was, right now. All the world, and the capital of the ulus was nowhere near his heart, or his head. He was usually better at resisting the pull of her sensuality. But when the light glistened on her lips just so, and her eyes grew wet and her shoulders drooped, limp with her own passions, he found himself leaping onto the pyre over and over again.

The last of the crowd were leaving with backward nervous glances, especially those who had heard her curse him for his neglect in the past. His advisers knew her desires well enough—not just the legitimacy of her sons, which he could give her, eventually, but her own place on the dais as his wife, his khaness. A political disaster he'd well avoided since becoming khan. There'd been other women, of course. Simpler, less demanding women. Even in death, however, they left their own complications behind. He'd have to do something about Eluneke soon. In the meantime, better the traps he understood than a stranger whose baggage cart he just hadn't seen yet.

The tent was almost empty now. Jochi stood with his back to the departing court, Sechule held in front of him. With an arm across her waist, he blocked her from the view of the curious. Disapproval carved a frown line between his brows, but Mergen didn't notice. His eyes were filled with Sechule, who was as beautiful as she had been the night they'd first run off to the river together. He'd have liked to do the same again, pretending to that youthful freedom from responsibility, but that wasn't possible anymore. Sometimes he wondered if she'd cast a spell on him.

Most of the time he knew what drew him back to her in

spite of good sense telling him to send her away: warm flesh that, no matter their quarrels in daylight, had always held him safe in the night. So he'd settle for the furs of his own bed, more forgiving of aging bones than the riverbank anyway. It didn't matter, now. Nothing stood between him and the only woman for whom he had ever felt such need.

Throughout the ger-tent of the khan servants had dimmed the lights. All lay in darkness and shadow except for one lamp on a near chest, and the glow of the firebox. In that pale light Sechule took her leave of Jochi and walked toward the khan, unclasping her coat with each step until she let it slide from her shoulders behind her. It wasn't her best. She hadn't intended to seduce him, which made him feel lighter, almost happy to invite her to join him in the blankets.

She smiled at him, her fingers working the fastenings of the elaborate headdress that spilled her hair like waterfalls at each side of her head. Jewels lay like a trail of crumbs behind her, freeing her hair to fall loosely to her waist as she stepped up onto the dais. When she was sure she had his full attention, she drew her dress over her head, heedless of the way her shift rode up over her naked thighs and hips. Then the dress dropped in a heap. In nothing but her shift, she knelt before him.

Somehow, modesty seemed meaningless with Sechule. Her hair drifted across his body like an army of delicate fingers; he wanted to feel it on his skin and worked at the bindings of his own clothes. She helped, freeing him with her hands while complicating his efforts with her sensual attacks on his face, his throat, each part of him as it was revealed from his discarded clothing. Finally, there it was, her hair, his skin.

He couldn't hold in the moan that built in his throat and he plunged his hands into the depths of the rich dark folds of her hair, fanned the long strands until they covered him like sable, all soft fur and prickles on his skin.

"Mergen," she said, and covered his mouth with her kisses. "Beloved khan. Love me, love me."

"Sechule." He was a wise man, and so knew himself for a fool, but he let himself believe her words meant what he wanted them to mean, that her body desired the same things he felt when she touched him, when her body slid under his and the power of their senses built between them. Because he couldn't give her what she wanted, he pretended not to know. This was enough. It had to be enough. It was all he had to give her. The rest belonged to Prince Tayyichiut, the son of his dead brother, and nothing could stand between the khan and that sacred trust. Not even Mergen the man and his lust for this one woman.

When the emerald green bamboo snake who was some-times the Lady Chaiujin, and sometimes Qutula's lover, woke again, Bekter had returned and lay snoring in his bed. Slithering under his covers, she curled around him in her snake form and turned back into a woman.

"Bekter. Beautiful, kind, wise, Bekter—" she made the words a breathy whisper in his ear, a promise of pleasures to follow if he would just open his eyes.

He snorted, batted aimlessly at his nose, and rolled over.

"Beloved, soft, sweet Bekter—" A little louder now, with a stroke of fingernails at the back of his neck.

He flopped on his stomach, burped long and loudly, sighing contentedly in his sleep when he was done. A bit of drool hung from his lip. Stretched. Broke away and fell into the furs he slept on. Her fingertips dug in, left little half-moons of blood between his shoulder blades, under a braid of hair slicked flat with sheep fat.

The false Lady Chaiujin had just decided that she had tried hard enough to seduce the insensate pile of blubber. Then he snorted, twitched like a shaman with a vision, and lifted his sleep-wrinkled face with a vague look in his eyes. "Huh! What?" he half rolled, and stared at her as if he had never seen a naked woman before. Which, perhaps, he hadn't.

"Who are you? I think you have the wrong bed. Qutula sleeps over there."

He pulled the blankets up as if to cover his nakedness, al-though he wore little less in bed than he normally walked around in.

"What makes you think I came for Qutula? Don't say you haven't had your own admirers before now."

"Strange women show up in 'Tula's bed, not mine." He took her hands away from the laces on his pants, then didn't know what to do with them. "Nothing personal, you understand, but I prefer to make the acquaintance of the women I sleep with before the fact, not after. In the daylight."

Or he imagined that's how it would go, she thought. He experimented with releasing her hands, grabbed them again when she set them back to work on his laces.

"Don't do that!"

He wasn't pretty like his brother, and his spirit of adventure seemed sorely lacking for a warrior. But his indignant resistance made her forays at his clothing more of a game than a seduction. "Why not?" she baited him. "Afraid of a defenseless woman?"

"Anyone who grew up with my mother would be a fool not to be," he muttered, then scowled, unwilling to have thoughts of his mother intrude on a moment already more disturbing than he liked. "For all I know you could be a demon sent to snatch me away to the underworld."

If only that were possible, she'd set her sights a bit higher, or better yet go home alone, finally and at last. Only they'd closed the crack between the worlds with their wars. She was stuck here. Qutula had been much easier to seduce.

Bekter wasn't just playing hard to get, though. While they'd been talking, his hand had inched slowly toward his sword. Whatever he thought her, he'd decided she was dangerous. He had no reputation for courage or brains for anything but his poems. She wondered, though. If he thought her just another camp follower, then he had neither and was lacking drives that made a virile man as well. If he really had guessed what she was, however, then he had more of both brains and courage than she would have credited even to Qutula. Interesting. But his fingers had reached the hilt of his sword. It was time to go.

"I'm sorry," she said, and kissed him lightly on the nose. "You would have enjoyed it."

Clothing was simple. She wished herself covered and she

was, leaving him bemused with the memory of their encounter growing less clear with each step she took away from his bed. When she reached the door, he would forget she had ever been there. Which was, she thought, a shame.

If Qutula couldn't bring his brother in line, he didn't deserve her or the khanate. Tonight her lover stayed with the prince, setting him on the short and painful road to his funeral pyre. But tomorrow, she would find him where he slept and remind him of the rewards awaiting him at the end of his own road. And soon she would make him an heir. She didn't know what the child would be—snake or human or demon—or which of her various natures drove her to create this strange new life. But on her way to the door she grabbed Sechule's silk coat that she had lately rested upon. It would make a fine soft lining for the nest she must soon make in earnest. Not yet, though. Her egg was not quite ready yet.

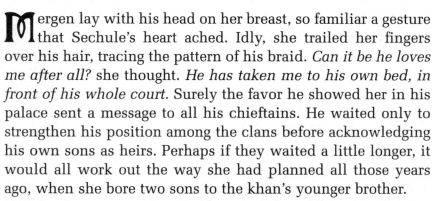

Mergen lay with his head on her breast, so familiar a gesture that Sechule's heart ached. Idly, she trailed her fingers over his hair, tracing the pattern of his braid. *Can it be he loves me after all?* she thought. *He has taken me to his own bed, in front of his whole court.* Surely the favor he showed her in his palace sent a message to all his chieftains. He waited only to strengthen his position among the clans before acknowledging his own sons as heirs. Perhaps if they waited a little longer, it would all work out the way she had planned all those years ago, when she bore two sons to the khan's younger brother.

Morning was coming. As she remembered from his visits to her tent, Mergen woke before the birds or the horses, before even the slaves had stirred about their breakfast pots. She felt it in a flex of muscle as he tensed beside her. Then his smile spread upon her breast. He kissed her lightly there, and pushed himself up to look into her eyes.

"Thank you," he said, and rolled away, scratching at his head where the braid was bound tight to the skin. "Jochi will escort you home; he's the most discreet of my guards. No one will know where you spent your night."

"I don't fear the eyes of the clans," she answered with a smile. "I would feed you breakfast with my own hands, as I used to do when you crept under my tent cloths all those years ago."

"I'm sorry," he said, seeing something in her eyes that brought instant regret to his own. "I shouldn't have asked you to stay last night . . ."

She saw it then, in the way he wouldn't look at her, but cast his glance over her shoulder. He'd felt an itch and called on her to scratch it for him. Nothing had changed at all. Curses bubbled up in her heart, almost made it to her lips. But a shadow fell over their bed. Jochi, impassive, waited for her to get up and sneak away like a baby stealer. Her dignity in shreds, she could do nothing but bow her head in acceptance of his command.

"Whatever you want, you have of me, my khan. I have only ever wanted to serve you."

Some emotion passed quickly over his face, regret, or discomfort that she hadn't taken herself away yet. Perhaps he didn't know himself. Jochi didn't allow her the time to persuade him to her preferred interpretation, however. With light pressure at her arm he moved her away from the dais, saying, "This way, my lady," as if a title she did not own might calm her anger at the indignity he did her.

"I only meant . . . Of course."

With a last bow, she turned and walked away, remembering last night how Jochi had shielded her from the eyes of the court. So they wouldn't know the khan had called for the services of his favorite whore again, she now guessed. And he would never make a whore's sons his heirs. Unless there could be no others. Qutula had the life of the prince in his hands already. She considered the herbs and medicines in the chest at home. If she could somehow reach the khan's food, he would find such visits as they just had few and unsatisfying indeed. Whatever marriage he made for politics or younger, softer flesh, there would be no heirs but Sechule's sons.

PART THREE

SONS OF
DARKNESS

Chapter Twenty-one

BEKTER STOOD BEFORE THE raven tent wondering how to explain his presence to the shamaness Toragana. He was supposed to be spying for his father, but he didn't have the skills for it, even to serve the ulus. He'd done well enough the last time, he supposed; the shamaness had seemed happy when he promised to return. Five days had passed since then, however. Tinglut-Khan's messenger had returned to announce the approach of a Tinglut prince, whose party would reach the tent city of the Qubal gur-khan in the morning. Tomorrow he would be called to attend to the duties of court; today he had a mission for his father.

Eye to eye with the raven guarding her door, however, he admitted to himself that he hadn't come back for Mergen Gur-Khan. He needed advice, answers to questions he didn't dare bring to Bolghai's attention even if he could find him. The court shaman appeared and disappeared on his own calendar, heedless of the khan's wishes or the needs of royal spies with disturbing dreams of their own. So he found himself waiting outside the shamaness' tent once again, his own worries simmering off the fire while he listened to the old tales she told to the children of her clan.

In his world, tales still seemed to come to life. A prince had fallen in love with a princess of the toads, or so rumor said, adding that he had sickened from the poisons in her skin. Bekter knew better. Prince Tayy spent one night with a gut ache—too much drink, or something bitter in the pies—and recovered the next day. Even now he sat with the leaders of the royal guardsmen, planning a great hunt to entertain the Tinglut prince. The girl existed, of course, no toad but an apprentice in training to the shamaness in this very tent and one of the reasons he had come. The prince had better sense than to fall in love with her, though. Soon enough the khan would give him a political wife to be the object of his devotion.

Mergen wanted to know everything about her, just in case. That was the spying part of his visit. Back the other side of catching the prince by the river with her, he'd thought the khan overcautious for his heir. But he'd seen enough between them to realize that she'd bewitched him, or the prince had fallen under the spell of her eyes if nothing more sinister. Even an innocent connection could end in disaster; adding magic to the mix made catastrophe almost a certainty.

A shamaness might choose to walk out to the river with a young man because the night was warm and the grass was soft. Even a warrior should have better sense than to bring a shamaness in love to a casual bed, however. For the girl loved the prince, of that he had no doubt. He'd seen love denied for politics in his mother's tent and understood why Mergen was so worried about Prince Tayy.

It seemed to Bekter that some things ran true in the blood, including a weakness for mysterious women with unearthly powers. He wondered what secrets 'Tula's woman hid. His own preferences ran to simpler things, or it least it had until now. Which brought him to the second reason for his visit. His dream. He hoped it was a dream. Didn't want to consider that the strange woman had entered his mother's tent and his bed to offer him—what? Her body, certainly, but she hadn't seemed that enamored of his person. What else she meant for him, he still didn't know.

Needing a deep, calm mind to share his concerns, he'd thought first of the shamaness. He'd forgotten about the children, though. They were back as well. He had no desire to make of himself a meal for the gossips again in front of them, so he waited while dark clouds gobbled up the sky. The summer rains had come; soon he'd have to find shelter. For now he listened through the creamy felted tent cloths as the shamaness recited the story of Nogai's Bear, or the part of it suitable for young ears. The death of the khan at the hands of the bear's son, raised as his own heir, made no tale for children.

Entranced like the children by her voice, he waited through the first raindrops until the khan of the story had received his wife back in joy and rewarded Nogai with the rank of general and a place at his side. When the children ran out, declaring themselves to be the khan, or Nogai—the girls, he noted, seemed disinclined to suffer as the stolen wife or her grieving husband but wielded stick swords as Nogai—he still waited.

Finally, the shamaness came to him still wearing her robes of office, with the keen dead eyes of the stuffed raven judging him from atop her headdress. Holding back the door with a smile of welcome and a question in her eyes, she asked, "What can I do for you today, poet of khans?"

"My mind is uneasy," he said, the proper formula when calling for advice on a problem that did not yet require a healing, and took from the purse at his waist a gold coin.

"Not gold, but a teapot," she answered the coin with a dismissive wave of her hand and set about filling the teapot in question with crushed leaves and water hot off the firebox.

Bekter understood the old riddle well enough and answered with a smile. "What stands between friends." Hospitality, that meant, and not a cash transaction. Then he saw the girl.

She sat on the layered carpets, weaving a little basket out of reeds. He recognized her instantly and should have been elated that he had a chance to observe her up close. Instead, he found himself frozen in disarray. He'd expected the shamaness to be alone and found himself torn suddenly between his own private errand and the need to learn more about the girl who had caught the prince's eye and terrified Qutula, two good reasons to make the khan nervous.

Looking up from the cups she set out on a small chest—just two, Bekter noted—the shamaness followed the direction of his gaze. "This is my apprentice, Eluneke," she introduced them with a question in the lift of her eyebrow. "Have you met before?"

The girl was watching him with wide, cautious eyes. She recognized him and wondered, he supposed, if he meant her harm as Qutula had threatened. He must have looked at her the same way. Qutula had seen her as a giant poisonous toad, after all. Too late to deny that they had met. Or, something.

"Only from a distance," he said, reining in his galloping imagination. "I'm a friend of the prince."

"I see," Toragana said, as if he had explained more than he might want her to know.

"You're the other one's brother, aren't you?" Eluneke gathered a collection of little baskets scattered at her feet and tied them to the strings that hung from her shaman's robes.

"Which other one?" Bekter asked the top of her head as she leaned over to scoop up the dried reeds she had used to weave the baskets. Remembering the rough treatment she had received at the hand of Qutula and his Durluken, he was suddenly reluctant to claim that connection.

"You know who I mean." She gave him a sharp glance from under her downcast lashes, not flirtatious but attending to the reeds she picked up from the carpets.

"Qutula is my brother, yes. I'm not like him, though."

"I know." She nodded, coming to her feet. "The question is, whose side will you come down on when the prince's life hangs between this world and the next?"

"What are you talking about? I'm no traitor!" Bekter drew himself up to his full, if unimposing, height. "And neither is my brother. But if you know something about a plot to harm the prince—"

"What if you're wrong?" she insisted. It shouldn't have answered his question, but it did.

"I am no traitor." But if it came to believing ill of Qutula, how would he fall? He really didn't know.

She searched his eyes for truth or falsehood and seemed content with what she saw for now. "All right, then," she said, and then, to her teacher, "Will you be long here?"

"I'll be where I need to be when it is time," Toragana reached out and smoothed the girl's hair in the loving gesture of a mother. "Until then, mind your own business, little flower, and trust me to mind mine."

Which should have sounded like a reprimand, but rather came out as some playful code between them. Eluneke smiled mischievously up at the shamaness before she made a bow to Bekter and departed. He knew he ought to follow her, but he had come for other business and Toragana was watching to see what he would do.

Bolghai's tent lay on the far side of the city. He wasn't waiting for her at home, though; Eluneke turned toward the open land and started to run. The next step of her initiation was too dangerous to approach with magic, so she kept to her human form as she left the thinning lines of tents behind her. The soft grass crushed underfoot released sweet fragrances as it cushioned her step. She settled into a pace that ate up the li without stealing her breath. She needed that to call her totem animals to her. "King of toads, king of toads, I need you," she chanted.

> *"By your oath at greatest need,*
> *bring your troops to guide my way.*
> *Heaven will reward you, king of toads."*

She had made of her headdress a comfortable seat for him, well guarded against a sudden fall by an elaborate casque of wicker. She owned few beads, but those she had—two coral ones small as seeds and a larger one of turquoise that had belonged to her mother—she had worked into the decoration of the headdress to honor the king who would make his seat there.

She had tied her baskets to the silver chains that hung from the slashed leather of her shaman's robes. Some small enough to suit a toad no bigger than her thumb, some to house a guest larger than her fist, they flew in many ribbons about her as she ran, leaving bruises where they bounced against her legs and hips and on her breasts. She didn't let the discomfort slow her pace, however. Bolghai was waiting, and heaven after that.

"**Y**ou can't go where she is heading, good Bekter. You must, I fear, make do with the errand that brought you."

"I'm no more a spy than a traitor!" he protested, but this time he couldn't meet her eyes. She would know, and how could he expect her to believe him after such a lie, even for the gur-khan?

"Of course you are," she answered, "But you're far too gallant to mean her any harm and even the gur-khan himself, I think, wishes only to protect her."

The thought that Mergen might care what happened to the girl had never crossed his mind. Hadn't crossed 'Tula's either, or he wouldn't have threatened her. His brother was impetuous, but Bekter wouldn't believe him a traitor. Now that Toragana had mentioned it, however, the notion planted itself and took root. How did the story reshape itself if Eluneke was more than an inconvenience to be rid of?

"Who is she?" he asked, and didn't say, *Why would Mergen care?* The possibilities terrified him. His father favored his blanket-sons and had seen that they rose in the court. Caution sank deep roots in the gur-khan's heart, however. He had never given any public sign of his affection, nor had he shown by any word that he recognized them as his heirs.

Though Sechule had been his favorite, they always knew their father had entertained other lovers. How much more cautiously would he protect a daughter from the schemes and attentions of the court? In Toragana's eyes he saw the reflection of his own thoughts, and the moment when he came to the conclusion she had meant him to reach. Once the notion seized him, he thought he recognized the gur-khan in the girl's dark eyes.

"Is she my sister?" he asked, in this unsettled moment telling her more about his own parentage than a lowly shaman from an obscure clan ought to know.

She didn't look surprised at his revelation about himself. Carefully as Mergen himself might do, she answered with another question. "Does the gur-khan say so?"

He suppressed a dismissive movement of his hand. "No more than he has acknowledged his sons."

It would make sense of the gur-khan's interest in her, though. A word to her clan chieftain would have taken the girl well out of the prince's reach, but Mergen hadn't given that command. Suddenly he wanted her close by. Available to the prince? Bekter didn't think so. But an emissary was due to arrive that night, in search of a wife for the Tinglut-Khan. He gave a little shudder in sympathy for the girl who might soon find herself wed to the old man who stood in uneasy alliance with her father. Was that why she pursued the robes of a shaman?

"You've heard the stories they are telling in the camp about her?" he asked instead. He doubted the foreign khan's interest in a poisonous toad for a wife. The thought that he might be related to one clenched a tight fist around his belly. If he could have shed his bloodline like a snake its skin, he'd have done so that very moment.

Toragana shook her head, not denying anything he'd said, but exasperated, he thought.

"Stories grow in the telling." She pointed him to a cushion on the rugs, near the firebox and away from the low stool for clients. "Sit, before you fall," she said, and filled a cup with tea.

He did as he was told but refused to be lulled with her answer. "We both know that tall tales grow from true seeds. Qutula saw her in the shape of her totem animal."

Flowers floated in the tea, which needed neither butter nor honey to improve the flavor. Idly he wondered if she had drugged him or merely sweetened the drink. "Could she poison him with her skin?" he persisted in spite of the snort of laughter he startled out of her. The notion that so dangerous a creature might be kin made him queasy all over again. "Qutula says she poisoned him when he touched her."

"And what was he doing touching her in the first place?" Settling the ruffled feathers of her robes, the shamaness rephrased his request. "Two questions, you mean to ask: 'can she poison with her skin?' and 'would she use such a taint to harm the prince?' "

Toragana curled her leg under her and sat among the carpets, separated from Bekter by a stray beam of dusty light that pierced the smoke hole in the roof. "Rest easy," she assured him, "The truth, as it happens, is 'no,' to both. Eluneke is no danger to your brother or your prince. She is a girl who sometimes wears the form of a toad, but who is always, at heart, a girl."

Her eyes were clear and gray as the Onga River on a winter afternoon. He would have said they hid nothing, but he knew better than that. A shaman was made of secrets, and she gave him a glimpse of them when she added over her tea, "Bolghai believes she may be the prince's salvation."

He'd never really thought the girl a physical threat. Tayy was a hero, after all. He'd made allies of dragons. And Eluneke seemed to care for him even if she was an unearthly creature with or without a poisonous skin. The prince could hold his own against a lovesick cousin, even one with shamanistic skills. But what was Bolghai afraid of?

"Salvation from what?"

Bolghai waited for her by an outcrop of rock that on a day with more sunshine glittered with mica. Today clouds had closed over Great Sun, turning the day almost to night. The rocks didn't glitter, but they did move, seething with a strange life of their own. When she drew closer, she realized the stones remained still and sleeping. Over and around them, however, crawled an army of toads.

"The king of the toads has kept his promise," Bolghai informed her, though she could tell that for herself now.

As if waiting for the introduction, the giant toad crawled out of the mass of his court and croaked a greeting at her.

"I don't understand." Eluneke cast a helpless glance at her guide. She had to find the tree at the center of the world and climb to heaven in human form, but she could only communicate with the toads when in the shape of her totem animal.

"That's all right," Bolghai assured her with a little pat on her shoulder. "He understands you."

That would do. "Welcome, Your Majesty," she said, and bowed low to King Toad.

"Croak!" he said in answer, and climbed into his seat atop her headdress.

Once he had taken his place on the throne she had prepared for him, the toad court swarmed to find their own places on her dress. She had made baskets for ten, but none seemed willing to stay behind. They climbed into the baskets in pairs and fours, and when there was no room in the baskets even with legs and arms sticking through the wicker, they climbed onto the silver chains that held the baskets, and the hide ribbons that made up her costume itself. Each toad weighed little by itself, but with hundreds of them clinging everywhere to her clothing, she found it difficult to lift a foot. Running was impossible.

"I can't do it!" she cried, "They are too many!"

The toads just clung more tenaciously, croaking their messages of encouragement or deep in their own noisy cross-conversations. The king of the toads said something, but not, apparently an order for any of the toads to disembark.

"In this journey, you will need all the help you can get," Bolghai encouraged her, though whether he somehow knew the language of toads and translated for their king or just added his own thoughts to the noise she didn't know. But the toads weren't leaving.

"All right," she said, and with great effort took her first encumbered step. Right, then left, then right, against the rain that had started as the gentle tears of heaven but had now become the blinding downpour of a raging storm. She tried not to think about where she was going, or how she was to find the tree at the center of the world. Bolghai had led her away from the narrow band of forest that lined the Onga. On the flat plain of the grasslands, no natural tree grew for li after li of waving grass and tearful wildflowers.

The shaman seemed to read her mind, or perhaps the perplexity that pursed her lips and drew her brows together. "The great tree will find you," he said. "All you have to do is run."

Toragana gave an apologetic tilt of her shoulder. It was hard, now that she had the ear of the gur-khan's own poet, to admit how little she really knew about the danger to the prince or the role Eluneke would play in saving him from the death that loomed ahead.

"In a vision Eluneke has seen a death's head riding the prince's horse. Now we're racing against fate and time to save him from what she has seen."

The breath went out of him in a whoosh. Toragana took the teacup from his hand and set it down, dabbing absently at the spill soaking into the carpets. She'd had time to get used to the notion, but her visitor sat with his eyes wide and his cheeks pale as he asked the question that burdened her own heart. "How?"

"The vision doesn't say." She took his hand in hers, willing him to listen and believe. "Let me tell you a story."

Bekter could walk away if he chose; she had already resolved to release him if he pulled his hand away. But he waited, patient eyes troubled. His presence gave her hope as she began the tale he already knew.

"When last you visited my tent, I was telling the children the story of Alaghai the Beautiful and the king of the Cloud Country. But some among the storytellers and shamanic orders know that the truth doesn't end with a wedding and a happily-ever-after."

"I know," he said, and bowed his head as if he bore some terrible burden. A wisp of hair had escaped its braid and Toragana reached out with her free hand and brushed it from his forehead with the backs of her fingers.

"When a wound festers, the evil spirits often veil their poisoned breath behind the illusion of ruddy health," she said. "If we wish true healing to occur, we have to cast out the evil spirits before they kill what they inhabit."

"I know that, too," he admitted. "But this tale cuts too close to my bones. I would not revisit it if I could help it."

She would have spared him if she could, but Eluneke's visions gave her little choice. "Sometimes the spirits of a sickness reside in the body," she reminded him. "And sometimes they reside in the soul of a people. To hide from them only gives them a dark place to thrive."

"Open the wound, then," he said, and turned his hand in hers, offering the smooth pale underside of his arm as a symbol of the cutting she would do to his soul.

He still attracted her, but now was not the time to kiss the flesh that rose so sweetly from his wrist. Toragana entwined their fingers for her own comfort as much as for his. Then she took up the tale.

"Alaghai had two brothers who saw the king as an invader," she began softly, "even if his weapons of choice were gifts and flowers. And so they hatched a plot between them. Luring their sister to a tent hidden far outside the city of the khan, they made her their prisoner and set guards around her from among their loyal followers. Then each set fist to the face of his brother and returned to the ger-tent palace with bruises to support the story they told, of an attack by bandits who seized the princess. They didn't know that Alaghai had stolen away for a night of passion with her lover, the king, or that he had sneaked under the tent cloths to be with her under the khan's own roof.

"When he heard the story of his sons set upon and his daughter abducted, the khan sent the gathered warriors of the ulus to search for the imaginary bandits. That first King Llesho likewise sent his most trusted aides to find the princess.

"The brothers had hidden their sister well. Weeks passed, and the king found no trace of his bride. But time made no secret of the babe rounding Princess Alaghai's belly. Her brothers soon discovered what she had done with the king. If allowed to live, the child might one day rise up like the son of Nogai's Bear to avenge their treachery and take the dais for himself. The brothers resolved to hold the princess in secret until she delivered the child and then kill it before its first cry. Only when they had secured their own positions with the murder of the babe would they lead the king to his death in battle for his bride.

"To kill the king, the two brothers concocted a plot out of magic and sorrow, a wonderfully carved spear they presented as a gift to show their love for the promised husband of their sister. But the spear was cursed."

"And so for generations the khan's family has been cursed with the blood debt of that terrible day," Bekter said. He shuddered, waging an inner struggle against some horrific memory of his own. Toragana had seen the like in men lately returned from the battlefield. The words that followed came as no surprise.

"We just fought a war to pay that debt," Bekter said, though she little needed the reminder. "I have seen the cursed spear in the hand of that king's descendant. Our own Prince Tayyichiut nearly paid the curse with his life. But where does the tale lead us? Back to two brothers who commit treachery against all they should hold most dear? And for what? An inheritance I have never desired? I would never hurt the prince! Never!"

Toragana held his hand more tightly when he tried to pull away. "I know you love the prince, Bekter. I know you would do nothing to hurt him. But someone does wish him harm. The prince will die, soon, if we don't figure out who, and how."

"Of course," he said, but his voice had grown wary and his eyes closed her out of his anguished thoughts. He gave up his efforts to untangle his fingers, however. She gave them a reassuring squeeze which he didn't return, but to which he didn't object. "But why this story? Why these brothers?"

"You tell me, poet." She didn't mention what they had both seen, Qutula with his hand around Eluneke's throat.

Outside the rain had begun in earnest.

Beneath Eluneke's feet the grass had flattened, grown slippery with the rain that beat against her shoulders and rattled the baskets where the tenacious toads clung. Growing accustomed to their weight, she gathered speed until she was running again, across the open plain where no trees waited for her at all. *Where is it?* she asked the darkening day. *How do you find the center of the world? Where is the tree that grows there?*

From the shadows of the storm lightning flashed, scattering branches of red and purple light from cloud to cloud and turning the vast and empty plain white and colorless as Great Moon Lun. Eluneke stumbled, righted herself amid the croaking protests of her riders. "I'm sorry, I'm sorry," she muttered under her breath.

She flinched as the thunder rolled over her. Not all of the water running down her face had fallen from the sky. Her own tears felt hot and salty with her terror next to the cold of the rain. No sane person went out on the plains during a storm. Thunderbolts from heaven scattered death at random. The gods used lightning to snatch the unwary right out of the mortal world and left them dead when they were done. She didn't want to end up like that, lying in a puddle somewhere with the sign of the tree burned into her breasts.

Oh. Of course. The riddle was simple, really. *A tree where no tree grows.* Lightning, its towering trunk reaching from earth to heaven, with great branches holding up a crown of clouds. She would climb the lightning. It was impossible, but being a shaman meant doing the impossible on a regular basis. The hair prickled on her arms and neck, rising in bumps of cold and foreboding, but she ran on.

High above her little tent, thunder rumbled across the sky. Toragana thought of her pupil and the task she must complete. She should be out there with the girl, guiding her as her own teacher had done. But Eluneke had Bolghai, and Bekter, too, had a journey to make. She would have made it easier for him, but knew they needed to drive all the evil spirits into the open before they could be banished.

"I know how the story ends." Bekter stared at their clasped hands as if he couldn't quite figure out how they had got that way. Or as if he were looking into a different time and place entirely. Toragana wondered if poets, like shaman, could travel in waking dreams. She held on more tightly, unwilling to let him go there alone. His face gave no sign that he noticed, but some of the tension went out of his shoulders as he picked up the telling for her.

"A servant, fearing for the life of the princess at the hands of her brothers, told the king of the Cloud Country where to find the tent where they had hidden her. With his armies out of the Golden City he came to her rescue just in time to see the two princes strangle his newborn child.

"When he raised the spear in battle, the cursed gift pierced him through with poison, murdering him. The brothers died in the war that followed. Their sister, it is said, wandered in madness for the rest of her life. A new khan was set upon the dais, and that is the line from which our own Mergen Gur-Khan is sprung. Thus, the debt of blood we owed the Cloud Country in the name of the Qubal people. A debt we owe no more, having won the Golden City in battle against the Uulgar, under the banner of the god-king Llesho himself. I know the story. But that is history, a debt we paid in the blood of our own Prince Tayyichiut. What can it have to do with Eluneke's visions?"

He heaved a very great sigh, and Toragana wanted to fold him into her arms and keep him safe there, but he wouldn't understand it if she did and—

His head dropped to her shoulder. Perhaps he would understand it after all.

"She cannot mean that I would hurt the prince. I would never—"

This time, it was her turn to say, "I know, I know.

"The old tales teach us hard truths, that sons will have their day and more than warriors suffer when princes go to war. But we are meant to learn from the old stories, not borrow their guilt. Bolghai and I are shaman, like the one who cursed the spear, but we would sooner die fighting such a curse than seal a man's doom with one. You are a brother, like the brothers in the tale, but you are a good and loyal man who would no more betray your prince than you would betray yourself. Eluneke is a princess, and she loves the prince. But she is more powerful by far than that long-ago Alaghai and is forewarned by her visions. If any hand can stop it, ours can, brought together out of a story, perhaps, but destined to change its ending."

"**Y**ou're right." Bekter straightened his spine, rubbing his eyes as he moved away from the shamaness. The skin felt stretched over his cheekbones, as if he were waking from a dream. Outside, he heard the thunder roll across the sky. It would be a muddy hunt in the morning. He couldn't avoid the obvious conclusions anymore.

"If Eluneke is the gur-khan's daughter, a lot of things make more sense. He wants the girl stopped. It's not just a romantic ballad; politically it's a mess. There are khans and emperors and apadishas from Pontus to the capital city of the Shan Empire watching to see what match the gur-khan will make for his nephew.

"Eventually, he will have to make more children or acknowledge some among those he's scattered in the camps of the ulus to soothe the nervous posturing of the losers in that contest for the heir's bed." With a bitter laugh he gestured at his own person. "A fat musician will be hard to shift. A pretty girl a lot easier, but not if she's a shaman."

"Not so difficult as that." She smiled in spite of the seriousness of their conversation. "If the fat musician has eyes as deep as the night sky and a smile soft as a spring day." She untangled their hands, trailing her nails across the pads of his fingertips. "And a touch that wrings music from a woman's soul."

His music was adequate at best, though he'd never tried a tune upon a woman. In Toragana, though, he was beginning to find harmonies he didn't know existed between men and women. But he still had the problem of Eluneke and the prince, and the tragedy of a tale caught up in a vision.

"Even a khan must sometimes choose between the thing he wishes and the thing he must have," the shamaness reminded him, reading the questions in his eyes. "If he wishes a daughter to trade for peace, he will lose an heir and that peace as well. That's the lesson for us in the story."

"You think Qutula will kill the prince."

"Unless we stop him, *someone* is going to kill Prince

Tayyichiut. But if we turn the stampeding horses at the wagons we don't have to repair the tents. At the least Qutula has threatened Eluneke, who may be the only chance we have to save the prince."

That was an easy enough riddle to solve. If they could find the assassin before he struck, they could fight him on their own terms with a much greater hope of success. He couldn't believe Qutula would plot murder—his brother loved the prince as much as he did—but it gave them a place to start.

He had forgotten something he had planned to tell her. But the rain beat on the tent cloths and the angry bellow of the thunder roared overhead, while inside the little tent he was warm and dry. Toragana looked at him with such heat in her eyes that she could only mean one thing by it. And, he discovered, he rather liked the thought of an older woman under his blankets after all.

"Stay until the storm passes." She reached for his hand, a gesture that had grown as familiar as his matching one, to twine his fingers with hers. She crossed the step between them, so close now that he could smell the herbs in her hair and the leather of her shaman's robes, and the warm and musky woman smell.

The raven watched him disapprovingly from atop her shaman's headdress, but not for long. Releasing his hand she lifted the nest from her head and set it away from the firebox. Her robes followed, carefully hung on a peg. Then she stood in nothing but her shift, a smile lighting her eyes. "It's cold outside, in the rain," she said. "Come, warm my bed a while."

The furs looked inviting, and by the heated glow of the firebox, Toragana's skin seemed flushed with youthful vitality. Not at all like—oh. The woman who had come to him in his dreams. He'd meant to tell her, but this didn't seem the time. "I'd like that very much," he said, and let her untie the strings of his clothes.

Chapter Twenty-two

"**M**Y PRINCE, we have to go!" Altan shouted.

Startled, Tayy looked up from the shrine that had grown up around the place where his father's pyre had burned. At Mergen-Gur-Khan's insistence, he had brought Qutula and Altan with him as guards. The two didn't get along—'Tula had wanted to bring Duwa instead—but Altan was Nirun, his own man. Duwa served the Durluken. They were just names for the games, but in the subtle push and shove for status in the court, the prince determined to hold the line for his own team in front of the khan. So it was Altan who first brought his prince out of his prayerful meditation with the reminder, "You will want to be off the grass before the Tinglut prince comes any closer."

The Tinglut-Khan's messenger had announced the arrival at sundown of Prince Daritai, second son of Tinglut's third wife, to discuss a marriage between their clans. Mergen had declared a great hunt for the morning to celebrate the visiting prince. But first they must receive him at sunset with all the splendor of the gur-khan's court.

"At least you get to wear silks," Qutula added with a mock grumble. "We guardsmen will be in half-armor until the Tinglut are back on their own ground."

"Count your blessings that you will have a place by the dais, inside the ger-tent palace," Altan challenged him. Fat raindrops started to fall on the stones of the shrine. "The rains are coming. I would not be on guard outside the doors tonight. We need to ride now if we don't want to get caught in the storm ourselves."

"The gur-khan will have our heads if anything happens to you," Qutula agreed, glaring sourly at Altan, as if he had usurped his better's place in sounding that alarm. The dogs would have done it, and considerably sooner, if they'd come with him, but he'd left them behind out of deference to the battle they waged with his cousin. Both of his guardsmen were looking back over their shoulders to the clouds roiling the sky to the north, however. Tayy did the same. A line of heavy rain dropped a gray curtain over the horizon.

"Let's get out of here," he agreed, and mounted his horse. Foreign prince or not, darkness was moving toward them from the south as if some terrible beast was swallowing the sun; already they could see forked lightning reaching for the heavens in the distance.

He knew more about storms now, having watched the approach of the like in the belly of a galley slaver. This one was coming in off the Marmer Sea. He half expected it to sweep him up as it had his friend Llesho in that terrible storm at sea. The gods used storms to pull human beings out of the living world into the sky, only to return them dead again of the experience. King Llesho—not the old legend, but the new one—had survived the experience, but it turned out he was a god himself so that didn't count. The prince tucked his head down against the neck of his horse and settled her with a murmur of reassuring words before letting her set her own pace. He didn't have to urge her, just pointed her in the direction of the tent city, and she went like her feet were on fire.

Qutula was ahead of him. Behind, Altan urged him to greater speed—"Hurry!"—but after that the rising wind snatched his voice away.

They were galloping full out now, all three of them. Altan caught up, terror blanching the color from his face. In the wind, Tayy heard the shrieking voices of the nine maidens, daughters of the great sky god who rode the storms in search of earthly lovers to snatch up into the heavens. Puddles had already begun to form in the rain and he guided his horse around them, one more hazard of the storm. The spirits of the restless dead could reach out and snag a man by the ankles, dragging him down into the underworld through standing water.

Cold and wet, he rode through a terrifying landscape where the underworld of the spirits and the heavens of the gods turned the mortal realm into wind and water and fire with no flame. He looked back, saw the branching stretch of lightning joining grass to dense black cloud. In the blinding white light that washed the air between black sky and blacker earth, he saw the silhouettes of two figures, running. He recognized the man as Bolghai by the skins flapping around his neck as he ran. The other figure, shorter than the man, seethed with no sharp outline to her figure, but instinctively the prince knew who it must be.

"Eluneke!"

Tayy hesitated. His guardsmen had ridden far ahead of his voice and didn't turn or show by any sign that they had heard. Eluneke and the shaman were still too far away to hear, but he could tell they were heading in the direction of his father's shrine. Toward the storm, which was bearing down on them as if it had a will to seize them for heaven.

Maybe they were looking for him, but he was as clear against their horizon as they were against his. And if that was Eluneke, the shifting movement around her could only mean that she had called the kingdom of toads to attend her. He didn't know what the shamaness in training was doing, but he wasn't about to leave her to the storm. Wrenching the mare around to face the lightning he drove his knees into her flanks and cried out, "Eluneke!"

The mare leaped and curvetted a moment, ran a few paces and dug in her hooves, refusing to go any farther. Her eyes rolled in her head and froth steamed at the corners of her mouth. Too much a lady to throw him, she stood her ground trembling and would not go on.

"You've got more sense than I do, girl," he agreed, soothing her with long strokes of his hand on her neck while the wind kicked grit in his eyes and whipped his braids where they hung below the silver cap of his royal helm. His guardsmen, confident that he was with them, had pulled well ahead and reason told him to follow. The Qubal people needed him alive, not dead in the grass with the tree burned into his chest. But he wouldn't leave Eluneke to whatever mad venture Bolghai had set her. Not in this storm.

"I don't know what you expect of me!" he shouted at the unseen gods advancing in a line of thunder and rain. With a frustrated sigh he slid from the terrified horse. "Go," he told her. "Find safety, and come back for me when you can." Foolish orders to give a dumb beast, but he slapped her flank with the irrational certainty that she had heard him and would obey. He didn't stay to watch her go, but turned and ran back toward the shrine. He would intersect Eluneke there, he thought, and put on a burst of speed that carried him back into the storm.

Rain pelted his shoulders and ran off his pointed silver cap. His boots kicked up gouts of mud in the beaten grass. Lightning passed from cloud to cloud, returning day to the grasslands in a flash that was quickly snuffed out by the rain. He was close enough now to see Eluneke, a hundred or more toads clinging to her shaman's robes while their king rode in state atop her headdress. The sight filled him with an unearthly dread even though he had been there when the pact was made. Hesitating, he slipped in the grass and fell backward, knocking the air out of his chest. Overhead, the clouds pulsed with the signal fires of the gods, rumbled with the drums of heaven that mortals called thunder.

The prince squeezed his eyes shut for a moment to clear them of the rain that filled them, then he dragged himself to his feet and started to run again. "Eluneke!"

She didn't hear him, or didn't acknowledge him if she did. Bolghai, however, turned his head. Dismay had rounded his mouth into a wide "O."

"Go back!" he shouted. "Go back!" Tayy didn't listen. Whatever fate the old shaman had planned for Eluneke, he wouldn't let her go through it alone.

She was almost there. Already the storm was focusing on her, on the shrine where the sky gods would call her. Eluneke didn't know by what sense she felt their presence, but Bolghai didn't stop her. Riding in his throne atop her head, King Toad seemed content with the direction she was taking his people as well. The sound of a familiar voice reached her in strands of fog torn apart by the shrieking wind and the thunder rumbling overhead.

"Stop!" Prince Tayyichiut cried, and she thought she heard him say, "Wait for me!"

He couldn't follow where she planned to go, however, so she ran faster, toward the shrine that rose higher each day on the plains. A toad shaken loose from its hold on the leather ribbons of her robes fell to the grass, and another, but most of their number hung on.

Lightning struck as she neared the low pile of stone in its circle of ash. It didn't flicker out, but held steady, linking earth to heaven. Another rose out of the ground beside it, another, until they circled the shrine, nine great trees of lightning with Eluneke inside the circle. *This is it,* she thought. *The gods accept me as a shamaness, or I die with the mark of the tree on my breast.* But which of the nine dancing trees of light was she supposed to climb? Which was the tree at the center of the world?

"Ribit!"

In human form she couldn't understand the words of King Toad. His meaning, this time, was clear enough, however. "That one," he must have meant.

Over the topmost point at the very center of the shrine the sky seemed to open in furious white light, and from the heavens came a searing purple bolt. Above, great purple branches joined cloud to cloud in a towering crown while below the stone of the shrine shattered with the sound like a rocket from Shan going off. The air itself, fleeing the wrath of heaven, blew her off her feet in the broken stone. Eluneke's hair stood on end.

Her skin lifted from her flesh in the way it does when a ghost passes nearby. She wanted to run away, to bury herself beneath the shattered shrine and hide until the terrible storm had passed. But that wouldn't win her the knowledge she needed to save the prince. Pulling herself to her feet, she glared at the tower of dancing light at the center of the destruction. "Now," she said, and took the few steps that brought her to the base.

She thought it would be difficult, and it was, but not in the way she'd expected. Though the tree of lightning seemed no wider than her hand from a distance, it grew unnaturally thicker with each step she took toward it. When she could bring herself to touch it, the life force of heaven passed through her, bringing every nerve in her body to painful life. There were no hand or toeholds to the eye, but when she set foot to the purple light, her toes sank in slightly and held. It was more difficult to plunge her hands into the burning tower but she took a deep breath, closed her eyes, and pushed. The tree held her, though by no solid substance she could identify.

She tried not to think about how high above the mortal world she must climb but focused on each arm as she reached over her head for the next handhold, each foot as she lifted it to the next unearthly toehold. And again, and again. Other girls of marrying age wore silk coats and beads of coral or jade in their ears, she thought, while she dangled toads for decorations. Other girls flirted with the wrestlers while their grandmothers made matches for them. She climbed the lightning to wrest the life of her intended from the gods—after which she must do the same on earth, with no grandmother to claim a prince for a shamaness and all the armies of the gur-khan to stand against her.

Below, she heard voices. Bolghai, she recognized, querulous, to Prince Tayyichiut's pleading. The prince wanted her to come down, but she wouldn't. She was doing this for him, after all. The king of the toads made some comment, ironic by the sound of it. The higher she climbed, the closer she seemed to understanding his language. Not yet, though. Not quite, but she thought it might be advice, and didn't look down.

"Eluneke!" The shrine to his father's memory exploded in a hail of dust and rocky fragments that peppered him with fine cuts and one bruise the size of his fist over his left eye. The lightning strikes didn't snap and fade as they should, but remained untamed and writhing in a circle like the nine dancing maidens around a central strike that seemed to swallow up the world around it. His heart stuttered in his chest and the hairs on the backs of his arms rose in fine points of flesh. Overhead, limbs of the great lightning tree turned Eluneke into her own shadow, climbing higher and higher.

Tayy knew he was in the presence of unearthly magic but he would not let her go into that danger alone. "Eluneke! Eluneke!" he cried. When she didn't answer, he threw himself into the circle of dancing light.

"No!" Strong arms wrapped across his chest and pulled him back. "It's Eluneke's path. Let her follow it!"

Bolghai. Tayy fought him with all his might, but the shaman had pinned his arms to his sides. When he kicked, the shaman picked him up in a bear hug, and when he tried to throw his weight to the side to escape, Bolghai let them tumble together into the muddy grass. Above them, the wind howled cold as night. Ice hard as stones fell from the heavens, pummeling them and littering the grass, some small as millet, some larger than his fist. And one, not ice at all, but a toad frozen solid.

"She'll come back. I promise. She'll come back."

Tayy shivered in the shaman's arms, accepting no comfort as Bolghai held him and smoothed his braids—Tayy's cap had rolled away when they had fallen.

"To become a shaman, she must find the tree at the center of the world and climb it alone, child. How else is she to learn the arts of healing from the gods who reign in the heavens?"

"You did this, too?" Tayy looked up at Eluneke, whose seething shadow had reached the first branching of the great tree she climbed. His fists clenched helplessly as the clouds dropped lower, it seemed, to swallow her up. But if Bolghai had survived it—

"We each find the tree in our own way," Bolghai answered, as cagey a way of saying "no" as the prince had ever heard. Tayy figured he could defend Eluneke in heaven even if he didn't survive the return to earth. That would be enough for him, if it had to be.

As if he knew what Tayy was going to say next, Bolghai added quickly, "This is Eluneke's path, not yours. Do you think she will thank either of us if I let you kill yourself against the lightning trying to stop her?" He released Tayy with a little shake, "To knock some sense into you," he said. "She will need us both down here when she returns. Up there, she doesn't need either of us."

"But—" Tayy rolled to his feet, ready to follow but too late. One by one the bolts of lightning snapped out until only the tree at the center of the world remained. High over their heads Eluneke vanished into the cloudy crown of the great tree and that, too, imploded as if all the world had become thunder. Tayy clapped his hands to his ears and stared up where it had been.

"Where did she go?"

"She is with the gods in heaven now," Bolghai answered.

The thunder had deafened him. The prince didn't hear, but knew the answer anyway.

"What do we do now?" He didn't need the answer to that either. *We wait.*

Chapter Twenty-three

THE LIGHTNING'S TRUNK grew more tenuous as Eluneke climbed. Great branching limbs spread out above her and she stretched, reaching for the sturdiest that blocked her upward path. From there she grabbed another, making her way into the great crown of clouds that billowed around her. The clouds were like ice, the lightning like fire. Trembling from the cold at her back and the brilliant energy crackling through her limbs as she climbed, she wondered which would cause her to fall back to earth first. Would she lose her grip because her hands had grown too numb to hold on? Or because the heavenly fire had burned through muscle and sinew to the bone?

"So this is heaven," the king of the toads croaked.

"Huh," she said, too focused on the task of surviving the climb to do more than acknowledge that suddenly she understood his speech. Nearby, one of the lesser bolts of lightning wavered and snapped out.

"Whoa!" her passenger observed, a bit breathlessly. "Not exactly my idea of perfect bliss."

He shifted in his seat atop her head and she snapped, "Keep still, unless you want to end up a smear on the muddy ground!" The words came out in foreign croaks that strained her throat, but King Toad stopped moving. She wasn't sure if he was following her orders or frozen in terror—or from the cold.

One by one the lightning bolts that had danced around their central tree collapsed until only the great tree at the center of the world remained, wobbling uncertainly under her weight.

"Are we there yet?"

"No," she gritted between clenched teeth, and wept silent, frozen tears as one toad and then another lost its grasp on her shaman's robes and fell.

But: "Yes," a woman's voice answered from above. Hands reached down and took hold of Eluneke's arms and shoulders, drawing her into the warmth of the summer sun just as the tree she climbed disappeared in an ear-shattering crash of thunder.

"Thank you." Unable to bow—the king of the toads still squatted precariously in a basket on her head—Eluneke curtsied politely to the beautiful young woman who stood watching her with a grim and forbidding countenance.

The woman was tall, so that the top of the basket on Eluneke's headdress came only to her shoulder. Her coats were of gold embroidered all over in silver dragons and in her hand she carried a spear. At her side stood another young woman of an equal height and dressed just as lavishly with all the animals of the grasslands embroidered in silver on her coats. In her hand she held a drum. Next to her another woman, with all manner of healing flowers embroidered on the silk of her coats and a laurel bough in her hand, studied Eluneke as if she were some new specimen that had not yet proved its usefulness. Nine in all, the women circled her as the lightning had on the stormy plains. Eluneke thought they must be the daughters of the great sky god of the heavens, but she was too polite to ask.

"Thank you," said the king of the toads, inflating his throat in a pompous balloon. Although he had spoken in the language of the toads and Eluneke in the language of the Qubal, they understood each other.

The women seemed to understand them both. "You're welcome," the first said with a smile but no bow. Eluneke and her totem were supplicants here, not equals.

"Here" did indeed seem to be heaven as the stories had described it. No sign of the terrible storm below disturbed the fragrant grass, where only soft breezes lifted the hair of the nine maidens in gentle waves. It should have been later in the afternoon, but Great and Little Suns both shed their light from the very top of the sky above them. An open door flap showed Great Sun to be a ger-tent palace of gold, larger even than that of the khan. The abode of the sky god, Eluneke figured, though she saw neither warriors to defend him nor the sky god himself. Great Moon Lun shared the vaulted heavens with both suns and her brother moons, an impossible sky in the mortal world, but here all things were possible, if one had the knowledge.

"May we ask why you left your own world for ours?" the woman of the drum asked. "The path is difficult for a reason. Humans aren't welcome here."

"Nor," her companion with the laurel bough added quickly, "do we welcome their toad companions."

"I wish to serve my people and my prince as a shamaness." Eluneke gestured at her distinctive robes as evidence of her calling. In her own small circle the toads who had accompanied her were leaving their baskets and crawling down her silver chains for the sweet grass of heaven.

"Following the teaching of my masters, I climbed the tree at the center of the world to beg the secrets of healing and long life from the sky god and his daughters." Eluneke curtsied again to show that she recognized the women to whom she spoke.

"A shamaness, perhaps," the first conceded, settling the butt of her spear on the ground. With the familiarity of a warrior, her hand wrapped the shaft below the leaf-shaped blade. "but I sense an urgency in your voice that few among your number have expressed on coming here. Fewer yet have the courage to climb the tree when it manifests as the lightning."

"A vision sent me."

The god's warrior daughter accepted this answer with a tip of her head and another question, phrased like a riddle: "A vision more powerful than the storms of heaven."

"The death of a prince," Eluneke answered, still cautious. But if the daughters were asking questions that Bolghai might, they weren't likely to throw her back to earth quite yet. She would have kept the rest to herself, but if the sky god sent her visions, then they already knew. "My husband."

"A hard path," the daughter with the drum muttered.

"It has its rewards." A little smile escaped Eluneke's lips. He was handsome, after all, and he took her communion with the king of the toads in his stride. If they survived the coming threat, she thought they might make a comfortable pair. As for the prince part, and the differences in their ranks, she just wouldn't think about that.

It seemed that the warrior maid had passed the questioning to her sister, for once again the woman with the drum spoke up. "I have greeted the totem spirits of many shamans before, but only in their empty skins." The animals embroidered on her coats shimmered in the sunlight as she peered curiously at the king of the toads. "It is a strange shaman indeed who lets her living totem speak for himself."

"We have an arrangement," Eluneke explained, which seemed to amuse the nine maidens.

"And what do you get out of this arrangement, toad?" The warrior daughter didn't seem perplexed. Rather, it felt like a test, which it probably was.

"My skin," the king of the toads answered, "safely where it belongs, wrapped over my bones and not shriveled and dangling from a string on a shaman's coat. The same for my people, of course."

"Nothing more?" the maiden asked again.

Toads don't have shoulders formed for shrugging, but he bobbed his head in his species' version of the gesture, admitting to an ulterior motive. "Even a toad can have a sense of adventure. How else would one of my kind climb the tree and see heaven, or greet the nine daughters of the sky god in person?"

In fact, his people had scattered widely, exploring by smell and touch and taste the rich loamy ground and the sweet green grass of heaven. With their raspy croaks they reported their findings back to their king: fat insects, soft earth, and—far off— trees bordering a river that flowed like the Onga through heaven.

"Then enjoy your visit, for it may be a long one," she said with a warning glance at Eluneke. "Climbing up the tree at the center of the world is difficult enough. Climbing down is more so."

"And learning the skills to banish evil spirits that cause sickness and death?" Eluneke asked. She knew better than to invite trouble before its time. If she were clever enough at her lessons, she felt sure that the maidens would teach her what she needed to solve the riddle of the way home.

"For that you must ask permission of our father, who rules the sky," the first of the daughters answered. Great Sun had begun his journey toward evening and the daughters turned to track his shadow across the flowing grass. Eluneke had expected the king of the toads to leave her as his countrymen had, but he remained on his throne atop her shaman's headdress and together they followed the nine magical women home.

Mergen's court buzzed with excitement, but the gur-khan paid little heed to the preparations going on around him. Prince Tayy had returned to the palace in the middle of the storm with marvels glittering in his eyes and would not say where he had gone or why he had abandoned his guardsmen. Bolghai hadn't returned at all, nor had Bekter, whom he'd sent to spy on the girl Eluneke. And scouts had come in reporting the appearance of the Tinglut prince Daritai and his party approaching from the north, come to seal the peace with a bride for the old khan.

It would matter little what carpet he sat on, or who waited to greet him, if he found no potential brides to choose from among the Qubal. Mergen had already sent General Jochi to find Princess Orda. Though she'd only seen seven summers, as the direct descendant of Chimbai-Khan and the sister of the khan-to-be she made the best choice for a long-term peace. And the old khan might be dead before they had to present her, at fourteen, to his tents. But the princess had spent all her short seasons fostered to a remote member of his brother's clans. The general could not return with her before the Great Hunt in the morning.

"What are you going to do if the old khan decides not to wait until the child has grown to a marrying age?" Lady Bortu paused in directing the servants to ask the question he'd been avoiding. If not the princess, they found themselves with few appropriate female relations to trade.

"Perhaps he'd like a wife of his own age," he taunted her. After the death of her husband, the Lady Bortu had freely taken lovers, but never again an ambitious husband. Now her opportunities were few and expensive.

"They never do, old fools." She scratched thoughtfully at a stray whisker that sprouted from her chin. "Yesugei's daughter has gone out of reach—"

He had thought Yesugei's daughter might do. She was pretty enough, but her father had taken her far to the south. He knew what the khaness thought of that. "Send the woman away, not the general who serves you," she'd complained. For Yesugei's service in the war and before it to Chimbai, however, Mergen owed his old friend this opportunity to advance his status. The daughter might yet prove useful as a match to one of his own sons, to bind the new khan more closely to his old ulus. Now, however, he had to count her out of his calculations.

"Eluneke," he said.

His mother pursed her lips, as much a denial of his wishes as she might make to a royal edict of the gur-khan. He wasn't stupid and he wasn't blind, however. It looked to him like his own mother had joined in a conspiracy with the Qubal shamans to make the girl one of their own. He feared they had bewitched the prince, whose shivering ague had wakened him again in the middle of the night. Though he declared himself well in the morning, Prince Tayyichiut's complexion had lost its healthy color, and he spent too much time moping about his father's shrine. The Lady Bortu wouldn't allow her allies to murder her own grandson. Short of lethal, however, he would lay no wager on how far she would go to achieve her mystical ends.

It only remained to discover whether his own son Bekter had joined in their conspiracy or had himself become their prisoner.

"Qutula!" he called to his loyal son, who caught his eye with a hawklike darting gaze over his own preparations as Prince Tayyichiut put aside his muddy clothes for the stiffly embroidered silks of his court dress. He, too, must have heard the prince's teeth-chattering moans in the night.

Qutula left the prince and stood before him in the blue coat of a guardsman. He wore his sword at his side and carried a spear in a sheath slung over his back. Mergen hesitated to separate him from the heir, but who else could he trust to find Bekter without spreading his actions throughout the tent city?

"My gur-khan," he acknowledged the summons, bowing so low that the top of his pointed hat brushed the carpets.

No one else, Mergen decided, and said, "I would have your brother's songs to entertain our visitors, but I see him nowhere among our musicians and poets."

He smiled, but his son read his displeasure in the wrinkles of his brow and the creases between his eyes. Bekter had disappeared on a mission to find out more about Eluneke and her shaman teacher. Mergen wanted his delinquent spy brought in front of him to give an accounting both of his mission and of his absence.

"As you wish." With another bow, Qutula turned and made his swift way from the royal presence. He would find his brother and drag him from whatever shelter from the storm he had found for himself, Mergen knew. Or he would report back that the gur-khan's poet, like his court shaman, had disappeared. Either way he would have his answer.

Chahar seemed most suited to his next errand. Mergen's own age-mate, he stood closest after General Jochi to the gur-khan in his guard. As Bolghai's son he had seen many wonders, but he possessed for himself little interest in the spirit world. The shamaness wouldn't frighten him with her magic, nor was he likely to fall under her spell. With a nod of his head he gestured for the captain to attend him.

"My gur-khan." Chahar bowed as Qutula had done.

"This shamaness, Toragana, has crossed my wishes. I don't care what her powers are. I want her brought to me."

"Yes, my khan." The slow lowering of Chahar's lids offered only agreement. The power of a shaman must be harnessed by the will of khan or chieftain or it grew wild and dangerous. If the teacher didn't bow to the orders of the gur-khan, Chahar would ex-

ecute her before she became a threat. That would be obvious to anyone who had survived the royal court, and to the son of a shaman
more than others. Mergen accepted the captain's obedience.

"Bring her apprentice as well, but make sure the girl remains unharmed." If the Tinglut prince refused Princess Orda
in the old khan's name, the whole court would know Eluneke
for his daughter. For now, however, he would keep his secret
and his hope for a more exalted match.

"As you wish." Again, the proper answer, given with the
proper bow, and Chahar, too, had gone. Mergen glanced up
then to see his mother watching him with secret calculations in
her eagle gaze. He said nothing but stood and let his servants
strip off his clothes and replace them with the more elaborate
silks he wore for court visitors.

First the servants dressed him in a full caftan of red-and-
yellow brocade, which they followed with a dark-blue sleeveless coat woven in the patterns that symbolized all the worlds
of heaven and earth and the underworld. At his knees, dragons
flew above the waves below which the underworld lurked at
the hem. White clouds drifted across a blue silk sky at his waist
while the diagonal stripes of a rainbow, the kingdom of the sky
god and his daughters, banded his breast. His cone-shaped silver hat and the ornate scrollwork on the fronts of the coat were
richly embroidered with gold threads. Chimbai-Khan had worn
the same court dress to greet visitors before him, and Mergen
felt the presence of his brother at his shoulder as he took on the
clothes of his office.

"What have you done to my son?"

He thought he heard the words whispered in his ear, but
that would mean Chimbai's spirit had become trapped here, between heaven and the underworld. Mergen didn't want to consider what such an omen might presage for them all.

Tayy watched his grandmother watching Mergen Gur-Khan
give his orders. His cousin's attentions weighed on his
shoulders of late, and he felt his breath come more easily when

Qutula departed with a purposeful swift step on the gur-khan's errand. The Lady Bortu seemed relieved as well, and he wondered what she knew, how many of his suspicions she might confirm. As if she felt his eyes on her, she turned her predatory gaze back on him, searching for something in his face. What she found seemed to worry her. Well, good. It worried him, too.

Surrounded by the bustling court, he could imagine that Eluneke was safe in the home of the sky god and would return soon with her toads and her secret knowledge. He hadn't quite figured out what would happen next, though. She came from the wrong clan and wandered bootless in the mud collecting herbs and simples and consorting with the lowest of creatures as her totem. Mergen would laugh at his infatuation and auction him off to some far-off princess in exchange for a treaty.

And when had he come to view his own arranged marriage with such bitterness? Bolghai made more sense as a mate—at least he had rank, though the memory of his smell sent a shiver up the prince's spine. Eluneke smelled warm and sweet, the scent of girl and sunlight and the moss they had rested on by the river, heated by the smooth rich skin at the curve of her neck.

He shook himself free of the direction his thoughts had gone, noted that his grandmother was still watching him, but with considerably greater interest now. Tayy knew he had to talk to someone about this feeling that somehow Eluneke was his destiny. Perhaps the khaness would understand. Maybe Bolghai had reported some whisper among the spirits that made sense of it all. But now wasn't the time. He veiled his gaze and turned away.

U p close, Eluneke saw that the ger-tent palace of the god was made not of felt but of the stuff of clouds, embroidered everywhere with golden sunlight. She thought it must be uncomfortably hot and damp inside, but the warmth of the embroidery seemed to keep the rugs and furs of the dais dry while the clouds cooled the intemperate heat at the center of the

Great Sun tent. The lattices were made of lightning and the decorations everywhere reflected the natural world as much as the
heavenly one. Stars scattered between the spokes of the roof
provided the light of heaven, but lakes and ponds rippled with
earthly breezes in the mirrors hanging from the lattices.

Chests taller than her head were carved each out of a single
tree. When she looked more closely at the scenes painted on
their sides, she saw the figures moved, men and women and
deer and herds of horses going about their days and nights
across the sky god's furnishings. She had never been inside the
ger-tent palace of the khan, but she guessed not even Mergen-
Gur-Khan could match such lavishness, or the splendor of the
sky god's retainers. Strange and terrible beasts wearing sky-blue
coats and pointed caps that glowed with moonlight guarded the
great ger-tent with their backs to the lattices. Nobles of the sky
folk in marvelous clothes, with planets for jewels dangling
from their ears, sat or moved about their business on the rich
carpets. Some looked just like people, but others wore strange
shapes of creatures Eluneke had never seen before. She met the
eyes of a woman dressed all in silver and recognized the dragon
nature looking back at her. Shivering, she dropped her gaze in
a proper show of respect.

On the dais the sky god himself waited for them. The nine
daughters had seemed very tall, but they looked like children
next to the god, whose cone-shaped golden cap nearly brushed
the roof of his palace. His coats were the hazy blue of a summer
day at the shoulders, deepening to the clear, deep cerulean of a
cloudless sky in autumn at their hems. Embroidered rainbows
of red and gold crossed his breast, and red-and-silver stars glittered at the tops of his deep cuffs. In his hand the god held a
thighbone as a staff with a horse's head carved at one end and
a flowing lock of golden mane at the other. Skins of silver
wolves and golden foxes covered the dais.

The sky god gestured for her to sit and she did, holding her
neck very still as the king of the toads climbed down off his
perch. When they had settled on the gold-and-silver furs, the
herbalist daughter handed her father a cup filled with pale yellow tea. Golden flowers floated in the cup. The sky god drank

sparingly and handed the cup to Eluneke, who sipped in her turn. The tea tasted of honey and sunlight, burning away the icy cold of her climb as it soothed the tingling that remained of the lightning's fire in her fingers.

"I would know the recipe and other herbal remedies for the ailments of humans and their creatures." She passed the cup to the king of the toads, whose sticky tongue darted out to taste.

The sky god's daughter whispered in her ear the secret names of the flowers and mosses and the barks of trees, and where they might be found. When she had told Eluneke all that she knew, she moved to take her place next to her father, making way for her sister. The daughter of the drum, whose clothes were embroidered in all the animals of the grasslands, followed next with food: the meat of some animal stuffed and roasted with coals and a bowl of sour yogurt for the sky god and Eluneke, a cage filled with buzzing flies for the king of the toads.

"I would know the secret languages of the animals," Eluneke said, taking her cue from the clothes and the drum and the dishes served by the hand of the sky god's daughter. "I would know how to cast out animal spirits and their diseases."

The god's daughter leaned over and whispered all the languages of animals, and she was surprised to discover that she already knew many of them. The stoat and the raven, the language of the toads, and the language of the golden eagle, though whose totem that might be she didn't know. When she had learned how to understand all the animals, the daughter of the spear murmured in her ear the secrets to casting out demons. She paled at this terrible knowledge, but did not faint, which the sky god's daughters would have scorned. Then another sister took her place, and another, whispering their secrets one by one.

Eluneke listened and learned.

Chapter Twenty-four

A S HE RODE AWAY FROM the ger-tent palace, Qutula slipped his hand beneath his shirt to rub absently at the tattoo of the emerald green bamboo snake. He had grown accustomed to the way his lady seemed to know his every move and used the serpent to punish or reward him, as his actions annoyed or pleased her. He had even come to welcome the way the inky green snake would uncoil herself and slither across his flesh, moving down his arm to peer out of his sleeve on her own errands, or wrapping herself below his belly as a promise and a warning.

Something—not him, he thought, but something—had happened recently to anger the lady, however. The serpent which was her sign burned steadily, like a poison eating its way through skin and muscle to his very heart. It only made him yearn the more for the cool heat of her body, he realized, which settled a chill of fear and longing in his gut.

He had no time for pleasure now, however, and the pain was getting in the way of fulfilling his ambitions. Mergen had sent him to find his missing brother before the party of the Tinglut prince arrived at court. Qutula had little time or patience for the task. Though the thunder had subsided, rain spilled over his cap and ran down his cheeks and his nose. Home seemed the most likely place to start. If Bek had taken shelter from the storm elsewhere, Sechule would know where he had gone. She wasn't a witch, but she had her secret ways to find her sons at need.

She was standing at the firebox, mixing some herbs that exhaled a noxious green vapor as they bubbled in a small stone pot. She didn't immediately greet him, but he saw her glance into the mirror she had set against the lattices and frown. Self-consciously, his hand went to the tattoo writhing on his breast.

The chest where she kept her minor poisons stood open with an uncorked jar beside it, so he knew Bekter wasn't home. Damn.

"Where is he?" Qutula growled at his mother while he futilely tossed the bedding stacked in the corner.

"Not here," Sechule answered the obvious then deigned to give him some information he could use. "Since before the rain. It's not the first time either."

Surely Bekter hadn't found himself a woman! But his mother tilted her head at him, one eyebrow raised in a silent question: *"Have I raised an idiot for a son?"*

So, a woman. "Who is she?"

He knew better than to poke his fingers—or his nose—into his mother's cook pots when she was brewing her little potions, but he paced the ger-tent like a pent-up wolf, kicking at a painted chest in his frustration. "The khan wants him in the palace with his songs ready when the Tinglut prince arrives. I didn't expect to have to hunt for him under some camp follower's skirts!"

"Were it that easy," his mother spat back at him, glaring as if it were his fault his brother made neither warrior nor hunter. "He went to see that shamaness, the one who teaches the prince's folly."

Qutula scarcely had time to register Sechule's answer before his lady's mark branded white heat across his skin. "Why?" He gasped into the empty air. The words came out in a raspy whisper.

"He had a visitor. It disturbed him, yet instead of talking to his mother about it, he went seeking advice from the raven woman." Carefully wiping her hands with a soft cloth Sechule turned to face him.

Suddenly, the serpent tattoo came to life with a fire more intense than any Qutula had felt before. He forgot his brother, his mother, everything but the pain and fear. This time she would not stop. He curled in on himself around the agony burning in his breast. This time she would kill him.

"Leave him alone, fool!"

He was too breathless to ask what she was doing when his mother reached for his shirt and coat and tore them open to expose his tattooed breast. Then her sharp nails dug deep, following the burning tracks of his lady's anger. Strips of flesh seemed to tear away from his body, screaming in a woman's rage above the sounds of his own agony. Sechule held the serpent, an emerald green bamboo snake, fast by the back of its head. The creature lashed at her with its tail and tongue, squirming in an effort to sink its fangs into her hand.

"Not so fast, my lady. We have a bargain!"

A bargain? What bargain had Sechule made with his lover, and how did she know about the token his mysterious lady had printed like a scent on his flesh? However it had happened, his own rage equaled that of the serpent.

"Don't!" he cried, bereft as the mark tore free of his breast. Though he welcomed the relief from the pain the creature had so recently inflicted on him, it felt as if his mother had torn out part of his soul.

But— "Don't be a fool!" she said, and popped the serpent into a jar that stood open on her workbench. "Cover yourself up! Next time I will let her sink those sharp fangs into you and welcome. Must I do everything myself?"

"You knew her by her token!" he stumbled over the words, busy commanding his hands, which would reach for the jar that imprisoned the serpent if he relaxed his control.

"Of course I did," she answered. Pounding the stopper into the jar with the heel of her hand she set it on a shelf in the chest that hid her poisons. "But that is neither here nor there. Your brother must be with us in the coming struggle to secure your father's love, not with the shamaness against us. Find him and return him to the palace before he commits treason! It will be over for us all if he throws in his lot against the gur-khan's interests."

Qutula bowed his head in obedience to his mother, but his gaze turned longingly to the jar where the serpent lay. His mother saw and cut off the request with a bladelike fall of her hand.

"Not now," she insisted. "You'll need your mind clear and unfettered when you talk to your brother. And it would mean disaster to bring the lady's token into the tent of the shamaness. The lady is more powerful, but to use that power would reveal too much before you are ready to act."

"I've acted already," he reminded her with a dull glare. The prince suffered nightly from the poison Qutula administered in his drink.

His mother made sense—until Mergen named him heir they could reveal no part of their aspirations—but her words seemed to come from too far away to matter. Only the mysterious lady mattered, and the gift of her name and her body she had promised him when he had taken the khanate. The serpent bound their conspiracy with the reality of her pleasure and her pain. He would allow no one to steal the mark of that bond from him—

Sechule stood between him and the painted chest, however, a fearsome look in her eyes. For a moment they stood that way, poised between mastery and rebellion. She was no witch, but she had powers of her own he didn't want to cross. And of course, she was right.

"I'll go," he promised, and left his mother with a kiss on her cheek and a backward longing glance at the chest of poisons where his lady's token slumbered. He would deal with his mother later, when he had the crown. . . .

Deep in the heart of the stoneware jar, the serpent demon roused from an intermittent slumber. Sechule's voice summoned her from the other side of human.

"I'm ready to let you go, my lady, but first you must swear not to bite me or hurt me in any way."

Once, the serpent remembered, she had walked upright

among the Qubal as the Lady Chaiujin. In her snaky form the
memory seemed to belong to some other creature. This wasn't
her true shape either, but the wiles of a serpent came closer to
her demon nature. She thought of herself only as serpent now,
and as serpent she slithered out of the jar with no thought more
than to sink her sharp, curved fangs into the hand that had imprisoned her and kill it. Perfectly still, she rested her beady
gaze on the woman, using her cold and lidless stare to freeze
her prey. She could tell by the heat radiating in waves off the
woman's skin that she was afraid. Sechule's heart thundered, as
loud to the serpent as the herds running on the plains.

In spite of her fear, the woman kept a firm grip behind the
serpent's jaws, calling her back to two-legged memories. "I mean
no disrespect, khaness, but feared that you would kill my unworthy child before he had served his purpose in our design."

Ah, yes. Revenge. And motherhood.

Floating beneath the surface of her thoughts, the false Lady
Chaiujin knew she needed this woman's cooperation. So it
wouldn't serve her in the long run to sink her fangs into the
meat of Sechule's hand, where the thumb met the wrist. The
serpent tongue flicked out restlessly, tasting food, though
hunter-sense said the human was too big. The jaws of a bamboo
snake would never stretch that wide.

"Do you hear me, lady? If we do not have an agreement, I
can make a stew of your flesh and use your skin for a lovely
pair of mittens."

Sechule gave her a little shake, rattling her right down to
her tail. The serpent was no lady but a daughter of the underworld. She had been gone so long that she sometimes forgot her
own name in that other kingdom, but she never forgot where
she belonged. So she bowed her head in submission while
promising her snaky self, *not for long*. The mortal was too big
to eat, but not too big to die.

Sechule seemed content that she had the agreement she demanded, however. "We still have the same goal. But Qutula is
the weapon we must wield to attain it." Biting nervously at her
lip, the woman put her down on the floor of the tent.

With a shiver that started at her head and rippled all the

way through her, the demon's serpent-self stretched until once again she stood in a woman's skin. Her scales became the fine embroidered silk of her coats which she settled around her as she sat across from her recent captor.

"Don't do that again," she said. "The serpent has a mind of her own, and she doesn't like you."

"I'll leave my herb chest open a crack, like this," Sechule negotiated a truce with a bow that indicated her regret without lowering herself to apologize. "If someone comes in unexpectedly, you can hide inside until they are gone."

The chest had a lock which might be turned to trap her, but the false Lady Chaiujin accepted that some risks came with every alliance. As Qutula's mother, the human female must be put off her guard until the son had attained the dais. It would be easier to kill her then. Until that time, she must convince Sechule they were allies. Friends, the humans called it. The word had uses when persuading an enemy to one's aid.

"Friends." She smiled at Sechule and took a cup of tea from her hands in a show of trust between poisoners. "I regret the pain I caused your older son, but I assure you his rewards are equal to his punishments. The younger, however, proves resistant to the charms of a stranger in his bed."

"Bekter is a fool," Sechule agreed. "But his loss at this time would rouse suspicions before we are ready to act."

"But later," the serpent-demon bargained in her human form. His rebuff had insulted her; she would not be denied her revenge.

"Later," Sechule agreed. Her eyes told a different truth, however, of serpents crushed underfoot and herself on the dais. The lady recognized the ambition, and didn't begrudge it in her ally. It was, after all, what she planned to do to Sechule, once she had planted her egg on the dais of the khan.

"Then our bargain still stands," she agreed.

Sechule bowed, dropping her lashes respectfully. When she looked up again, the lady had vanished into smoke. As vapor she watched a moment more, but Sechule went back to the potion cooking on the firebox. And the lady found that she missed the warmth of her lover's breast.

As Qutula rode deeper into the camp in search of his brother and the shamaness, the tattoo made itself felt as a missing part of himself, falling into place beneath the shard of jade he wore by a thread beneath his shirt. He had found the jade outside a cave in which the hideous king of demons had died at the hand of the god-king and had picked it up for luck. Once it held a coiled serpent incised on it, but the carving had faded or the lady had taken the jade and had replaced it with a talisman of her own while he had slept beside her in the grass.

He had grown into the habit of worrying it when he sensed the absence of his lady's attention, but now his hand dropped to his side. The low hum of the returning presence tingled through his nerves with a kiss of warmth that carried the promise of her anger. He wondered what had caused her fury, but hesitated to invite her retribution again with the question. Perhaps, when their bodies locked in lovemaking, the lady herself would more freely give up her secrets. Now, however, he had his brother to consider, and their father waiting impatiently with dangerous guests on the way.

The shamaness was easy enough to find. There were fewer of the lower ranks remaining in the khan's city every day. He recognized her tent by the raven feathers sewn to the felt covering and the raven staring at him from over her door. Dismounting in the wind-driven rain that tore at his clothing, he left his horse to graze what it might from the beaten grass between the scattered tents and entered without announcing himself, as one might do among lowly neighbors. The shamaness knelt at the firebox, making barley tea. Though it was midday, the bedclothes lay in an untidy tumble on the floor. Qutula saw no sign of her apprentice or his brother.

"May I help you?" She rose unhurriedly and reached for her shaman's robes, which hung from a peg on the lattice. It seemed like an accidental brush of her hand that turned the mirror on him, but under his clothes the tattoo shrank in on itself, so cold on his skin that the shamaness had to ask the question again to pierce his distraction.

She had put on the robes and her headdress. He knew the raven was dead and stuffed on top of her head, but still he saw it blink its beady eyes at him. "I can help you with the demon you carry," she said, and stretched a finger to his breast.

"I don't know what you're talking about. It's a decoration, just ink." He drew back as if hers were the poison touch, while the emerald green bamboo snake burrowed into the flesh above his heart. "I'm looking for Bekter, the gur-khan's poet." Annoyance at his brother cut through the distraction of the lady's token.

The shamaness reached for her medicine stick. "And to what purpose?"

He wondered if they had met before, though he remembered no such encounter. For whatever reason, she didn't seem to like him, not surprising if she had designs of her own to use her apprentice against the prince and gain the dais for herself. Mergen had already seen through that ploy, however. He had only to find his brother before his father sent guards to arrest her.

"The gur-khan has need of his services. If you know where I can find him, it will go better for you to tell me now." She had begun to mutter some incantation beneath her breath when two things happened at once.

The rumpled bedding heaved like an earthquake.

"Better how?" Bekter's head appeared over the blankets, followed by a naked shoulder. He rubbed absently at his tangled hair, loosening the braids even more than a roll in a shamaness' bed had done, but his gaze was sharp with questions.

At that moment, the door was swept aside to reveal Mergen's blue-coated guardsmen, Captain Chahar at their head.

"Captain," Qutula ground out between clenched teeth, though he managed to produce the proper bow between equals in rank.

Chahar returned the courtesy, "Captain," with the same precisely calculated bow. His eyes, however, absorbed every detail of the scene, including the court poet, Qutula's brother, diving under the shamaness' blankets in search of his clothes.

"What is going on here?" Bekter grumbled when he appeared again a moment later, still shoving his arms into the sleeves of his court silks. He had made no effort to disguise himself for his lover and Chahar was no fool. This was exactly the confrontation Qutula had wanted to avoid.

"I know why Captain Qutula has come," the shamaness added her own questions, showing in her glance that she understood more by that than Qutula's search for his brother. "But to what do I owe the pleasure of your visit after so many years, Captain Chahar?"

"No pleasure at all, my lady shamaness," Chahar announced, half stumbling in an aborted bow much deeper than Qutula thought proper for any errand of the court in this tent. "I have come as a matter of honor between my lord the gur-khan and my father's tents, to take you into custody, together with your apprentice, the girl Eluneke."

"You mean, he wants to arrest her." Bekter had pulled himself to order and now he stood between Chahar and the shamaness.

"I'll attend the gur-khan and be honored to do so." She stepped away from Bekter's offer of protection with a sweeping gesture to demonstrate that the little tent was empty, except for her disheveled lover and the khan's various emissaries. "But as you can see, my apprentice isn't here."

"And does her disappearance have anything to do with my father's absence from his place at court?" Chahar asked.

Before Qutula could chastise his fellow captain for usurping the gur-khan's right to question his prisoner, the shamaness herself rebuked him.

"You know I can't answer that," she told him, more gently than Qutula would have done it.

That seemed to be all the answer Chahar needed, however. "Everyone doesn't have to become a shaman," he complained, confirming Qutula's suspicions about the girl.

"For some, there is no other choice." She spoke as if this were an old argument between them. Worse news: though Bekter seemed uneasy with her answer, he didn't seem surprised.

"It will go ill for you. The gur-khan would not have chosen

that road." Chahar shook his head, trying, Qutula thought, to rid it of the inevitable conclusions he had himself drawn. Whatever plot the shaman folk had to use the girl as a lure for the prince, Bolghai was a part of it. It only remained to ask how deeply they had ensnared his brother, Bekter.

But: "Ill or well, it must be faced," the shamaness said. She already wore her robes and she ruffled out the feathers that hung from every leather strip.

"I'll be there to speak for you if need be," Bekter promised her.

"I know you will." She smiled more like a proud mother than a lover, but kissed him with enthusiasm. Then, in a flurry of robes and feathers, she disappeared.

Captain Chahar peered up at the smoke hole over the firebox. "I expect she'll meet us there," he said, and shepherded his guardsmen on their way.

Bekter, too, stared up at the smoke hole for a moment, but then he seemed to come back to himself. "Best not keep the gurkhan waiting," he said, as if he hadn't been doing just that.

Qutula seethed with fury at his brother, a fury fueled by the token of his lady on his breast, which had woken to renewed pain.

"If you have ruined all our plans with your choice of bed partner, I will kill you myself," he said.

Bekter looked at him as if he were a riddle he was only now beginning to solve. "Perhaps you should rethink your plans," he said, but softly, more to himself than Qutula.

There seemed nothing else to do, then, but turn on his heel and leave his brother to follow. But as he took up the reins and headed for the ger-tent palace, Qutula resolved to turn the shamans' plots to his own use. He'd have felt better about that plan if he knew where Bolghai had taken the girl.

T he storm had nearly passed when Bolghai turned away from the shrine that marked the pyre of the fallen khan. Great Sun was setting, the low slanting rays creating arches of rainbows beneath the solemn clouds. The prince had demanded his promise to keep an eye out for the apprentice Eluneke, but the most dangerous part of the trip was over. The gods hadn't rejected her, or he'd have found her close to where she vanished, dead with the sign of the tree burned into her breast.

She'd be gone for three days, he figured, and if the past was anything to go by, she would find her way down again any place but where she'd climbed the tree. He figured the prince's nature would call her home eventually. He could wait for that as easily in the comfort of the ger-tent palace as in the cold of a summer night. Besides, he missed his dinner. With that last grumbling thought, he fixed the palace in his mind, turned into his totem animal, and made his way home by the road between the worlds.

Chapter Twenty-five

PRINCE DARITAI of the Tinglut ulus sat in state as an honored guest on the steps of the dais of the Qubal-Khan. At the right hand of Mergen, who now called himself gur-khan, Prince Tayyichiut rested his back against the shoulder of a guardsman with a quick and wary eye. On his left the Lady Bortu, khaness of her son the gur-khan and Great Mother to the clans, leaned her chin on her knee and froze the Tinglut ambassador like prey beneath her eagle gaze.

At the khan's feet, but still above the firebox, sat Mergen's court. Daritai's own nobles had an honored place among the nobles and chieftains of the Qubal clans at the right of the dais, just below the little gathering of musicians, shamans, and fortune-tellers tucked away to the side. The shamaness in the raven robes had caught the khan's attention, not happily, but he said nothing and politely kept his gaze from straying too often in her direction. Daritai figured he'd need to learn more about what was going on there before he made any recommendations to his father's court.

While he sat among the Qubal in their ger-tent palace, his honor guard set up the Tinglut camp outside the city. He'd brought his eldest son, a sturdy hunter of twelve, along with five hundred warriors to set against ten thousand of the Qubal, if there was trouble. Around him, fifty of his picked warriors sorted themselves among the blue-coated Qubal who girdled the ger-tent palace with their backs to the lattices. An equal number guarded their fellows against a stray spear through the felted tent cloth from the outside. But if trouble came from within, Daritai was dead, as simple as that, though his men would see that he didn't die alone. If the Qubal overran his camp, he had another son at home to inherit his property.

Not for the first time Daritai cursed his conniving half brother. Hulegu had the greater skill at diplomacy and should have been the negotiator for Tinglut-Khan's new treaty-wife. But Hulegu had ambitions; he had seduced Tinglut's warlike character with impossible schemes to conquer the Shan Empire. Then he'd remained at home, whispering poison in the khan's ear, while Daritai was sent to accomplish the hopeless task and return in failure.

Daritai had fought the plan and lost. As he had known from the start, his ten thousands were a mere handful against the empire, already on the march to war in the Cloud Country. In a rage, his father had stripped him of his honors, including his place on the dais as heir. Hulegu now wore the silver cap and sat at his father's right hand, his intention from the start.

Tinglut had other sons, however, and Hulegu wouldn't risk his newfound favor with an absence from court, particularly to negotiate a marriage treaty. A new wife might mean new heirs, after all. So once again Daritai found himself confronting an impossible task for which he was ill suited, at which Hulegu doubtless wished him to fail.

He was a soldier; no strategist, just a tactician whose diplomatic skills narrowed to one: in his youth, Daritai had made an excellent spy. Face blandly free of his opinions, therefore, he let his glance travel over the decorations that adorned the foreign palace, collecting data for his khan. Mirrors in elaborate frames hung from the lattices. They hadn't kept the demons out or saved the Lady Chaiujin, Daritai's half sister, but they reflected the lamplight, giving an unearthly sheen to thick tapestries of silk and fine wool that covered the latticed walls in every direction.

The Tinglut-Khan preferred to express his love of war with

many weapons both antique and modern as his decorations. Mergen's blue-coated warriors, at attention along the lattices, carried sufficient armaments to balance the more peaceful appearance of his ger-tent palace, however. Daritai resolved to keep his guard up and gave a nod to one of his own warriors sharing duty along the lattices.

Imperceptible to any who didn't expect it, the gesture marked the place where he would run if he needed a fast escape. The man set his hand casually on his knife hilt to show that he understood his duty, to slash an exit through the densely embroidered tent coverings at need. Planning for trouble had kept Daritai alive on the battlefield. It couldn't hurt on a diplomatic mission either. Satisfied, he gave his attention to the dais, where servants had appeared bearing trays of food and drink.

The Lady Bortu, Mergen-Khan's old witch of a khaness, was still watching him. To let him know that nothing escaped her attention, she turned with exaggerated care to the guardsman he had lately signaled. Then she repeated his own gesture, but with the large movements of an epic singer, setting the cascades of precious jewels that dripped from her ears and the horns of her matron's headdress to clacking sharply one against another.

"I trust our cooks have understood the wishes of your steward, young prince." The lady motioned at a tray with a gnarled hand, each twisted finger circled with a heavy ring. *Nothing escapes my notice, boy*, her eyes told him above a smile false as her teeth. Though he had seen more than thirty summers and fought in battles for half of them, he didn't contradict her. Only that long experience kept him seated, though all his instincts told him to run when she looked at him that way.

"Excellent." He picked through the bits of roasted meat and crumbled cheese displayed on a tray held out to him by the serving girl. Pies and other artful dishes also circulated among the khan's party, but Daritai's steward had made known to the Qubal cooks his preference for unmixed foods. Particularly in a foreign camp, such dishes were harder to poison. His steward had said nothing about the motives for his tastes, however. It wouldn't do to give any ideas to this Mergen, who called himself gur-khan.

The old khaness knew, of course, just as she knew where he would run if negotiations went very badly. And what she knew, Mergen knew as well, though the khan's smile was all a host's welcome should be. If Tinglut-Khan chose war over marriage, he'd have to take out the old lady first thing, because Mergen took all his cues from her. Daritai kept his eyes downcast on the tray until he had his thoughts well hidden.

The serving girl provided the distraction he needed, leaning over him so that the back of his hand brushed her breast as he hesitated between choices on the tray. He knew that women found him a handsome man. His wives had often commented on the heat of his gaze, the manly proportion of his chest and thighs. And he had worn his best coats of beaten silk, black as night when Great Moon Lun had chased her little brothers over the horizon and embroidered everywhere with silver stars in the pattern of the summer sky, Great Moon herself emblazoned in an auspicious house. So he might have thought the girl favored him for her own pleasure. The Qubal-Khan looked on with a benign smile, however, offering more than mutton and curd for his satisfaction.

If he'd been inclined to ardor, Mergen's interest in it would have dampened his enthusiasm. But he had more important matters on his mind, and old Bortu was looking at him as if he were a tasty rabbit. He imagined she might swoop down on him and snap his neck with her strong, sharp beak. Daritai therefore made his choice of meat and cheese and dismissed the girl, not unkindly, but with no invitation for later.

Casting about for a suitable conversational gambit, he settled on the sculptures in bronze and silver inlaid with coral and lapis that stood on carved and painted chests scattered above the firebox. One in particular drew his notice, a bust of Llesho, the god-king of the Cloud Country, whom the artist had depicted as an older man. The god-king had many allies, including the emperor of Shan who, while traveling to war against the South, had uncovered Tinglut-Khan plotting with the Uulgar raiders to overrun his empire.

In spite of their quarrel with the emperor of Shan, Daritai had led the Tinglut horde in the wars of the foreign gods to defend the mortal world from demons. He'd helped to win that one, but it hadn't stopped his half brother from usurping his place next to Tinglut on the dais. Now he was reduced to bargaining over wives for the failing khan.

"I understand you traveled with the god-king Llesho himself." He addressed the young Qubal prince with just a hint of a question and a wave of his hand in the direction of the bronze head. He'd never met a god himself nor any man who had. But the Qubal had a special bond through Prince Tayyichiut the Orphan. So he'd heard and the bronze head seemed to prove.

A twisty little smile touched the Qubal prince's lips, not for Daritai, but for a memory painful for all its warmth. "He saved my life," the prince said, rubbing absently at his belly.

Daritai recognized the track of Prince Tayyichiut's hand. Some old wound lay hidden beneath the princely clothes; on occasion Daritai had followed that same anxious path of sword or spear across his flesh. Even now, like any soldier watching the prince, he was reminded of past pain, the old reflex to soothe it. *Does it still hurt much?* he wanted to ask, but courtesy forbid him even to notice the prince's actions.

"Please pardon the Princess Orda's absence." With a careless nod, Mergen Gur-Khan ordered the dinner trays taken away. "I have sent for her, but she was visiting with relatives in a distant clan. I expect her party to return by morning."

It was doubtless past her bedtime anyway, Daritai mused, though he didn't phrase his objection in quite those words for the khan. A child bride, the Princess Orda would be an inconvenience until she reached a marriageable age and, brought up far from the court, could offer no useful intelligence to her new clans. He had such a one of his own to offer in reciprocal trade.

By the khan's order, Daritai's daughter of but four summers, who held his heart like a treasure box in her tiny hands, might go as a future bride to Mergen-Khan or his heir. The thought of his daughter raised among the Qubal, forgetting her beloved father and her own people, chilled him to his very liver. He didn't think this khan would suffer such qualms about Chimbai's girl child, but knew better than to trust the face a master such as Mergen Gur-Khan put upon a bargain.

"The child is sweet-natured and eager to learn." As the Princess Orda's grandmother, Lady Bortu made the offer. In the normal course of lesser matchmaking among the clans, the husband's grandmother would dismiss the offer or show her interest in the prospective granddaughter-in-law. Then the negotiations for a dowry would begin in earnest. But Tinglut-Khan's grandmother had been dust before Daritai drew his first breath. No ulus would have entrusted the Great Mother of the khan's royal clan to a foreign power anyway, even under treaty.

Daritai sipped his kumiss and smiled to take the offense out of his next words. "Do not take my answer amiss," he prefaced his response to the khaness with a diplomatically apologetic lift of his shoulder. "But time being what it is for the grandfathers among us, the Tinglut-Khan needs a wife for today, not a child to raise for tomorrow's bed, even if she is the true child of the famed Chimbai-Khan, who now reigns in state among the ancestors.

"We might, of course, consider a match for the future at a later date." The youngest of Daritai's brothers, not much older than his own daughter, would need a wife eventually. But he hadn't come to bind a treaty with the marriage beds of the next generation. His father was looking for the freshness of youth to rejuvenate his generative parts, as if he lacked heirs from among the ten legitimate sons and daughters he claimed by his current and former wives and concubines.

And then there was the intelligence, of course. Did Mergen Gur-Khan plan to hold the reins of the Qubal forever, or turn them over to his heir? Did he plan to legitimize his blanket-sons and set up his own dynasty or take a wife and make new heirs? Did he plan to marry Prince Tayyichiut to some great power who would give him the strength to conquer all the grasslands? All were questions that touched on the security of the Tinglut, and his father had charged him to return with answers, or not at all.

According to his spies and messengers, Mergen kept no young female relations at court. Daritai could find report of few female relations at all. The Lady Bortu, of course, but Tinglut loathed her with some old, undying fury. The dead Chimbai's young daughter had remained no more than a whisper of a rumor until the Lady Bortu had offered her as a wife to the Tinglut-Khan.

As for other female relations, none could claim more than a distant blood kinship to the gur-khan, and none had fostered among the intrigues that sprouted like wild grass around the dais. He expected Mergen to counter with the offer of a poor relation who smelled like the sheep and had a temperament to match. Which would probably suit his father just fine if she had a fair face and a youthful figure.

It was still early in the negotiations, but he already missed his own tents, his wives, and his sons and daughters. He was starting to wonder if his father had sent him more to be rid of him than to negotiate a marriage when Mergen Gur-Khan spoke up again.

"There will be time tomorrow to talk of treaties and marriage contracts. Tonight, let us entertain you with drink and music, and in the morning a hunt in honor of your name. You can meet the Princess Orda and consider other eligible women of noble blood who might prove more acceptable to an eager husband.

Daritai saw the Qubal prince cut a doubtful frown at his uncle from under his dark brows. Whatever he meant by it, he kept to himself. The old grandmother Bortu said nothing, nor by the twitch of a muscle let her feelings be known, but still he thought she wasn't pleased with Mergen's offer. Secrets here, he realized, and wondered how that boded for the Tinglut-Khan.

The musicians had taken their signal to bring out their instruments, however, and he turned politely to listen to the first song, one his spies had reported about the prince and a giant bear. Exaggerated, surely, but he sensed a seed of truth in the prince's long-suffering sigh. He settled himself to listen and remember the song for his father.

Tayy rolled over in his bed of furs and stared up at the great radiating spokes that held up the roof of the ger-tent palace.

It was still night. For a change he hadn't wakened with his belly on fire, which gave him a blessed moment of peace to think. Great Moon had risen high in the sky before Daritai's guardsmen had boosted their prince into his saddle. They'd led him back to his own tents still mumbling Bekter's song that had come to be known as "Prince Tayyichiut's Bear."

It had been a good effort until the foreign prince pulled his head up and swept his gleaming glance over the white tents of the gur-khan. Counting, Tayy thought, and not tumbled in his cups at all. That made him smarter than he'd let on, which was considerable in itself. Likable too, which might be just another weapon or might mean something deeper.

In the dark, he listened to the blue-coated warriors rustling with small movements to stay awake as they guarded the gur-khan and his court. Nearby, Mergen slept in his usual watchful silence and a little farther away, the Lady Bortu snored soundly, interrupted only by the occasional snort as she lay deep in some grandmother-dream. Other noble retainers like-wise slept scattered through the great tent.

Peaceful, except that Bolghai hadn't roused him from his blankets, so Eluneke must not have returned yet. "How will we know when she's back?" he'd asked the shaman with the rain falling on their shoulders and the thunder all around. Tayy liked warm and dry better than cold and wet any day, but he wouldn't abandon her to an unknown fate.

"Don't worry. She'll find a way to let us know."

"So it's not that dangerous—" Maybe he was overreacting, though it seemed unlikely. People didn't just disappear up a bolt of lightning every day, but perhaps her calling protected her.

"Not dangerous?" Bolghai had looked back at him as if he were mad. "Of course it's dangerous. I should think it's the most dangerous thing a human being can do, outside of being on a galley ship in a storm like this one, of course," he added, as if he'd just remembered Tayy's own recent brushes with death. "But we can't do anything right now. It's up to Eluneke."

It seemed a thin excuse to abandon the watch, but Bolghai would hear of nothing else. He'd mumbled something under his breath about headstrong princes making life complicated and then he'd run. It would have been a long, wet walk, but Tayy's horse had turned and stood her ground some distance from the unnatural fireworks at the khan's shrine. Bolghai had disappeared then, leaving him in the care of his mount. He'd made it home to the angry fear of his uncle and the knowing silence of his grandmother, who had ordered dry clothes and hot food for him but asked no questions about why he had abandoned his guardsmen once again for his own perilous adventures in the storm.

He thought she already knew and didn't want the words spoken aloud in front of the gur-khan. Then Chahar had brought in Toragana, under arrest. Bolghai had objected, Chahar had looked miserable. Mergen had relented, but only a little. He'd released her into the custody of his shaman and the guardsman Chahar, who was Bolghai's son, with the words, "I need the girl; she must be presented to me properly attired for court when we return from the hunt tomorrow."

"Where she has traveled no mortal, not even another shaman, may follow," Bolghai had answered, demonstrating, if Mergen hadn't known it, his complicity with Eluneke's teacher.

"Find a way to end this madness at once, or suffer the consequences, which fall to the ulus as well as to yourself, shaman."

Bolghai had said nothing, but his expression said it all. There was no turning back from where Eluneke had gone. Mergen had cursed very thoroughly under his breath. "You don't know what you may have cost your people," he growled.

"Ah." Bolghai had given the half-mad grin of the spirit-possessed when he answered, "But what have we saved the Qubal people?"

What, indeed? How had Eluneke become the prey his uncle and the shaman fought over like two hunting dogs? Bolghai confirmed his guess when he added, "She is not for the Tinglut-Khan. The spirits have made other plans."

"And what good is she to me wed to our own prince?" Mergen had demanded, so he knew something about Tayy's meeting with the girl. In his anger, it seemed that he'd forgotten the prince, who listened furtively to their low-voiced argument.

The Lady Bortu didn't stop them but cut her glance to his uncle when Tayy looked at her. Attend, her gaze told him, and he did, while shaman and khan debated his future as if he weren't there.

"For that matter," Mergen had gone on with his low-voiced rant meant only for the ears of his shaman, "what good is the prince to me if he is already attached within the ulus. We have alliances to seal with weddings. I have a Tinglut prince on my doorstep, old man; who do you leave me to trade for peace?"

"The spirits don't ask my permission," Bolghai pointed out with a little bounce to set the stoats of his shaman's robes in motion, a reminder of his office.

Tayy had felt some mysterious bond form with Eluneke from that first shared glance. She had stood in the doorway of Toragana's tent with her broom and watched him ride by with his hunting companions. Her eyes had pierced him like a lightning bolt; he hadn't wanted to look away. That sense of destiny had grown stronger with each chance meeting. Tayy could well believe the spirits had a hand in it. Nice to hear it from an expert, though.

He'd known from the start the girl's status would prove an issue with his uncle, but this debate hadn't taken the direction he'd expected. Mergen had the more pressing matter of a bride for the Tinglut-Khan to consider and he didn't need to hear prophecy with an uneasy ally riding to parley.

Toragana had stood silent as a stone, her face a graven image until then. She spoke up now, however, giving the gurkhan what little comfort she had to offer one who crossed the wishes of the spirit world. "I believe they are meant to survive," she said. "Before she even met him, the girl believed her purpose was to save his life." She turned to Tayy himself then, with a reassuring smile. "She's a stubborn girl. If she is meant to keep the prince alive, she'll find a way to do it. Right now, she's pursuing the 'finding a way' part."

"You don't fool me. She's pursuing a set of robes like your own." But at the mention of death something in Mergen's eyes had shifted. "The Tinglut prince is on my doorstep."

Even through his shock, Tayy had understood his meaning.

Neither Bolghai nor Toragana had an answer for him, however. Finally, Mergen had dismissed them both with an angry growl, "Watch him."

Why did his uncle want to see Eluneke *now?* Tayy balked at the only logical answer. Chimbai-Khan had sent his brother into many tents. Qutula and Bekter had resulted in one such tent. But what about the others? Eluneke? Mergen's daughter? His cousin? Had he screwed up that badly?

Bolghai had known, that was clear, and so had Toragana, but he thought not for as long. Why hadn't they told him? Cousins didn't marry. It was legal, barely, in the royal family, but Mergen was right. He needed all the able-bodied young he could lay hands on to seal the alliances begun in the war for the Cloud Country. There was the part about saving his life, of course, but that could be anything. Mergen was right. That didn't mean Tayy'd give her up, though—certainly not to wed Tinglut-Khan. Not for anyone.

The Tinglut prince had come and gone for the night, making no threat. Lying there awake, Tayy imagined Eluneke in the heavy silk coats of court, riding away with Prince Daritai. A newly familiar burn churned his stomach. He thought of old Tinglut-Khan touching her and a red haze filled the darkness. It would little serve his uncle's peace if he murdered the royal husband in his bed, but for a few gut-churning moments he could think of nothing else.

First things first, however. He was worried and tired and still amazed at all that he had seen by his father's shrine. Daritai seemed a small obstacle to someone who could climb the lightning and return with the knowledge of the sky god. And it seemed unlikely that the old khan would accept a shamaness as a wife. Eluneke hadn't returned yet, of course, and if he were telling the truth, to himself if to no one else, he was wounded that she had left him behind. Even the toad people climbed to heaven with her by riding on her shaman's robes. *I would have stood beside you,* he thought, *I would have defended you against gods and demons.*

But she'd gone without him. Waiting for the hunt that would begin with the dawn, he worried that her role as a shaman would put a distance between them more uncrossable even than the needs of the ulus for political marriages.

Time passed strangely in the heaven of the sky god and his daughters. Eluneke drank tea and ate yogurt with the gods while her mortal body, attuned to the world below, felt the passing of the storm and Great Sun's descent into the underworld. "I should go home," she said, having listened to each sky daughter in turn and acquired all their knowledge. "Though I'm grateful for all that you've taught me, and for the wonders I've seen in your realm."

"As to that," the sky god answered, taking up a piece of cheese, "You have shown great courage and determination in visiting me, and my daughters tell me you're wise beyond mortal skill and an amiable companion as well. You're welcome to stay here, where the rain only falls at night and the sky is always full of rainbows."

"You flatter me beyond words that gratitude can express." Eluneke set her cup down with deliberation. "But, alas, I came to borrow the wisdom of the gods to save my future husband, a prince in the world below. All that you've taught me warns me to return as soon as possible. He may be in mortal danger even as we sit in comfortable conversation over our tea."

"Then you should go," the daughter with the drum answered kindly, and offered her instrument as a parting gift. "Take this to call the spirits at need."

"And this." The daughter who knew all the herbs and medicines that grew on land added her own gift, a laurel bough, and the next and the next. Each added the accoutrements of her own special knowledge to Eluneke's shamanic burden, until the next to last, the daughter of the spear, who offered Eluneke her weapon, "To help you save your husband from the underworld," she said. "The demons fear it above all terrors to their kind."

When they were done with their good-byes and the giving of gifts, Eluneke wondered how she would carry all these things with her, but the last sister gave her a pouch small enough to hang from her belt. And into the pouch she placed each of the other gifts, which would not have fit in the mortal realm, but each shrank down until it was small enough to join the others at her waist in the world above. And when she had them securely tied, she bowed to the sky god and his daughters and prepared to take her leave. The king of the toads, who had accompanied her and had himself received numerous presents for his people, climbed up into his seat in the basket atop her shaman's headdress.

"If you would have a servant guide us to the place where we might descend again into our own world, we'll leave you in peace now," she said.

The sky god stretched his hands out, to show that they were empty, and he did not smile. "If you chose to stay, I would have gladly given you all the comforts you might require," he said, "but this one thing I cannot do. The paths of the gods are not open to mortals. Those rare few who find their way to my realm must likewise find their own way home."

Like a dream on waking, the ger-tent palace of the suns and moons disappeared, and with it the god and his daughters. Eluneke found herself alone with King Toad on a plain more vast than the grasslands of the Harn. Nowhere did she see even a rabbit hole that might lead her down into the world below.

"What do we do now?" King Toad asked in his own language.

"We walk," Eluneke answered. Somewhere out there where the suns and moons shared the same sky, and rainbows arched between them, there had to be a way home.

Chapter Twenty-six

QUTALA WOKE AT HIS PRINCE'S side with plots seething in his mind. He had a sister, of all things, and it looked like Mergen was going to legitimize her above the sons who sat at his side in the ger-tent palace for all their lives. Prince Tayy wandered out to relieve himself. When he returned, Qutula was ready with clothes for the hunt. He slipped a linen shirt over the prince's head and waited while the prince tucked in his arms and pulled on his leggings.

It could have been worse, he decided. The gur-khan needed the girl as trade goods to keep the old Tinglut happy and out of the way. He'd seen her—nearly strangled her and was glad now that he'd stopped in time. She'd be out of the camp almost as soon as she showed up and he hadn't incurred his father's un-expected wrath over her.

Tayy had done just that, though for different reasons. Falling in love with the girl had put him head-to-head with his uncle, and the two of them were locking horns like two rams in springtime. That could only work to Qutula's favor. He held out the prince's leather hunting jacket, tied the strings at his waist and offered a boot, toes upturned over the wooden sole as nearby, Chahar did the same for the gur-khan.

The only person in more trouble than Tayy right now was the khan's shaman. Toragana hadn't known Eluneke's true identity when she took the girl as an apprentice, but Bolghai had. Qutula wondered how the gur-khan planned to keep Eluneke's shamanic training a secret long enough to marry her off to the Tinglut-Khan. He wondered what secrets a shamaness might have to extend the life of an aging mortal, and if the old khan might wonder the same things when confronted with such a wife. The more he thought around the angles, the less he saw a downside for his plans. Prince Tayy, on the other hand . . .

"**I** love her. I didn't plan it, wouldn't have chosen it, but it happened." Tayy pulled his boot on, brushing aside the quiver held in Qutula's outstretched hand.

"I'll find you a wife, soon." Mergen Gur-Khan raised his arms, let Chahar tie the strings on his jacket. "But this girl—my daughter and your cousin, mind you—is out of your reach, for politics in this tent and taboo in any other. She goes to the Tinglut, if they'll take her."

Grabbing up his spear, Mergen had muttered, "If we find the damned girl," under his breath.

Tayy heard him anyway and the reminder tied another knot in his gut. Eluneke hadn't returned. Bolghai didn't seem to expect her back yet, but he couldn't think of anything good coming of her prolonged absence. Maybe she had fallen back to earth somewhere out beyond the camp. She might be lying somewhere dying while he prepared for a day of sport. But where would she go if she were hurt and confused? Not Toragana's tent; someone would have come to alert them if she'd shown up there.

The dell near the river, where they'd bargained with the king of the toads for the aid of his people. Of course.

"I have to go," he said, worry tight in the flesh pulling his cheeks into a grimace. "She could be hurt." He kept his dignity enough to walk, not run, past the nobles and chieftains gathered on either side of the firebox. He owed his uncle more than that, however, and gave a nod to acknowledge it over his shoulder. "I'll be back in time for the hunt—"

Mergen took a step as if to follow him from the dais, but the Lady Bortu laid a hand on his elbow. He glared at her, but he stopped. It was his uncle's daughter, after all, and the khaness' granddaughter. If something had happened to her, he figured they must want someone looking for her who might know where she'd go to ground. Just, it seemed, not the heir. Bolghai or Toragana might have been able to find her, but they didn't seem inclined to look. So Mergen tilted his chin, pointing him out, and he went, his Nirun forming up behind him.

The gur-khan held steady under his mother's firm hand, but his heart flew after his nephew. He felt something for the girl. Not love—he hadn't seen her since she was small, not until the afternoon when Tayy had stumbled on the shamaness' tent. But tucking her away with a remote clan was one thing and losing her to a shamanic initiation was another. Too much rode on her delicate shoulders right here for her to go dream traveling with the gods. He needed her back, now, before the Tinglut prince discovered his father's bride had disappeared.

"I'll take my Durluken and follow him." Qutula turned to his father with a bow, long-suffering affection in the tilt of his lips when he added, "We'll make certain he meets the hunt before our visitors take his absence as a slight."

Mergen nodded, unsurprised at his blanket-son's devotion to his prince. "He should have his most trusted companions about him," he agreed, and was pleased when the rest of the young guardsmen fell in step with his son as he took off after his cousin. His mother's voice, soft as a whisper but more dire, shook him from his satisfaction, however.

"Blood is coming," she said, warning him of the greater game moving on the grasslands.

He thought a messenger might have come, bringing news of an insulted Tinglut prince returning home empty-handed or worse, an outrider bringing doom from General Yesugei in the South. When he looked in the direction her gaze led him, how-

ever, he found that she followed the path of the Durluken, passing the firebox on their way to find the prince.

"Blood?" he said, watching Mangkut set his shoulder to his
captain's and Duwa lay hand to the hilt of his knife.

The Tinglut made their tents on the other side of Chimbai's
shrine. But for the warning his mother whispered in his ear, he
would have said they warded against an imaginary threat
within their own camp. The Lady Bortu might have been a
shamaness herself, except that was too much power in a
khaness. Sometimes she still spoke in shamanic riddles, however; he wondered if she delivered some arcane message from
the spirit world.

"How do I stop it?"

"Make them whole," she answered and he thought she was
going to leave it at that, as undecipherable in her riddles as Bolghai himself. But she was first the khaness, Great Mother of the
most powerful of the Qubal clans, and second the mother of
khans. She put her duty to her people above the capricious demands of the unruly spirits, so she answered her own riddle for
him, or at least gave him enough clues to answer it himself.

"The boy needs the girl. The sons need a father's hand."

He was starting to believe the first, with mounting exasperation. "You should have spoken yesterday. I have promised her
to the Tinglut."

"Would words have mattered?"

"Probably not."

Tinglut-Khan was the last remaining threat on the grasslands. Mergen had stronger ties with the Cloud Country than he
had with his own neighbor and he had to fix that. The girl
would appreciate the jewels and furs and other presents she
would receive as a wife of a khan. She had the sense—and a
shaman's training to aid her—to practice patience and to make
her own connections among the Tinglut for the day her aged
husband went to his ancestors. If that meant exposing the heir
to risks from which she might have saved him, well, they had
shamans of their own and many ten thousands of warriors to
protect him. Mergen would just have to persuade him not to
run off without his guardsmen about him.

"As for the other, you know my mind on that." However much he privately wished to acknowledge his sons, her second warning hinted at threats he would not accept. "Soon enough, Bekter and Qutula will have what they most desire from their father. In the meantime, they love their prince even if they cannot call him cousin."

"It curdles in the bones left too long simmering at the back of the firebox," she answered with another riddle.

This one he understood well enough. Love unacknowledged, she meant, might turn to envy and sour like an old broth. "Soon," he answered. Prince Tayyichiut was ready to be khan. Mergen would make the treaty with Tinglut, and then he would step down, giving as his gifts to his brother's child peace with all his neighbors, and cousins for his closest allies.

"Soon enough?"

There was nothing to say to that, and his nobles and chieftains awaited his call to horse. So he gave the order to mount with the exhortation, "A hungry people depend on your prowess today. Let the grass run red with the success of your hunt!"

"Hurrah!" they called back in unison. With spear in hand and bow and arrows slung on his back Mergen strode from the dais. The hunt fell in behind him.

W hen they approached the dell where Qutula had threatened the girl for her interference with the heir, Prince Tayy raised his hand to bring his guardsmen to a halt. The horses could only take the slope at a gallop, which would hardly suit the present need, so the prince dismounted and gave his reins into the hand that reached for them. Duwa, Qutula noticed. A furious Altan jostled him for the honor and lost the contest.

"Wait here," the prince commanded all the gathered guardsmen to silence. "The shamaness may have returned hurt or confused from her dream travel. I don't want to startle her."

"If she's hurt, she may need our help." Pretending to worry,

Qutula narrowed his eyes and peered into the gloom of the forested dell. He had nudged his own horse between that of Altan and his master, as his Durluken had intermingled with the Nirun, to watch their rivals and be among the first to protect the heir.

"I'm hoping she just needs a familiar voice to bring her home," Tayy rushed to assure him. "I'm more worried about the Tinglut wandering our camp. If there's trouble below I'll call for you, but I need you here more, in case we were followed."

"Leave the rest on watch on the plain above, then." Qutula didn't want the Nirun interfering but let his cousin believe he acquiesced to his royal wishes, save only for his own concern: "Someone should guard your back in case the Tinglut have come before us." He handed his own reins to Altan, who hesitated but could not refuse in front of the prince. Mangkut, who watched with subtle understanding, tilted his chin to accept the unspoken order to follow. Duwa would stay to remind the Nirun of their prince's command if they wavered.

Satisfied that his own Durluken would hide themselves among the trees to await his own word, Qutula turned again to convincing the prince. "I cannot claim her openly, but we both now know that Eluneke is my sister," he whispered so that none but the two of them could hear. "How do you think I will feel if something has happened to her and I stood useless and unsuspecting up above? How would you feel if you were in my place?"

It was a dangerous question, inappropriate for someone of Qutula's station, and he immediately withdrew it with a downcast head and apology. "I do not presume to know the mind of my prince."

But they were kin, even if that bond had never been acknowledged, and his question, artfully retracted, reminded the prince that he shared a close tie of blood with the shaman princess himself. How could Tayy fault him for his brotherly concern?

"Come," Tayy said as Qutula knew he would, giving in to his cousin's urgent plea with a sigh. "But watch from the trees. I don't think she knows who her father is. Certainly she knows nothing of the court or armies. I don't want her to feel threatened."

"Of course, my prince." Given permission to follow, Qutula usurped first place on their downward climb, "If some enemy lies in wait, let me be the first to feel the sting of his arrow," he reasoned. "Of us two, whose absence would the clans feel most?"

"My uncle would wish us both to come home," Tayy objected, but both the Durluken and his own Nirun added their arguments in Qutula's support, except for Altan, whose wary frown boded ill.

He had asked only what the gur-khan would have demanded, however, and the prince had little choice but to agree. Leading the way, Qutula headed down into the dell. Both knew they must tread carefully down the steep slope, and so they fell silent, watchful but still given to their own thoughts. When the land leveled out again, the prince set a hand on his cousin's shoulder to signal that he should wait, and went on alone. Qutula did as instructed for a moment, but then followed, silently as in the stalking hunt, until he found a tree behind which he might hide himself, close enough to the river to see all that transpired.

Then he settled to wait, scratching idly at the place where the tattoo of the emerald green bamboo snake usually tingled under the skin. He didn't feel it now, he realized, and knew that if he looked under his shirt the mark would be gone. He missed it, missed the warmth of her reminders and the sting of her displeasure. Had she tired of him, or had he displeased her with his failure to murder the prince? Had she abandoned him, to mark a new lover with the fire of her love bite? Surely she must understand that murder required the right moment. He wanted to be khan, not buried alive for regicide. . . .

Frustrated, Sechule set the bedding back against the wall. Foreign dignitaries were visiting the tent city again and feasting and celebrations were planned to honor the Tinglut prince after the Great Hunt. Her sons attended the gur-khan and his heir. By the grace of their attachment to the court, she would gain entrance to the entertainments of the ger-tent palace itself. Remembering the humiliating dismissal she had lately suffered at Mergen's hand, she had determined that this time when he summoned her to attend his sleep, she would plead a bellyache. She would conquer the conqueror with her beauty and leave him panting in his barren bed for the rich sensuality of the body she withheld from him.

For the plan to work, however, she must appear before the court at her most bedazzling, fully adorned in her best silk coats and with precious beads hanging from her hair and ears. But her best silk coats were missing. A search of the tent had uncovered a lost earring and a dagger that Bekter had missed, but not her silk coats. She hadn't seen them for some days. Not since . . .

"My Lady Sechule. Take a moment for tea."

Not since the last time the Lady Chaiujin had come calling. Sechule set down Bekter's dagger and smoothed her hands down her aprons. Before turning to face her visitor she took a deep breath and looked into the mirror that hung over her workbench. As she had suspected, the creature who looked back at her from within the bronze frame bore little resemblance to Lady Chaiujin, whose voice she had heard. Though the shape in the mirror was blurred, Sechule made out the flick of a restless forked tongue, the delicate tracery of scales above the lady's dark and lidless eyes.

"You don't want to do that," the voice chastised. "Our purposes require each other regardless of the form I take. Wouldn't you rather we met as friends than as hostile allies?" That word again, friends, though Lady Chaiujin had never befriended the mistress of her brother-in-law when she sat beside her husband on the dais.

"I may take a ram for an ewe, but it will give me no milk," Sechule answered with a riddle clear enough in its meaning. If they were indeed hostile allies, better to know it and set one's defenses accordingly.

"Then know me for my milk." The lady Chaiujin's dark eyes

glittered with malice as she waited for Sechule to decide how to take the rejoinder—as an answer to the riddle, or a warning. The milk of the emerald green bamboo snake's fangs had killed more than once in the tent city of the Qubal.

"Of course, my lady." Bowing her head she accepted both the offer and the warning. She didn't need the mirror to show her the lady's snaky form. She had seen the serpent-demon with her own eyes and held it prisoner in her cabinet. The opening moves thus dispensed with, however, she brought out cups and filled the pot with leaves and hot water from the kettle on the firebox.

"If you are looking for my son Qutula, he is attending the gur-khan and his heir at the Great Hunt." Bekter likewise accompanied the hunt, eager for a new song to inspire him. She didn't mention her second son, recalling his disappointing reticence on finding his brother's lover in his bed.

The lady took her cup and smiled as between confidantes. "Qutula can manage the hunt on his own. Can't two sisters of the mind share a quiet conversation without bringing the men into it? We have better things to discuss between ourselves."

"Certainly," Sechule agreed. "Such as?"

The demon-Lady Chaiujin must have heard the hesitation in her voice, but she gave no appearance of offense. "The girl," she said. "I am of two minds about the girl, and would like to hear your opinion."

"The girl." Sechule sipped the hot tea to give herself time to think. What girl? The Lady Chaiujin was herself Qutula's only lover, or at least the only one his mother knew about. As for Bekter, he confided nothing to her of such things. Sechule thought perhaps he was too much in love with his round-bellied lute to give thought to natural women. She doubted the lady much cared about him since her failed seduction there. That left the apprentice shamaness who had formed a relationship with the prince well beyond her station.

Setting down her cup, the Lady Chaiujin confirmed Sechule's conclusion. "The little shamaness. If Mergen sends her off with the Tinglut prince, we are rid of her interference, and with the gur-khan none the wiser about our little plot. If he decides to keep her for his heir, Qutula must dispose of her, of course."

None of that made sense. Mergen might allow his heir to keep the girl as his mistress, of course, but why would he try to seal a treaty with the Tinglut by offering some penniless shamaness to their khan? Neither of her sons had returned from their duties at the ger-tent palace before the hunt, so she'd had no report of what had transpired at court the night before.

Sechule's carefully neutral expression gave no sign of her ignorance while she considered this tidbit of information. Something had clearly changed in the status of the prince's folly, however. Even as a nobody a shaman was a danger to their plans. If the girl had somehow found favor, she posed a serious threat. Or an opportunity.

"Dead, of course, she can cause no trouble," Sechule agreed. Then, cocking her head as if the thought had come after her agreement, she added, "Or we might use her as bait, to draw our prey?"

"Bait, indeed, dear friend." Both women smiled as if they had come to one mind, though Sechule wondered why the demon—snake or woman—had stolen her best coats. As for the girl, she would need to speak with Qutula before she set her own plans in motion.

Perhaps, buried together in the furs of his bed, Mergen might confide in her and she would guide his thoughts about this girl. . . .

Tayy made his way down to the river with the hairs on the back of his neck standing on end, waiting for the arrow between the shoulder blades that never came. He missed Jumal, whom he trusted above all his companions, and wished he'd had time to talk about the oblique warning that had ended badly when Mergen sent him south with General Yesugei. For that matter, he wished for the general himself, who might have had advice about the danger that Jumal had seen where others hadn't looked. He didn't think Qutula would try to hurt him with foreigners in the camp, but he had lost faith in his cousin to thwart some other threat.

Fortunately, he didn't expect any danger to himself this morning. But Eluneke's absence worried him. Bolghai had expected her no sooner, of course. That didn't comfort him any more than the Tinglut prince did, waiting to take her away to wed an enemy old in years as he was in past enmities. He thought that, if he had a way to do it, he might warn her to stay where she was, abiding among the gods who at least would present a fairer face than the husband politics intended for her.

Humans didn't survive long away from the land and air of their own mortal world, however. She'd fare no better in the heavens, so he fought his way to the riverbank. The king of the toads had hidden behind this tree and there Tayy found the patch of moss where he and Eluneke had sat together, debating the life and death of the toads she needed to complete her shaman's costume. Here he had watched her turn into her totem animal to negotiate her treaty with their king.

Bolghai would cover the other possibilities, but he thought she would come back here. She had taken the toads with her on her spirit journey to see the sky god, and she had come to know the prince here as well. If she lost her way, her heart would call her back to him in this place.

Dropping to the moss, he curled his legs to wait. Above him on the slope of the dell he heard a twig snap and knew Qutula was watching him. He'd have rather had the dogs for company, but they had gone with the pack for the hunt, where he should follow before the Tinglut took insult. Except for the sound of his guardsmen, who had not stayed where he left them but had fanned out in a circle with himself at their center, the wood remained unnaturally still. The toads were gone, and the frogs, silent. Even the river ran quietly. The whole world of gods and mortals held their breath, and superstitious fear crept over him, that Eluneke was waiting, too. She would not return, bringing with her the life of the forest, as long as his soldiers watched the place where she must enter the mortal realm.

"Go," he called to Qutula, the heat of whose eyes seemed to burn a hole in the back of his head. "And take the rest of the guard. You can see there's no one here but ourselves. Tell the gur-khan I'll follow as soon as I can."

"The gur-khan gave me different orders." Qutula said in his ear, close enough for a knife, or a confidence.

"I know. Tell him that your disobedience is on my head." Dropping his voice so that only his cousin could hear, Tayy added, "Mergen is at greater risk from our Tinglut guests than I may be among the trees. How could I forgive myself if something happened to my uncle while you sat in the branches watching the moss grow on my behalf?"

He could hear the hesitation in his cousin's restless feet against the old fallen leaves. "She is shy at the best of times," he added, though he didn't think it was exactly true. Cautious, he guessed, and wary of a danger warned in a vision. But he wouldn't share that with the cousin who had nearly strangled him in a competition of wrestling. "She'll be disoriented after her long visit to the heavens. With so many people around, she may be afraid to return at all."

"You're probably right," Qutula acceded agreeably enough. "I'll send the rest away." Mangkut had come out of the trees. His captain passed him an order with a hand signal to which he bowed in acknowledgment and turned to gather up the Durluken who had filtered down through the wood. "I'll stay out of your way, but I won't leave until you do. The gur-khan would have my head. So I'll guard the path out of these woods—I can't abandon you with only the river for your escape."

"No!" Tayy wasn't going to win this one. Even his Nirun, who had gathered with the Durluken, took Qutula's side. But he wouldn't give in without having his own way at least in part. "The khan needs you at his side." They both knew the greater danger rode with Mergen now. Qutula wanted to be with the khan, Tayy could see indecision tearing at him in the restless searching of his eyes, stealing furtively to the grassland above.

"Leave Altan with the horses," he urged his cousin. Tayy wanted someone he trusted completely to watch his back. Jumal had gone, so that left Altan, whom he trusted as much as anybody, though not with Eluneke's secret. "Any threat would have to come from up above anyway." Any but his cousin. If someone wanted to hurt him, they'd have to come down off the high plains and that meant passing his guardsman on the path above. And from there Altan wouldn't hear or see anything that happened below.

Qutula brushed absently with his fingers at the jade on its thread around his throat. If his mother could give him a potion to effect the transformation, Qutula would have split himself in two, leaving his shade behind to watch for an opportunity against the prince while his physical presence lavished devotion on his father. Unfortunately, Sechule had no such power hiding in her cabinet. He couldn't reject the prince's plan without revealing his own secret plots, however, so he offered a compromise, "I'll go if you let me leave Mangkut to stand guard." Mangkut would watch with eyes pledged to Qutula and whisper in his ear what he saw of the prince and his forbidden princess.

Unsurprisingly, Altan objected, his hostile glance saying more about his distrust of the Durluken than his words, "I'll stay, as my prince bids me."

But Qutula disagreed, with an emphatic jerk of his chin in the direction of the waiting guardsmen. "You're the prince's lieutenant; who else can lead the Nirun in his absence?"

To object would have revealed too much. Tayy nodded, accepting the Durluken as his watchman on the path. It worried him that Qutula might not care if the prince knew his cousin had designs on his position. He went, which was the important thing for the here and now.

Like a weight lifting from his back, Tayy felt the eyes of the Durluken pull away, until he was alone with the river and his thoughts. They were grim as he sat there. When he had Eluneke back, he would figure out how to salvage his relationship with his uncle's blanket-sons. First he had to get her back, which was proving more difficult than he'd hoped.

Once he would have confided in Bolghai, but the shaman answered only in riddles and seemed never to take him—or anything—seriously. Bortu was wise and she loved him, but he thought she loved the Qubal more. She didn't know Eluneke anyway, and had never shown sympathy for putting emotions above political necessity. He couldn't talk to her, and Mergen was the problem. Eluneke understood him, though, with all his hopes and fears. She wasn't here, but he could talk to her, and maybe she would hear him in heaven and follow his voice home.

"I won't let them take you away," he said, the most important first. "We can run, or we can fight, but I won't let them part us."

" **. . .** **I** won't let them part us . . ." Out of her despair the voice rose from somewhere near Eluneke's heart. A human voice, in danger somewhere, she remembered through the dim thoughts of her toad mind.

The sky god and his daughters had given her their secrets and then abandoned her to find her own way home. She had searched and searched in human form and then in the shape of her totem animal, until she lost the notion even of what she was looking for. She thought that she had once been human, but what that meant had faded with the rainbows.

"Ribbit," the king of the toads said from his throne in the basket that once had ridden on her head. She squatted low on her haunches and bobbed in submission to his rule. A fat and juicy fly hummed by and she caught him on her tongue, swallowing him down still beating his fragile wings against her gullet.

"You said we were fated to be together," the voice continued. "You said I was your destiny, that we met because the spirits had sent you to save my life. I don't care about that, Eluneke. If you're lost, Qutula can strangle me or this Tinglut prince can pierce me with his arrow. What difference will it make?"

What difference? The fate of the ulus, that's all, to say nothing of her own heart, which had begun to swell and burn as the words found the love she had hidden there. She had to get back—out flicked her tongue to catch a mosquito and pop, down her throat it went, still buzzing indignantly.

"You have to come back," the voice continued, and this time it had a name, Prince Tayyichiut of the Qubal ulus, heir to the khanate. A face drifted across her toad mind, half-flesh, half-bone. "I've lost too much already to let you go as well."

He sounded bitter, and she remembered the grimace of pain that had dragged his lips back off his teeth, the ache of old wounds he carried on a body too young to know such terrors. His parents had died of treachery, and he would follow them if she didn't save him. The death's-head vision left no doubt of that and suddenly her breakfast of insects sat uneasy on her toad belly. She had to go home, right now.

That had been her problem before, she realized. To go home, you had to have a home to go to. And she hadn't, not in Toragana's little tent among the clans that had fostered her with growing irritation. Her mysterious father's wealth and power never materialized to provide her with a dowry or themselves with the price for keeping her. Like Prince Tayy she was an orphan, homeless except for the prince, who was home and life and destiny in one.

"This way!" she called to the king of the toads, who gathered his people in turn, all the hundreds who had climbed with Eluneke up the tree of lightning to the gods. And like a tangled vine she crawled back down the lilting sorrow of the prince's voice.

Chapter Twenty-seven

"CAN I COME with you?"

Daritai closed his eyes against the importunate twelve-year-old voice at his back. The sounds of the camp preparing to ride faded into the background like the wind tangling the braids below his princely silver cap. He'd left the boy sleeping in his tent, had almost made a clean escape across the field where the horses and riders were gathering for the hunt, because he didn't want to answer that question. *No,* he wanted to say. *It's too dangerous.*

But Tumbinai, his eldest son, had hunted with the warriors for over a year now. To leave him behind would signal to his own men too many of his secret thoughts. There was more going on in the Qubal camp than Mergen-Khan let on. More, probably, than the gur-khan knew himself. How he might use to his advantage the unrest—the veiled hostilities—he had sensed in the tent city Daritai hadn't quite figured, but he knew the boy was his own weakness. Mergen might mean the Tinglut clans no harm, but factions in the Qubal court might see in his youthful heir a weapon to use against him as a hostage, or worse. And yet, what better show of peace than his unblooded son at his side in the enemy camp?

He'd feel better about the whole mission if he could figure out why his father had insisted he bring the boy in the first place. Hulegu already held Daritai's seat on the dais. He didn't think Tinglut-Khan meant to wipe out his line to ensure the new heir's position, but he couldn't entirely dismiss the thought. If that were the case, then perhaps his father didn't expect him to return at all, let alone with a treaty-bride.

The endless possibilities for betrayal on this mission almost paralyzed him in front of his own son, in the face of the simplest question—"Can I come with you?"—that he should have answered differently a hundred and more li back, in his own tents. He couldn't answer as his heart wished now, however: *Take half a hundred of my most trusted guardsmen and go home, as fast as horse may carry you, into the arms of your mother and stay there until I come for you, be it through storm and blood and murder.* Whatever the game, he had to play it out to the end.

"Of course, you must attend me and make your courtesies to the foreign khan," he agreed.

"Thank you, Father! I'll get my horse . . ."

"Yes, go. Don't let manners keep you!" He drew his lips back in a wooden smile at the familiar joke that Tumbinai, clever boy, might have seen through on another day. But on this morning, with the clear blue light of Great Sun filling his heart with anticipation, he turned his back on the bleeding anxiety in his father's eyes, running to ready his mount with innocent joy.

"Stay with him," he instructed a guard who followed at his elbow. "Make sure that no harm comes to him."

"With my life, my prince." The man asked no questions, not even with a furrowing of his brows. He bowed deeply to bind the vow and went after the young princeling.

Time to go. Daritai found his own mount readily enough and greeted his closest guardsmen who had accompanied him to victory and defeat through all the years of his youth and adulthood. Too soon to have saddled the horse after their conversation, Tumbinai joined them, nudging seasoned warriors out of his way to take his place at his father's side. He was trying, Daritai noted, to retain a serious and regal mien, but in his excitement a grin kept escaping the boy's control.

Let him survive, he begged the spirits as they rode to meet the Qubal gur-khan. The appointed place of that meeting, the shrine of the murdered Chimbai-Khan, now lay fractured by storms, an ill omen if ever he'd seen one. *He doesn't have to be a prince,* he thought, *just let him live to be a man.*

Mergen waited until his scouts told him that Prince Daritai's party had arrived at Chimbai's shattered shrine before he led out his own hunters. Scouts had also reported sighting Jochi's returning party in the distance. Their large central tent flew a banner in Chimbai's colors to show that a member of the royal family resided within. He'd had success in finding the Princess Orda, then, for all the good it would do them now. Daritai didn't want the girl and he wondered what success Prince Tayy had had in finding their next offering to the Tinglut-Khan for peace between them. If Tinglut had any sense he'd have taken the little girl to raise her in a tent friendly to his interests. But the old ram had other plans for his dotage.

The party he'd sent to bring back the hope of that compromise was approaching with the speed of a summer squall. Let the Tinglut prince wait, he thought, while he gathered his own younger generation about him: his heir and the young warriors who would form their own phalanx in defense of their prince. And the princess, his daughter, summoned from whatever shamanic ritual Bolghai had set her. He knew he ought to be hoping that Eluneke did nothing to dissuade the emissary. He found himself wishing instead that she might confound this Daritai with some shaman's trick that sent the Tinglut prince home with his jaws agape and his face pale from terror. So much for peace.

But Qutula greeted him at the head of that party, with news he could have done without. "We saw no sign of the princess, though Prince Tayy seemed certain that she would come to him if he waited. He refused our company, however, afraid our presence would frighten the girl away, and said the steep slope of the dell and the Onga River itself provided all the protection he needed against any attack."

Qutula must have seen the anger gathering in Mergen's eyes, because he added in his own defense, "I convinced him to keep Mangkut on guard with the horses. And I confess I disobeyed his direct order, though I hoped to win your pardon for my crime. I left another guardsman from among my own cadre hidden within the trees."

"You have my pardon, and gladly," Mergen assured his son, letting go a little of the tension that had built between his shoulders when he saw neither prince nor princess returning with the others. He gave the signal to move out and asked, "You haven't found the girl, then?"

"Not yet."

In her serpent form, the false Lady Chaiujin slithered through the grass. She didn't think she needed Sechule's help persuading Qutula to murder the girl. He'd already shown himself willing. That was before he knew her as his sister, of course, but family feeling hadn't extended to his cousin, the prince. She didn't think the girl would stir any greater love. It seemed he used his heart to course blood through his veins but for little else. In this he reminded her of a serpent. She felt the egg taking shape in her belly, and tingled in anticipation of the moment when her child would quicken in his shell. But not yet. Not quite. There were murders to perform, and a lover to cajole.

She thought of his breast and formed the desire to rest there, to sink her inky teeth into his flesh and hold fast to him with his desire matched to hers. In her demon thoughts she made her desire real.

Qutula sidled his horse in between the khan and his agemates who guarded him. Restlessly his hand went to his breast, returned to his side under his control again. The lady of his mysterious nights burned her impatient message over his heart again and he welcomed the pain as a reminder of the deeds he had promised her. Soon, soon.

Chahar, Bolghai's son and the warrior who rode closest to the khan in Jochi's absence, made room for him, but the guardsman's expression was troubled. He had grown up in a shaman's tent and had a subtlety that bore careful watching. Killing, if necessary, though a murder so close to the khan would heighten the vigilance of his guards. Letting no part of his thoughts show, Qutula shrugged a shoulder to disavow his next words. "The prince thinks she'll come to his call if there aren't a lot of people around to frighten her."

"Let's hope so," Mergen agreed, riding comfortably, it seemed, with his own son at his side. Qutula kept a triumphant smile from his lips with difficulty. Soon, Mergen would be forced to acknowledge him as he had the girl Eluneke. He would ride at the side of the gur-khan as his right. Then a terrible accident, and the gur-khan would follow Chimbai and his heir. He might, with cunning, avoid a war altogether. Qutula would take Mergen's place at the head of the clans.

Perhaps he would bring the Tinglut under the Qubal sway as Mergen himself had swept up the Uulgar. He would rule the grasslands from the valleys of the Shan Empire to the mountains of the Cloud Country. He said nothing of this, however, as the gur-khan's hunting party stopped to greet the Tinglut prince—auspiciously for his plans, he thought—across the ashes of the murdered khan.

"I've lost too much already to let you go as well." Tayy buried his face in his hands. However lost she became in her initiation rites, he didn't think Eluneke would forget him, but he was afraid to look and find that it was so.

"Ribit." A little toad with a high, rusty voice like a badly hung gate plopped on his boot. "Ribit!"

"Eluneke?" Tayy leaned far over so that he stared eye to eye with the toad that perched on his upturned toe.

"Ribit!" she answered, sounding more desperate than she had a moment before. She bobbed her head in a little dance but didn't turn back into the girl he knew.

Suddenly, plop, plop, plop, toads were tumbling all around him. A great rain of toads spilled out of a sky as clear and blue as the silk of his best court robes. As they fell, the wood filled with the sounds—high and deep, croaking and bellowing—of their voices. With their return the crickets and cicadas came to life, mosquitoes bit, and flies lit on his arms. The little toad on his boot looked hungrily at a fat insect that flew too close, but she refrained from eating it. Tayy was glad of that, since it was hard enough to harbor romantic feelings for a toad. He might have to resort to keeping her fed on such fare if she didn't find her own true form soon, but for now he'd rather not think about such things.

"Don't worry," he soothed her, though his own heart trembled in his chest. What would he do if she never remembered how to become human again?

Daritai sat his horse at the center of his five hundred and waited for the gur-khan's hunting party to draw near. In the aftermath of the rain, no dust blurred the Qubal approach, At least a thousand in that line, he guessed. They had all—Qubal and Tinglut, too—come from battle too recently for any easiness with the sight. Like a nervous habit, his hand shifted to his bow. Others among his picked guard did the same but none was so ill-trained as to set an arrow. At least, not in the front ranks. His men would take nothing for granted in this meeting.

Tumbinai, smart boy, nudged closer on his mount. Given the choice, he would have sent the boy to the lower ranks with instructions to stay out of sight. The Qubal-Khan might take affront if he found out that the Tinglut emissary felt a need to hide his children from his allies, however. That meant his son front and center, at his side, preferably not shifting quite so wildly between excitement and terror.

"The gur-khan has no reputation for serving leg of visitor

baked in coals," he said, trying to settle the boy. "Be polite, try to look stupid if he asks anything you shouldn't answer, and beyond that, you've been to court. I trust you to know how to behave."

"He guts his enemies and buries them alive so that the horses beat the dirt down on top of them," the boy muttered with a shiver.

Daritai had heard the same rumors, had also heard they weren't true. Having met the man, he wouldn't put it beyond him at great need, which was better than he could say for the boy's grandfather, whose enemies were better off plunging the dagger into their own livers. He didn't plan to offer the gur-khan a reason for displeasure and felt confident in reassuring his son, "Stories for stormy nights. Mergen Gur-Khan is an honorable man and would never harm an unblooded youth."

Unlike your grandfather, he thought, who might want to clear his own ger-tent palace of too many heirs. He couldn't think of that, however, not and do the job required to keep them all alive at home. The Qubal party had neared enough that he could make out the features of the gur-khan at their center. Daritai nudged his horse forward to greet his host, his son following a few paces behind. He didn't look back, just hoped the boy had smeared an appropriately friendly expression on his face.

Mergen stepped out of his line as well, to face him with a welcoming tilt of his head, no more for a lesser son. Prince Tayyichiut wasn't there, and for a moment Daritai's heart turned over. Treachery, he thought, and would have sent his own son flying. But it was too late, the boy was too exposed. *What have I done? I've killed my son . . .*

"The prince has a sore head, but will join us shortly," Mergen lied with a tip of his hand to pantomime a cup. Drunk, then. His ironic smile shared the lie between them with no expectation of belief, just reassurance that the prince's absence meant nothing in the scheme of Daritai's mission. Or so he meant his adversary to believe.

The guardsman who had ridden at the gur-khan's right hand set his unblinking gaze on Tumbinai. He might have been a viper coiled upon the saddle. Qutula, his name was, and dependable report said the gur-khan's blanket-son. Did the absence of the old khan's prince mean a change in the royal succession in the wind? The young guardsman didn't take the place of the heir in the greeting as Tumbinai had done. Resented it, too, by the look of him. Not the danger he'd anticipated but more, perhaps, than he had counted on. He didn't think this one would stand on honor to preserve his father's agreements. Daritai was glad he'd rejected the old khan's child, but he wondered if any bride Mergen offered would serve for more than warming old Tinglut-Khan's bed.

He kept his thoughts to himself when he greeted the gur-khan however. "A fine day for a hunt!" he said, his face turned with proper appreciation into the wind-drenched sunlight.

"A fine day, indeed," Mergen Gur-Khan answered. "Would you have a wager?"

"First shot," Daritai agreed, meaning the first game brought down between them. The Qubal hunters outnumbered his own by too great a number for betting on the greatest catch.

"Done."

With the wagers between the first of the hunters concluded, the lesser members of each party broke into their own groups and pairs, setting wager against wager with a low roar like distant thunder.

So the Tinglut prince had brought a ready-made hostage with him. As he listened to his father make the first wager, Qutula set a cold and thoughtful eye on the boy, Tumbinai, who looked back with a combination of terror and fascination difficult to resist. *Whose idea were you?* he wondered, half aloud.

At his breast, his lady whispered "Fathers, sometimes, wishing to be rid of troublesome sons, invite their enemies to feast on kinship's bones."

She could have meant the Tinglut prince, or his own father for that matter, but he didn't think so. He wasn't the one who had fallen under Mergen's displeasure this time. As for the Tinglut pup, Qutula saw the moment of panic when Papa Daritai counted up the players and realized the Qubal heir hadn't added into the sum while his own offspring was flying in the breeze, a banner to be taken in the games of statecraft. He ought to be able to make something of that. Tilting his head at a regal angle he'd seen Tayy pull off far too often, Qutula let the Tinglut wonder why he rode at Mergen's side. *Look your fill,* he thought. *Soon enough the contest will come to us two.*

A line opened then to let the beaters and the handlers through with the dogs, who milled about baying and nipping at each other in their own drawing of ranks. Just like their human counterparts, Qutula observed, they jockeyed for position. And like the old dogs, the older guardsmen had settled their places in the pack long ago; Mergen's followers rose among the ranks while Chimbai's found themselves drifting to the rear or, like General Yesugei, sent away where he could have no influence on the court.

Qutula's own Durluken guardsmen followed the lead of their elders, crowded at the right hand of the khan. The absent prince's Nirun muttered blackly under their breath to see their adversaries hold the place they had claimed for themselves as the heir's favorites. Altan, the prince's own, nudged his horse closer to the khan as if he might preserve his prince's place with his own person, but Duwa pushed him back. Words were spoken. Altan set hand to his dagger and in the same breath, Duwa had cleared his own sheath. Neither moved then, as if the seriousness of what they had done in the gur-khan's presence paralyzed them in their saddles.

Qutula saw the displeasure his father otherwise hid from the hunting party.

"Save the daggers for the conies, we do not need them between friendly rivals," Mergen chided the young guardsmen. Each dropped his head in shame to have brought censure on Nirun and Durluken both, but satisfaction gleamed in the eye Duwa turned on his captain. Qutula knew better than to share with his followers his private plans for the khanate, but it seemed that if he chose to fight, he would have willing accomplices. Good. With no outward sign that he approved his henchman's actions, he gave his full attention to his father's speech.

"Instead of bickering uselessly among yourselves, turn your rivalry into meat for the cook pots," Mergen proposed. "Whichever team brings in the greatest catch will win for their captain the praise of the singers of the royal court. Bekter himself will compose a ballad in the winner's honor. Is that not so, good poet?"

Bekter, who had ridden with little attention to his place in the line of the gur-khan's hunting party, worked his way forward at the mention of his name. "Of course," he said, bowing from the saddle with all show of acquiescence though Qutula was certain he hadn't heard what Mergen had promised in his name. It was enough to cool the hot heads among the younger guardsmen, however.

"Do something," the snake tattooed on his chest whispered in Qutula's ear. Mergen had turned the confrontation into a formal contest; now he could show his appreciation for Duwa's silent promise with his own reward. "And to sweeten the pot, a coral bead the size of the knuckle on my right thumb, to the Durluken who brings down the first branchy game." Buck or roedeer, he meant by that, game worthy of a prince.

A shout went up among the Durluken, who raised their bows above their heads to salute the prize. Then Bolghai came forward with his rattle and his drum, singing the low ululation that called the game. The stoats at his throat flying about him as he whirled, the shaman danced with little hops to signify the conies and jerboa, and all the small animals who scurried close to the ground. With swoops and the flapping of his arms he mimicked the birds and with huge gallops summoned the greater game, the roe deer and wild ram and other fleet, four-footed prey.

The blessing ended and the beaters took up their own drums and clashing bells, surging forward with their wild and terrifying noise. The master of the hunt, with horns blowing, set the order of the day for the waiting hunters. The lake formation, as in battle, would sweep across the grasslands. The gur-khan's party, with the Tinglut prince beside him, would lead from the center where they would find the best hunting. His guard captains, acting for his absent generals Yesugei and

Jochi, would take the wide sweeping arms on either side, encircling their prey and driving it toward the waiting arrows of the royal huntsmen.

When each knew his place in the order of march, the hunt moved out

Chapter Twenty-eight

IF NOT FOR the Tinglut warriors who rode among his own forces in numbers sufficient to make a bloody mess of a clear blue day, Mergen would have enjoyed the hunt. The rains had tamed the dust and the breezes were cool against his face as he rode. Beneath him he scarcely felt the strike of hooves on the soft ground. And ahead, among the lesser game, the beaters had spotted a ram standing as tall as his horse at the shoulder, with horns curled on themselves in a circle which he could scarcely have measured with both arms spread wide.

He would, on another day, have drawn his own bow for a shot at the beast. But the youngest warriors had forged ahead, shouting their allegiances to Nirun or Durluken, or to the prince of the Tinglut, each promising to bring down the wild sheep for the glory of his hero. Qutula paced him on the right, letting his Durluken run ahead for his honor, while on his left, the Tinglut prince, Daritai, rode with his own son close to his flank.

The boy rode well, as any born of the grasslands would. The moods careening across his face, however, spoke of a sharp mind behind the childish face. Smart enough to understand the danger, at least, and adventurous enough to enjoy the day in spite of it. His father need only teach him to keep those feelings behind his eyes, defended against enemies who would read

him like a well-marked trail. A pity the boy wasn't the groom
on offer. He'd have suited Princess Orda when they both had a
few years on them.

A compliment might seem like a threat under the circumstances, so Mergen kept those thoughts to himself. He followed
the hunt for the ram, letting the drama of the chase unfold ahead.

"**B**olghai will know what to do," Tayy promised the toad-
girl, and put out his hand. "He'll want to see you right
away."

He had tried everything he could think of to return her to
her natural form, but Eluneke remained stubbornly toad. She
stepped into his waiting palm, however, as he added, "He'll be
attending the hunt to bless the catch. I should be there myself—
my uncle will have my bones for soup spoons for staying away
so long."

She listened gravely, then leaped from his hand onto his
hunting jacket, nudging the edge where it crossed his breast.

"Oh, yes, of course." That was clear enough. He loosened
the fastenings to cradle her inside, close to his heart. As he
climbed away from the river he tightened the strings again to
keep her safe. "Just don't make any noise until we find him. I
don't want to have to explain you to my uncle in this shape."

She croaked some answer, though if she meant it as indignation or agreement he couldn't tell. They both fell silent as he
climbed. When the lip of the dell was in sight, Mangkut called
down, "Who goes?" He'd set an arrow to his bow, pointed at
Tayy's breast.

Is this the moment? Tayy asked himself. Would Qutula
prove now, with murder he could disavow, that his hands
around the prince's throat had been no accident but assassina-
tion, thwarted by the skills Tayy had learned in his travels with
foreign armies?

He answered Mangkut's challenge calmly enough—"It's
only Prince Tayy"—and waited for the arrow to prove . . . something.

"The hunt has begun," Mangkut informed him, and pointed his arrow at the ground. "I can hear the dogs in the distance."

Tayy mounted his horse with a nod to his cousin's follower. Mangkut didn't ask about the girl. It wasn't his place to do so and the Durluken followed Qutula's lead, who perhaps had never expected the prince to find her. Tayy kept his own counsel about the small toad riding in his coat.

The young warriors, Nirun and Durluken and a few of the Tinglut as well, had driven their prey to staggering exhaustion. While their lesser fellows contented themselves with smaller game, more than a hand of young warriors had pulled taut the strings of their bows in hope of bringing down the ram. As Mergen bore down on them with the rear guard, they let fly over the heads of their horses.

A strike, there on the flank. The ram, already running, surged ahead. Another arrow, glancing off the horn, fell harmlessly to the ground but a third caught him in the neck. The ram staggered to his knees, rose again as more arrows pierced his shaggy hide. A drunken step, another, as if the creature did not own the legs that carried him. Unchecked, his forward motion brought him down on his great spiral horns as the young horsemen drew up around him, Altan and Duwa among them, which boded ill for a peaceful day.

Altan drew his arrow from the neck of the beast and held it over his head in victory for the Nirun. Duwa snarled something, curse or challenge, over his shoulder while he cut his own arrow from the ram's breast. Whatever he'd said carried sufficient heat that the others who had come to retrieve their own arrows drew back in a wary pack.

Withdraw, Mergen wished of Altan, who might have had the right of it, but who always lacked for tact. Altan, of course, didn't hear his khan's thoughts, and acted as he always did, with an instinct for the killing shot. He laughed. Duwa's face suffused with bloody-minded rage.

If Qutula had ridden with his followers, he might have

stopped it, but his blanket-son had remained at Mergen's side, his eye on his own soaring prey. His arrow flew, a bird fell from the sky, and a little farther ahead, Duwa raised his knife.

"Don't do it . . ."

Qutula didn't seem to hear, but the Tinglut prince turned sharply to stare at him as the knife found its mark over the body of the ram.

"What—?" Daritai began, but their line was breaking around the fallen in front of them. Mergen would have wished the foreign prince with their flank, following the game and none the wiser. Instead he stopped, the child at his side, while the gur-khan on his steaming horse drew up to take accounting of the tragedy before them.

What have you done? he wished to demand of the young man who stood with bloodied hand before him. *What have you brought down on your house and clans by your rash actions?* But a khan could show no such human weakness even for the boyhood companion of his blanket-son. Not when Altan, the pride and heir of his own general Jochi, lay dead beside the ram.

So, so, so. "Find his father. General Jochi must be told," Mergen instructed Qutula, whose man had committed murder over a dumb beast for the cook pot. "Tell him I sent you to stand guard over the princess; he may come at the will of his gur-khan."

Qutula gave him a sulky look, as if he was being punished, which Mergen supposed he was. Later he would talk to his son and his heir both about letting rivalries grow into blood feuds, but now he had justice to administer, and a general with powerful clans behind him to appease. Duwa was himself the child of clans who had set their hopes upon their son's position in the ger-tent palace. Now those hopes would die, as Altan had died. Except, of course, that luck and time might see fortune return to Duwa's family some day. Altan would not rise again.

"My lord gur-khan." His head properly bowed, Duwa fell to one knee in the mud awash with the blood of man and beast, but he showed no contrition as he complained, "It's not my fault. He mocked me in front of all the court—in front of foreigners!"

"Silence," Mergen commanded. At his most killingly furious his voice dropped almost to a whisper and it did so now. Only those nearest—Duwa himself, and the Tinglut prince, who looked like he would rather be anywhere but in this company—could hear. Duwa had hung from Qutula's coat sleeve since they were children, however, and heard the deadly warning in that gentle tone. He blanched and held his tongue.

While they waited for the dead boy's father to claim his body and his vengeance, Mergen called a guardsman to him. "Find the chieftain who rules this one, and bring him to me," he ordered with a tilt of his chin at Duwa. "Someone will have to pay for this."

A protest reddened Duwa's cheeks, but he kept the words he might have spoken to himself. *Restraint now, too late to do you any good,* Mergen pondered. Prince Daritai looked pale, and Mergen remembered the child who rode with him, who had sensibly kept his mouth shut and his eyes open. He would have given the man leave to find his own tents but needed all his witnesses present when the fathers came. And he could find no way in front of both their guardsmen to make the assurances of safety the Tinglut prince needed to hear. They wouldn't have been true anyway.

"I saw nothing, my lord gur-khan, nor did my son," Daritai muttered, reading Mergen's intentions with a courteous bow. If he wasn't a witness, the gur-khan needn't require his presence.

The boy's sudden sharp breath told him otherwise. Daritai pretended not to notice and the boy wisely thought better of his objection. It gave him a pretense to free the foreigners from an embroilment in Qubal politics, something he wished for both their sakes. But Daritai had heard him send for the general. The man was no fool, but a likely spy as well as emissary. Mergen might yet need the child as a hostage for his father's silence.

Too soon the gallop of approaching horses heralded a new arrival. There hadn't been time to bring the general; Prince Tayyichiut entered the unhappy circle, Mangkut the Durluken following. With a glance from one side to the other, the guardsman took in the hostility, if not the cause, between the teams.

Quietly he fell back, unwilling, it seemed, to draw attention to his allegiance in the conflict.

They hadn't brought Eluneke with them—just as well under the circumstances, Mergen thought. Though he dearly wished to know where she had gone, he wouldn't have chosen to introduce the Tinglut-Khan's prospective bride to her potential son-in-law this way. No one spoke as the prince walked his sweating horse toward the felled ram.

"What happened?" Tayy recognized his own Nirun marshaled in a glowering line across a fallen ram from the Durluken, who stared back with war in their eyes.

"Tragedy," Mergen answered.

Something else spoke in his eyes. Murder, Tayy guessed. His own dogs had shouldered their way past the guards and they paced a worried path between their master's horse and the young warriors gathered around their prey. Tayy dismounted and brushed his way past a guardsman who would not meet his eye, drawn like the hounds to the rich scent of blood at the center of the circle.

Ah; that explained it. Altan, his face still contorted with the shock of his death, lay with his arm outflung across the shaggy back of the fallen ram. His blood had ceased to drip and formed a crusting armor like a starburst across his breast.

Senseless, senseless death, and for what? A slab of meat and a pair of horns? Or the first move in a war that was no game at all? When had the teams formed for honorable contest in the games become opposing armies? And where was Qutula's hand in this? Suspicion had grown into surety; his cousin's mind must surely have guided this move, even if his palms were clean of blood. In time each question, like a stone, must be answered carefully with his own moves on the board. But first, his friend . . .

"Altan—" Prince Tayy fell to his knees, reached for the knife that lay beside him. He knew that knife. Strategy would have served him better, but desperate, grieving rage overwhelmed all his political calculations. The storm of powerful feelings set his heart to beating in strange and terrible rhythms.

Suddenly he was on his feet with no memory of rising, a single thought drumming in his head.

"I'll kill the man who did this," he swore, looking straight at Duwa, who gazed back at him with growing unease but little remorse.

"Altan?"

General Jochi hadn't been a part of the original circle, but he was here now, Tayy realized, and had the greater claim to vengeance. Following a few paces behind came Qutula, with a practiced apology on his face, and across the general's saddle sat a little girl. The Princess Orda looked about her with fearless curiosity.

His hand with the knife clasped in it dropped to Tayy's side. Terrible fury swelled his heart unabated, but he could not stain his sister's unblinking innocence with Qubal blood, even that of a murderer.

"He wouldn't leave her behind," Qutula shrugged a helpless shoulder. Watching his cousin with clearer eyes, Tayy figured he hadn't explained why the general was needed at the hunt.

"Let me hold her for you, sir," a child's voice interrupted the tense drama. The boy held out his arms. "I have a little sister at home and I've carried her before me lots of times."

It was easy enough to see where the boy got his face, but where had he come from? And what was a Tinglut princeling doing here? Jochi's attention lay wholly on his son, however. Tayy held his breath when the general absently passed the Qubal princess into the hands of the foreign boy. Mergen's eyes widened with alarm, but he clamped his lips so tightly shut that wrinkles pleated his mustaches. His horse danced a little under him, but quickly came back to hand as the khan regained his watchful composure. Jochi noticed none of it.

"How did this happen?" the general demanded, his eyes fixed on the body of his son.

"Murder," said a Nirun, who glared at the Durluken gathered behind the guilty Duwa.

"Quarrel," a Durluken objected. "Hasty words, a deadly insult answered."

"Too much haste all around," Mergen judged.

Inside Tayy's shirt the toad he had carried from the river scrambled to be let out and he loosened his ties and set her down beside the cooling body. "Can you help him?" he asked, inexplicably to the gathered company.

The toad bobbed and hopped. Then she turned into a girl with tangled hair and a smudge of dirt on her face, dressed in the shaman's robes in which she'd disappeared. Now the baskets she had woven for her totems dangled bruised and empty from the ribbons of her coat, hardly suitably for a shamaness let alone a lady of her father's rank. Mergen looked like he'd bitten into something rotten. She didn't know he was her father, of course. She'd been in heaven, talking to the gods, when Mergen had revealed that bit of family history.

"I'm sorry. He's gone," she said, meaning that Altan's spirit had severed the invisible cord that tied it to his body. "Where is Bolghai? Evil has been done here; I feel the demon spirits drawing near already. This place needs blessing and a pyre to send him on his way as soon as possible."

"First a matter of judgment, daughter, then the proper sending of my general's heir to the ancestors. This ram for which he died will pay his way among his ancestor spirits."

Prince Tayy knew the look she gave the gur-khan. He had grown up on the like from Bolghai. Eluneke made no acknowledgment of the rank he had given her, but with a lowering of her lashes took it in to contemplate later, when matters of the dead did not require her urgent attention.

Mergen knew the look as well. He withdrew from that contest with a tilt of his chin to cede to her the temporary victory of her shamanic station and turned to the Tinglut boy. "You aren't in trouble," he said, pretending not to notice the rejected child bride in the hands of a foreign princeling. "You have done nothing wrong. But to make a fair judgment, I have to know what you saw."

The boy said nothing.

"My lord khan—" The prince, Daritai, nudged his horse a step closer to the gur-khan. From every point in the circle swords shrieked from their scabbards. Holding his hands carefully away from his sides, where sword and dagger rested, Daritai rolled a desperate look in the direction of his son, who held tightly to the Qubal princess with no notion of the danger he was in.

Or perhaps he knew too well, Tayy thought. His grip on the little girl wasn't threatening, but of the two, it seemed the princess did the comforting, and the Tinglut boy the asking.

"No threat," Daritai promised. "I'll tell you anything you want to know, but please don't hurt my son."

"I don't torture children," Mergen answered him with asperity and, exasperated, begged of his court, "will someone with the rank to do so take the Princess Orda into custody before I am obliged to notice and assume the Tinglut have taken her hostage?"

"I was just trying to help!" Shocked, the boy would have flung her from the horse to save himself from the accusation. Only her small round arms clinging like vines to his neck saved them from another inadvertent disaster. Qutula reached for her, but she wouldn't let go, resisting him instead with her raised voice and with the curled toes of her little boots until Eluneke came and collected her.

In the midst of turning Altan's death into a sorry farce, Duwa's chieftain arrived with the guardsman's father and uncles. Eluneke retreated, the little princess in her arms, as the men of Duwa's clan picked their way through the gathering crowd to face the khan. The crowd fell silent, waiting for judgment. Tayy waited with them, measuring his uncle's deliberation against his own need for retribution.

Impassively, Mergen greeted the chieftain of the Dobun-Qubal, who guided his horse to stand before the gur-khan. He knew Dobun for a good leader, sensible in his way and not given to ambitions for advancement in the ulus. In a court lately infected with assassinations, he valued the man's modesty. A young warrior like Duwa, however, who had grown to manhood in the light of the dais, might have dreams that reached beyond the limits of the growing herds and the thickly wooled sheep of his family and his clans.

And so we are brought to this, good Dobun, he thought, *and you are flung, unwished and unsuspecting, into the blazing sun of the gur-khan's notice.* Though he might have preferred to do so, he could not, in front of all the clans and the dead boy's father, forgive the murderous actions of the young lieutenant for the loyal service of his chieftain.

"A warrior has died here," he said. With a gesture of his bow he parted the gathered Nirun and Durluken to reveal General Jochi bent on one knee over his son. Prince Tayyichiut knelt at his side; neither wept, but vengeance crackled like lightning in the air.

Duwa's father cast a beseeching glance at Qutula, saying more about the spring at the source of Duwa's ambitions than he might have liked. Mergen's blanket-son had taken a step away from his companion, however, distancing himself from his follower's crime.

"A fine young man, son of my general, companion of my heir, has been murdered and his murderer stands accused by his own bloody hand and his bloody knife.

"Witnesses, then?" Dobun bowed deeply, dismay carved in the downturn of his mouth. This was politics far above his inclinations, about to cost him a nephew.

"My own eyes," Mergen nodded. "And these." Stretching out his hand he took in the gathered armies of the Nirun whose sword hands itched for vengeance and the Durluken, whose stubborn necks would not bend to accept any blame.

Dobun tugged anxiously at his mustaches. "What price?"

Jochi had risen as the moment for judgment came. He stood a silent witness with the drying blood of his son painting his fingers as the khan handed down his sentence.

"From the Dobun-Qubal, two herds of horses and one of sheep, to become the property of the clans of the Jochi-Qubal. Half the tents of his father with all their household goods now belong to General Jochi, as compensation for the loss of those things which might have come to his family through his own son who now lies dead."

The Dobun-Qubal clans would survive, but Duwa's family was ruined, impoverished possibly forever. The worst re-

mained, however. Knowing it, Duwa's father spoke up, asking
the question that as a father he must dread the most.

"And my son?"

"My lord general?" Mergen turned to Jochi, the injured
party. Tradition dictated the answer, and the general gave it.
"My servants need a servant." Duwa would become a slave in
the household of the general.

"For as many cycles as the accused, Duwa, has fingers,"
Mergen agreed. On occasion a murderer might be returned to
his family quickly, with all his fingers severed, but Mergen
didn't think his general would stray so far from honor.

The chieftain accepted this judgment with tears in his eyes.
"You will have your herds and tents by nightfall," he promised
the general and with a final bow to the gur-khan, departed in
the company of Duwa's uncles. His father remained, though he
refused to watch as Duwa's wrists were tied and he was led
away. He made no apology to the general, but spat a speculative
hawk into the dirt and silently followed his chieftain.

Jochi would receive the oldest and sickest beasts from
among the Dobun-Qubal herds, but most of the animals would
be sound and the tents well mended. He would, of course, have
given it all up to have his son sit up and curse them roundly for
making such a fuss at a mere scratch. Altan didn't move, though,
and wouldn't be sitting up this side of the underworld again.

"Travel in peace to the land of your ancestors, and make a
place for us when we follow," Mergen prayed his farewell. Tayy
had regained his saddle. The track of drying tears had cut their
own path through the streak of Altan's blood that crossed his
cheek, but after a moment he started moving toward the forest
that bordered the river. Together with the gathered hunters,
Nirun, and the older bands with allegiances to the khan, they
would collect the trees for Altan's pyre. In the deceptive mo-
mentary peace, Mergen prayed for time to break his unruly
children to his hand before they set chaos loose across all the
grasslands.

At a little distance, and in his totem form, Bolghai watched the Durluken as by ones and twos they slunk away. Finally only their captain remained, close by his father's side, contemplating the Nirun pyre with a cold eye. Trouble was coming; the stoat's black button nose twitched with the stink of it. Conspiracy. Eluneke had been right all along.

Fortunately, the sky god and his daughters had been kind to her. After his own visit to the heavens, Bolghai had spent three days as a stoat before remembering how to be human again. The girl'd had help, of course; the prince had called her home as well as any shaman might. Still, the fact that she'd returned to herself so quickly spoke well of the power of her gifts. Which reminded him . . .

Stretching, the shaman shaped human arms and human legs, and drew his spine out straight and long. With a last thought for his robes, he stood up and made his presence known in answer to his gur-khan's call.

"I'm here," he said, "though your own daughter seems to have the matter well in hand."

"She shouldn't be here at all. She's a royal princess, you old fool. She had no right to choose this path and you had orders to stop it."

Danger rumbled in the words. Bolghai didn't think the gur-khan would have him killed, but the part about being an old fool gave him the edge in their argument, especially the old part, though Toragana would doubtless tell him it was the fool part. Because he was ready to die, if he could leave the ulus in the hands of a shaman powerful enough to protect it. Like the gur-khan's daughter. Now was not the time to have that discussion, however.

"The hungry spirits grow fat on our disputes," he rebuked Mergen gently. "When we have sent this brave young man to his ancestors, you are welcome to flay me as you choose."

"Don't think I won't, old man." Mergen delivered the rebuff as an insult, with his back turned to the shaman. The argument wasn't over.

Bolghai sighed and untied his drum from the strings where it hung at his sides, and the drumstick made from the shinbone of a roebuck. Demons and lost souls drawn by violent murder had gathered thickly around the quarrel. With his drum and his dance and his prayers, he set about dispersing them while Eluneke, with the dead khan's daughter still in her arms, directed the construction of the pyre.

Chapter Twenty-nine

A TOAD. THE GIRL whom Mergen-Khan had summoned to wed the Tinglut-Khan was a toad. Gazing in dismay over the shambles of his mission, Prince Daritai had to admit that his father might have been right about the Qubal all along. He'd never believed the explanation Mergen-Khan had given for the disappearance of the Lady Chaiujin. Murdered, Tinglut had guessed, by a Qubal hand and not a serpent-demon.

"Mergen cost me a royal daughter," the khan had reminded him. "He owes me a royal wife, something pretty and young to warm my bed in winter." Though he wouldn't say as much in front of Hulegu, Tinglut wanted heirs with royal Qubal blood. He would use those children to claim the Qubal ulus in the war he planned, to install himself as regent for the sons he planned to get. The present heir possessed all the skills he needed to foresee his own downfall if Daritai succeeded. Hulegu, of course, would expect the mission to fail.

The treaty had offered an opportunity to spy out the truth about the Qubal's intentions. It hadn't taken Daritai long. At best he could report that the proposed bride was a dirty-faced shamaness with no court manners, a ridiculous totem, and an overbearing manner. Tinglut wouldn't have minded the dirty face if she were pretty enough, which she was. He might even find the skills of a shamaness useful for prolonging his vigor.

But the khan his father would never accept a sharp-tongued toad in his bed.

It seemed clear that Mergen had never intended to claim her and that he did so now only to pacify his neighbor, who would have accepted the girl in ignorance of her lowly station and her calling. And, it seemed, if he read the direction of that wind correctly, that the prince himself had interests in that quarter. From the careful way he moved around her, Daritai thought they hadn't slept together yet, but it seemed likely to happen soon. The Qubal prince didn't mind the toad part either, which Daritai didn't want to think about. So much for honorable intentions.

As for murder, the young warrior with the knife in his chest gave clear evidence that those closest to the khan were still busy killing each other. He thought the general's son was just the first move in the latest game of Qubal politics, and wondered how long Mergen had before he followed his brother onto the pyre. Sooner than later, if the gur-khan didn't do something about his blanket-sons. Tinglut would have solved the problem by strangling them in their sleep. Daritai sometimes waited sleepless in his own bed for the soft tread of the assassin.

His own father wasn't the issue now, though. He had seen too much, and so had his son. Mergen knew it; his personal guard glared at the Tinglut forces across a divide no greater than a single step, yet fathoms deep in mutual suspicion. The hostile tension of the armies had settled like damp in Tumbinai's bones. The boy sat rigidly erect in his saddle, dark eyes wide, afraid to make a move that would tilt the balance into violence. Daritai had trained him for warfare, but they were too outnumbered to call it anything but slaughter. Tumbinai would know that, too.

Whatever happened to Daritai, he was determined to bargain or beg for the life of his son. When the gur-khan had dismissed his old shaman to his duties, he nudged his horse forward, keeping his hands in view of the guardsmen who surrounded him.

"We should return to our own tents and leave you to your grief." He bowed to acknowledge the mourning court, but said nothing of his intention to pack up his tents and his son as quickly as he could and slip away like Mergen's own Durluken.

The gur-khan cast a brief glance at him but his opaque gaze fixed on the dead boy with his arm flung over the ram. The silence between them stretched like a bowstring until Daritai could endure it no more. Breaking every rule of hostile diplomacy, he slid from his horse and knelt at the foot of the mounted khan. With head bowed, he filled the silence with his bargain.

"If you need a hostage, I will stay, and vouch for the discretion of my men. I ask just a small party of his most familiar guardsmen to take my son home."

"And what will keep the boy quiet when he finds himself the target of his grandfather's questions?"

Still on his knees, Daritai tilted his head back to face Mergen. Great Sun, he noted, had begun to fall, and it shone like a gathering of spirits around the impassive gur-khan. "He knows you'll kill me if he breaks his word."

"A good argument if he cares. What if your death means nothing to him?" The golden light behind him cast Mergen's features in shadows from which an emotion as powerful as it was fleeting escaped his glacial eyes. It seemed he was not so unaware of his own peril as Daritai had suspected.

With a wry half smile the prince answered the emotion behind the question. "Then I'll die, but Tumbinai will be as safe as I can make him."

"Not safe enough."

The wistfulness of Mergen's tone robbed it of any threat. They both knew they stood on the brink of war, with only the love of their children as common ground between them.

"Send half your guard with him." The gur-khan nodded permission and Daritai bowed deeply, slack-muscled with relief. This time, maybe, love would be enough.

But Tumbinai said, "No."

From his precarious position among the horse's legs, Prince Daritai had lost the advantage of perspective that Mergen

held from the back of his gelded bay. So he couldn't see the
boy's growing horror as his father offered his life for his son's
freedom. Daritai wouldn't have noticed that Tayy had returned
and listened sharply or that Eluneke had drawn closer with the
Princess Orda still in her arms. Or that the little girl had fixed
the Tinglut boy with a stare that sent a warning shiver straight
up Mergen's spine.

The gur-khan had seen it all, however, and he wasn't
pleased with any of them, least of all the boy Tumbinai, who
was looking back at Princess Orda with a fierce protectiveness
that seemed equally to enfold his endangered father. So when
he said, "No," to the gur-khan's offer to hold his father prisoner
in his place, Daritai was surprised. Mergen wasn't, though they
shared a common displeasure.

"I won't leave my father. And the little girl needs someone
to watch over her." Stubborn and headstrong, the boy firmed
his quivering chin and met the gur-khan's stare with a level
gaze of his own. He'd grown up in the court of the Tinglut-
Khan, that look said. He knew about throwaway lesser children
and he wasn't going to let anything happen to the Princess
Orda.

At that moment, Mergen could cheerfully have wrung General Jochi's neck. The boy had held the little girl in his arms,
stirring all the instincts in him to defend the weak. Mergen in-
dulged in a little silent swearing while the father tried not to
show his terror and the boy swallowed a lump the size of a wal-
nut in his throat. Prince Tayyichiut, of course, was watching
him with all the terrible knowledge of his own experience in
his eyes. Tayy had seen the murders of his father and mother,
his own enslavement by pirates, and the deaths of his friends
in battle. And now he trod a careful path through the uncertain
threats of his own court.

None of them wished their own prince's history for this
child. Mergen just wasn't sure how he could prevent it. They
were at an impasse until, in a quavering whisper, the boy
Tumbinai said, "I don't like my grandfather."

The boy's father might have turned to stone. He didn't
panic, but something desperate and dangerous coiled inside his

stillness. *Don't draw your sword,* Mergen prayed, *let him finish.* They'd already lost a boy today. With luck and a little common sense, nobody else had to die.

"My father doesn't either."

Prince Daritai said nothing, but the coiled springs of his muscles all relaxed at once. His eyelids slid down, rose again without hope, as he pulled himself upright, his chin held up, his chest thrust out, ready for the sword or the knife.

Don't be a fool. Mergen couldn't make the warning out loud, or tell the man, *At this moment we are allies in getting this child home alive. Don't mess it up.* He could, however, learn over his horse's neck and whisper conspiratorially to the boy, "I don't like him either. But I do like Princess Orda. If you go with your father, I will make sure that nothing happens to her."

The look that came back at him shook him to his boots. Tumbinai didn't think this khan would live long enough to protect his little niece.

"You see too much, boy," Mergen warned him. "Get those eyes of yours under control if you want to survive your grandfather's court." He let a little of his own cunning reach his eyes but didn't wait to see what effect he'd had on the boy. "Go," he told the father.

With a precise bow Daritai mounted his own horse and grabbed the reins from his son. Then, without another word he turned and led the boy away from their avid audience. His guardsmen followed, and Mergen sent a handful of his own to see them on their way. As mistakes went, he thought he'd just made a big one. The boy was innocent, but his father was a spy, going home without a treaty or a bride for the Tinglut-Khan. He couldn't bring himself to regret it. And when he heard Tayy's soft, "Thank you," at his side, he was glad.

Prince Daritai rode with sedate dignity toward the Tinglut camp. Mergen would have his own spies watching and he didn't want to arouse more suspicion, or interest, than the gur-khan had already shown. Unfortunately, this left Tumbinai with the leisure, and the breath, to talk.

"I can't believe you did that." The Tinglut court was a harsh school, but Tumbinai had learned his lessons well. In spite of his obvious distress, he kept his tone flat and emotionless. "Did you think I would leave you in enemy hands and run home to my grandfather like a frightened ewe?"

"I expected you to behave like a soldier and do as you were told. Clearly, I expected too much of you. That is my failing." Daritai had learned restraint at the same harsh knee. His heart twisted in his chest for the things he could not do—hold the boy safe and protected in his arms, rage at him for risking his life, weep for the peril which required such bravery of a child. He should be proving himself with blunted short spears at jidu, demonstrating his prowess at wrestling or in horse racing, not defending his father in an already bloody situation.

He hadn't planned to teach this particular lesson so soon, but dire need might settle it the more firmly in both heart and head. "You're fortunate that the gur-khan is a wise and a merciful man. If he'd decided to punish you for your impertinence, I'd have been honor bound to stop him. And he, to save face before his court, would have punished you even if he had to kill me to do it."

As he had hoped, Tumbinai was measuring the truth of the words, his agile mind all in his eyes. Mergen was right; he'd have to control that. Tomorrow would do for that lesson, but no later. They still had Tinglut-Khan himself to face. But the boy was adding up the afternoon and the total was tugging down at the corners of his mouth.

"He wouldn't kill us, there'd be war."

"Think, boy. Do you see a princess coming home with us?"

They had entered their own camp. Daritai spoke more sharply than he otherwise might have done, between orders to break camp and move out. Servants ran to drag down the felted tent cloths. Urged on by the sharp end of his tongue, his warriors leaped from their saddles to help in the bundling of the lattices and the packing of the wagons. At the very center of this furious burst of energy, Tumbinai sat and thought.

"We don't have a treaty," he said slowly. "I liked the toad-girl, but I don't think Grandfather would marry her."

"I think he'd be damned insulted at the offer," Daritai agreed.

Tumbinai fell silent, mulling over all that he'd seen and heard, while his father made plans and cast them aside as quickly. He had to get his son out of here, before Mergen changed his mind. Going home meant Tinglut and his half brother Hulegu, and the dangers that came of being one heir too many.

Daritai thought he might have another answer, but he had to move fast and gather more soldiers before Tinglut-Khan had a chance to react. A displaced heir was a threat to the backside sitting on the dais; he was surprised that Hulegu's assassins hadn't murdered him already. But a prince who claimed for himself the Qubal khanate became a power to be dealt with on his own terms, and if that prince claimed the title of gur-khan, khan of khans, for his father, they both might prosper.

There was the problem of the Uulgar clans in the South, whose army had gone home under a Qubal-Khan in Mergen's name. But he thought that he might strike a bargain there. The man could keep his new title and answer to no overlord. The Uulgar were, after all, far away and of no consequence to the Tinglut-Khan or to Daritai. And if, in the future, Daritai should cast his eye in that direction, he would do so for the glory of his father, with all the horsed warriors that the two ulus together, Tinglut and Qubal, could muster.

"What will happen to the gur-khan?" Tumbinai asked, and made a face. He knew the board and how the stones must lay or be swept away. Mergen might fall at the hands of a Tinglut warrior, but he was more likely to die as his brother had, of ambitious relatives, before Daritai had mustered his army. Living seemed the longest odds. "I promised the little girl she'd be safe."

It was on the tip of Daritai's tongue to remind the boy not to make promises he couldn't keep, but something stopped him, a warning in his son's eyes. They were young yet, but Chimbai's little princess in his own household, as the future wife of his son, would legitimize his claim to the Qubal khanate. His father wouldn't be happy about it, but with an ulus behind him, Daritai could deal with old Tinglut-Khan.

"That's right, you did." Daritai smiled. "We will just have to make sure that you keep your promise."

Tumbinai looked uneasy, but he slapped the boy on the shoulder. "Don't worry. The girl will be safe; that's what matters."

He left his son in the care of his guardsmen and galloped to find his own captains.

"Hurry!" he cried, gathering his warriors around him. A few of his forces must move at the pace of the wagons. The rest would travel to the tent city of the Tinglut-Khan at speed. There were armies to raise, and quickly, before Mergen brought his unruly princelings into line and the opportunity was lost.

Chapter Thirty

GREAT MOON LUN RODE HIGH in the sky, veiled by the smoke that had taken Altan to his ancestors. In the shadows cast in her pure white light, Altan's pyre stretched black and smoldering across the beaten grass. The men of the hunt had spent the day gathering turves and felling trees to supply the pyre. Tayy had worked beside them, hauling brush and logs roped to his saddle from the river. By late afternoon Bolghai had set torch to kindling; the night had passed watching the pyre burn. Midnight saw the flames fallen to glowing embers crumbling into ash.

After paying her respects, the Lady Bortu pleaded weariness and returned to the ger-tent palace. By ones and twos, the warriors and chieftains who had stayed with the khan's army followed her lead to find their own tents and their rest. Mergen had stayed until his general, with much gratitude for the honor shown his son, had led his household away to suffer their grief in privacy, and then he, too, had gone, to his bed. Perhaps to one offering more human comforts, but Prince Tayy didn't want to know about that. Sechule had wandered among the lesser mourners, leading the gur-khan's gaze like a tame lamb until she attached herself to a knot of women making their way home while the flames still burned. Goodwives, they didn't acknowledge her presence among them. Given the power of her whispers in the court's ear, neither did they turn her away.

The prince noted it all with maddening clarity. The three shamans conferred over the fire and his cousin the poet with a lute in his hands plucked out some song to commemorate the life returning in smoke to its ancestors. With his face closed and secret, Qutula had stayed at his side for most of the night. Pleading only a desire to support his prince in his sorrow, he had allowed no one to approach until, as Great Moon shone down on them from the very top of the sky, he had drifted to the edge of the thinning crowd and quietly slipped away.

Tayy thought he ought to send someone to watch him, but the only person he trusted with the errand lay in cinders on the pyre. He wanted Jumal back in his own company, and General Yesugei to guard his uncle while Jochi digested the bitter herbs of his grief. But they were far to the south with the Uulgar prisoners, now vassals of the Qubal. The death of one soldier seemed hardly sufficient to require their return.

"Grim thoughts for a grim day." Bolghai had come upon him silently, while his mind had lingered on his departing cousin. As with everything the shaman said, his words held a riddle connected at their center to Tayy's own thoughts.

"I think he wants to kill me," he said. "I think he worried Altan would figure that out. Duwa must have guessed as much and solved the problem for him."

"Clever boy," the shaman approved while Prince Tayy watched the woman, Toragana, approach his cousin Bekter with a promise in her smile. Bekter seemed not to mind the stuffed bird nesting on her head; his answering smile was warm and full of memories. So. The royal poet slung his lute onto his back. Taking the hand of the shamaness, he led her away from the crowd. Tayy didn't begrudge them their happiness, but he felt like he'd swallowed a coal from the pyre, and that it had lodged beneath his breastbone where his heart should be.

"Am I going to die?" he asked more of the blighted night than the shaman. But the shaman heard, and answered anyway.

"Of course," he said. "But as to when, who knows?"

He did know, though. Tayy could see it in his eyes. "Will it matter?" He qualified the question. "To the ulus? To anyone?"

"Oh, yes. I can assure you that your death will matter." Bolghai gave him one of those enigmatic smiles with more mischief in it than seemed called for under the circumstances. Then, with a little hop in his step, the shaman walked away.

"It will matter to me."

Eluneke. She'd come up behind him, silent as Bolghai had been, and had heard the conversation he'd meant only for his own ears, really. He felt like a whining fool when he remembered it, but she took his hand in hers and said, "Your death means everything to the ulus."

She didn't say it wouldn't happen. In fact, she said it as though it already *had* happened. So, again. At least he knew. He let her draw him away from the dying embers, down to the place they counted as their own by the side of the river, where the light of Great Moon scarcely penetrated the mossy trees.

Qutula rode out past the glow of firelight. His heart felt light and he grinned in anticipation as he left behind him the gloom of a court in mourning. His lady was pleased with him. The fizz she sent through his limbs, like a well-fermented kumiss, might have addled the mind of a lesser man, but it spurred Qutula to greater feats of clearheaded machinations. Dead or sent away or in mourning, the greatest threats to his conspiracy now littered the field of the vanquished. Power fueled his sleepless energy. He would have laughed at the exultant pleasure of it, but restrained himself that much, to ride in silence. He didn't own the night yet and wouldn't have his plans ruined by a chance ear.

He found a place protected in shadows cast by an outcrop of rock and filled with flowers that had lost their color in the moonlight. There he dismounted and laid his coat on the ground. This time, he knew she would come and threw himself down on his coat to wait with the smell of the flowers in his nose and the pleasure of a plan well begun coursing through his veins. He had stripped the prince of his protectors; soon Tayyichiut, son of Chimbai, would be dead. With his rivals out of the way, the khan would look to his son for an heir. The thought warmed him and, in spite of his intentions, he slept.

It was no surprise that Toragana led him to her shaman's tent. They'd left the girl, his sister it now seemed, at Altan's funeral pyre. She couldn't have arrived before them except in her totem form, but Toragana assured him she wouldn't take that route. "It's much too soon," she said as they passed under the watchful eye of the stuffed raven over her door. "The risk is too great that she would lose her way."

By that, he thought she meant that the girl might turn into a toad and stay that way, permanently. There were other hazards to that calling as well, however. Only the initiate, and the occasional foreign god, might know the mystery of dream travel, the nether region between their world and the next by which the shaman moved through the mortal realm. He'd never heard of a shaman who entered the dreamscape and failed to return, but he supposed it could happen. As a poet, the tragic possibilities captured his imagination. As a brother, however, the same images made him shudder with dread. Sensibly, he figured Eluneke would walk home.

"I didn't know she was my sister the last time we met," he reminded the shamaness. He'd thought her a threat to the prince's standing, if not his life. Now he didn't know what to think. "I'd like to talk to her again, now that I know we're related."

"And you will." She took the lute from his back and leaned it against her worktable, then drew him to her bed of feathers and furs, her mind and her nimble fingers focused on the ties of his coats. "But not tonight."

She was with Prince Tayyichiut, he guessed, and figured he ought to be more worried about that. Mergen needed them both for marriages of state and he'd charged Bekter with keeping an eye on her. But Altan was dead and Duwa a slave. Things seemed to be falling apart and he knew enough of legendry and the old songs to recognize the signs of disaster that followed when kings set their own will above the will of the gods. He would never accuse his father of hubris, but an excess of caution could prove just as costly.

Toragana had taken off his coat and was working on his breeches. Politely he had begun to slide her shaman's robes from her shoulders, but his heart wasn't in it. Tonight he felt too sad for the pleasures of her flesh.

She must have read his thoughts in the hesitation of his fingers, because she stilled him with her hands over his heart. "My spirit is heavy with many sorrows, too," she told him, "but if you would do me the kindness, I would wish to be held a little before you go."

He hadn't known until she asked, but it was exactly what he needed as well. He told her so with a kiss and lute-string roughened fingertips upon her skin. Lying face-to-face, with arms and legs entwined, her forehead resting lightly on his brow, he felt the tightness of his grief ease a little bit. When his fingers began to relearn the map of her skin, she didn't complain, but stroked his own more coarsely drawn country with her lips. They didn't laugh the way they had before; desire became a drowning thing, with sorrow left on the shore like old clothes for a little while. Not all magic, he realized, required a potion or a spell.

"My sons have gone to the beds of strangers, my only daughter to the heir. All that I've worked for is coming undone, Sechule, and once again I find myself back here with you."

He had followed her blindly to the tent she shared with her children for no reasons of secrecy, but out of blind need where she led him. It was smaller than he remembered, two lattices crowded with bedding and the worktable where she mixed her herbs, but with few of the luxuries he should have provided for the mother of his sons. Chimbai had wanted no claims on his younger brother, but Chimbai was long dead now, back the other side of a war they had fought and won without him. And without him they must go on, though the world seemed to fall like the ash of Altan's pyre around them. Perhaps his mother had been right all along.

As if reading his mind, Sechule answered the melancholy litany of his thoughts, both spoken and not, with an old challenge lightly laid. "Perhaps you should take that as a sign from the gods and marry me."

She stroked his face, her eyes dark with invitation. Her lips fell lightly apart, drawing his attention to the rush of her heated breath and he thought, *Yes, perhaps it's right this time.* He knew it was a weakness, to forget the fights and her ambition. But Mergen's body clenched with the promise of solace in eyes that seemed to swallow him whole. He could have her beside him for all the nights of his life, desire quenched with no greater effort than to reach his arm across the blankets . . .

"Yes," he said, and met her light tone though it cost him, because the sorrow was still there like a blight on his heart. "Perhaps, when the prince has been made khan, and I have stepped down to live out my days as a well-loved adviser, we can marry and grow old together with our sons and our grandchildren around us."

It wasn't what she wanted to hear, and he couldn't figure out what he'd done now. She'd known, from the beginning . . . she couldn't have thought . . . He would give her all he was and all he had to himself alone, but she must know that she would never be khaness, her sons would never follow him on the dais. He owed that duty to his brother.

That she had not known, or had not accepted this simple fact, showed itself in the cooling of her ardor.

"Don't think about it now." She gave a little rueful laugh, as though she had come out the butt of some cruel joke, but her fingers paused only a moment as they stripped him of his sword and dagger, and his clothes. "Who knows what the future will bring."

The way she said it, he thought perhaps the rumors about

witchcraft had more truth in them than he had ever believed.
What do you know? "Can you read my fortune in the bottom of
a cup, then, and promise me a wife with skin as soft as butter,
with hair like the mane of a fine black mare?"

"And fine strong sons to give offerings to the spirits for your
soul."

With Altan lately dead he thought the promise of sons to see
him on his own way to the ancestors less than tactful. But she
drew him down into her soft bed and welcomed him into her
arms with an indulgent smile. "Think later," she admonished
him. "You can be gur-khan in the morning. Tonight, you are my
intended husband and entitled to an accounting of what I bring
to this match."

She meant her body, and he took possession like a husband
while he planned the campaign to capture her soul, which remained remote and out of his reach. As he fell asleep between
her breasts, he thought perhaps when they had married, she
would open that door to him as well.

B y Great Moon Lun, Eluneke could see the Qubal heading
back to the tent city of the khan. Bathed in that stark white
light, the pyre of the prince's follower, Altan, showed stark and
black. The descent into the little dell where the Onga River ran,
however, became a descent into moist and earthy darkness.

Taking his hand, Eluneke led the prince carefully down into
the pitchy night that wrapped the trees. "Not magic," she assured him as all the details of leaf and tree disappeared into the
darkness.

He knew that, of course. "I wish it were," he answered, and
she heard the pain of his loss and the knowledge of more to
come tighten the words in his throat. "We could hide down
here in the dark until it was all over up there."

She understood the sentiment, but there was no hiding
from fate. Before her mystical eye, his face was losing its flesh,
the beautiful young warrior she loved fading to flensed bone as
each step took them deeper into the darkness. Above, a dry leaf

rustled with a purposeful tread. They had picked up a guard, possibly an assassin, but she didn't think so yet. Qutula was occupied elsewhere. Tears welled in her eyes, but she didn't stop. Didn't need to warn the prince either. Though he divided most of his attention between the treacherous climb and her face, he stole a glance back at the moving shadows where the sound had come from.

"I don't think Qutula can afford to lose another man yet," he said, which summed up her own thoughts on their unwanted companion.

Between them, they knew the lay of the land along the river better than any of Qutula's Durluken, or the Nirun. The spy, or guardsman, came no further as Eluneke and her prince made their way by touch among the dark and looming trees. Finally, she knew by the soft press of moss underfoot that they had come to their own special place. Tayy folded his legs and sat with his back against the tree sacred to King Toad. Eluneke followed him, pensively resting her chin on the arms crossed over her knee.

"So are you a real shaman now?" he asked, "I saw a lot in my travels, but never someone climbing lightning before." He'd seen wonders, however, and this one, she recognized, had frightened him only for her sake.

"Not yet," she answered glumly. Eluneke still had one more task to complete. She had to travel to the underworld and return with the knowledge to lead the dying to their ancestors. This was the last, most terrifying step: to travel with the dead and learn their secrets, and return unscathed. And she would have to cajole the soul of the prince back to the living with her.

"I am committed to saving you," she said, knowing the trap his mind was caught in.

"I don't know how," he answered glumly. "My uncle won't see the danger, or if he does, refuses to believe his eyes."

Eluneke winced at the mention of the gur-khan who was, it seemed, also her father.

"I'm sorry." He hurried to apologize for hurting her with the reminder, but she didn't shy away from the thought.

"It doesn't matter what he wants, you know, or who he

would see us marry to secure the peace. You're my husband by the gods' light." Her visions had made that clear enough, so she hadn't given much thought to his feelings in the matter. Hadn't given much thought to her own feelings come to that. She'd accepted it as she accepted that her hair was thick and her hands square and more useful than pretty.

He was a prince, which was nice, but he was about to die, which wasn't. She had felt herself drawn to him at first sight, but hadn't expected the way her body went still and watchful whenever he came into view or the unthinking way she moved to meet him with all her nerves tingling when he looked back at her. From that first vision in the doorway of Toragana's tent, however, she had known the urge to rage and weep at the sightless skull that came between his face and her eyes. If she couldn't save him, how could he be her husband? If she couldn't save him, how could she live without him?

Her husband. He'd accepted her from the first and had joined in her loving conspiracy to save him without understanding why she was worth fighting his uncle for. They still had to work around the whole dead thing, though.

"Then we have to convince my uncle, your father, very quickly, before the gods have made you a widow."

"Don't joke about it." She hadn't meant to sound so angry, but she wouldn't hear him give up. If she had to follow him onto his pyre and drag him away from the gods by the force of her arms and her will, she wouldn't let him go.

"Sorry." He ducked his head to hide his confusion and misery, but she sensed it rolling off his skin in waves. "Altan is already dead. I should be glad my uncle sent Jumal away, or he'd be dead now, too, I think. So I have to ask myself which is best: do I fight my cousin, and my uncle, too, if necessary to stay alive, knowing that it will cost the lives closest to me and that I will die anyway? Or do I give Qutula the opportunity he's waiting for and end it quickly, without the loss of all the innocent life that stands between us."

"Don't say it! Don't give up, don't ever give up!" She took his face between her hands, as if she could impress on him the absolute necessity that he fight even a losing battle against his cousin. "The gods gave you to me, and you will fight until I give you permission to stop, which will be never. If the task were truly impossible, they would not have promised happiness at the end of it." Fate had promised her a husband. The happiness part she came up with on her own, but she was determined to make that happen as well.

"It doesn't have to be impossible," her prince corrected her, his own hands trailing fingers through her maiden's loose tresses. "It need only be unacceptable." He kissed her with tears and fierce longing and she knew she would be his downfall and wept.

"Not for me," she berated him. Her knees tucked under her chin, she rocked inconsolably. "Do *not* trade your life for mine, I forbid it!"

"You have taken to the role of princess with remarkable speed, but I am still the heir." He joked gently, brushing her hair back and wiping the damp from her cheeks. "I give the orders here, and I command that you stop crying this instant. I'm not dead yet, and until it happens, we won't know how we are meant to stop it."

"I don't think I'm going to be a biddable wife." She wrinkled her nose at him to show her displeasure at his lordly manners but brought the argument back to the urgent promise she required of him. "But I'll make this bargain with you. If you don't make any stupid deals with your cousin, I'll try to be an obedient wife."

He tilted his head so that it rested against the tree at his back and looked up into the graying sky. "No you won't," he said with a little smile on his face.

"Probably not," she agreed. "But I'll do anything I can for you if you just ask."

"I know." He took her hand in his, kissed her knuckles with the breath of a sigh. "Sit with me," he asked, "until I have to go."

"Always," she said, meaning: "I will always be here for you, no matter what."

He seemed to understand all that and more that she hadn't even put into thoughts yet. He didn't exactly relax, but he let her carry some of his burden. Between them, they found some peace in that. That peace seemed short-lived. Nearer at hand than any assassin should have been able to approach unheard, the leaves shifted lightly.

"Ribbit."

With the keen insight of the shaman, Eluneke saw that King Totad, with his crown of leaves, had crept down his tree and settled nearby, contemplating them with kingly measure. It was too dark for the prince's eyes to make out the shape, but he had heard—Eluneke saw the shifting of shadows as he turned his head toward the voice in the dark.

"What did he say?" Tayy asked, "Is it King Toad?"

"Ribbit," King Toad repeated.

"Yes, it is." Her time with the sky god and his daughters had taught her many things, and among them the languages of the animals, so she understood that he was offering his own cautious support.

"His majesty says he's had enough of adventures but will defend this place, his own realm, with all the power of the toads."

"Ribbit!" King Toad swelled his throat, which flushed with a florid warning of the poison exudations of his skin.

"We are welcome here, to share in the peace of the mossy trees under his protection." Eluneke translated, and again, when the prince asked, "Thank him for me, please," with the formality of one royal to another.

"Croak!"

With a bob of his head to acknowledge the courtesy, the king of the toads withdrew, leaving them with the illusion of privacy, though Eluneke knew more than one set of toady eyes were watching them. They were her totem, however, closer to her in some ways than her own skin. In her totem form, they *were* her own skin. So she rested under the prince's arm, her head leaning on his shoulder, and said nothing of Great Moon Lun chasing her brothers from the sky.

Qutula woke with the smell of moist earth in his nose. By the drugged heaviness of his limbs he guessed that he had slept for some time. The stars that had glittered in a clear sky above the rocks where he'd lain his coats had vanished, but the dark remained, more complete than any night he had ever known. His coats were gone, and so were his clothes and his weapons, but beneath him the softness of silk cradled his naked back. No breeze stirred. He lay alone, surrounded by stone, with only the fragment of jade from the battlefield sprawled by its golden thread across his heart to cover him.

"What?" He tried to rise; the question had escaped his sleep fogged senses. With a moment to orient himself, he knew the truth. Only his lady of mystery could have found him in the shadows cast by the tumbled stones, and only she would have troubled to remove his hunting clothes. But where had she brought him? And where had she gone?

A cool, firm hand, lightly cupped over the jade talisman, pressed him back, then lifted, leaving him bereft even of her shadow. He didn't try to rise again; didn't think he could, so there wasn't much point in trying except to make a fool of himself.

"Where are my clothes?"

"Safe." He'd never disrobed in her presence before. It felt dangerous to do so now and his body tightened with the anticipation.

He heard a sound like the snapping of fingers, smelled sulfur, and a lamp leaped to life, its flame quickly hidden behind its shutters. By the smothered light he saw that she had set it on an outcrop of stone that roughened the otherwise smooth curve of a low-roofed cavern. Underground. How had she brought him there? Beneath him lay his mother's best coat—he recognized it in the half-light—and about him other items of silk or gold set with precious stones, that he recognized from the camp. Then his lady crossed into the light.

Though her long dark hair hid her face from him, her emerald green coats hung open from her shoulders, lamplight gilding her naked curves. Her legs remained partly in shadow; he made out just the suggestion of their long, curving sweep, outlined in the golden light. Almost absently her hands met across her belly, kneading softly the flesh over her womb like an invitation. Never before had she made herself so vulnerable to his eyes.

Qutula's arms felt heavy when he reached for her. "Let me hold you." He meant to command her, but it sounded too much like pleading in his own ears to please him.

This time, however, she allowed it. "Of course, my beloved."

He could see her smile behind the drape of hair that crossed her cheek. Then she came to him, dropping the coats she wore in a heap on the ground before standing astride him. The lethargy that had overwhelmed him on waking had gone, but looking at her, he couldn't breathe for a moment. In the half-light of the shuttered lamp, what he could see of her was as beautiful as feel had taught him in the dark and he wanted to touch her again, to relearn the delicate sensations of her skin against his rough fingertips, against his belly and thighs.

Her ankles rested on either side of his hips and he took them in his hands, smoothed the skin of her calves, following that curve like a swan's neck to her thighs. He pulled her down so that she must kneel to him, over him. Her breasts came within his reach and he took them, soft in his hands, and drew her down to bury his mouth in them.

"This time tomorrow, it will be over," he said, meaning the prince's death.

And, "How," she answered back. "How will it be done?"

"By poison. The vial in my sleeve."

Her fingers traced the knife-sharp bones of his face and he turned his head to kiss her wrist where it poised near his lips. She would, he supposed, return his coats with the prince's death folded in the cuff. "Already I've dosed him in small amounts. The whole court believes he suffers some malady of evil spirits. When he dies suffering the same ache in his gut, they can have no suspicion. I have eaten the same food as he, after all, and drunk from the same bowl."

His mother had provided him the antidote, which Qutula had taken with great care. No suspicion would fall on him.

"And if he doesn't eat or drink the tainted food? Or if he

survives the poison?" Her voice was muffled, her face buried in his neck then lower, trailing a flicking dry tongue over the taut flesh that banded his rib cage. Not a human tongue, but when her fingers were so busy elsewhere on his flesh, it was hard to remember why that might matter.

"Then war," he answered, thinking, *One, two, three,* and *who knew he had so many ribs?* Not enough of them, if it meant she had come to the end of that careful addition of their sum. He had other parts, however. His belly, his hip: she found each with her mouth and explored it with her fingertips, leaving the bloody traces of her sharp nails to show where she had gone.

"Steal the girl," she murmured into the hollow of his throat. "If the poison fails, the prince will look for her. You can draw him away from the court and kill him then."

She was right. A hostage would simplify the murder of the prince, if it came to a fight. Qutula hesitated to tell her so; he hated taking orders from a woman, even his mother, who had worked all her life to put him on the dais. He didn't want this one to think she could control him with her ideas.

"Of course, I may have misjudged you." Her cool belly brushed against his softly, but she withdrew from him with her voice. "She is your sister, after all."

And his father had acknowledged her before either of the sons who had served him all their lives. "As Tayyichiut is my cousin," he agreed at least on the kinship. "She is one more obstacle between my father and his true heir." Once the prince was safely murdered, the girl would follow him to the ancestors. Killing her would be easier than holding her hostage, though.

"She's a shamaness and I am no bridegroom kidnapping his willing bride. She can vanish into the dreamscape and travel anywhere at the speed of thought. How do we take and hold her against her will?"

As he talked, he traced circles insubstantial as a kiss around the pink nipple that brushed his fingertips.

"With this." From around his neck the lady of mysteries plucked the gold thread and passed it over her own head, so that the smooth jade fragment rested gleaming over her burnished breasts. "Let me keep it for a little while; you will have it back soon enough. When the time comes, set the talisman around the girl's neck. At our command, the power it binds will pin her to the mortal realm, invisible to her teachers in the dreamscape, until she goes to meet her ancestors. Which will, I trust, be soon."

"Then we are agreed."

Though he felt more naked in its absence than he had from his lack of clothing, Qutula didn't ask when she would return the jade talisman, or how. A lifetime spent in the tent of his mother had taught him not to question certain powers but to command them through others, by cunning. Now, the thought of such powers in his hands fed his desire. He would have tipped her over and taken her in one sweep of his strong body, but she nipped him more than playfully on the shoulder and he felt a cold like death spread from the wound.

"I will give you the means to take the dais of your father," she said, though as yet she had done little more than suggest the ways by which he might do it for himself.

He owed her nothing, but it cost him less to humor her, at least until the princess his sister had gone to her ancestors. He might need her help for that. So he lowered his lashes humbly and answered, "I am in your debt, my lady."

"I know. And tonight you will give me my heart's desire in payment of that debt."

Her voice, imperial and desperate, fired his senses. "You already have it," he assured her. "The prince will die tonight, I swear it." The bargain cost him little. He had already told her of his intention to kill his cousin that very day.

"Not enough, not enough," she groaned into his ear. Frustrated in his desire to have her, it was on the tip of his tongue to rebuff her demand and override her objections by force, if necessary. But: "It's time," she moaned, her voice rising in an anguished cry of desire more powerful than any he had felt in her before.

"Oh, gods, my fathers, it's time!" With those strange words she took his willing body inside her, rocking with little moans, "Mine, mine."

He thought she meant himself, her willing property at such moments, and answered, "Yours, yours."

Suddenly, she went very still over him. He would have screamed, or strangled her until she had no choice but to serve his body or die, but the cold on his shoulder was spreading. She might kill him if he tried.

He needn't have feared, however. She said only, "Do you mean it? Mine?"

How could she doubt? When she had him in this way, at least. "Anything," he answered, "I have sworn my life to you. Anything I am is yours." The thing about promises, he had already learned, was that they were so easy to make when they served him, and so easy to break when that served him better.

He could tell by her sigh of satisfaction, by the renewed interest she showed in his body, that she had believed him. When finally he had spent himself inside her once, and again by the power of his youthful vigor and her eager encouragement, she lay across him weak with her own pleasure.

"You, too, have made promises, my lady," he said, and brushed her hair aside with fingers gone slack with satisfaction. "Before I leave this place, I must know who you are."

"Time," she agreed, and lifted her head. Suddenly, it seemed as though a hood had been lifted from his eyes, so that he could see for the first time.

"My Lady Chaiujin!" His heart stuttered in his chest, for reflected in her human eyes he saw the slitted obsidian of the serpent. Framing her sweet oval face he saw the faint tracery of a serpent's green scales. A part of him, he realized, had known all along that it was she, or something very like the serpent-demon who had taken the Tinglut princess' place in his uncle's bed. Torn between a natural terror and covetous lust, he wondered if Chimbai-Khan had seen the demon behind the human face of his second wife, and if he had courted the danger in the pleasure, until it killed him.

She must have seen the confused lust in his eyes, because she smiled and revealed to him the forked tongue that flicked pleasure where his neck joined his shoulder. Her sinuous hands stroked him and he felt the smooth dry shift of scales against his skin when she wrapped her legs around him.

Qutula grinned up at her, then quick as any snake rolled her under him. "With you beside me, and your power in my grasp, we can rule the world." He took the globes of her breasts in his hands; through the pale green of her skin, a rosy blush deepened at their tips as he mapped the paths of his conquests on her flesh. She wanted him, and by her acquiescent smile let him know that she would allow his dominance this once.

He took what she offered, kissed her mouth with its strange tongue and plunged deep between her parted legs. Still a woman there, she could not become fully serpent while he pressed her thighs apart. Then he was done, gasping for breath while his sweat fell, drop, drop, drop, on her dry, smooth skin. Her fingers soothed him, tracing the fall of his braids on his shoulder.

As he drifted to sleep, he felt the slither of a serpent cross his flesh. Reaching out with the last strength of his arm for her, he let the smooth scales glide effortlessly through fingers growing numb and heavy and strange. Without knowing quite how it had happened, he surrendered consciousness to strange and pain-filled dreams.

Chapter Thirty-one

IN HER SERPENT form the false Lady Chaiujin left the comfort of her nest for the grassy surface. Great Moon Lun had set, but Little Sun had not yet risen; she moved by starlight too pale to aid a human eye, and the vibration of the air, which she sensed with her flicking tongue. Wrapped around her green scales she wore the golden thread, with the fragment of smooth round jade balanced on her back.

Once that fragment had formed the bottom of a drinking bowl, the match to a wedding cup carried by the god-king Llesho. At the bottom she had incised her image, a coiled rune that tied her demon soul to his more godlike one. He'd used her badly in his war against the demon-king, but that was over now. The cup was broken, her mark carved in skin instead of jade. A new war began; if she moved the stones on the board just so, she might go home or, barring that, place on the dais of the khan the son now growing in the egg she carried. What that child would be she did not know. Already, however, she felt the power of his demon kind stir within her womb.

But first she must remove the obstacles to his ascendancy who littered the ger-tent palace: the khan's heir, and the khan. Then Qutula, her lover, must die to make way for his own demon son. She thought perhaps she would eat him when the time came, and feed bits of him to his son, to give him strength in the nest. And, of course, the girl who stood to defend the heir, and who might produce her own offspring of power to contest the dais with Qutula's son—first, she must be rid of the girl.

She had come to the place she had intended and, hidden by the darkness, returned to human form. Around her the painstakingly slow process of rebuilding, stone by stone, hand by hand, the shrine of the khan her former husband, had begun. No one had touched the tumble of shards from which the sliding hiss of a thousand serpents whispered on the night air.

Before she rested, she must rid her nest of the human she had used to fertilize her egg. Then she had one last task. Drawing the round flat circle of jade from between her breasts where it had fallen, she called to her serpent brethren, summoning a demon of her own kind. "Brother serpent, sister snake, my father bids you come to me."

She repeated the incantation not once but a hundred times, until the ground beneath her feet seethed with snakes, coming not only from their nearby nests within the ruin of the khan's shrine. Far across the grass she saw the undulation of their backs, so that the grass itself seemed to blow against the wind. All of these were mortal snakes, kin with the power to kill, but not the skills of a demon to block the magic of the shamaness. These she sent to find the human hidden in her underground nest and carry him on their backs to the surface, to the cover of sharp upthrusting rocks where he had thought to await her. She forbade them his murder, but commanded that he must be gone before he awoke. He must never find her nest.

When they had slithered away to do her bidding, she took up her chant again, searching the fading night with more than sight for one of her own kind. Most of her demon kin had been cast back into the underworld by the combined armies of gods and humans during the great battle high above the Golden City. Finally, however, when she feared the loss of darkness to the dawn, an answer came.

"Mistress." A snake, thick and black, with markings on its

back, rose up on its tail to salute her. "I bow before you and your child." He dipped his head to her belly and continued, "What would you have of me?"

"Your power, for a day, a week," she answered, imperious in command. Her father was a king in the underworld, and she would soon be mother to a khan in this. "A girl, to be hidden, her power muted for a while."

Qutula had promised to kill the prince soon. She would have done it herself more efficiently, but needed something by which to control her lover. Murder of his father's heir seemed a likely tool, and he had promised that his plan would escape suspicion, or a costly war. But just in case he failed, she added, "We may need her later, so don't do any damage."

"As you wish," the serpent answered with another bow of his wedge-shaped head on its long neck.

With that, she took him in her hand and with his own sharp fangs carved the coiled rune into the bottom of the shattered cup, which like a coin now lay on her palm. He grinned at her and poison dripped from his fangs onto the fresh carving.

"You may go now," she told him, setting him down in the grass. "You'll know it when the token finds its way onto the throat of the girl, and you will come to my bidding as if I had summoned you that very moment. She must not use her powers, nor may shaman or magician find her. If any human comes near who is not bound to myself, or to my Lord Qutula, they must see only grass where her tents are raised, and only sheep where her guards stand watch. None may find her by magical or earthly means."

"As you wish, my lady." The black serpent writhed into a knot of courtesy as a lesser demon to the daughter of a king, and when she released him, sidled away in the grass. He wouldn't go far, she knew. There were gaps among the broken stones where he might rest and many female snakes who wriggled enticingly nearby.

The wan light of Little Sun had begun to touch the sky with false dawn. She quickly made her way to her sleeping lover, now lying among his scattered clothes in the grass where the snakes had left him, and replaced the jade token on his breast.

Then she adopted her serpent form again and returned, unseen, to the borrowed comforts of her nest.

Languorous in satisfaction, Mergen, great gur-khan of the Qubal and the Uulgar clans, yawned and scratched absently at his crotch. "If we are to wed," he told Sechule, "I should start wooing you with presents."

Sechule smiled with downcast eyes as she handed him a cup of tea. He had already forbidden her the prize she wished, and now he proposed to buy her with trifles. But scorn would come later, when her son had won for her the place her lover had refused her. Now, she gave him a flirtatious smile through gritted teeth and teased, "A fine silk coat then, or, no, two fine silk coats, with the most elaborate embroideries." She could at least replace the finery that had vanished lately from her tent. "And a jewel bead for my hair. I must at least compete with the other noble wives."

"You will be the most elegant of wives," he promised, "All the coats and gowns you wish, and I'll choose the beads personally to enhance the glory of your hair."

He was teasing her, she knew, as well he meant it, too. She kissed him and helped him dress, thinking, she would have all the silk coats she wanted, and the headdress of a khaness if not a wife, when her son defeated him and took the dais and the ulus with it from his father's dead hands. The thought of murder lit her eyes with pleasure that he took for admiration. With one arm he drew her close and kissed her while she thought, poison, or perhaps a dagger to his kidney, once Qutula had begun his war.

PART FOUR

THE SHAMANS'
WAR

Chapter Thirty-two

"**O**UR GUESTS don't come to us today," Lady Bortu commented, over her breakfast, needling him between bites of crumbly cheese and millet stew. "The treaty which would have bartered your daughter for peace remains unpledged."

Mergen had noticed. "The Tinglut packed their tents while our noble Altan made his journey to his ancestors. By now they are doubtless halfway home." He had offered as a bride for the Tinglut-Khan a shamaness who traveled in the shape of a toad inside the coats of his heir. Daritai would have seen the insult of that match on so many levels that he might not even have considered the murder in his decision. Mergen admitted to himself that the negotiations could have gone better.

"And what do you plan to do about it?" The beads of his mother's elaborate horned headdress clacked and swayed as she spoke, a reminder of the power of her station. She had made more than one khan, and could make another of her blood if not her womb.

Smothering a sigh, he glared in the Lady Bortu's direction, careful not to meet her eye, however. He didn't want to have this conversation now. Didn't want to have it at all until he'd dealt with the unruly youths of his court, and they hadn't shown up yet. She would not, however, leave the thing undone.

"You need Yesugei."

She didn't accuse him of a mistake in sending the general away with his ten thousand of Uulgar, but it was in his own mind that he had. He would certainly need Yesugei and those conquered troops if he wished to use force against the Tinglut where marriage had failed. Picking over the breakfast for which he had no appetite, he considered whom to send as messenger to bring them back. Not Jochi, who was needed here and whose grief put him at risk in a mission of personal danger. He gestured instead for Chahar, who came forward with a deep bow. He had, Mergen noted, his father's eyes, though with none of the shaman's otherworldly gaze.

"Take a message to our beloved Yesugei-Khan," he said. "Tell him that his gur-khan wishes his company, and that of his armies."

Chahar bowed and left, carrying with him a turquoise bead as a gift for the general and the understanding that he would report all he had seen and heard for the general's intelligence. Turquoise meant the threat of war, though not at imminent approach. Yesugei would come with his armies, in good order and fresh for fighting.

Mergen would not attack his peaceful neighbor. Marriages might, after all, still join the uluses in one blood within a generation. But if there would be war, he had no doubt who would win it. His heir would take his place as gur-khan over all the grasslands, an emperor to rival that of Shan. The Lady Bortu, noting the turquoise bead, grinned at him and ate her breakfast.

His mother was out when Qutula returned home late in the day to change into the blue coat of a guardsman. The firebox was still warm, but his mother's kettle was empty. At some time during the night, while dreams of a thousand vipers seething in the grass troubled his sleep, the Lady Chaiujin, his once-secret lover, had taken away the smooth jade shard he wore. In its place she had returned the token he had carried from a distant battlefield, with its coiled ruin carved on its face. Or she'd replaced it with another like it, though he'd thought it a rare piece when he'd picked it up. This one itched like bees swarming where it touched his skin.

Sechule kept a mirror pointed at the doorway to repel demons, or so she might tell the clients for her potions. Their own faces, reflected in the polished silver, were said to terrify the evil spirits into flight. Not all the mirrors in the ger-tent palace had stopped the Lady Chaiujin from becoming the khan's wife, of course. Buckling his sword at the waist of his blue coat, he cast a glance in that direction, half expecting to see the reflection of his lady's obsidian eyes. The strange serpent staring back startled him. Qutula had come to terms with his lover's other nature, however, and accepted the sinister-looking demon as her acolyte.

"Welcome," he greeted the creature.

"How did you know I was here?" Mangkut slipped over the threshold, staring about him for other spies in the shadows.

"I didn't."

"Oh."

Mangkut hadn't seen the serpent, which had vanished as soon as he turned away from the mirror, and Qutula chose not to enlighten him. *Let him be nervous,* he thought, as his follower licked his dry lips. *Fear will keep him sharp.* Duwa he considered a necessary loss, to part the prince from his closest allies, but he couldn't spare Mangkut as well. At least, not yet.

"What report do you have?"

As he expected, Mangkut had gathered for his captain the intelligence of his Durluken, posted throughout the camp. He drew out a cord with small beads tied at regular intervals and fingered the first of them as he spoke.

"The Tinglut have run off. Scouts have scattered to track them," he said, and his fingers moved to the next bead. "The gur-khan has sent for General Yesugei."

Qutula gave a nod to acknowledge the news. "And our Prince Tayyichiut?" He had assigned Mangkut to watch the prince and report on his movements through the night.

"With the Lady Eluneke, as you surmised." Mangkut's fingers slipped to the next bead on the cord. "They spent the night together by the river."

"Have they returned to the palace?"

"Not yet. They talked through the night." Mangkut smirked. "I left when they fell asleep."

Qutula hated the little dell with its dense and tangled span of forest where the river ran, waiting to drag him down into the underworld at the first misstep. The thought of sleeping on its banks raised the hairs on the back of his neck. Prince Tayy seemed to like it, but with the girl he'd given Qutula a powerful tool to use against him.

"The gur-khan won't be happy. He has political marriages in mind." He didn't mention the toad part. That couldn't have pleased his father either. Qutula had no such inclinations, either to become a toad or to wed one.

"If the prince won't honor the gur-khan's wishes," Mangkut suggested, "he has more loyal kin to whom he may look."

"I can't speculate." Qutula dropped his eyes, properly abashed. He had no right to claim his father yet. Once he freed the gur-khan from his obligation to Chimbai's son, however, he would make of himself a more dutiful heir.

"And I can only serve." With his tight grin and his bow, Mangkut showed that the Durluken likewise planned for the day when their captain might lead them from the dais instead of beside it.

Qutula recognized the offer for what it was. "I'm late already to take my place at court," he said, and drew the jade talisman on its gold thread from his neck. "With my Durluken, follow the girl. When you have her alone, slip this over her head. It will dull her powers so that you can hold her. Don't hurt her if you can help it, but she must be hidden away for a while. I mean only to protect her, should the Tinglut try to answer the insult by harming her."

He expected his own plot to succeed and wouldn't need a trap to bait for the prince. But if she remained unchecked, the girl could make a nuisance of herself when Qutula wished the gur-khan focused on his own claims to be heir.

Mangkut took the jade and Qutula saw the moment when he thought to wear the talisman under his own clothes. But already the creature that inhabited it burned the Durluken's fingertips. Mangkut considered the thing with distaste and then slipped it into the deep cuff of his coat. With a final bow, he darted out of Sechule's tent to gather his companions and complete his mission.

Qutula stood a moment, lost in thought with a hand laid lightly on his mother's worktable. If nothing else, Eluneke's disappearance would occupy the shaman Bolghai, who might otherwise uncover the poison dose before it had murdered the prince. With Prince Tayyichiut dead, he would ride out with the Nirun to free the princess and destroy his own followers as renegades. Caught between grief and gratitude, his father would have no choice but to raise him to the dais. And anyone who might have told him otherwise would be dead. Settling his coat more comfortably about his shoulders, Qutula left his mother's tent for the sumptuous palace of his father. Soon, that, too, would be his.

His mother was there ahead of him, sitting above the firebox with a clutch of matrons who eyed her with frozen hostility. She returned their regard with a haughty lift of her head. The gur-khan was busy with the current Tinglut crisis, but he seemed preoccupied, stealing bewildered glances which his mother returned with cool dignity. He'd expected her to be happier about something. Sechule, for her part, seemed to be masking a simmering rage which she vented only in the way she held herself disdainfully apart from the other women.

Pretending not to notice, Qutula bowed and took his place at the foot of the dais. He looked around, but the prince had not yet returned from his night, and most of the morning, with the shaman princess. *See, Father, who is faithful and who is not,* he thought.

As if reading his mind, the gur-khan called him forward. "Have you seen your cousin the prince this morning?" he asked.

Cousin.

The world turned on the word. Mergen had spoken softly; his voice carried no farther than the dais, but General Jochi raised an eyebrow over the maps. It was a declaration; never before had he mentioned their relationship, even indirectly. At first, Qutula couldn't answer. His mind had gone numb from the shock.

"Not since last night," he finally stammered out while Mergen waited patiently for him to pull himself together. It was even the truth, though Qutula wasn't ready to mention the intelligence of his own spies yet. "The prince sent us away to be alone . . ."

Not so alone, he wished to convey, but hesitantly as if he didn't want to get his cousin in trouble. Perhaps he didn't have to commit murder after all. Mergen might be angry enough about the Princess Eluneke to supplant the heir with his own son at last.

"He's with Eluneke."

The gur-khan hadn't exactly asked, but Qutula confirmed his guess with an apologetic little shrug. "They were together the last I saw them." He would have preferred the news come from someone else, but Mergen seemed to place no blame on the messenger.

"Find him, and bring him to me. As for Elenuke, she is motherless and has no proper guide in the shamaness Toragana. Take her to your mother."

A quick glance showed Qutula that Sechule had gone.

"Ask the Lady Sechule, in my name, to prepare the girl for her place as a princess in my court. She may direct our servants to obtain for her the things she will need, the beads and silver, the silk coats, for a proper presentation. And tell her to choose the best gowns for herself as well. I want her to be the girl's guardian at court and as for more, I will let her tell you herself. Then come back and join us in our deliberations. The Tinglut have gone—"

"As you wish, my lord gur-khan." Qutula bowed and took his leave, wondering if he had time to stop Mangkut. It seemed that after his planning for war or murder, he might have his wish from the benevolent hand of his father after all. "You will be khaness yet, Mother," he muttered under his breath. The gur-khan, it seemed, was more susceptible to crotch-thinking than he had guessed, though how his father's new regard might have angered her remained unclear. But their quarrel, whatever it might be, mattered little. By tomorrow, he would be his father's heir and then, as quickly as he could safely manage it, he would be khan.

They had talked through the night, falling asleep on the soft moss when the gray of false dawn was lighting the grasslands above them. When Eluneke finally woke, the sun was high enough to strike golden sparks on the ripples of the river. Prince Tayy had already wakened and sat with his back to King Toad's tree, watching her.

"Good morning," she said, then reconsidered her greeting. "Good afternoon. Or, midday; have you been awake long? I didn't mean to sleep at all—"

"I've only been awake a few minutes."

She thought he might be lying about that, but he seemed peaceful, as if he were holding at bay for a little while the concerns of the day. Altan was dead, and not likely for a simple quarrel.

"I have to go to my uncle." The prince twirled a leaf absently in his hand, his thoughts far from her in that moment. "If our suspicions are true, the whole ulus is at risk."

"The gur-khan must be told," she agreed, though it was hard not to knock him on the head or slip him a potion, anything to keep him under her watchful eye and that of the toad people, away from the danger that circled the court.

"You'll be all right if I leave you here?" He had subtly shifted the way he carried himself, hunching his shoulders in around his heart. Peace had fled, leaving in its place the indrawn tension of one with sorrow behind him and danger ahead.

"I'll be fine," she answered. "I may not be a soldier, but I can run away better than almost anybody." She let him see the little toad of her totem in her eyes, a reminder of her powers as an apprentice shamaness. One more journey stood between her and the fullness of her station, but she had recovered well enough from her travels in the heavens and might easily escape any mortal threat through the dream realm.

"I don't want to go," he admitted, laughing a little at himself, but with so many emotions in his living eyes that they almost overwhelmed the death's-head turning his wrinkled brow to bone. Then, swooping down on her like a nervous bird, he kissed her on the lips. "I won't let him sell you off to the old Tinglut-Khan."

"That's all right, then." She tried to smile when she answered him. "I'm not sure which dismayed his emissary more—my totem form or the dirt on my face when I returned to my human shape." She didn't mention riding in the prince's jacket, the warmth of his flesh against her skin, the beat of his heart in her twiggy bones.

"I will fight for you," he told her, the words no less forceful for the speed with which they rushed from his mouth.

That wasn't what she wanted to hear. Taking his face in her hands she gave it a little shake to make sure he was paying attention to her, not the images of battle in his head. "I don't want you to die for me," she commanded. "Don't die."

"I can't promise that."

She was crying in spite of her efforts to be brave, the tears dripping off the tip of her nose. "Try," she said, and returned his kiss. But all she felt were the bare teeth of his grinning skull.

"I'll try," he agreed on the compromise. Opening fingers of bone, he released her for the upward path to the grasslands above the dell.

"Good-bye," she whispered as he went. The next time she saw him, she knew, he would be dead.

When he had passed out of sight, she turned to face the Durluken warrior hidden among the trees. "I know you're there," she said. "What do you want?"

"No one wants to hurt you." She didn't recognize him when he stepped out from behind the branches. "My captain just wants to speak with you."

"Qutula?" she asked, though she knew he must have sent them. If anyone meant her harm, it was he. She couldn't cry out. Who but the prince would hear her? She had just extracted a promise that he shouldn't risk his life for her.

Eluneke turned to run. Already she felt her totem form taking shape in her mind. It would take only a step or two, and she could escape into the dream realm. . . .

"Qutula," said a voice in her ear. Mangkut. She should have heard him coming, or felt his presence behind her, but he remained a dangerous void in her mind even now, when his hand clamped around her wrist.

"Let me go!" She kicked out at him and aimed a blow at his nose, but he dodged it, twisting her wrist painfully behind her. Another kick. He held her with her back against him, so she didn't have a good angle to do any damage. Bolghai had taught her how to run in her mind, however; if she could just distract him for a moment, she could escape, warn the prince that his cousin had moved against him.

She closed her eyes, briefly, to set her imaginary feet in motion. It was a mistake. A chip of stone suspended by a gold thread dropped over her head and evil settled like a weight over her heart.

"What?" she groped at the talisman, a fragment of jade. Her fingers couldn't seem to reach it, though her nails dug garnet rivers in the flesh of her breasts.

"Don't, don't." Mangkut grabbed for her free hand and she eluded him, swinging at his head again. The thing around her neck had clouded her perceptions, however, and the blow glanced harmlessly off his jaw. Then he had both her hands held at her sides.

"The pain will stop soon. In the meantime, my orders are to deliver you unhurt, and I will, if I have to tie your hands at your sides to do it." He was crooning as if to settle a nervous horse, but she thought he must be lying. She could abide the pain, but already the thing had robbed her of control over her body.

Why? clashed with *What have you done?* in her mind, but she knew part of it already and doubted her captors understood even as much as she did herself. The creature who inhabited the stone whispered in her ear, obscenities to which she refused to listen. She knew his kind, if not his name. She had seen his like in a green mist towering over Qutula in the wrestling match.

With the help of the grasslands and their neighbors, with dragons and magical beasts Prince Tayy had described to her, the god-king Llesho had defeated the demons' reign of terror against the gates of heaven. They had killed the demon-king in his lair and closed the crack between the worlds that had allowed him passage from his rightful domain below. On that mountaintop high above the Cloud Country, many of his minions had also perished. Some had escaped, however, and some had found their way into the world of mortals long before that fateful battle. One such had murdered Tayy's father and mother. Another, or perhaps the same, had lent its strength to the captain of the Durluken against the prince.

"Not her," the creature of the talisman whispered in Eluneke's ear. "She is the queen of us all now that the king her father is dead."

The rune carved in the fragment—she saw now it was jade—began to uncoil. A grinning serpent's head rose on a jeweled neck. She struggled to escape it, but Mangkut pulled her wrists up tightly behind her back.

"Now, now," he said, and may have crowed more, except that the creature struck, sinking fangs into her breast. She knew the effect of a viper's bite. The searing pain didn't come, however. Sleep, instead, swept over her head and she sank to her knees, the pain in her shoulders from the wrenching of her arms grew distant and meaningless. Then she didn't feel anything at all.

"I *liked* Altan." Bekter sat on the low stool the shamaness reserved for patients and picked out a random tune on his lute. "With Jumal gone, the prince needed him. His loss will hit his father hard, as well."

"An evil wind sighs through the grass," Toragana agreed in the riddle form of her calling. "Soon, it will howl."

Bekter looked up, surprised. They had spent the night as man and woman, not poet and shamaness. Now, and without warning, his innocent observation had moved them back into the professional. Her meaning seemed pretty clear, however. Altan's death had been no crime of passion or accident of temper, but murder, planned and carried out in cold blood. Not the first piece removed from the board, but the first in the current round to be swept away so unalterably. Jumal could be recalled, but Altan's return would take more seasons than the prince could spare. What greater evil awaited them he could only guess, and prayed that it didn't involve his brother.

He remembered the emerald green bamboo snake tattooed over Qutula's heart and how dismayed the khan had been to see it there. His brother had passed it off as a reminder of past injuries, perhaps a mistake brought on by drunkenness, but Qutula never drank to excess. And Altan had died at Durluken hands, so he put scant hope in that prayer.

"When do you think this evil will strike again?"

Bekter was looking into Toragana's eyes when he said it, so he saw the very moment when her gaze grew distant, then troubled.

"Now," she said, and swept up her robes from their peg on the lattices and her tall shaman's headdress with its prescient raven glaring down at him from its crown. "I have to find Bolghai."

Bekter set his lute down. Panic wouldn't help anyone. He had to ask her, though, "Has something happened to my fa . . . the gur-khan? Or the prince?"

"Not yet." She shook her head, more as if to clear her ears than to emphasize her negative, which had not carried much force behind it anyway.

"Then what?" he pressed, guessing by the controlled tension with which she prepared herself that catastrophe had struck very close to the dais.

"Eluneke has disappeared. I can't sense her presence anywhere."

The gur-khan's daughter, recognized by her father and offered as a bride to seal the treaty with the Tinglut only the day before. His own sister, come to that, but more importantly, the prince had fallen in love with her.

"Have the Tinglut kidnapped her?" he suggested. Bride capture sometimes happened even between consenting couples. But it seemed unlikely that, rejecting the girl as unsuitable, Prince Daritai would snatch her up and take her with him when he left. He might have wanted her for himself, of course, but had shown no sign of it on meeting her. The Tinglut prince had seemed truly dismayed to discover the princess, offered to his father in matrimonial bond of the peace between them, in the shape of a toad carried about in the pocket of Mergen's heir.

Toragana had more pressing reasons for believing otherwise. "I don't mean she's not here in this tent, or that she has gone from the gur-khan's camp. She is a shamaness in training under my care. I can tell you exactly where she goes and what she is doing at any point in the day, wherever she travels in this world or passing through the dreamscape. Her presence is with me always, as a part of the fabric of the universe. And now that presence has vanished like the shuttering of a lamp."

"Dead?" he asked, concerned first for his father, then for the girl herself. Evil moved, as surely as Toragana had predicted.

After a moment during which her eyes rolled back in her head and she stumbled so that he had to steady her, the shamaness shook her head. "Not dead," she assured him, though she seemed little relieved by it. "I would feel her departing spirit. The Tinglut could not have done this."

He should have taken comfort in that. If the Tinglut prince could not have accomplished whatever had been done to Eluneke, then neither could Qutula. But when he thought of the tattoo on his brother's breast, he guessed that might not be true.

"I have to go," he said. "The gur-khan will need me." Mergen would hardly desire his music, but Bekter could offer him the comforting presence of a son. As for Qutula . . .

"I'm going as well." Toragana strode over to open the door. A stoat leaped through and chittered at her briefly. Bekter thought he must be spending too much time with the shamaness; he plainly read the worry in the bright intelligent eyes of Bolghai, the gur-khan's shaman, in his totem form.

"Good luck," he said.

"Remember Alaghai the Beautiful and her brothers," Toragana answered back, though Prince Tayy was the girl's cousin and not a foreign king.

"I'll try." Bekter promised only that much, wishing it were not so easy to believe that Qutula had a hand in his half sister's disappearance. He was pleased that he managed to control his reaction when Toragana turned into a raven and flew away. The stoat had likewise gone, by routes Bekter didn't wish to explore. He had obligations as well, so he gathered up his lute and went to find his horse.

"**P**rince Tayyichiut! Prince Tayy!"

Tayy reined in his horse and waited for the riders to come up to him. He recognized Qutula's voice and wondered if his cousin had ridden out to kill him before he reached the safety of the palace. There were too many in the approaching party to fight, however, and they were too near for him to run. Fortunately, his own Nirun rode among the newcomers, their faces showing only the proper concern of guardsmen who have been thwarted far too long in their efforts to protect their charge.

"Has my uncle sent you?" he asked, "I was on my way back anyway."

"The gur-khan has sent me to request your presence," Qutula affirmed. "My father has also asked that I send a picked hand of guardsmen to escort the Princess Eluneke to the tents of the Lady Sechule, my mother, to be properly prepared to take her place at the foot of the dais."

Tayy said nothing while he calculated the import of that statement. He knew the gur-khan had acknowledged Eluneke in order to barter her as a bride with the Tinglut, and wondered how long Mergen's favor would last if they defied his wishes. As for the other, clearly his cousin's fortunes had changed in his father's court.

"He's acknowledged you, then." He turned his horse and fell in beside his cousin. Managing a smile, Tayy wondered how it would influence the plots of Mergen's blanket-son to be recognized as his father's true offspring. He might choose to delay his plans, hoping for greater favor through his superior devotion to the khan. Or the khan might have set his son above his nephew already. But Qutula gave a slight shake of his head.

"Privately only," he said. "And possibly in error."

Mergen didn't make such errors, of course. Qutula was covering his hasty appropriation of a station the gur-khan had not yet announced to the court. But if Mergen wanted Eluneke in Sechule's care, it meant he had changed his mind about his mistress as well.

Tayy was still contemplating the possible meanings of Mergen's change of heart when his cousin added, "Jochi was there."

Not so privately, then, if not a formal declaration. He wondered what Mergen had offered Sechule. His own guardsmen had ringed him about, however, and he saw not more than a face or two of Durluken—his cousin was waiting with a wry smile for him to finish taking the measure of the force that had come for him.

"My followers have cost you greatly in your friend Altan," Qutula granted with an apologetic bow of his head. "I've chastised them already, but I wouldn't insult you by asking you to ride among them."

His cousin was lying, and didn't care if he knew it. The Durluken were doubtless on some errand of mischief. But the Nirun were Tayy's own, which meant his personal safety was assured at least until they returned to the palace. Anything else would have to wait until he had talked with the gur-khan. Which was better done sooner than later. He nudged the mare's flanks with his heels and let her have her head. Qutula did the same and they raced, the tails of their horses flying out behind them, for the ger-tent gleaming in its silver embroideries.

Chapter Thirty-three

PACING DIDN'T HELP, but Eluneke's frustration pushed her to measure the small tent with her steps anyway. The count never changed, however many times she repeated the circuit of the single lattice, batted with ragged felt on the outside and with a dirty rug and a cold firebox within. Qutula's Durluken stood guard at the door but would neither speak to her nor allow her to look out. They fed her at irregular intervals, leaving her to go hungry as often as not. Sometimes Qutula himself led the guardsmen. Sometimes Mangkut or another she didn't recognize took turn and turn about as moonlight followed sunshine through the smoke hole at the top of her tent.

For news, she had only the movement of that dappled beam of light to tell her how the suns moved in the heavens, and the soughing of the wind in the trees rising above the rush of water nearby. They had hidden her in the forest near the Onga River, she deduced by these clues; not in the dell where she met with Prince Tayy but farther along its banks, where no one would think to look.

Since entering her apprenticeship, she'd had the comfort of knowing that wherever she went, she carried her teacher with her. That sensation of Toragana watching over her shoulder had vanished, however, when Mangkut slipped the jade talisman over her head. The shamaness would be looking for her pupil, though. And Prince Tayyichiut would have sent the Nirun to search for her as well.

"The prince will find me," she'd warned her captor. "He'll bring the forces of his Nirun and the armies of the khan with him when he comes."

Mangkut had laughed at that. "My master has his own plans for Prince Tayy. He'll find his ancestors before he finds this tent!"

"Your master suffers the pride of many fallen traitors, counting his corpses before they are laid to the pyre." She'd faced down the sky god himself and refused to show her captors that they frightened her. "The prince has survived more powerful enemies than his cousin."

The sky god hadn't knocked her down on a filthy carpet or stood over her threatening rape or worse.

"Qutula will kill you if he comes back and finds you've damaged his bait." Her shoulder hurt where she'd fallen on it and she rubbed at the soreness, settling her panicked breathing. It was a small injury compared to the ones he wanted to inflict, but her reminder stopped him.

Tense and angry, Mangkut had clenched his fists into tight balls and walked away, but at least now she knew why they were holding her captive. Qutula feared that her skills as a shamaness might defeat their plan. The court had its own shaman, with deeper wisdom than she could hope to possess, but Bolghai had also been her teacher. He'd be torn between his obligations, to a student and to the court. Eluneke hoped he had enough sense to stay at the gur-khan's side and not fall into Qutula's trap by joining the search. So far no one had brought news of the prince succumbing to illness or injury, but she couldn't count on that for long. If their plan didn't work soon, she had no doubt that Qutula would use her to lure the prince out where he might be murdered in private.

She had to escape. The talisman prevented her from shifting into her totem form or traveling through the dreamscape. She'd been trying for days. Though she thought she was growing stronger in the struggle, time was running out. Trying to fight her way through in human form had earned her some bruises and an angry red ring around her throat, where Mangkut had choked her with the gold thread around her neck. But she had to do something.

Fretfully, she stroked the rune incised on the jade talisman. She could, she had discovered, touch it as long as she left it where it lay. When she tried to remove it, however, it slipped maddeningly out of her fingers. "Damn it!" She dropped to her stomach and tried to escape between the crossed lattices, but her fingers burned when she touched the felted tent cloths.

"That won't work, my lady. My mistress has bid me keep you here, and here you will stay."

"Who are you?" she asked the creature who inhabited the jade. "Who is your mistress?" She had thought Qutula commanded the talisman as he commanded the guards who watched her.

She heard a chuckling in her head, and then a voice dripping acid. "A nameless minion, bound to do the bidding of my lady. I'm sure you know her name."

Eluneke didn't believe the nameless part, but he sounded too bitter for the second to be a lie. "The Lady Chaiujin."

He didn't deny that she had guessed correctly.

It took all her concentration to focus her shaman powers on the conversation, but she knew what to do. Settling with one leg crossed under her on the filthy rug and the other bent with her chin resting on her knee, she turned her vision inward, to confront the voice that rattled in her mind. "What does your mistress want, nameless one?"

"Power, of course, and revenge. The little prince will pay, as many others have before him, for standing between the lady and her desires. But he enjoys the favors of a toad; perhaps he will likewise enjoy the kiss of her fangs!" He snickered, taunting her. Eluneke refused to let him upset her.

"I understand revenge." She nodded her head as if encouraging a patient to list his complaints. "I myself grew up an orphan in a weak and impoverished clan while my father sat upon the very dais."

The facts, which the creature might read on the surface of her mind, were true. Since he was a creature of evil and so expected the same in others, the demon of the talisman accepted that the lie about her feelings must be true as well. One thing raised his suspicions, however. "Your affection for the prince . . ."

"Your lady herself sat on the dais with the prince's father. Did she then trade her affections for the khan's position, or merely offer the use of a body not even her own for access to his power?"

"Ah," the creature cooed in her ear like a turtledove.

"With your help, between us we could take for ourselves what the lady would use us to win for herself." Toragana would know how to defeat the creature who inhabited the jade circle; Eluneke needed only to escape the tent where Qutula had hidden her.

But: "Noooo," the demon moaned. "She would not like it, and her reach is long."

Eluneke's hand slid over the disk. Distracted by her arguments, for a moment he didn't notice. She whipped the golden thread over her head and flung it at the door, then dived for a tear in the felt.

"I don't think so, my lady toad." Mangkut grabbed her by the hair and shook her until her teeth rattled.

She thought herself a toad, felt herself shrinking and let out a croaking call before the talisman descended again. Her own magic met the magic of the demon in the jade, clashed, and she screamed, tearing at her throat. Caught in transition, her form remained half toad, half human.

"Ugh!" he released her, but by then it was too late. She could not escape with the talisman on her breast and knew that if she did, she would be stoned to death as a demon, the very thing she fought.

Prince Tayyichiut strode into the ger-tent palace of his uncle, dripping with rain that had obscured even the light of the stars to search by. Dropping his wet coat in the hands of a servant, he approached the dais. At his back the Nirun fell onto the carpets below the firebox, weary from a day of searching for the shaman-princess. For days they had looked, in the shadow of every rock and behind every tree. In every tent they found the same answer: no one had seen Eluneke. The troops who went out every day had given up on finding her well and now hoped only to find her alive.

Tayy kept to himself and his Nirun the belief that Qutula held her prisoner. His cousin was too clever to lead him to Eluneke. He knew that, but had assigned men to follow him anyway. Qutula would expect that. For himself, he had begun by riding out on an alternate shift, following the Durluken in the hope that someone would slip up and lead him to her hidden prison. His own experience matched the reports of his Nirun, however. He would follow Mangkut or another of his cousin's men as far as the wood where the Onga rose out of the dell, then would lose them as if they had fallen through the river into the underworld itself. They always rode out of the wood again at shift change, but none of his own could ever follow them to where they searched, or where they might guard Eluneke as Qutula's prisoner.

At first, they'd all spent long hours at the search, but as the days in the saddle produced no results, fewer stayed out to exhaustion. He still saw his cousin very little, but that owed less to strategy and more to the fact that he kept no schedule now but rode until he could stay in the saddle no longer, and returned only long enough to restore his strength to ride again.

Tayy staggered slightly as he neared the dais. Bekter, fingering an old, half-forgotten tune in the corner, laid a hand across the strings of his lute to silence them. Bolghai was absent still. The empty place by the musicians ached like a missing tooth, but many of the chieftains and nobles had gathered above the firebox, watching as he advanced. He saw Sechule in a new purple coat sitting among them. Chahar was gone, on an errand of his uncle's to Yesugei, but Jochi had returned to his place by the gur-khan, a low table covered in maps between them. It didn't take a map to find a girl lost in the tent city, but they had enemies on their doorstep, and half of their army far to the south.

"We've found no sign of her," Tayy said, with a nod to his cousin Bekter to acknowledge the courtesy of his silence. He thought the song might have been a warning, if only he could remember what it was. Outside, his dogs howled their distress, but in front of his uncle's court he kept his own voice cold as stone. "No sign, either, of the Tinglut."

Qutula had returned ahead of him, and was already seated at the foot of the dais. His eyes were wide and dark with a false concern. "I fared no better," he said.

The gur-khan nodded, accepting the report, but his glance at his blanket-son hid questions he wasn't ready to ask before the whole court. Tayy would have asked them with a sword, but killing his cousin wouldn't find Eluneke.

"Come, sit by your grandmother and calm her weeping," Mergen invited him. Lady Bortu was doing nothing of the sort, but Tayy accepted his place beside her. She looked not much better than he guessed he must himself, but kept her thoughts, tight-lipped, to herself.

"Rest," Mergen ordered them all. "You can't do anything more until the rain stops. Then perhaps Lun and her brothers will help us find one of her own."

Great Moon watched over shamans in their dream travels. Tayy didn't think that would help Eluneke now. Humans had taken her. He didn't think it was the Tinglut, though not from Qutula's assurance, "I sent Durluken to follow Prince Daritai. They returned today, but report no sign of my sister on the march."

"Wisely done," the gur-khan thanked him, though he must have wondered, as Tayy did himself, why Qutula waited until now to tell him. His cousin's eyes were gleaming, though he kept his mouth turned down as if in sorrow.

He enjoys our grief. He did it to see me flinch. The prince reached that conclusion even through his exhaustion. He'd already dismissed the Tinglut as the thieves, though like his cousin he had sent a precious few of his Nirun to shadow the movements of Prince Daritai. The one report he'd received had given him nothing about Eluneke, but he'd learned that the Durluken were watching. Mergen Gur-Khan's scouts had fol-

lowed the Tinglut forces as well, but they wouldn't find what
wasn't there.

No, someone closer to home had taken her like a bride thief,
or a murderer. Whatever he had done to her, Qutula's face gave
nothing away as he watched, with false concern, Tayy fall
loose-limbed with weariness to the dais.

Servants were called then, food and drink brought. Tayy
chose a pie from a laden silver tray, but Qutula took it from
him, bit into it and swallowed before he offered it to the prince.
Tayy didn't trust his cousin, but he didn't think Qutula wanted
him dead badly enough to poison himself first. So he ate when
Qutula found his food safe and sipped when the kumiss bowl
came to him. His mind, however, was on Bekter's tale.

"Play," the gur-khan asked with a gesture to his blanket-son.
"Let music ease our minds a little, if it can."

The usual court entertainment had been dismissed for the
duration of the crisis, but Bekter's music always seemed to
soothe the gur-khan's distress. He came forward, his instrument
in his hand, and made a low bow.

"As you wish, my lord."

A servant brought a low stool and Bekter sat on it. If his
mouth were as choked with secrets as his eyes, Tayy thought,
he would never get a song out. Presently he began to play the
song he had practiced earlier. As he listened, Tayy realized the
poet's secrets were all there in his voice.

"Long ago a princess lived,
A child among warriors.
Alaghai of seven summers
bright with blood and sword
Walked barefooted among the dead,
weeping for their fate."

Tayy set aside the kumiss, concentrating on the meter. He
knew the story, a popular one from childhood, of the little
princess who was later known as Alaghai the Beautiful. Beside
him, Mergen picked up the cup the prince had abandoned.

" 'He's gone to his ancestors,
magnificent in battle,
With sacrifices of enemies
to pay his way
And crowned with a silver cap,
the bloodied khan.

" 'Until I see his crow-pecked eyes,
and touch his mortal wounds
Your words are the wind to me,
crying false sorrow.'
She left them, to search barefoot
through the red fields of her father."

In the end, of course, little Alaghai would find her father the khan, wounded but living on that dreadful battlefield. Because of her timely aid he would survive. An appropriate, if somewhat pointed, choice for a party resting from a search, it reassured that their efforts would not be in vain. Like the child princess, they would also have success. One might even smile at the reversal of roles in the tale in which a princess sought a khan to amuse their own khan seeking a princess.

The tale might mean nothing more, except that Prince Tayyichiut remembered another night when his own father Chimbai-Khan had told the story of the grown Alaghai the Beautiful. Angry at her choice of the foreign king Llesho the Great as her husband, her brothers had kidnapped her and murdered her child before her eyes. Her husband, that foreign king, died of spell-crafted murder when a cursed spear turned in his own hand and killed him. The brothers likewise fell, in the war they had begun. Only Alaghai had survived, but as a madwoman alone in the tent of her captivity.

Few in the court would connect the hopeful story of the little princess saving the life of her father with the tragic aftermath of betrayal and death. Tayy wouldn't have done so himself, except that he had traveled in the company of that foreign king's successor and repaid that debt of long-ago murder with the wounds on his own flesh. But he thought, looking into Bekter's eyes, that the poet remembered, and that he sang the early tale only because he daren't sing the later. Beside him, he heard a groan, and turning, saw his uncle wipe his lips.

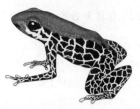

Chapter Thirty-four

QUTULA BEAT with his fist on the support next to door to his mother's tent. It was still night, but with a snap in the air that spoke of false dawn just off the horizon.

"My Lady Mother!" he pounded on the support again and cast an impatient glance at the troop of Durluken massed behind him. "Saddle Bekter's horse, and my mother's," he instructed two he trusted least. "The rest of you stay here unless I call for you." He ducked his head and went in.

"Mother! My lord, the gur-khan, needs you!" he said, conscious that he could be heard easily through the tent felt.

Sechule seemed to have few such concerns. "Even the gur-khan doesn't always get what he wants." She had risen, and set a taper to a lamp. In the yellow glow she reached for the new purple silk coat Mergen had given her. "This is hardly a proper errand for a son."

Curled on his side of the firebox, Bekter made a noise in his sleep like a yak in heat. He rolled over in his bed, burying his head in his blankets.

"The gur-khan has fallen ill," Qutula explained. He hadn't come as Mergen's procurer. "No one knows what to do."

He tried to warn her with his glance to listen past his words to the meaning he couldn't speak out loud.

"I'll come with you, of course. But the court's shaman has a reputation for his skill," she added, playing her part, though with real concern behind it. If he'd been there, the shaman might have recognized the poison and even figured out who had dosed the gur-khan. Or, if he didn't identify it at once, Mergen might have died while he cast about for a likely cure. "Surely he must be able to help more than I."

Qutula shook his head. "Bolghai has disappeared." No surprise that the old stoat had vanished. He'd abetted the toad-girl's training, after all, and now she was missing. The shaman's absence could only work to Qutula's benefit, however. Murdering the gur-khan hadn't been part of Qutula's plan. At least not yet. And he wanted none of the blame to tarnish his own name.

"Bek, wake up!" He strode over to rouse the lump hidden in the bedcovers. "The gur-khan needs your help!"

"Anything, of course." Bekter rolled out of his blankets, bleary-eyed but tracking. "What's the problem?"

"Mergen is sick. The Lady Bortu thinks he may be dying." He omitted his own certainty of it. His brother knew nothing of the plots he had hatched with their mother and the Lady Chaiujin. For his brother, and for the court, Qutula had to appear the concerned blanket-son, frantic to help his beloved, if only clandestinely recognized, father.

"Bolghai is off looking for our sister, so we need you to find the ragged shamaness who trained the girl and bring her to the palace. Our father may die without her help."

"She's not there." Bekter grabbed for his coats where they had fallen from their peg onto the carpets. "She's looking for Eluneke, too, but in the sphere of dreams. Time runs funny there; she could be back yesterday, or a week from now."

"For your father you have to try," Qutula insisted. He might have said more, but Mangkut knocked to tell them the horses were ready.

Bekter yawned, but he was moving with a sense of urgency now. "I'll check her tent; she may have come back while I was asleep. But if she's not there, I don't know what I can do."

"You'll do your best, I'm sure of it." Qutula added an encouraging slap on the arm and assigned a handful of his own men to accompany him. He urged his brother to speed, confi-

dent that their mother would have the matter under control before he actually found the raven woman.

Sechule had begun to gather herbs and other things from
the jars and boxes on her workbench. "What are his symptoms?" she asked for the Durluken witnesses.

"He suffers much the same as the prince's recent disease,
only to a much more serious degree: a clenching of the belly
and nausea, headache. Even the light of a candle brought near
causes him to scream in anguish. The Lady Bortu has tried all
the cures she knows, but nothing seems to help. Most just make
the pain worse. The prince is frantic with worry."

Mergen had drunk the kumiss meant for Tayy and it was
killing him instead of the inconvenient prince. He thought
Mangkut might have guessed what had happened, but didn't
risk the truth in case his band of Durluken harbored a spy.
Sechule had nodded her understanding as he recounted the
symptoms, however. Of course, she would know them and
know what they meant. When he had done, she asked, "Is anyone else ill?"

"No one else seems affected. The prince says nothing of his
own condition, but I believe he suffers his usual mild version
of the disease. We fear he may worsen." No one said the word
"poison," but Qutula felt it as a question on every mind.
Sechule, of course, would realize that Mergen hadn't taken the
full amount. She had calculated the dose for a younger heart,
however. Qutula feared the gur-khan might be dead before they
could reach him with the antidote. If that were to happen, it
would mean war over the succession. Until he was certain that
his original plan had failed utterly, however, he needed to play
out his part as a loving son and cousin. His Durluken, reporting
as gossip his desperate efforts to save his father, would allay
any suspicion against him.

"I tasted every drink and dish for the prince, and Jochi did
the same for the gur-khan. If something found its way into the
food, we have failed our duty."

With a glance at the painted chest where she kept her poisons and potions, Sechule let him know that she knew he had
done it, and something had gone wrong. "Don't take it on your-

self." She followed his lead and acted her concern for the benefit of his companions, who needed very little to secure their trust. "Of course, we may find that Jochi has also fallen ill. But if neither of the tasters has suffered, it means the dose, if any, can be strong enough only for mischief, not murder.

That might have been true if Qutula hadn't taken the antidote, but it would convince his men, who would spread that gossip most convincingly.

"I am more concerned that the dark spirits have brought ill luck into the house." Sechule finished gathering her herbs and flowers and picked up last a pot of leaves pounded into a paste.

"I'm ready," she assured him, and led him from the tent.

"Aaaaahhhhhhh! Aaaaaaaaaaahhhh!"

Tayy paused, his hands arrested as he buckled his sword belt around his waist. Closing his eyes, he shut out the sight of his uncle's anguish, but nothing blocked the sound of his wretched cries.

"You are not well yourself, my prince," Jochi reminded him in low tones. No one else had dared to remind him that he was himself mortal and subject to whatever evil beset the gur-khan. Over the sweat-soaked head of her only remaining son, Lady Bortu had watched him prepare as if for battle, but she had not chosen to stop him. None of the chieftains still assembled at the court had the rank, or the death wish, to stand in his way. General Jochi, however, had both position and his own grief to use against him, and the wisdom to know that sleep would be impossible in the palace.

"You might rest more comfortably in a friendly tent. My own are at your command."

"I don't need rest." He shuddered at another piercing scream from his uncle, who had suffered sword wounds in the past without a whimper. "I have to find Bolghai."

"With a sword?" Lady Bortu looked up from tending her son with questions brooding in her eyes.

"I have to find Eluneke." When he said it, his fingers

clenched around the hilt of his sword. "I have to find out who has done this to my uncle, and stop them."

Mergen had passed into delirium, tossing his head restlessly against the fever that soaked his braids and sweated his brow. "Sechule!" he cried.

Tayy took a step closer. "What about Sechule?" he asked eagerly. If Mergen knew who had done this to him . . .

But Jochi stared long and hard into the darkness that filled the bottom of the ger-tent palace. "Your uncle has lately renewed his interest in the Lady Sechule," he said, as if he expected salvation to walk out of the shadows. "He calls for his pledged wife. I sent Qutula to bring her."

He must have let his feelings show because Jochi, misinterpreting them, hurried to reassure him. "Your uncle never intended to displace you as his heir, but hoped, when you had taken his place on the dais, to follow his heart with the lady. He wished very much also to repair a grief he has long felt for his nameless sons."

"I wasn't jealous." But he couldn't say what he'd been thinking, that his uncle had cried out the name of his murderer and not his lover. The Lady Sechule hadn't approached the dais that evening, but her son had. With his own stomach churning, Tayy wondered suddenly what poison had come to the gur-khan, a wedding gift from his pledged wife, through her son. And then he wondered if Mergen had been meant to die at all. Qutula intercepted all of Tayy's food, not his father's.

Lady Bortu wiped Mergen's neck and shoulders. "He's dying," she said. He had fallen into a muttering stupor, his eyes showing white beneath the half-closed lashes. "Nothing I do helps him."

"I'll bring Eluneke back," Tayy promised, "She'll know how to help."

"Find her," Bortu agreed, but she said nothing of saving the life of the gur-khan.

Qutula passed him in the doorway, escorting his mother who carried with her an assortment of remedies. Tayy didn't wait, but acknowledged his cousin's bow with a nod of his head that bordered on insult.

"You acted too soon," he murmured under his breath as he knocked Qutula's elbow in passing. "If he dies, you receive nothing. Except the point of my sword."

The chieftains who had gathered to await the outcome of Mergen's illness hadn't heard him, but they watched with interest as Qutula answered in a voice meant to carry, "Your grief makes you rash. I have not heard you." With a deeper bow still Qutula signaled his unwillingness to engage in open conflict in anger.

A murmur of approval went up among the watchers. Qutula seduced them with false candor, but he didn't fool the prince.

"I *will* find Eluneke," he said, again too low for any but his cousin to hear. "You won't get away with this."

"Watch me." This time Qutula, too, spoke just between the two of them. Prince Tayy would have drawn his sword, but he had already offered combat. Qutula had refused it and he had no evidence to justify a seemingly unprovoked attack. Had no evidence to convince anyone in the court to keep Sechule, his uncle's chosen consort, away from his sickbed either. But Eluneke was out there somewhere, counting on him to rescue her as much as he counted on her help to save his uncle. So he went.

Somewhere his body lay in pain, but Mergen didn't feel it anymore. He had become spirit, and spirit rose out of the shell that ceased to writhe when he left it. He still breathed down there in the fever and sweat, with a belly corroded by whatever poison she had given him. Through her son, no doubt. He couldn't believe it of Jochi, though now he wondered at how natural the idea felt, that Sechule and her son had murdered him, when only hours before he had been arranging his life around his love for them.

They had come, of course, like the carrion crows to peck his liver. Only Tayy had guessed what she had done. The rest seemed bent upon drawing her nearer, to repeat the dose if this one took too long about its task, he thought. She was weeping prettily, just the occasional teardrop as her choked voice gave directions to those who tended him.

"Have this made into a tea, please. And don't mind the smell. Sometimes the bitterest herbs produce the sweetest results." She gave over to a servant enough of the mixture of curled leaves and blackened stems to brew a large pot with the instructions, "All who attend the gur-khan should take a cup as well, to protect them. When the evil spirit is expelled, it will look for a new home."

"No!" Mergen shouted. "She poisoned me!" But they couldn't hear him and soon each of those near the dais had taken a cup. Qutula sipped with the rest, so perhaps this time she meant no harm. In fact, as the evil drink trickled down his own throat, he saw the rigid tension ease out of his convulsing muscles. Curious, he allowed the apparent calm of his own face to draw him back.

Pain! Terrible, terrible pain. The drink had softened his muscles, relieving the outward signs of his disease while making it impossible to control his limbs. Inside, however, the poison continued to eat at his liver while his gut turned to water.

"Now a cup, very clean, half full of cool water," she instructed someone over his head, and soon he felt the cup pressed to his lips, spilling drop by drop over his tongue so he had no choice but to drink or drown. Not water, she had doctored the drink in full sight of all the court. He recognized that bitter taste—it had tainted the kumiss which Qutula had poisoned the night before—but he was helpless to spit it out.

"Drink, my love," he heard her whisper in his ear. "It won't be long now. I"m sorry it has to hurt so much. I didn't plan it this way. It was supposed to be the prince, to clear the way for your own son's ascension to the khanate.

"Qutula will be unhappy with me, since your death will doubtless mean war with the prince. And he truly wished for your love." Softly crooning words of madness and hate into his ear, she fed him sip by sip from the poisoned cup, while the first relaxing draft kept his spirit trapped inside his body. "Your power, too, of course; even that would have been evidence of your love. But who can argue with fate? Certainly not I, who would have been khaness but for your scruples. Now I will be the mother of a khan and you will be dead."

NO! he thought. Then, when the pain grew worse than he imagined possible, he thought, "Yes, gods and ancestors take me, I cannot endure this anymore."

His bowels had let go early in his sickness. He would have hidden himself from the shame as each clenching seizure loosened his gut again, but he had lost the power even to turn his head away.

"Blood!" he heard, curses and prayers and weeping. Sechule was weeping. "I can do nothing but make him comfortable now," she said, "I am too late. The evil spirits have chewed his vitals to the spine. I do not see that he can live so!"

"My lady," he heard the sounds of comfort given to his murderess while he vomited more blood and the dark red pool spread across his bed.

"My son, my son," his mother had reclaimed her place at his head while the woman he would have made his wife lay weeping in the arms of the son who had put her deadly potion in his drink.

"Is he in much pain?" Jochi asked, and Sechule answered, "None at all."

It was a lie, as all her words were lies. He thought he must have died of the pain, and that it had followed him into hell itself to chew through skin and bone. Blood gushed unchecked from his body. He was cold, very cold, and desperate to say something that would unmask his murderers. But the spirits of the dead, the lost, the voracious spirits began to hover and among them loomed one living face of comfort.

"Mother," he said, a whisper, barely a breath, for by then he had little breath left him. Then he had none.

His mother rocked with his head cradled in her arms, but he didn't feel it. Her wails of grief rose up to heaven, but he heard them only as a distant, passing breeze.

"Well, brother," Chimbai said, waiting for him in the pure white light of Great Moon Lun spilling through the smoke hole. "Between us, we are singularly bad at choosing women."

"It could've been different." The pain was gone now, and

the filth and the blood. He walked beside his brother through the thick grass scattered with wildflowers in the sunlight.

"Maybe," Chimbai made it known by his tone that he conceded not an inch. "But a woman who would hand a man his bleeding heart and grind his guts to ribbons in the bargain because he didn't also give her an ulus for a wedding gift is no great loss."

Like his brother, Mergen refused to concede the point. "So, I suppose if you are here, I must be dead. Have you come to show me the way to our ancestors?"

"Dead, yes, I'm afraid so." In spite of this momentous pronouncement, Chimbai seemed preoccupied. "As for accompanying you to the ancestors, not yet, I'm afraid. I have work to do here first, to secure the ulus. Soon, though."

Mergen nodded, accepting that answer. It had been on his mind as well. "Can I help?" Even as he asked, a shiver passed through him, carrying a memory of unspeakable pain.

Chimbai noticed. "Not yet," he said. "Not this fight."

Another nod. In life Mergen had always followed his brother's lead, and he did so now, when Chimbai-Khan released him to his death in peace. "Later, then."

They lingered, perched on an outcrop of glittering rock as morning turned into afternoon and the pyre was gathered and lit. Sechule wept. Qutula let a tear escape his eye as well, but Prince Tayy showed none of his grief or despair on his face. Mergen saw his nephew's emotions like a garment that he wore, from the darkest to the brightest. He thought to ask if the boy would be all right, but already his attachment to the mortal world was fading. Coming toward him through the rising smoke, he recognized his father then, and Otchigin. His grandmother, and all the friends and ancestors who had come before him, beckoned.

"Go on," Chimbai said. "We'll be along soon." He laid his hand on the head of a red hound Mergen recognized as one of Tayy's.

"Oh," he said, and smiled. "I see, now."

An unearthly hand reached out to him and he took it, following the smoke of his pyre to the spirits of his beloved dead.

Chapter Thirty-five

THOUGH HE had traveled far in his totem form looking for the girl, Bolghai felt the tremor in the ether that meant a death of some consequence in the mortal world. Sniffing the air, he found in that death the smell of a life familiar to him. The gur-khan, he realized, and in terrible pain. A proper shaman, he had made a bond of service with the souls of those he treated on a regular basis and so he winced in sympathetic pain as the gnawing agony resonated in his own gut. Poison.

He should have been there. Guilt crushed his tiny stoat form, adding to the grief he felt at the loss. Mergen had the wisdom and passion to fight and win a war his brother had handed him, but even the Lady Chaiujin's murders had not imbued him with the necessary suspicion to keep him alive in his own court. As when his own son died fighting the stone giants, Bolghai curled his little paws around his black button nose and wept.

Not for long, however.

"What is it? What is it?" A raven popped out of the dream-scape and hopped nervously on the grass for a moment before it shook out its feathers and turned into Toragana, the shamaness.

"I felt something, like a wave of darkness passing through the dreamscape," she said, preening her shaman's robes. "What happened?"

Bolghai dried his little stoat eyes and shook himself all over, setting the skins on his collar flying in a shivering dance. Human again, he told her what he knew. "The gur-khan has died," he said, "Murdered, I believe, by his own kin. We have to get back."

"Of course," she said. "The prince will be alone now, and in danger."

He hadn't mentioned which relation had murdered the khan, but Toragana, he realized, had not for a moment suspected Prince Tayy, who would have profited most from the death of his uncle.

"Does he have anyone near him he can trust?" she asked, her mind traveling the same path that his own had taken. Tayy had much to gain with Mergen gone, but the gur-khan had planned to step down in favor of his heir anyway. The prince had only to wait. But others who might covet the dais had only eliminated one obstacle to be faced with another in the prince himself. Which made him the next target.

"Jochi." He hesitated, certain of his loyalty, but said, "The general still suffers the loss of his son, and harbors in his own house the murderer, a slave with ties to Qutula."

"You think Qutula murdered his own father, then." She seemed unsurprised and added, "I'm sure he has taken Eluneke; he's seen her for a threat since the first time he laid eyes on her."

"I think it most likely, and that he had the help of his mother, the Lady Sechule." The searing pain he had sensed most surely had come from a poison, and he knew the lady for an expert in the use of herbs both wholesome and less so. "I wish Mergen hadn't sent Chahar on his errand to Yesugei-Khan," he mused. Chahar had his father's talents, if not his father's inclination to the shaman trade. But with the understanding that comes of looking backward on the path that has led to crisis, Bolghai knew that not even his own skills had given him the foresight to protect the gur-khan. Chahar hadn't seen the threat any more than Jochi or Bolghai himself. If not all, then no one of them could be blamed for not preventing it.

"I have to go," he said, shaking off his own regrets.

"Do you need me?" Toragana asked, but Bolghai shook his head. "Not now, alas. Find the girl if you can. The prince will need her."

"And for her own sake."

"For her own sake." He bowed his head, humbled by the reminder that the girl's life, too, hung in the balance. Then, with a twitch and a twist, he took his stoat form and followed the scent of grief.

Softly, Eluneke moaned to herself. Caught between her human form and her totem, she shunned the light. She had no need to avoid Qutula's guardsmen, however. The most forward of them, and Qutula himself, had been absent all morning. Those who remained kept a superstitious distance, though she heard them muttering to themselves about smothering the monster with stones. Caught as she was by the demon in the talisman, she had only the shadows to protect her.

Smoke drifted on the air, and in it the smell of burning flesh. Another pyre, which would explain the absence of Qutula and Mangkut and the others closest to her half brother. She wondered who had died now and prayed to the gods of the sky and her ancestors below that Prince Tayy still lived. She knew Qutula wanted him dead but thought she would know if the prince had passed from this world to the next. Her heart must wither like old fruit if he died.

The guardsmen who remained had fallen silent as the smoke thickened. Their unease penetrated even the mind-numbing horror of her state. Rescue became a dim hope. If Tayy still lived, Qutula would use her against him. If Qutula had succeeded in murdering him and had taken his place on the dais, then what? How could he return her to the gur-khan knowing what she did about his part in her abduction? He must realize that if she lived, she would devote her life to exposing him for a traitor.

Escape seemed her only option, but she had no success in engaging the demon of the talisman again. Even her efforts to touch the jade fragment with its strange coiled ruin had failed. Until she was free of its evil influence, she didn't dare leave the protection of the little tent. In her present form, she could expect only murder at the hands of any who saw her.

In despair, she dropped her misshapen head into her webbed fingers and wept.

"Ribbit!" A little toad slipped under the tent felt and cocked his curious head at her.

"Ribbit!" Another, red and poisonous, joined him, and another, larger and green, and another . . . One, missing a toe lost in a fight with a weasel, she recognized from her visit to the sky god and his daughters. She was a member of King Toad's court and a leader in his harem.

"Ribbit!" King Toad's wife said.

The demon made it difficult for Eluneke to practice her arts, but caught as she was half in toad form, she understood the Queen Toad:

"This is unseemly, girl! Last night your mind-cries tumbled into chaos a court concert to the moon. And now, sent by my husband to demand an explanation, I find you neither toad not girl, nor any part of your spirit animating the realm of mortal creatures. What do you mean by it?"

"I am held prisoner by this talisman." Eluneke sat up and dried her eyes. She gestured at the jade fragment tied around her neck by the gold thread. "It holds me in this tent and, I think, must hide my presence from my teachers. Otherwise they would have rescued me by now."

"So take it off," Queen Toad instructed her with some asperity. She had accompanied Eluneke on her trip to the sky god's kingdom, however, and possessing great courage herself, she had recognized the same in the young shamaness. She waited now for an explanation free of any shame to the girl.

"I tried." Eluneke strove to keep the doleful whine out of her voice, but Queen Toad wrinkled her upper lip in distaste anyway. Eluneke took a deep breath to settle her fears and began again, offering as unemotionally as she could her attempt to escape first in human and then in toad form. The consequences of her efforts were clear in her round, bulging eyes and the green of her wide-stretched lips.

"I see," said Queen Toad, bobbing her head to show that she both understood and sympathized with Eluneke's plight. "I would bite through the thread that holds you prisoner to this thing, but as you can see, I have no teeth."

"Until I am free of this demon, neither have I," Eluneke mourned. "And while I sit here, neither human nor toad but some monstrous thing between them both, Qutula plots against the prince. He will murder him. He may already have done so."

Queen Toad had demanded courage of her, and she willingly gave it. She feared little for herself, but she couldn't stop the tears that leaked from her toady eyes when she thought of the danger to Prince Tayyichiut. A disgusted sigh let her know that this display of emotion had not gone unnoticed, but Queen Toad refrained from a more pointed rebuke.

"Can't you take it off over your head?"

Eluneke showed how her hands slipped past the talisman and its thread, leaving crusting marks on her own green skin.

"Lean over," Queen Toad demanded. But Mangkut had tied the cord too tightly around her throat. Human fingers might have worked it off, but the toads had neither the strength nor the dexterity to free the princess.

"It would seem we are at an impasse," Queen Toad observed, "since those creatures with the teeth to chew through the golden thread seldom stop to converse with the toads. They are more likely to eat us first and wonder not at all if there might have been a question worth asking."

That was true. Mostly. A shaman would have the power to understand the toads, though. "If the king of the toads would send an emissary to my teacher's tent, she would listen," Eluneke suggested. The toads had given her hope for the first time in a very long time.

"The Lady Toragana is a good shamaness," the Queen Toad agreed, "But in the realm of animals she flies the skies as a raven. Like the toads, she has no teeth to bite the thread."

"And like the toads," Eluneke added glumly, "she would

quickly become the prey of any creature with teeth sharp enough to be of help."

"I'm sorry," Queen Toad sympathized.

Eluneke bobbed her head in acknowledgment. A fat black fly flew near and her long tongue flicked out, snatched it out of the air and flung it still buzzing down her too human throat. "Ugh," she said, and clapped both hands to her mouth. "I can't believe I did that!" she mumbled between her webbed fingers.

"Well, if you didn't want it, you could have left it for your betters," Queen Toad croaked and slapped one webbed foot indignantly. "But it is clear that something must be done quickly."

"I told you that."

Queen Toad glared at her but otherwise kept her thoughts to herself.

"Of course! Bolghai! He's the most powerful shaman I know." Why hadn't Eluneke thought of him before? "In his totem form he travels as a stoat, so his teeth will be sharp and strong. If you can't find him, you can ask Toragana to look in the dream realm."

Queen Toad quickly instructed minions to look for Bolghai, and others to find Toragana.

"But warn them not to tell Prince Tayy," Eluneke begged, "Qutula stole me to use as bait to draw the prince into his trap and murder him."

Adding this to her instructions, Queen Toad sent the toads out onto the grasslands to search for the shamans and deliver her messages. Then, with another haughty croak she slipped away under the tent cloths and Eluneke was alone again.

T he fires of the funeral pyre had fallen to angry embers the color of the cloud-choked sky. In the distance, a light rain had begun to fall, a drape of silver beads that shone in the low red light of Great Sun on the horizon. Great Sun would rise again in the morning, of course, just as Mergen's spirit might return some day in another form. But the gur-khan, ruler of the Qubal and the Uulgar people, was gone forever.

"Call the chieftains together." Tayy might have phrased his request to his uncle's general more diplomatically, but he wasn't feeling diplomatic at the moment. His cousin had vanished, taking with him his Durluken and a greater number of Mergen's troops than he'd expected.

"They won't come," the general advised him. "Mergen sent for Yesugei before he died and the chieftains won't move until he returns." Jochi hesitated, and Tayy cast a piercing glance at the unhappy man walking at his side, silently urging him to continue.

"You know I have no love for the gur-khan's blanket-son or his Durluken." A Durluken had murdered his own son, Altan. "But we have no proof against him."

"And the army?"

"Yours. They would follow the Warrior Prince to the underworld itself and fight demons in your name if you asked them to."

"With any luck we can limit the fighting to the mortal realm, though I wouldn't be surprised to find an old enemy of my family mixed up in it somewhere."

"The Lady Chaiujin?"

Tayy shrugged. "Maybe. Or maybe I'm just trying to justify my own failure. He has Eluneke, I know it. I just can't figure out how he's hidden her from all our searches."

"If Bolghai can't find her, you may be right."

Hearing it didn't make Tayy feel any better. Saner, maybe, but Mergen was still dead, Eluneke still missing, and he still didn't have a clue. "I was a fool to think it was a game," he admitted. "But I know better now. I should have died last night. Mergen drank my cup."

"I wondered." Jochi didn't look the least surprised. "I think at the end the gur-khan hoped by marrying Sechule to bring his sons to feed more tamely from his hand. Bekter, of course, has always been content with his place at court, but his brother yearned for his father's recognition. Or so Mergen believed."

"It seems he preferred his father's place on the dais, however much he shortened Mergen's life to get it." His uncle's announcement that he would marry Sechule had come as a shock, but Tayy would have given his place to his cousin gladly before letting this happen.

"The gur-khan never intended to name Qutula his heir," Jochi said. "He would have married Sechule only after the chieftains had named you gur-khan."

The general stared into the setting sun and Tayy gave him the time he needed to put his thoughts together. "In the end, I think you may be right that Qutula meant for you to die and not his father. Mergen's death brings him no nearer his goal. Sechule, however—"

"Could have saved him, but didn't because he wouldn't name her khaness?" Tayy nodded, finishing the general's thought. "I think you're right. I want her found—who knows what mischief she has in mind." He didn't say he wanted her dead, but Jochi would know it. As for Qutula, "Tell all our men he must be taken alive, along with his closest minions. Until we find Eluneke."

"We won't fail you." Jochi paused, as if pondering the wisdom of what he would say next. "Like those who rode away with him, some of the chieftains will side with Qutula against you." He cast a nervous glance to see what Tayy would do.

"Not everyone liked my father," Tayy agreed. "Some will think the succession should have gone to Mergen's line when he became the khan."

"Only because they don't know the part Qutula played in his father's death," Jochi assured him. "You can persuade them. Yesugei will help."

"I don't know what Yesugei will do," Tayy admitted. "He loved Sechule and may still believe my uncle sent him away so that he'd have her for himself. He may even blame me for all that has happened. No one saw Qutula poison my drink, but everyone must know by now it was my cup that killed the gur-khan."

Jochi shook his head, denying this emphatically. "Yesugei may have made a fool of himself over the woman, but he isn't blind and his loyalties have never been in doubt."

"I hope you're right." They walked a little farther. The chieftains had moved their tents away from the main camp, waiting and watching. Only the warriors loyal to the khan's heir remained with their families and other retainers. Passing between the tents, Tayy saw men sharpening their blades and women preparing to move. They were waiting for his order, but he had one more duty to perform for his uncle.

"I have to sit with Lady Bortu tonight," he said. "Find out for me which side Bekter has come down on, and send him to join us if he remains loyal. We are all the family she has left."

"It's a terrible thing to outlive your children." Jochi bowed his head, hiding his own sorrow. "I'll find out."

Tayy waited until the general had walked away before he turned to the ger-tent palace where his grandmother awaited him, surrounded by the ladies of her court. A soft head slid under his hand and he stroked the red fur, greeted the black as well, returning from some doggy errand of his own. To the surprise of his guardsmen he brought the dogs with him into the palace. The Lady Bortu did not object, but buried her face in the thick black fur and wept with brokenhearted sobs into the dog's neck. The prince gritted his teeth to keep his own moans inside, but the dogs whined their answer to his distress. Tomorrow he would go to war. But tonight, with his own hand resting on the flank of the dog lying at his feet, he joined his mourning to his grandmother's.

Chapter Thirty-six

"WHERE'S BEKTER?" Qutula stormed into his mother's tent, his Durluken following. The serpent-demon he carried as a tattoo on his breast burned, inflaming his rage.

Sechule glanced at him in the mirror over her worktable. Her face tightened and he wondered which image of his lady she had seen there. She said nothing of the demon in the mirror when she turned to address him, however.

"Your brother is out with the rest of the camp, searching for the girl. Or so he told me, though you might find him with the shamaness he's been bedding."

For a moment his heart stuttered. But Eluneke wasn't the only shamaness in the camp. "Toragana?" whispered a familiar hissing voice in his ear and he repeated the name.

"She dresses in feathers and honors the raven." Sechule waved a dismissive hand. She gave no sign that she had heard the whispering voice. "Her name may be Toragana; he doesn't talk about her."

"Bitch." Qutula swore quietly under his breath, consigning the shamaness, his mother, and his half sister all to the underworld. He didn't trust any of them, not even the lady who rode as an inky serpent over his heart. Certainly not his mother. At a gesture, his Durluken began turning the bedding over and jabbing the points of their spears into all the likely hiding places.

"My lady khaness," he said, and bowed deeply to lay the silk at her feet. It pleased him to think that he could hold what Chimbai-Khan could not. He was a boy, of course, and didn't believe in the mortality of his own flesh.

"My lord," she answered, smiling, and took his face in her hands to kiss him. As she did sometimes, she let him taste her serpent tongue, narrow and strange to his human mouth.

"Let me see your body," he tugged at the ties of her coats, releasing her breasts. "Come to me," he moaned into her mouth and drew her down onto the purple silk.

She was a demon and a serpent, suffering no human emotions to cloud her purpose. In all their former encounters she had held her lover a little apart, even in the heat of passion, turning him away at will or calling him at her pleasure to exert her dominance over him. She controlled him still, with her cool thighs and her soft breasts. But where he touched her now, his fingers left trails of longing. Her own desires swept her like a wildfire.

How could this be? She demanded his touch and he gave it, demanded his mouth there, and there, and his body, fitted to hers, the cloud of purple silk like moonlight on her skin. She wanted, wanted, and it would have frightened her, that desire, except that her lover groveled between her thighs, more lost in the heat even than she.

Finally, when he had exhausted himself, she turned him away. "You have to go," she said. "The prince will lead out his armies soon. You need to be ready."

"I'm ready," he assured her, but he rolled over and began to pull on his clothes. "One last kiss," he demanded and, when she gave him her human mouth, he asked for the serpent. "For all your forms are pleasing to me." He breathed the words on her skin and would have fallen down beside her when she licked a trickle of sweat from his throat with a long, forked tongue.

"Go," she said, before finding his mouth and tasting out its contours. "Our army awaits."

She withdrew her touch from him then, and gave him only a mocking smile when he would have demanded more. When

he had gone, she gathered up the purple silk coat and carried it
to her nest, where she added it to the other she had stolen.
Sleep beckoned in the cool chamber hidden among the stones.
She shaped scales and fangs in her mind and willed the transformation into her snaky form.

A fluttering as of bird wings rippled deep in her belly, but
her form stubbornly remained human. Her egg had grown too
large to be contained by the serpent's body, she thought, and
hated the changes fast coming over her. But, as a mist, nothing
could hold her . . .

Again, nothing. The egg bound her to her human form as
surely as chains bound the slave to the whipping post.

"Nooooo!" she wailed.

Tearing her hair, she fell, screaming her rage onto the
heaped silks. With demon strength she tore the purple coat to
shreds, screaming, "No, no, no!" with each rending tear. But
none of her imprecations or any of her skills would break the
curse of flesh that bore a child of human blood.

"If we don't turn around now, we may be too late!" Jumal
broke off a piece of hard cheese and dipped it in his tea
while Yesugei considered for the hundredth time in a week
how to answer his young captain. No matter how he counted
up the stones, his place on the board never changed.

"We are under orders to proceed south. If we turn around,
we commit treason, a crime punishable by a more horrible
death than I hope you ever see, let alone suffer." He'd seen Mergen use the threat of such a death to wring a confession out of
a prisoner and he had no doubt it would destroy the gur-khan
to carry out such a sentence on the boy, but he kept that part to
himself.

"And if we're too late?" Jumal knew better than to speak his
fears by name in front of all of Yesugei's captains, but they both
understood his meaning. What if Qutula murdered the prince?
What if civil war had already broken out? Could they save the
ulus without destroying the khanate?

Yesugei hadn't trusted the boy at first. He'd roundly cursed Mergen under his breath for burdening him with a Qubal problem as well as the young Uulgar chieftain whose father had died at Mergen's own hand, a gift with teeth and claws if he'd ever seen one. The gur-khan had sent Jumal south to get him away from the prince, and Yesugei had wondered what kind of danger the boy might represent to his own party. Over the weeks of travel south, however, he'd come to know both young men better. He now trusted them as far as their experience permitted.

Gradually, he had drawn out Jumal's story. The weight of their combined suspicions had caused him to slow their progress, in case they might be needed nearer home. To turn around against Mergen's direct orders, however, would set him in opposition to his gur-khan. With the one exception of the woman Sechule, that was something he would never do.

"My lord Yesugei-Khan—" His second challenge, the Uulgar boy who had taken the name of Otchigin to honor Mergen's dead anda, burst into the command tent and skidded to a halt on the carpets. In taking on the name, he'd taken the devotion to the gur-kahn as his own as well. And as the living heir of their executed khan, he had pledged the loyalty of all his fellow prisoners, who he now named Uulgar-Qubal.

He'd been on duty guarding the perimeter. His sudden appearance, breathless and anxious, could only mean one thing. Yesugei didn't have to look at Jumal to know the young captain had come to the same conclusion even before the young Otchigin had finished his announcement: "A messenger from the gur-khan to see you, my lord khan."

The messenger hadn't waited but had followed the young captain into the war tent and gave his own precise court bow. Otchigin bounced nervously on the balls of his feet, his hand drifting to the hilt of his sword. No defense was required, however. Yesugei knew this messenger well.

"Chahar!" He rose to greet the newcomer at once, clasping the messenger's arms in a welcoming embrace. "Rest here beside me," he said, bidding the messenger to take a seat on the thick carpets layered to make a soft floor for the war tent. "You look like a man ten years older than the last time we met."

Chahar sat heavily and accepted a damp washing cloth from a servant. In the few weeks since Yesugei had left the gur-khan's court, worry had creased new lines in the familiar face. The muscles in Chahar's arms quivered with a fine exhaustion when he wiped the dust from his face.

"First your message, then food," Yesugei instructed his old friend, glad that he hadn't made greater haste southward.

His young captains waited at attention with their blue-coated backs to the lattices as proper guardsmen to a khan. He trusted them, and their companions who defended him, to follow any command and to take to the grave any secret they heard in his tent. But the gur-khan hadn't offered such trust when he sent his messenger, and so he dismissed them with a command he knew would soon be necessary. "Prepare the camp to move out. Send the hunters ahead—we'll need to feed a hungry army on the march. We head north when Great Sun leaves no shadow."

Jumal cast a doubtful glance at the messenger, but they both knew Chahar would never serve the enemies working against the gur-khan. With a calming word to his Uulgar second, he gathered his guardsmen and left his khan to his private report. Yesugei had no doubt he would remain to guard the door, but no one else would hear what went on in the command tent.

"Tell me why you look like the hunting hounds of the underworld are on your heels," Yesugei said when he was alone with the messenger. His weeks in discussion with Jumal had shown the new khan greater dangers within the ger-tent palace itself, so he felt prepared for whatever he might hear.

"My message—" Chahar stammered and stopped, his eyes suddenly empty of the deep intelligence Yesugei knew in him. At first he thought the man suffered from an exhaustion so extreme that he had temporarily lost control of both memory and senses. But with a bitter little laugh Chahar pulled himself together.

"The gur-khan sent this message: 'Tell him that his gur-khan wishes his company, and that of his armies.'"

With that Chahar handed him a tourquoise bead, the signal for a threat of war, though not an imminent one. It was clear the man had missed more than one meal reaching the southbound camp at speed, however. A handful of steps brought him to the door where Jumal waited, as he had expected. The servant with a tray of food, already standing just beyond the carrying of their voices was a welcome surprise.

"He didn't look fit for much." Jumal passed off his foresight with a little shrug. "I thought this might help."

"I'm sure it will."

The servant followed him into the tent and set his tray on the floor in front of the newcomer, leaving Yesugei and the gur-khan's messenger alone. Chahar helped himself to a cup of tea and a chunk of hard cheese, chewing for sustenance but also to gain time. He would have had the weeks of travel to order his report, so this continued hesitation knotted the breakfast in Yesugei's belly.

When he had gathered his senses, Chahar began to tell his tale. "After you left on your errand to subdue the Uulgar South, Mergen revealed Eluneke, the apprentice shamaness, to be his own daughter . . ."

The news about Mergen's offer of his daughter to the Tinglut-Khan and his emissary's subsequent refusal came as little surprise. Yesugei had known about the girl since her birth and had shared her father's dismay that she had apprenticed herself to a shamaness. He remembered the day of the hunt, when Prince Tayy had first set eyes on her. That they might have grown to love each other, while unfortunate, came as no surprise after such a fateful meeting. It was just more bad luck, perhaps, that Prince Tayyichiut and the princess had appeared at their absolute worst in front of the ambassador. But Yesugei was certain that Mergen's ill fortune had a darker purpose behind it. Chahar's next revelation confirmed all of his and Jumal's suspicions.

"Last night, as I lay sleeping, my father came to me in a dream. He wore his totem form and wept, but in the way of dreams I understood him. The worst has happened. Mergen himself is dead, murdered by his own son Qutula, perhaps with the assistance of the Lady Sechule, whom the gur-khan had lately agreed to wed."

The air went out of Yesugei's lungs, as if he'd received a blow to the chest. "Sechule?" he repeated. Though he had believed Jumal that Qutula was dangerous, he could hardly credit that Sechule would aid in his schemes. Except, she had always championed her older son.

The jealousy he expected at the thought didn't come. It seemed some part of him had already accepted the truth of Bolghai's message and he mourned the loss of his dreams about Sechule almost as much as he mourned his gur-khan. How could he have been so wrong?

"But why? If Mergen meant to marry her . . ."

"He meant to hand the khanate to the prince and then marry. Which would have removed all hope for Qutula to win the dais for himself, or for his mother to become khaness. Or so my father deduces. Qutula has fled; his mother likewise cannot be found, but my father says he saw her spirit roaming lost and bitter between the worlds and that she, too, must be dead. He says that Eluneke has been missing since the Tinglut left, and he can find no trace of her in any of the realms open to his shamanic senses."

"Is she still alive?" Yesugei was having trouble processing it all, but one thought rested uppermost in his mind: his duty to defend and protect the legitimate gur-khan and his family, whoever that might be. Eluneke was part of that.

"Bolghai has found no sign of her among the dead." Chahar picked a cautious way through his point. "But he can't find her among the living either. He is at a loss to explain it, but fears that Qutula may be conspiring with demons."

He hadn't thought it could get any worse. "The prince?" he asked.

"Safe when last I heard. But he searches for the shaman princess while there is light and mourns his uncle in the dark. My father worries for his health as well as his safety."

Yesugei accepted this report and recalled his captains. If Tayy still lived, he was gur-khan now, or would be when Yesugei arrived to uphold his position. And he was determined to do so before Qutula had shed more royal blood. "Leave a small force to support the camp followers," he told the captains when they had rejoined him in the command tent. "We ride to war in the name of Tayyichiut Gur-Khan."

"Tayyichiut Gur-Khan!" Jumal's exclamation carried equal parts of dismay and devotion. Like the new Otchigin at his side he understood the terrible loss the ulus had suffered. More than any of them, however, Jumal owed his allegiance to the new gur-khan.

"And the Uulgar prisoners?" the young Otchigin asked, with more questions than he dared ask in his eyes. Mergen had spared his life and the lives of the ten thousand Uulgar taken in the recent war for the Cloud Country. He had pledged his people and his life to serve the gur-khan, but Mergen reigned no more.

"There are no prisoners in this camp," Yesugei assured him with a clasp on his arm. "We are all Qubal now and we ride together to defend the gur-khan."

"As my khan orders." Otchigin bowed so low that the crown of his cap brushed the floor. When he followed Jumal from the command tent, his face had flushed deep wine with pride.

Trust, Yesugei thought, was a dangerous weapon. Mergen's trust in his son had led to murder and war. He hoped his own faith in the boy chieftain was not so misplaced.

Chapter Thirty-seven

TAYY PROPPED HIS HEAD on his hand, elbow resting on a map of the grasslands spread on a low table. The dogs had slept the night through at his feet but were raising their heads again in the doggy ordering of priorities: a visit outside and then breakfast.

"Go," he told them. They both hesitated, whining their distress at leaving him before leaping from the dais. In the gray dawn filtering through the smoke hole, he watched their tangle-legged run for the door. The shadowy light had dulled the glow from the lamps but provided little illumination for the maps he'd been studying. He closed his eyes for a moment, but it didn't help. The details, blurred and indistinct, had burned themselves onto the backs of his eyelids.

After another wakeful night of mourning, his grandmother had finally fallen asleep, allowing him to turn his attention to his general and the maps spread out between them. Like Jochi, most of the guardsmen in their blue coats and the gathered advisers who offered their opinions in respectfully lowerd voices had belonged to his uncle. Once his own cadre had guarded him. He'd expected to rely on his age-mate captains then, but Altan was dead and Jumal far to the south. And Qutula . . .

"You're *sure* Prince Daritai didn't kidnap her?"

"As you requested, I had the Tinglut party followed. The

prince set a careful watch and his force moved quickly to leave Qubal lands, both reasonable precautions given the failure of his embassy." No one mentioned that General Jochi was just repeating the significant facts he'd already covered in his report. "The Tinglut could scarcely prevent our spies from observing their progress, but none of our people saw any sign of the Princess Eluneke in their camp, nor did they sense any undue secrecy in the Tinglut's movements."

Prince Tayy nodded. "So Qutula has her, as we thought, and likely murdered my uncle as well." Staring down at the scraped horsehide map, he idly traced the branded lines that represented caravan routes and grazing boundaries. If he were Qutula, where would he go? Where would he find allies?

Beyond the ger-tent palace, the sound of horses going through their paces in the practice yard rumbled like distant thunder. His army prepared for war against an enemy who had until recently been a captain in their own ranks; who had sat on the very steps of the dais. Now he seemed to have vanished from the grasslands.

"Has anyone discovered Bekter's whereabouts?" They would have told him if they knew, but Tayy couldn't yet accept that Bekter had conspired with Qutula to murder their father. "Do we know if he's hiding? Could he not know we're looking for him?"

"I don't have an answer yet." Jochi shrugged a one-shouldered apology. "Until Yesugei comes, our armies are spread thin. But we'll find him; it just takes time."

"Do we *have* time?"

Trick question, when they had no choice. The general didn't even try to answer it. They still had people out looking for Eluneke and others tracking Qutula. And, of course, Jochi had insisted that a large contingent of their warriors remain to guard the prince himself. With the gur-khan murdered and Eluneke still missing, Tayy didn't even try to argue that point. But he needed to know where Bekter stood. And he needed to be out there looking for Eluneke himself.

"Perhaps the shamaness Toragana will know where my cousin is." It had seemed to him that Bolghai had trusted and respected Eluneke's teacher. But Bolghai had appeared to perform the necessary services for his uncle's spirit only to vanish again as the funeral fires had died. Tayy wondered briefly if his own shaman had sided with Qutula, but dismissed the thought as unworthy. He didn't want to think about his chances for victory if all the spirit world arrayed itself against him.

With an impatient sweep of his hand the map flew from the low table and fell on the steps of the dais. "I can't sit here and wait like a child or a coward for my cousin to come to kill me. I have to find him."

"And his followers?" Jochi asked, trying to sway him with the logistics of going against his cousin. "Your chieftains are correct in this at least—you'll need the full force of Yesugei's armies if you want to defeat Qutula."

"You must mean *my* armies, brought home at my murdered uncle's command by our general and vassal khan," he corrected Jochi coldly. The man might have served Mergen well, but Prince Tayyichiut, heir to the khanate, could afford no doubt about his own position. If the chieftains wanted Yesugei as their gur-khan, they could elect him with their cups and stones. In the meantime, Mergen had named Tayy his heir. To free Eluneke, he needed the armies and the power to command them that came with his rank.

The general met his bleak and deadly gaze evenly. When Tayy didn't back down, he accepted the rebuke with a humble bow. "The gur-khan's army," he said, giving Tayy the title although the chieftains had not yet voted.

Prince Tayy accepted the apology with a stiff jerk of his chin. The general hadn't mentioned that if Qutula had indeed aligned himself with demon allies they might have no hope of defeating him at all. Tayy knew it already; he'd barely survived a war against inhuman foes with no particular interest in him. On rainy days the scars he wore from that time still ached, reminding him of the cost. His own safety mattered little to him while Eluneke suffered captivity or worse, but the thought of such powers arrayed in full force against the Qubal people tied his already abused gut in knots.

Something of what he was thinking must have shown itself on his face, because Jochi laid a restraining hand on his forearm. "You can't command an army from the wrong side of the funeral pyre. To lead, you need to stay alive."

"I have to find her. If I'm so easily removed from the board, Yesugei can take up the battle in his own name." Tayy threw off the gentle restraint. "Let the chieftains elect a new line for their khan. It won't matter to me then."

Jochi shifted, placing his body between Tayy and the steps from the dais. "It will matter to your people," he said.

Nearby, the Lady Bortu's predator's dark eyes opened slowly and closed again without rousing from sleep. Pitching his voice low so that he didn't disturb her, Tayy growled a warning to his general. "If you try to stop me, I'll have you killed for the affront."

With a jerk of his chin he summoned the closest guardsmen, who approached with eyes wide and fearful. "I will step over your steaming corpse if I have to, but I will still go." He had ridden with Jochi in battle and so his general would know he made no empty threats.

The general conceded, his frustration barely restrained in a graceful bow. "Don't think that I value my own life over protecting yours, my prince," Jochi assured him, "but I prefer not to ruin this poor soldier by testing his loyalties in a campaign I've already lost."

"I know." Now that he had won his point, Tayy took a precious moment to salve the wounds of the spirit he had tried. "But I could sit here and mourn 'if only' until the sky turned green and it wouldn't change what has to be. Sound the call to arms. We ride."

He didn't wait for the general but strode toward the door down the long center aisle, past painted chests with the history of the ulus displayed on them. The bronze head of the Thebin king, Llesho the Great, once had meant no more to him than a prop to enliven the epic tale of Alaghai the Beautiful and her ill-fated king. Then the orphan king Llesho had stepped out of the tales to beg the Qubal's aid in rescuing his country from the invading Uulgar. Chimbai-Khan had gone to war to repay the debt the Qubal had remembered for generations in its tales. Now it felt like Tayy himself was caught in a legend. Bekter, court poet as well as cousin, would understand about such things. But Bekter couldn't be found.

Instead, he had a scattering of nobles rousing from their sleep on either side of the aisle. The ger-tent palace held six hundred when the clans gathered; now he counted just a scattered few, most of them too old to fight. Messengers had been sent with news of Mergen's death, but it would take time for the clans to return. Some, he knew, would wait and watch while others did the bleeding, and would pledge their cautious loyalty to whoever remained alive and standing at the end of it.

But he had Jochi to advise him and Jumal would be returning with Yesugei. The Uulgar prisoners would fight for their new khan, he thought, to retain the freedom Mergen had granted them. When he found Eluneke—he refused to think of it as "if"—he was pretty sure he'd have his own allies in the spirit world to help him. He just had to find her.

Out of long habit he scarcely noticed the guardsmen who left their places along the many lattices of the palace to form a defensive phalanx at his back. But he'd lost the friends of his own age who should have been his captains, so he had no one to stand shoulder to shoulder with him when Mangkut entered the ger tent palace, blocking the doorway as Tayy moved to exit.

"A message from General Qutula, my lord," Mangkut said, elevating his captain well beyond his rank. "I have been instructed to deliver it privately."

"With a knife?" Jochi asked. He had followed Prince Tayyichiut from the dais, and at his signal fifty guardsmen drew their swords and surrounded the intruder.

"You have nothing to fear from me," Mangkut begged off with a bow. "Mine is not the hand that moves the stones on this board." He lifted his arms away from the weapons at his side.

Tayy believed him that far. "He won't kill me," he assured his general. "Qutula will reserve that honor to himself."

"As you say, my lord." This time Mangkut smirked when he bowed. Jochi was less trusting. At a meaningful glance, two of the guardsmen set aside their own weapons to search the messenger and relieve him of any threat he might have carried. Sword and spear were taken from him, and several knives uncovered and set aside. When they were done, Mangkut reached inside his coat and brought out a delicate piece of Shannish paper.

"You will hand the paper to me, and I'll decide what is to be done with it," Jochi said, and held out his own hand.

The prince understood his reasons. The packet might have held a scorpion or some other danger might reveal itself when he opened the paper, though Mangkut didn't seem nervous enough about holding it himself to cause much concern. Surrendering with a little shrug, he gestured for Mangkut to do as Jochi commanded.

The paper had a single fold and, when released, a lock of hair slipped out. Tayy ignored Jochi's glare and grabbed the long dark strands out of the air before they could drift to the ground.

"My lord Qutula instructs me to say, 'follow, alone, or he will kill the girl,'" Mangkut recited.

"Trust Qutula? He'll murder them both, if he hasn't already killed the girl." Jochi's words might have been an ice-knife to his heart. The prince trusted Qutula no more than his general did, but only Mangkut could lead him to the hidden camp where Qutula held Eluneke prisoner.

Fortunately, Tayy was beginning to have a plan. "Kill him," he said, and turned away in contempt, his voice colder even than Mergen had sounded when he executed the Uulgar chieftains.

Immediately, his guardsmen tightened their hold on Mangkut's arms. Tayy remained torn between rage against his cousin and his terror that his actions might cost him Eluneke's life. He let that conflict show on his face. Suddenly Mangkut was afraid; when Jochi drew his sword, he began to struggle.

"I'm just a messenger," he cried, "I have no say in the message."

"You follow Qutula. That's reason enough to eliminate you."

"He deserves to die," the general agreed, his blade resting at the join of Mangkut's neck to his shoulder. He would willingly kill for his khan; he had his own reasons to hate as well. But there was a question in Jochi's eyes: would Tayy act as an enraged lover, or as a khan? Would he see the advantage they held in their hands?

"Tell me where he's hidden her and I'll let you live."

"I can't tell you." Mangkut ceased his struggles; calculation sharpened in his eyes. "I can only show you."

"On a map, then, willingly." Tayy finished the thought softly, as if to himself. "Or later if you prefer, in your own blood. If you don't want to die with your entrails in your hands, you'll tell me what I need to know."

As it did during the hunt, the prince's senses tightened until the whole world narrowed to his prey. Mangkut's eyes dilated and his breathing gathered hectic speed. Tayy smelled the fear rising in acrid waves from the messenger's clammy skin as he pleaded, "You don't understand. I *can't* tell you. Lord Qutula bribed a demon to hide his camp. I don't *know* how I will find it again, only that he will let me see the way because his lord wills it."

In his own petty way, Mangkut was as evil as his master. There was no point in trying to judge the honor of his words. But his terror stank of sincerity.

"So I'll follow you," Tayy agreed, "but not alone."

At his command, Mangkut's hands were tied. "Qutula wouldn't expect you to bring me to him on your own. Where are the others waiting?"

"Scattered along the road. They're to join us as we pass. By the time we reach the wagons on the outskirts, they should all be accounted for."

It made sense. "Then that is where my own guard will ambush them and take their places." Forwarned, maybe he'd even stay alive until Jochi arrived with his army.

"Take him out. Put him on a horse and tether it to my own," he commanded, and then addressed a warning to Mangkut himself: "If you make a move to warn your followers, I will gut you and stampede your horse. Qutula may still kill me, but your living entrails will be scattered from here to the Tinglut. Do I make myself clear?"

"Qutula said you were weak." The words still carried the bravado that Mangkut had begun with, but a line of sweat beaded his lip.

"He was wrong." For all their sakes, the prince hoped Qutula's captain believed him.

Mangkut said nothing to that, but he dropped his eyes, his shoulders hunched as if he might make himself invisible. Good. Tayy had seen his father and his uncle both use fear to save an enemy's life before, but he hadn't expected to need the lesson so soon.

"Get him out of here," he said, and when his guardsmen had taken Mangkut away, he turned to General Jochi. "I have a plan, but we don't have much time. . . ."

Bleary-eyed, Bekter rolled out of bed, wondering for a moment where he was. Not home, that was certain. But . . . a stuffed raven stared down at him from the spoked ceiling. Ah. He remembered now. Mergen, his father, was dead, and he'd heard whispers of poison. Who might have wanted to murder the gur-khan, or how they had managed it, remained a mystery to him, though there, too, he had heard whispers. He refused to believe Qutula capable of patricide. Didn't see anything to be gained by it, for one thing. All of his brother's hopes depended on his father staying alive long enough, at least, to repudiate his heir. As for the other whisper, Tayy had no motive at all. Mergen'd been preparing to step down in his favor, a smoother path to the dais than murder.

Sunk in his own grief, Bekter had come looking for Toragana. She'd been out looking for Eluneke, so he'd settled in to wait. She hadn't come back, and at some point he must have fallen asleep. If he had any sense, he'd be sleeping still.

Now that he was awake he shoveled dried camel pats into the stove and found the tea while the kettle heated. As he was pouring the boiled water over the tea leaves, a rustle of black wings signaled Toragana's arrival. The raven ruffled her feathers and turned into a woman, the warmth of welcome lighting her weary eyes.

"I didn't expect anyone to be here." She took the cup he had lavishly laced with honey and inhaled the steaming vapors with a deep indrawn breath. "Ahhhh. You can't begin to imagine how much I've been longing for a cup of tea."

"And I thought that welcome was for me." Now that she had returned, Bekter relaxed enough to tease.

"So it was," she answered in kind. "A man who can make a decent cup of tea *and* compose a heroic epic should be prized above all riches."

For a moment they smiled at each other in perfect harmony, the cares of the world banished from the comfortable tent. But the disasters that had befallen the Qubal court were never far from either of their thoughts.

"I'm sorry I couldn't be here for you when your father died. But Eluneke . . ."

"I understand." Bekter accepted her apology, but his chin sank mournfully to his breast. "Have you found any trace of where she might have gone, or why?"

Toragana shook her head, only then remembering that she still wore her shaman's headdress of feathers with a stuffed raven nesting on her crown. She took it off and set it on a painted chest, then hung her robes from their peg on the lattices. "I had almost convinced myself that the spirits of the underworld might have lured her into the river to drown. But there was a moment when I thought I sensed her presence in the mortal world, like the sun through a break in the clouds. It vanished before I figured out where it might be coming from—I've spent the night flying over all the lands between the palace and the river looking for her, or any place she might be hidden."

Bekter rubbed his face with both hands as if he could wipe away his own sorrow like so much dust. "How is it possible to hide a shamaness from the sight of her teacher?" he asked.

"Her captors must have otherworldly help."

"Demons?" Bekter's head came up at that. Both Toragana

and Bolghai followed the white path of the shaman. But dark magics had troubled the grasslands before.

"The false Lady Chaiujin?" He shivered, remembering Chimbai-Khan's deadly wife, and the strange woman who had come, uninvited, to his bed.

"It's possible. I'm running out of other ideas." Toragana's gaze drifted. She seemed to look into a different world all of a sudden, and he wondered if she would turn back into a raven and fly away again. Presently, however, she gave herself a little shake and reined in her farseeing vision. "We are about to have company. And, maybe, some answers."

Bekter listened for the sound of approaching horses. He heard nothing but the whisper of small creatures in the grass. Toragana was looking down at the carpet, however, and at the back of the tent rather than the door. When the fat green toad with one missing toe slipped under the tent cloths he reached for his sword.

Toragana stopped him with a warning. "You have nothing to fear as long as you offer her no threat."

"He or she, the toad is poisonous."

The shamaness waved his objection away, apparently unconcerned that the floor of her tent was filling with toads of all sizes. Not all were poisonous, but enough of them made Bekter nervous. Toragana, however, answered his concern without turning her attention from the regal toad who approached at the center of the hopping mass of green and brown and red. "Let me introduce the queen of the toads," she said, "who has come as a messenger from her husband, who rules the realm of toads."

"Greetings." Bekter made a polite bow, but he wondered if perhaps Qutula had been right to fear for the prince. With no such fears, Toragana squatted down in front of Queen Toad and planted her elbows companionably on her knees. "Ribbit," she said

The toad responded, "Croak!"

They proceeded to converse in a language that made Bekter's head ache. Though he understood not a word of what passed between them, he recognized the seriousness of the debate from the sharp fan of frown lines marking Toragana's brow. When the debate concluded, the shamaness stood up and put on her headdress again. The frown remained, her brows tilting like the wings of the raven on her head.

"The toads have found the Princess Eluneke, but we will need Bolghai to free her."

"I can help . . ." Bekter was already reaching for his seldom-used sword, but Toragana shook her head, rejecting his offer of assistance.

"If a human could get near her, I would gratefully accept," she said, assuaging his injured pride. "But the queen of the toads tells me that Eluneke's captor has set a demon guard to hide her from human eyes. If you should find a way past this unearthly glamour, the demon would destroy you, body and soul.

"The toads, not being human, are untroubled by the demon's spells. They've seen Eluneke and have spoken to her," Toragana assured him. "She is still alive, they tell me."

"Alive, but a prisoner of a demon!" He didn't say at the command of his brother, though he knew it must be true. "If she's so well hidden, what are we to do?"

"Queen Toad has come up with a plan. I think it will work, but it requires the stealth of Bolghai's totem creature. And his sharp teeth."

They needed the stoat, not the human shaman, and his sharp teeth for gnawing through bindings. One thing above all else he had learned in battle against strange forces, however; it always helped to have a backup plan. The demon's spell might hide Qutula's camp from his human sight, but he could follow the toads, who knew the way. His sword would sever rope or leather more quickly than the sharp teeth of a stoat. And, as Qutula's brother, he might have a chance at reasoning their way out of this mess. Or at least surviving the attempt.

He watched, growing accustomed to the transformation, as Toragana turned into a raven and flew out the smoke hole of her tent. When he looked down again, the toads were leaving as well. He did the same, by the door, and rounded the little tent in time to see that some of the toads had scattered. A line of disturbance in the grass pointed like an arrow toward the little dell through which the Onga River flowed, where the King Toad had his dominion. A greater wave pointed him farther down the river's bank, however. These, he thought, must be returning to assist in Eluneke's rescue. Mounting his horse, he followed at a distance, determined to do no less.

D aritai stroked the neck of his mare but succeeded only in communicating his own tension to the beast. She sidled with dainty lifts of her feet, not willful but like himself unable to settle. As he'd expected, Tinglut-Khan had taken badly the insults of the gur-khan but had listened with an avaricious gleam in his eye when his lesser prince set out his plan.

"The Qubal are in disorder," he'd told his father. "They've sent their best general to the south with half their army and all the prisoners they took during the war for the Cloud Country. Mergen Gur-Khan's second, Jochi, is distracted by the death of his own son and there is no love between the Qubal prince and his first officer, the gur-khan's blanket-son."

"They'll fight?" Tinglut-Khan had asked sharply, his hand straying across the map spread on a low table on the dais. At his side, Daritai's half brother, Prince Hulegu, watched him with unblinking tension.

"They already do. The dead boy was no accident." Daritai had driven the point home with his index finger, tapping the map where the Qubal usually grazed. "The cousin stands first among the prince's retainers by rank, but leads his own band of followers he calls the Durluken. The dead boy was a champion of the prince's own Nirun."

"The Sons of Darkness against the Sons of Light." Tinglut tugged at his long thin mustache. "So they play at spirit games and legend in their wars." He chuckled softly, slanting a glance from one son to the other, as if he knew the same warfare might break out between his own heirs if he slackened his hand on the reins. "How did that son of yours do?"

"Brave, observant as you would expect." He understood the

threat behind his father's casual question. He had wives, children, who would die first in any conflict with his father or the chosen heir. He'd thought of that. With any luck his most trusted guardsmen had already hidden them away.

"Ah, there is the boy now."

Tumbinai strode forward between two of Hulegu's most terrifying followers, one with a face so scarred that Daritai himself had difficulty looking at it. His son seemed unperturbed, though he had lived at the court of the Tinglut-Khan long enough to understand the threat. He smiled sweetly and kissed his grandfather first on one cheek and then on the other.

"Your father says that you were brave and observant," Tinglut challenged him. "So what did you see? Report, like a good scout!"

"Eluneke was pretty," Tumbinai said, "even if she did ride around in the shape of a toad sometimes. But she's already in love with the prince and he's in love with her, of course." He wrinkled his nose as though he found the idea of love very strange, which made his grandfather the khan laugh out loud.

"And did you notice anything besides the pretty girls?" he asked, a little of the malice leaving his grin.

"Prince Tayyichiut was upset about his friend dying. His cousin said he was sorry, but he wasn't. There was something funny about him."

Tumbinai frowned and a cold hand clutched at Daritai's heart. Sometimes the boy saw more than he should, but he usually had a good sense of when to keep his observations to himself, especially around his grandfather. He shrugged, as if he had no words to describe what he felt or saw, and ended lamely with, "I didn't like him."

"And did you like the prince, then?" Tinglut used a teasing tone, but he was watching his grandson carefully.

Tumbinai shrugged again. "He was sad about his friend. I guess that's nice."

"I'm sure it is." Reassured in some way that the boy posed no threat, Tinglut ruffled his hair with a bejeweled hand. "Now go find your bed. You'll be riding out with your uncle in the morning."

"You mean I can go to battle like my father!" the boy's face lit up with excitement, only to have his hopes dashed the next moment.

"I wouldn't risk you to the battlefield, child. You'll ride with the wagons and help Prince Hulegu to guard the women and children in case of attack. And when your father returns, you will take your place among the nobles in the palace."

A hostage, then. Tumbinai flashed his father a nervous glance but bowed to show his obedience to the khan. "As you wish," he said, and made a great display of yawning, which drew another laugh from his grandfather.

"Take this boy home to his mother," Tinglut roared, "and find what comfort there you may tonight, my son. Tomorrow you will ride for the glory of your khan and your people!"

And so Daritai found himself horsed again and riding to war. If he succeeded, all the grasslands would come under the sway of the Tinglut-Khan. As reward, his father might permit the return of his son. If he failed, he figured he'd be dead, and so would have little to say in the matter.

The armies were loyal to him as their general and he tried not to think about what that might mean past the present battle. His unruly imagination, however, thrust a tangle of possibilities on him as he rode. Returning victorious from the conquest of all the grasslands, he might seize the dais for himself, freeing his family forever from the threats his half brother Hulegu urged in the Tinglut-Khan's ear.

He could hold all the conquered lands in his own name, and live as gur-khan, filling the ger-tent palace of the Tinglut with the wives and children he had removed from the reach of the khan. All he had to do was sacrifice one child to Tinglut's revenge. For Daritai had no doubt that his father would torture and kill Tumbinai before his men could reach the boy.

Hulegu would have done it, if he'd had the stomach to do his own fighting at all. Daritai, however, would trade the grasslands and all he possessed for the life of his son. A frozen corner of his heart told him even that might not be enough to save his child.

Chapter Thirty-eight

"**D**ON'T LET HIM FIND ME. Don't let him find me. Don't let him find me." Eluneke chanted her private mantra like a prayer. She would have danced and beat her hands together to simulate a drum, but the demon that resided in the talisman resting over her heart had broken her legs the last time she'd tried. Oh, they hadn't really been broken. He'd have to leave the carved jade fragment and take corporeal form to do that and Qutula still needed her reasonably intact anyway. But when she had tried to dance a shaman's prayer, he'd convinced her mind that shattered fragments of bone were grinding agonizingly against each other. For a moment he'd even tricked her into believing that she saw the fractured points jutting from her flesh. She'd stayed mostly in her corner since then.

Except for direct invocations of the spirit world, which he punished with equally painful reminders, the demon made no objection to her chanting, taunting her with the uselessness of her efforts instead. "No one can hear you," he whispered in her ear. "The mortal world believes you dead, the spirit world cannot find you at all. So beg all you want, little girl. Only your jailer can hear you, and he is little inclined to mercy."

Qutula wanted Prince Tayyichiut dead and he'd be happy to kill her as well once he had what he wanted. Eluneke had given up trying to escape, but she still held out hope that Tayy wouldn't find her. At least not until he'd defeated his cousin in battle. Qutula's death would free the demon, who would have no further use for her. He might try to kill her, but she didn't think he'd stand and fight against her shamanic powers unless he had to.

"Is the monster still in there?"

Eluneke flinched at the caustic words meant for her. She knew the voice well enough: Duwa, the Durluken who had killed the Nirun captain Altan. One of Qutula's favorites, he'd escaped General Jochi's tents and run to his chosen master. When she opened her eyes, she saw that he still wore the iron band around his neck that marked him as a slave. More to the point, he had brought her breakfast.

Duwa, like the rest, approached her with dread and only when his master required it, like now. He entered the tent with a sneer on his face but kept to the lattices, well away from where she huddled on the filthy carpets.

"Ribbit," she said, just to annoy him.

He dropped the steaming bowl of millet boiled in whey, where it spread new stains across the muddy patterns. "Catch your own, then," he snarled at her, backing out of the tent.

Through the felted tent cloths she heard him say to someone outside the door, "I won't go back in there, no matter what you do to me."

"If that's the way you feel, then of course you won't have to go back," Qutula's voice answered. Then Eluneke heard a scream which ended suddenly in the thunk of something hard hitting the ground.

"Anyone else having second thoughts?" Qutula inquired, his voice cool and unruffled. No one volunteered an opinion. The blood seeping under the edge of the tent cover made the reason for that perfectly clear.

"Oooohhh," Eluneke wept. Wrapping her arms across her stomach, she clasped her shaman's costume tightly around her and rocked and moaned. They hadn't fed her the day before. Qutula hadn't been there and no one would come near her unless he forced them to it. She would doubtless starve to death if he didn't murder her first. Eluneke didn't like the idea, but she was starting to learn the limits of terror on that score. She knew he had sent for Tayy, however, and that she couldn't bear.

"Toragana!" she cried. "I need you! Where are you?"

As if in answer to the apprentice's prayer, a raven flew through the smoke hole and landed on one of the spokes that held up the roof. She shifted uneasily from one foot to the other on her perch. Though she didn't fly away again, neither did she change into the woman Toragana.

Qutula nudged the head of his follower Duwa with his toe. It rolled a little bit and he worried for a moment that it would fall into the pit his followers had dug for the prince. "Someone get rid of this."

As if they had been turned to stone, no one moved. Except Duwa, or his head, at least. It stopped when his nose hit a tuft of grass, which seemed to startle the life back into his army. Enough, at least, to drag the corpse away.

With a little nod of satisfaction, he turned his attention to his sword, carefully wiping the blood off with a soft square of cloth. When he had removed the last speck from the blade, Qutula dropped the cloth into the pit and slid the sword into its scabbard. He was almost ready.

In the distance he could see a smudge against the horizon that he figured for the prince coming at his command. His cousin had a reputation as a hero, but even the "bright shining one" couldn't overcome two hands of guardsmen sent to accompany Mangkut. Once the great Prince Tayyichiut was dead, he wouldn't need the girl. It would all be over soon.

He hadn't heard his demon lover join him until her hot breath whispered, "Kill him," in his ear. Now that they were so close to their goal, she had come out of hiding and stood beside him as a woman for all the camp to see. He missed her presence on his breast, missed the gift of pleasure that laced itself through his bones at the prick of her inky fangs and the voice riding in his head that had become a part of him. But he loved the fear and envy he saw in the eyes of his warriors when they recognized her for the Lady Chauijin, who had murdered the khan in his bed and who now chose to put Qutula in his place.

"I will," he promised, "But the army will fight for him. My brother has seen to that with his stupid songs."

"My people will help you." With a nod she showed him where the grass moved with a hundred and a hundred more of her snaky kinsmen.

His own heart stuttered in his breast. With an army of vipers he scarcely needed his human riders. And yet, who would follow a khan who openly ruled such creatures? Qutula suppressed his own terror at the slithering doom he saw approaching. The lady had murdered a husband before, and she was easily offended.

"Let the humans die for us," he suggested. "When we have won, I will build a new religion that honors the serpent-demon above all other spirits."

"And will you worship me in your tents, O great khan?"

He felt the threat in her fingers sliding to the back of his neck. Felt the promise as well when she drew his mouth down for a kiss.

"I will worship you in my tents, or anywhere you come to me," he sighed into her mouth.

"And will you worship me in the tall grass and among the stones, and anywhere my people gather?" she asked, and he said, "Yes, yes." His hands moved to her breast and he sought the serpent's tongue and the serpent's teeth in her mouth.

"We have time," she said, and Qutula let her lead him away to the tent he had taken for his own. Her serpent minion who watched over the shaman-princess would make sure that there was time. No one would find them until he chose to let them. His lady was proving to be a demanding lover, but he only had to satisfy her for a little while longer. When he was khan . . . but he mustn't let the thoughts come too close to the surface, where she might read them in his mind.

So far the plan was working. Prince Tayyichiut had delayed his departure with Mangkut while Jochi set a large force in place among the wagons that ringed the outer perimeter of the tent city. They had easily taken Qutula's small group of guards. Too easily, Tayy thought. They'd all been young and untested; some had seemed relieved of a great burden when they handed over their weapons. Qutula had been far away then, unable to control his nervous followers with threats or punishments. The next part wouldn't be as easy.

Mangkut had said nothing since they'd put him back on his horse. Several times Tayy caught him staring out of wide, blank eyes. Once, it seemed that the pupils of his eyes had narrowed to slits, as though a serpent were looking out of them. Perhaps, Tayy thought, she was.

"My Lady Chaiujin?" he inquired, but Mangkut's lips peeled back in a rictus of a smile and then he turned away. Not the emerald green bamboo snake-demon then, but another. Mangkut had said there was another.

"My pardon," he tried again. "I mean you no harm. I only wish to rescue the lady your master holds prisoner against her will."

"I have no master." The voice was not Mangkut's. He could read in the serpent eyes that the creature lied. Perhaps Qutula's soldiers were not the only ones who would betray him for their own freedom.

"Under my rule," Tayy promised, "the khanate will hold no creature slave against its will."

"Tell that to your horse," the demon replied. Contemptuously, he turned away, ending the conversation. Mangkut's shoulders sagged then. Released from the demon's control, the man began to tremble so fiercely that Tayy worried he might fall.

He had more important things to think about, however. A small tent city half hidden among the trees at the edge of the Onga had appeared as if out of nowhere. Mangkut had brought them through the demon's glamour which ringed the camp like a barricade of wagons. While there were few tents compared to the gathering under the gur-khan's banner, there were far too many to confront with Tayy's small force. He called a halt and slipped from the saddle.

"Where does he keep her?" he asked, dragging Mangkut after him.

"It's the one a little apart from the others; you can barely see it for the trees."

Not only did the tent stand alone, but it seemed that the warriors in the camp took care to stay well clear of it when they had to pass that way. Among the clans, only their shaman dealt easily with the spirit world. Tayy knew only Qutula who willingly treated with demons. That would work in their favor.

"General Qutula will have seen us coming," Mangkut remarked, promoting his captain, though not yet to the rank of khan. A small force had set out from the camp to intercept them but with no urgency.

"Mangkut will come with me." He tugged the traitorous captain from his saddle by the bonds that tied his hands. "I'll need five men to watch him, and to make sure no one comes into the tent while I release Eluneke."

"You'll have to get past my lord Qutula's demon first," Mangkut pointed out. "Once you see her, you may change your mind anyway." His sneer would have been more convincing if he'd managed to stop shaking.

"What has he done to her?" He didn't need the messenger any more. It would be easy to kill him.

"Nothing!" Mangkut shrank away from him, caught between terrors. "She's not hurt, just ugly as old Bortu's butt, and she did it to herself! It's not my fault!"

"It became your fault when you followed Qutula from the palace, and when you helped him kidnap her."

"I made a mistake! I'll do whatever you ask!"

Though Mangkut's eyes were round and human, the prince could see why the serpent-demon had found a comfortable home inside them. He wouldn't know the truth if it stepped on his foot.

"Take him," he said to one of the warriors who had dismounted to follow him. "As for the rest of you—"

"We know, Lord Gur-Khan." Their captain repeated his part

of the plan. "We hold your horses for your escape and guard the perimeter of your rescue."

"Your bravery will not go unsung." Prince Tayy clasped the hand of each man who would hold the way open for their retreat.

"My lord."

With a last salute, Tayy crouched low in the blowing grass and led his cohort around the camp. They would approach Eluneke's tent under cover of the forest that clung to the river.

The toads were still there, moving through the grass like a determined horde. Bekter was beginning to doubt the wisdom of following them, however. For one thing, he regretted not filling a waterskin for the journey which, at the rate toads traveled, seemed unlikely to put him in his brother's camp in time to do anything useful. For another, a storm was coming. Thunder rumbled ominously behind him. With his luck, he'd probably step in a puddle and find himself sucked into the underworld, or he'd be swept up to the heavens by lightning and left dead on the grass at the end of the storm.

He'd have done better to go immediately to the ger-tent palace. He should have told the prince what he had learned; General Jochi would have known what to do. *He* wouldn't have set out alone, but would have had the sense to bring his own horde with him. In spite of the bright sunlight, the thunder had settled into a steady roll that rumbled in his chest and shook the ground beneath his feet.

Oh. Not thunder, then. Half afraid to see what was following him, he turned around. Though still too far away to recognize by their features, it was easy enough to Hell that there were riders coming. A lot of them. For a heart-stopping moment he thought they would ride right over him. Then he realized that they were slowing their pace, stumbling around as if they had lost some trail they followed. Bekter could sympathize. He even figured that proved they were on his side. A handful of Qutula's people had passed him earlier, riding with no hesitation until they vanished before his eyes.

He'd have been more confident if he'd been able to figure out how a whole army had gotten this far without a magical toad to lead them, but it was worth turning back to find out. They would doubtless have water on them as well.

Bekter was not a small man and, mounted on his horse, made a large target against the bright blue sky, but the horde didn't seem to notice him. He flapped his hands over his head to draw their attention with no better success. *Hmmm.* That suggested he had passed within the influence of Qutula's demon, though not so far that he could actually see the Durluken camp. Not one to look a gift horde in the mouth, he turned around and headed back the way he had come. He worried about losing sight of the toads, but they seemed to understand his purpose in following them. A few had slowed their own frantic hopping as if waiting for him to catch up with them again.

It was easy to tell when the gur-khan's forces finally saw him because the horses in the front of the line reared up and would have unseated less skilled riders. Once the mounts were under control again, General Jochi, thank the gods and spirits, rode forward a few paces and rested his arms on the pommel of his saddle.

"And what are you doing out here alone, poet?"

The general didn't sound happy. Bekter didn't figure he'd like the answer much either, but there wasn't much he could do about that. "Following the toads," he said, and pointed to the ground.

The general had raised his hand but stopped mid signal. The warriors closest to him had started to move toward him, but stopped, confused both by their general's aborted command and by the grass ahead of them boiling with toads.

"We've been looking for you for the past two days."

And not for a chat or an epic, Bekter guessed. Jochi's fingers curled in what could only have been a choking motion. Not hard to figure what throat he imagined between his hands.

"I was with Toragana," Bekter explained. "Since this morning, I've been following these toads. According to Toragana, they know where my sister is."

"Your sister—" Jochi looked shocked that he had used the word, which made sense, considering that Qutula had kidnapped her. And suddenly he understood why they'd all been looking for him.

"I didn't help Qutula steal her. I don't know her well enough to know if I like her yet, but she's my blood, and the prince loves her. I can't believe you would think I would hurt either of them that way!"

"Then why are you here?"

"For the same reason you are, to find her and get her back."

But they hadn't been following a horde of toads. Suddenly, he had hope. "Do you know where she is?"

Jochi's frustration told him otherwise. "We were following the prince, then he disappeared."

"The prince—" It was unmanly to faint, Bekter reminded himself, but he nearly did it anyway.

"Water!" the general called, and one of the warriors formerly singled out to arrest him instead propped him up in his saddle and offered him the waterskin.

Bekter drank gratefully. It even helped his light-headedness enough to offer a suggestion. "The prince, I gather, was farther ahead of you than I was."

Jochi nodded, his eyes tense and watchful. "He had a guide from Qutula's camp. We were following at a cautious distance, but suddenly they disappeared. We continued in the direction he seemed to be heading, but we haven't seen them again."

"Well, if the prince's guide was taking him to Eluneke, and the toads are leading me to her as well, if you follow the toads, you should find the prince."

It struck him then that horses of the general's horde would trample the toads into the ground. But if the horde hadn't seen him until he stepped toward them, they must be close to the boundary of the demon's influence. They couldn't be that far from the camp.

"I'll follow the toads," he amended his suggestion. "Your army can follow me. When I disappear, you will know I can be no more than a step or two from where you last saw me. You ought to see me again as soon as you cross the spot where I vanished. It won't be fast, but when the camp comes into view, the toads can go to ground, allowing the horses to run."

Jochi clearly didn't like the idea, but he had little choice.

The prince, heir to the khanate, was on the other side of that invisible barrier. Going back without him wasn't an option for any of them.

With a nod, the general gave his permission to continue. Bekter turned around and followed the last of the toads through the demon's invisible shield. Behind him he heard swearing, but he held his mare to her steady pace and let her pick her way carefully among their warty guides.

Below, on the filthy carpets of the tent where Qutula held her prisoner, the shaman-princess Eluneke huddled in a heap and hid her sobs with a knobby hand held over her toady mouth. Within her breast, the shamaness Toragana wept for her pupil. Perched among the umbrella spokes of the roof, her totem form didn't know how to cry tears. She didn't dare to utter the bird's cry of desolation either, for fear of bringing Qutula's guardsmen with their bows. Toragana would be just as dead with an arrow through her feathered breast as she'd be in human form. So she hopped from one foot to another, lifting her sooty wings in distress, but kept her beak firmly closed.

She had a simple problem: find Bolghai and bring him back to free the princess from the talisman. But the demon's spell had clouded her vision even in her totem form. She had found Eluneke's prison only with the help of the toads and had no certainty of retracing her path on her own.

"Criii-kit!" squeaked a very small toad.

Wiping the tears from her eyes, Eluneke lifted her half-toad head to listen. "That might work," she agreed once the toad had explained their plan to rescue her with the help of Bolghai's sharp stoat's teeth. "But how will he find me?"

"Cri-yi-yi!" the toad responded.

Toragana fixed the creature with a long and thoughtful stare. He was certainly small enough to ride on her back while she searched out the shaman, and he could whisper the directions in her ear when she needed to return. She had to balance that against how tasty he looked for supper.

It was, of course, an unworthy consideration, and a reminder that she had held her totem form a bit too long. Fortunately, Eluneke didn't appear to have guessed what was going on in her raven's mind. The look she cast on her teacher was so full of hope that Toragana had to busy herself preening a feather so that her gaze did not give her away.

It took only a moment to bring herself around to it. Toragana hopped from the spokes of the umbrella roof and lightly flitted to the ground. Bowing her head, she accepted the little toad on her back with no more than a ruffle of her feathers. Then she was off, struggling to fly through the smoke hole and then gathering speed in the free air.

"Caw!" she warned the toad. She thought that when she passed into the dream realm the creature would be drawn with her. If she was wrong, however, he would fall from where her back had been, a long way to the ground.

"Criyiyi!" The little toad assured her that he was ready.

Flap, flap, flap, like running in the air, she reached for the dream world and suddenly, there she was.

"Criyi-kit!" The toad politely informed her that he had not fallen, though she would have known it anyway by the weight on her back.

"Bolghai!" she called. "Bolghai! I've found Eluneke, but I can't free her without you!"

She thought it might take a long time to find him, but he heard her call and appeared on the dream landscape that passed below her flight. When he stood on his hind legs and signaled her, she spiraled down to a landing made clumsy by the toad on her back.

"You have to come right away," she said. "Qutula has placed Eluneke at the mercy of a demon! We need your help."

The stoat looked for a moment as though he couldn't decide whether to leap on the raven and snap her neck for dinner or swallow the little toad whole. With a tremble that shook his fur from the tip of his nose to the end of his tail, however, he turned back into his human form and squatted on the grass. "Tell me everything," he said. "With a little effort, we should be able to get back before you left."

Chapter Thirty-nine

IF THE PLAN HAD GONE perfectly, Jochi would now be descending on Qutula's camp with three thousand of Tayy's own horde. The attack would have drawn off Qutula's forces, leaving his small cohort free to rescue the princess.

Tayy's part of the plan had gone smoothly enough. Mangkut had led him to the tent where he promised they would find Eluneke. "Prepare yourself for a shock," he had warned them with a smirk. "She is not the beauty you remember."

Tayy wanted to hit him, but he couldn't afford the commotion. "Bind him, and cover his mouth," he whispered to his companions. "Then tie him to a tree for his master to find."

Mangkut's eyes widened in terror. For betraying him, Qutula would surely have him killed as slowly and horribly as the prince had threatened. He gathered breath for a shout to rouse the camp but Tayy was there first, clamping a leather-gauntleted hand to his mouth. "There is more to this plan than you know," he whispered. "Be quiet and you may yet live. Make a sound and my companions will happily crack your ribs like a pigeon and draw your struggling lungs out through your backbone before they go to their own doom. Don't think Qutula will help you to a swifter end when he finds you."

Mangkut nodded to show that he understood. Tayy didn't

trust him, but before he could draw another breath, one of the Qubal rescuers stuffed a cleaning cloth for his sword into his mouth. Another secured a thong between Mangkut's teeth to hold it in place while a third tied his feet. They had never released his hands; Tayy left them to complete securing their prisoner and slipped under the tent cloth.

He didn't see her at first. When he did, he couldn't control the instant recoil.

Eluneke covered her distorted face and moaned softly into her hands. "Don't look at me," she whispered. "Leave me here—you have to go. He means to kill you."

"I'm not going anywhere without you," he promised, and cursed himself at the hesitation in his voice. Eluneke still had the general shape of a woman, but her face had been grotesquely transformed into the features of a frog. Thin strands, a travesty of her own thick dark hair, fell across large, protuberant eyes and partly covered the mouth stretched in a debased parody of a grin. Her hands, where they tried to hide her features, were mottled green and brown, her fingers gnarled and covered with warty yellow knobs of skin.

From the first time he had set eyes on her in Toragana's doorway he had loved her natural beauty. He loved her spirit more, however, and had accepted her totem animal long ago, conversing with the king of the toads and carrying Eluneke herself as a toad near his heart. But in all their past encounters she had chosen the form she wore; he found it impossible to accept the shape Qutula's demon had forced on her.

Eluneke watched him through her fingers and wept when it must have appeared to her that he could not look at her face. She flinched when he reached out to hold her.

"I'm sorry," he said. Her fear of him pierced his soul like a dagger, but he refused to be deterred. "I'm getting you out of here; Bolghai will know what to do when you're free."

"I can't. The demon . . ." She bobbed her head like a toad, refusing to accompany him while she urged him to his own escape. "Go, while you can."

"Not without you." *Patience*, he told himself, and was rewarded with her hand, tentatively reaching for his.

"Not so fast there, toad lover!" Between them, the form of a serpent materialized, fangs dripping vaporous venom.

Instinctively, Tayy pulled his sword, but the viper swirled away in a mist when he struck at it, leaving nothing behind but the hissing bark of its laughter.

"What difference does it make whether you still want her?" the creature hissed in his ear. "You're here, aren't you? Soon enough you'll be dead, and I'll be free."

His sword raised, Tayy whirled, tracking the sibilant voice. But the viper drew its insubstantial neck out of reach.

"Frankly, I didn't think you'd be such a fool," it taunted.

Tayy brought his sword down in a slicing move that should have severed the head from any material beast, but it slid right through the vaporous scales.

"That wasn't very friendly."

Before he could pull his hand back, the serpent found the thin bracelet of flesh exposed between the prince's riding gauntlet and his coat. Grinning, it sank its dripping fangs into his flesh. Venom pulsed fire into the wound. When the viper withdrew, one sharp tooth remained in the wound, lodged between the bones.

"No!" Eluneke screamed.

The effect of a demon's sting didn't always parallel the creature whose form it embodied. This time, Tayy realized, it did. Already his arm had begun to blister and bleed. His heart beat in strange rhythms and his breathing came in short, rapid gasps. He didn't have much time and, alerted by the sounds of struggle, Qutula's warriors had come boiling through the door of the tent.

"Ugly, isn't she?" Qutula stood smirking in front of him, his clothes hastily tied and his sword held carelessly in his hand.

Swaying on his feet, Tayy painfully raised his sword and charged, though he knew that the desperate action hastened his own death. It scarcely mattered now. Jochi hadn't come, and there were too many against his handful of guardsmen. But he could defend Eluneke until he fell. He moved in, feinted left, and cut Qutula a slashing blow that left his sleeve dangling but did little more than scratch the arm beneath.

"You son of a bitch!" Qutula snarled, and struck back.

Tayy intercepted the blow. Their swords slid blade against blade until they came to rest in a clash of cross guards. The prince's arm trembled, blood-choked from the serpent's bite and swelling with blisters from the venom. His sword grew impossibly heavy, but damaged muscles refused his commands to disengage.

Where was Jochi? Around him, weapons rang against each other as Tayy's small raiding party held off the tide of the opposition. Though Qutula's forces vastly outnumbered them, they had limited their approach to the doorway, so far at least not thinking to unmake the tent around them and so come at them from all sides. They might go on like that until their arms tired; eventually the prince's small cohort would stagger and the overwhelming numbers against them would triumph. But Tayy wouldn't be there to see it. He fell to his knees, blind and breathless, the pain in his arm so overwhelming that he hardly knew if he still held his sword.

Qutula's blade followed him down. "Your line is dead," he said, "You have no place here anymore." Then he plunged the sword into the prince's undefended back.

Tayy fell, arms spread on the dirty carpets, his life's blood adding to the stains that already crossed them. The last sounds he heard were Eluneke's sobs, mingling with the keening wail of his hounds somewhere out on the grasslands and the beating of drums in the distance. Too late to save the prince's life, Jochi had arrived. It had been too late since the serpent had struck, of course. He couldn't breathe: couldn't find the air to fill his lungs and his last sucking breath seemed to be leaking away with the blood flowing from the wound in his back.

His mother was frowning and he waited patiently for the scolding that didn't come. She was dead, of course, and he was long past the age when she might correct him like a child. He would have liked to know what had displeased her so, but lacked the energy to ask. But he easily went into her arms when she offered them, and laid his head against her heart the way he had as an infant. How he had missed her. Chimbai was there too, looking thunderously angry. He said nothing, however, and might have sighed, but Tayy's senses were fading. . . .

Chapter Forty

THE PRINCE'S MEN had fought with desperate energy and his own dead and wounded lay scattered among them, but Qutula's superior forces had won the day, killing or overpowering the little band of rescuers. The fighting hadn't ended, however; battle drums sounded in the distance. He wasn't surprised that Tayy's army had followed their prince, but the serpent-demon's failure to throw them off the track disappointed him. He would have to devise a suitable punishment. In the meantime, he took a moment to savor his victory over his cousin before mustering his army.

"We're under attack," he advised his closest followers who sorted their wounded while they waited for his next orders. "Tie the prisoners and throw them out where the good General Jochi's horde must pass.

"And leave this for him to chew on." With the last words, he picked up Tayy's sword from where it had fallen.

He would have liked to keep the weapon for the jewels in the hilt. Its presence with the prisoners—proof of the prince's death—would slow the horde now descending upon him, however; he needed that time to muster his own troops. With any luck, General Jochi would accept that his mission had failed and give his allegiance to Mergen's true son. Qutula didn't count on that, but any delay worked in his favor.

"Throw him in the pit." He nudged the body with his toe, rolling it over so the prince's unseeing eyes stared up at him. "Cover it and tether a horse or two to trample the ground; We don't want anyone digging him up again, now do we?"

No one answered—he'd expected no less—but the dead prince was taken up by his arms and his legs and carried out of the tent. Presently the satisfying sound of muddy earth falling heavily on leather half-armor reached him.

In the recent wars in the Cloud Country, Qutula had seen the result of allowing a hero's soul to return generation after generation in search of justice. He had no intention of letting Prince Tayyichiut's vengeful spirit disturb his rest now or in any future generation. Imprisoned in the carrion of its own buried corpse, Tayy's soul would make easy prey for the hungry spirits. Those unhappy tatters of captive souls would devour the living essence of the prince and turn him into one of their lost kind, devouring other luckless spirits in a neverending circle of torment.

So caught up in his own thoughts, Qutula almost forgot the toad-girl sniveling in the corner. Though it pained him to look at her, he needed something to trade for his life if it came to that. With Tayy dead, he didn't have many options.

"Are you carrying his child?" he asked.

She controlled the darting of her tongue with an effort, but gave no answer by word or the tremor of even an eyelid. That told him something in itself. She hadn't always been this hideous, of course, but the prince *had* suffered from more honor than sense.

"So in all those nights spent on the river he never rode you at all. Pity. Pity you aren't prettier or I'd give you a taste of what you've been missing."

Her eyes burned and he was glad of the demon he'd bound in the talisman at her fat toady throat. No gratitude at all for the fact that he'd just decided to spare her life. For the present. He might have to reconsider that decision, though. She had powers that amazed even Bolghai. If she ever got loose, he figured Jochi's army would be the least of his troubles.

But right now the general was his problem, so he turned

and left her there to listen while his guardsmen entombed her hero's soul.

The Durluken would meet the general's horde out on the grassland, well away from his own tents thanks to the spell his tame demon had cast over the camp. Qutula therefore directed only a small force to patrol his perimeter. For the rest, he sorted them with little confusion. Duwa's thousand he took under his command, in addition to ordering the movements of his whole army. As for Mangkut's company . . . the patrol had found his captain. They had freed his ankles so that he could walk under his own power, but his hands remained bound.

"My lord." Mangkut bowed deeply before he added, "I understand you have found the gift I brought you, and have dispatched it as you intended."

"You betrayed me to save your own skin," Qutula pointed out reasonably enough. The warriors who held the prisoner paled with fear, but Mangkut answered with a cocky grin.

"Not at all, my lord. Your orders were to bring the prince. Our plan for doing so unfortunately met more obstacles than I could overcome, so I had to improvise on the spot. He would not come as my prisoner, but I easily led him to your justice by making it seem that I believed myself at his mercy. Either way, I knew the outcome would be the same."

"And so it has been," Qutula agreed. He waited a moment to give his judgment, wanting to see Mangkut sweat for the risk he had taken—or the betrayal he had plotted. But he needed captains and Mangkut had followed him since they were on leading reins.

"Go," he said. "You made one error in your calculations. The general followed you with his army."

Mangkut grinned at the news. "And doubtless wanders in amazement outside your demon's glamour," he scoffed. "Until you fall on him as if from the sky, and disappear again to terrify his horde and send them running for their tents to hide their faces under their blankets. With their hero dead, who but our own Lord Qutula can win?"

"With such confidence, who could lead us into the fray but our own Captain Mangkut?" Qutula ordered the Durluken's hands released and returned his grin with malice lurking at the corners of his eyes. "I honor your thousand, who will lead the assault," he said.

Mangkut paled, understanding as Qutula knew he must the perilous role he'd been given. But he was the sort of captain who led by driving his men from behind rather than drawing them after him in the charge. He would consider his losses well spent if they accounted for his own survival. "My lord." He bowed his head in submission before heading off to locate his company and give his orders.

Qutula watched his departing back for only a moment. His horse in full caparison stood for him to mount. The sun shone brightly, a light breeze played with his braids below his cone-shaped helmet, and Jochi awaited him on the battlefield with an ulus already half lost. It was a fine day for a slaughter.

Bolghai followed Toragana through the dreamscape. Blind to Eluneke's spirit, he depended on the raven, with the little frog guide on her back, to find their pupil. Suddenly a darkness rose up across the horizon. Bolghai flinched, but the little toad urged the raven on, through the dark storm that blotted out all dreams and all the worlds of the living and the dead where shaman freely roam. He trembled, knowing the blight for a demon's spell, but trusted Eluneke's totem creature to lead them through.

It was a bumpy ride, filled with the voices of hungry spirits, and the lost, but then it ended, tumbling them into the bright light of their spirit-senses. They had passed the boundary of the demon's spell. The toad had brought them to Qutula—below, the soul of Mergen's blanket-son roiled the dreamscape with his dark purpose. It was this more than anything of the demon's own devising that had fed the shadow spell.

Though Bolghai now saw the tents of the enemy clearly in the dreamscape, Eluneke remained hidden from him. With the aid of her toad passenger, however, Toragana quickly found the tent where the demon held the shaman-princess prisoner and leaped into the mortal sphere. Bolghai thought himself inside the tent and scampered, nose twitching, into the world of the living on Qutula's soiled carpets.

Toragana fluttered helplessly around the girl's head a moment before landing on one of the umbrella spokes that held up the roof. Like the raven, Bolghai remained in his totem form, drawing power from the creatures of the earth to protect him from the demon whose presence he sensed in the tent. Even here, so close to her, he caught no reflection of Eluneke's bright soul in the misshapen creature, half toad, half girl, pressed weeping against the single lattice.

A tear welled from his little stoat eye. Disaster had struck, and it was his fault. If he had guided her more rapidly through the trials of her training, she might have fought off the demon who possessed the talisman around her throat. Or perhaps he was just being a fool.

She noticed him then, looking up from red-rimmed eyes that clashed vilely with her brown-and-green skin. "You're too late," she said, barely able to make the human sounds in her toady throat. "He's dead. My half brother murdered his own cousin and threw him in a pit. For all your vaunted powers, your prince's very soul lies rotting in the mud while horses pound the dirt over his head."

Bloghai shuddered and the fur rose on end down the length of his spine. The despair in her tormented voice chilled him, so that his liver quivered in his belly.

"Prince Tayyichiut?" He twitched his beady little nose questioningly, though she could mean no one else, with such wrenching tears.

"His soul is perishing, even now torn to pieces by the hungry spirits!" Eluneke clutched the thin strands of her hair with gnarled fingers. "I have to help him!"

Her anger shook Bolghai in his dismay. He had a task to do, a princess to rescue, and a prince to save from a fate more terrible than the death that presaged it. Toragana had explained to him that the demon would stop a human enemy of Qutula's from freeing the girl. So Bolghai must be something other than human when he approached the golden thread that bound talisman to spell.

In his totem form, therefore, he beckoned the spirit of the stoat and released it from his human control. In his own place he left not a thought but an impulse, to gnaw the thread and rid Eluneke of the jade disk at her breast. Then he crept into her lap and began to chew.

"Hurry!" Toragana cawed at him as he bit down on the golden thread. "There's no time!"

The toads had returned, nudging their way under the felted tent cloths. Gathering in hundreds around the center pole, they climbing over each other in their need to be near the shaman-princess. King Toad himself joined them, his demeanor solemn.

"How can we serve you?" he asked, and reverently bobbed his head, for Eluneke had taken the toad people with her to visit the sky god and he had himself frolicked in the grasses of heaven for a while.

"Can you dig?" Eluneke asked.

"We will do what we can," King Toad promised, though his people preferred trees by the waterside and grass for their homes.

With a last snap of his teeth, Bolghai parted the thread. "I can dig." He looked up from his work and grinned to show his sharp stoat teeth. Still more beast than man in spirit, he flexed his clawed hands, admirably shaped for digging burrows.

The gleaming jade of the talisman caught the attention of the stoat mind while the carved rune of a coiled serpent on its face drew Bolghai's more subtle shaman thoughts. He grasped the broken jade of the talisman in his paws and examined it. He'd seen that rune at the bottom of a wedding cup the Lady Chaiujin had given the god-king Llesho, back the other side of the war, when Chimbai still lived. It had certainly caused enough mischief then, so it didn't surprise him that even broken into bits it retained its ability to harm. He wondered if Qutula had known what he was playing with when he found it, or if the lady had bent an otherwise straight twig to shape a tool for her vengeance.

But now was not the time to contemplate what might have

been. He took the disk and scampered to the lattice with it, then hesitated, unwilling to risk the influence of the thing by keeping it nearby, but equally dismayed to leave Eluneke to her fate while he disposed of it.

"I'll take that," the king of the toads offered, seeing his distress. "What do you want me to do with it?"

"Throw it in the river," Bolghai suggested. "Let the demon's own kind draw it back down into hell."

The king of the toads bobbed his head in agreement and summoned a hand of his most trusted subjects to drag the thing away by its broken thread, trailing the talisman behind them. The snake that was the demon in the rune screamed in his rage, but he could do little to harm them from the bottom of the Onga River.

Eluneke shook out her besmirched sleeves and found her human form again; her eyes returned to their orbits, and her cheeks grew familiar under her smooth brown fingers. "It wasn't the Lady Chaiujin," she said.

"It would have been too much to hope," Bolghai agreed. He, too, returned to human shape, though his body felt strangely stretched and awkwardly large after days and weeks in his totem form.

"He was one of the lady's servants," she confirmed. "The lady herself whispers in Qutula's ear, and in his bed."

The ulus was in terrible danger. One demon might be defeated, or beaten back as they had beaten the Lady Chaiujin before. If she gathered followers, however . . .

"At Qutula's command, the demon-serpent murdered Prince Tayy or injured him so mortally that Qutula's sword seemed almost a mercy."

The princess seemed not to notice the tears running down her nose. It was, of course, no mercy at all, and when she told him what had happened, Bolghai dropped his human head into his hands and wept with her for the child he had loved and the man he had admired and the khan he might have been.

"I have to save him," she said, and he frowned, not sure he understood.

"You mean they buried him alive?" The thought of their brave, beautiful prince suffocating beneath the horses' hooves while his wounds bled into the dirt distressed Bolghai so much that his shape wavered and he found himself with his human hands drawn up like paws to shield his face from his own sorrow.

Toragana fluttered to the ground and when she had turned back into a woman, set a comforting hand on her pupil's shoulder.

"No!" Eluneke shook her off, rejecting any comfort. "You don't understand. Tayy's death was just the first half of my vision. He's supposed to be my husband; somehow, I have to bring him back."

That had always been the crux of it, Bolghai knew. Fate meant them to be matched, but how? He'd never heard of the like, even among the feats of the greatest shamans of legend. And Eluneke was just a girl, not even a full shamaness yet. . . .

Then it struck him: that was the point. "You're right, of course. You have to go and get him."

Her final test. They didn't usually come at quite so high a cost. Bolghai wondered if he had grown too old to serve as shaman to the royal household. He'd lost two khans, after all, and the prince before he even took his proper place at the head of the ulus. Had the fates intended Mergen's daughter to challenge the underworld for a life the hungry spirits must already have claimed for their own? It was too much to bear.

Eluneke peered out the door and pulled her head back with a grimly satisfied smile. "The human guardsmen are gone. They've been relying on the demon to control me for too long, it's made them careless."

"Will your totem animals willingly attend you on such a trip?" Toragana asked, while Bolghai was still trying to figure out if his own love for the prince was strong enough to find him among the tormented dead of the underworld. Eluneke'd had little time to gather skins of the naturally dead among the toads. Their kind usually slid down some gullet to die in the belly of a larger beast.

That didn't shake Eluneke's determination. "If not," she said, "I'll go alone."

But the queen of King Toad's harem would not hear of such a thing. "Ribbit!" she said. "The toads did well enough in heaven and would like to see for themselves this underworld of spirits and demons. So I'll go, and my fellow wives will come with me. A harem is a boring place to live, after all, even for a toad. We wish for adventures to entertain our lord. And true love is our specialty."

The little baskets that hung from Eluneke's shaman's robes had splintered and broken, but the toad wives wove them into makeshift nests and tucked themselves away in such numbers that it seemed Eluneke could scarcely move. This was how she had traveled to the sky god, Bolghai remembered. He liked the symmetry of it if nothing else. They slipped outside, but no one stopped them. The camp, it seemed, was empty.

"I'll lead the horses away," Toragana offered, and then they were left with the beaten ground.

"What do I do?" Eluneke asked.

"Use the gifts the gods have given you," Bolghai instructed her, "And dance."

The Lady Bortu sat among her women and the nobles and chieftains past the age of fighting battles. One granddaughter was missing. Eluneke might still live, but she had disappeared from Bortu's inner vision. At her knee the other, Princess Orda, had curled in a restless sleep. Mergen should never have sent for her. Old Tinglut had wanted a woman, not a child bride. They'd torn the little girl from the only home she'd ever known and, in so doing, had revealed the existence of Chimbai's daughter to an enemy for nothing.

Like Chimbai himself, Mergen had paid for his mistakes, of course; Bortu had given both her sons to the funeral pyre. She mourned them both with open eyes, however. The ulus was still paying. As she stroked the princess' tangled hair, her eyes took on the flinty, black light of the eagle. Long ago she had discovered her totem animal in the dream realm, but had turned away from the path of the shaman to mother khans instead. She had never doubted her decision. But gifted with the insights of her abandoned calling, she felt the child of one son die at the hands of the other. Prince Tayyichiut, her beautiful Prince Tayy, was dead.

And Princess Orda had cried as though the world were ending until, exhausted, she had fallen asleep where she lay. The name she called in her dreams didn't belong to her foster family, however. "Tumbi," she'd whispered under her breath. Bortu knew no one by that name among the Qubal, but Prince Daritai had a son called Tumbinai. Her spies had reported sighting Daritai's army, camped the other side of a rise in the grasslands, waiting, she guessed, until the Qubal forces had exhausted themselves on each other before seizing the leavings.

"I'm too old for war," she muttered querulously under her breath. Her ladies-in-waiting questioned her but she hadn't meant for them to hear.

At her feet, the little girl turned in her sleep. "Not too old," the princess murmured, though she couldn't have understood the Lady Bortu's weariness with a life that had outlasted all she loved. She spoke with such perfect confidence even in her sleep, however, that Bortu wondered if the spirit of a shaman didn't move within the child as it moved within her grandmother and her brother. Prince Tayyichiut had never recognized his powers, though he had drawn on them at need. If the child spoke prophecy, then perhaps there remained a reason why Bortu still lived. At the least, she thought, she might save Princess Orda when the Tinglut horde swept over them. The little girl gave her hope that she might yet contribute more than dead sons to the honor of her name before she joined the ancestors.

"My lord."
          Qutula turned at the sound of his lover's voice. Somewhere, Lady Chaiujin had found herself a horse which cantered over to bring the lady to his side.

"What are you doing here?" he asked with a little less confidence than he would have liked in front of his gathered army. He might need her demon powers if Jochi's experience should prove him the abler general, but the horde was no place for a woman. Why hadn't she coiled her inky serpent on his breast, where she had been in the habit of traveling?

The cold condescension of her features did not invite the question.

"We ride hard into bloody battle," he reminded her. The demon's face and figure seemed a little out of shape today, with the faint tracery of scales almost visible where her coats fell back on her wrists. "If you are unwell, my lady, I can find a servant to attend you." His mother might have been able to help, but he'd killed her. "Or my sister Eluneke . . ."

"The blood of battle is all I need," she said, and it was clear to him that she was as anxious as her mount to enter the fray. No human power could keep her in the camp if she chose to ride, so he gave up trying to dissuade her. The emperor of Shan, after all, had ridden to war with his own supernatural mistress at his side. Raising his arm to signal the advance, he decided that the comparison boded well for his success.

"Ayyeee—ayaaa! We ride!" he cried, and his captains took up the order.

Though his army was sadly reduced, still the thunder of four thousand horsemen with their replacement mounts charging into battle is a wondrous thing. The ground shook and the banners of his thousands lit the fire in his belly. Between his legs his mare stretched out, her hooves beating a battle song on the grass. Behind, the drums rumbled and the trumpets blared in terrifying cacophony. Dark as storm clouds and loud as thunder, their arrows swift and bright as lightning, Qutula's army advanced.

The great dark line of Jochi's force faltered. They had stumbled on the survivors of Prince Tayy's failed rescue, no doubt. The general wouldn't stop to hear the whole of the tale, but he knew now that the man he had hoped to rescue with his attack lay dead under the ground, food for the worms and the hungry spirits. He fought for no living khan, against Mergen's true son, the only heir left standing.

Stealing a glance in her direction, he saw that his lady's eyes were gleaming. Pride, he guessed, and the exhilaration of riding against a man who was defeated before the battle had began.

""Ayy-ayaaa-eee!" he cried, and drawing his spear, held it aloft so all who followed him might gaze upon the bright point casting sparks of sunlight like a challenge.

Jochi, he saw, had lifted Tayy's sword as if it were a talisman in his hand. It would fail the general as it had failed the prince. With a sound like mountains colliding, the armies met.

Chapter Forty-one

THE GIFTS OF THE GODS. Among the baskets and other decorations of her shaman's robes, Qutula hadn't noticed or recognized the value of the little pouch where Eluneke had stored the gifts from the daughters of the sky gods. Commanded to dance, she drew out the drum and horse-head drumstick. As she danced, she remembered. The daughter of the drum had taught her all the languages of the animals, but more importantly, Eluneke had learned from the daughter of the spear the skill of casting out demons. Like most of the skills of a shaman, they only worked on other people, so they hadn't helped her much with her own demon. Tayy was dead, something altogether different, but she hoped that while she tried to rescue him the incantations would protect them from the demons and hungry spirits that roamed in search of fresh souls.

With renewed confidence, she quickened the hopping steps of her totem dance while, clinging from her robes, the harem of the king of the toads urged her on. Once she had struggled to find her totem shape; now she set all her skill and concentration to finding the underworld in human form. It would have been easier as a toad, but Tayy had turned away from her monstrous face. She could not bear such a rejection again. To escape the world of the dead, he must follow her freely, so she danced as the girl he loved. When the urge to drop to her haunches and hop about on green-and-brown legs came over her, she fixed her mind on her purpose and the prince and set human feet on the path of the drum until, with one step, her foot passed through grass and earth like they were mist. With the next step she sank into the smothering darkness.

Nervously, Eluneke took a breath. Musty and damp though it was, she was relieved to find air, not earth in her throat. All around her was black as the bottom of a lake. With a hand held out in front of her, she trod as carefully as if through water, but met no resistance. She could see well enough if she didn't think too much about the contradiction of it: a landscape of mountains pointed their roots at the sky, their whitecapped tops hanging precariously over her head.

Above her, a river like a mirror flowed through a roof of silver grass. Reflected in the water she saw the world of trees, and leaves blowing in breezes that stirred the land of the living. She thought she must be walking on the clouds, or their reflection, that must take the place of solid ground here in the underworld. Afraid of what she would see if she glanced down, however, Eluneke looked straight ahead.

Shapes without limbs or faces moved out of the darkness and passed without seeming to notice her. The harem of toads shifted uneasily in their baskets but, not surprisingly, were unwilling to leave her for their own explorations. Then something brushed against her leg.

"Ah!" she let out a little yelp, quickly suppressed before she called the attention of those gliding shapes down on her.

A nose butted against her hip while, on her other side, a second of the spirit creatures nudged its soft, triangular head under her hand. Dogs, she realized, and looked down at them to confirm her guess. Tayy's dogs; the red whined anxiously and tugged at her sleeve, pulling Eluneke along.

"I'm coming," she promised. The dogs seemed to glow with their own unearthly light in the darkness and it struck her that they had never behaved quite the way mindless beasts ought.

Who are you? She didn't say the words aloud, but it seemed that in this realm one had only to shape the thought to be understood. The black dog looked up at her with his tongue hanging from the side of his mouth, his eyes wide and wet with dismay. Then he shook himself and his limbs began to lengthen and straighten. He'd been a large dog, but Chimbai-Khan had been a big man, and that was who sat at her feet. Or so Eluneke guessed, since her clans had stood too low in the ranks of the ulus for her to have seen his face when he had lived. But he wasn't Mergen, and she didn't know who else would wear such elegant silk robes or the silver helmet of the khan.

Even with a pyre and ceremonies performed with utmost care, spirits sometimes found themselves tied to the earth through some unfinished task or a bond in the mortal world they couldn't quite let go of. For the spirit of the khan, that bond was to his son. He dropped his head into his hands and wept with dampening sorrow.

"Come, come, we don't have time for indulging our grief!" A woman stood at Eluneke's side. There could be no doubt of her identity either.

"My lady khaness," Eluneke acknowledged the dignity of the lady with a deep bow. "Your son, Prince Tayyichiut, looks very much like you," she offered as an explanation for her greeting. Then, "Did," she amended with dismay, her own eyes dangerously near to tears.

"Tayy was always more handsome as a boy than I ever was as a woman," the khaness waved away the compliment. "But we have little time for pleasantries. My son's life hangs in the balance."

Eluneke was not in the habit of conversing with the spirits of the ancestors; she was still an apprentice shamaness and this was her first visit to the underworld and she had expected humbler souls to teach her. She didn't know the niceties of breaking bad news to such exalted spirits, but couldn't go on while the lady suffered such a misapprehension. "I'm sorry, my lady, but your son is dead. Qutula has imprisoned him, body and soul, in the cold earth."

"And you have come to save him. Of course. Did you bring your horse?"

Eluneke just looked confused at that. The lady examined her with a critical eye and took the horse-head drumstick that dangled forgotten from her hand. When the spirit touched it, the stick transformed itself, growing four legs and stretching its neck with a shake to settle its mane.

Chimbai-Khan had risen from his tears and by some magic of the underworld held the reins of two horses with eyes of fire, one black and one roan. "He can't have gotten far," he agreed with the Lady Temulun, his khaness. "But finding him will prove the simpler part of the task."

They would have to fight the hungry spirits, Eluneke thought; already the faceless wraiths of forgotten ancestors were tugging at her clothes and tangling clawed fingers in her hair. Not wanting to hear the answer if it proved dire, she nevertheless had to ask, "Is Mergen here with you?"

Chimbai shook his head, but a new sorrow marked his bold face. "I chose wrongly in the ordering of my brother," he admitted, and sighed, a sound more terrible when uttered by a spirit. "Only regrets bound him to the mortal realm, and those are quickly severed when the proper rites are performed. He has followed the path to the ancestors. In his next life, I hope he enjoys a greater peace of spirit than I ever left to him in this."

Eluneke nodded, glad that her father had escaped the traps that might have bound him in torment as a hungry spirit. She worried a little on that score for the khan and his khaness, but they had neither the red and hungry eyes of the lost nor the rapacious apetite of those who would devour the living. She had to find Tayy before that could happen to him.

Reading her mind again, it seemed, Chimbai mounted his fire-eyed black steed. His lady took her place in the saddle of the roan and Eluneke climbed onto the back of her own mount, smoky pale as bone. With a cry, they were off, riding across a landscape of darkness with the silver grass over their heads bending in their passing, as if from the impact of galloping hooves.

The noise was overpowering. Battle cries clashed with the screams of the wounded and the frenzied calls of the horses caught in their own battle madness. Bekter hated it, just as he hated the smell of blood and fear that sharpened the sweat of man and beast. Once he'd led Jochi's army past the demon's spell, however, he'd had no choice but to wrap a silver band around his arm and join the general's horde in battle.

He raised his sword over his head and brought it down in a slashing blow that took the arm off a man he vaguely recognized as an archery trainer in Chimbai-Khan's army. In the midst of the chaos of battle, they'd stopped and stared at each other for a moment. Then the archer raised his bow and Bekter knew the silver band around his arm for a trick. Jochi had ordered his army to wear just such a band to identify them as the khan's own.

Qutula had dressed his army with a band of green the color of the tattoo he wore on his breast: the emerald green bamboo snake that had caused the Qubal so much pain. By wearing silver, however, the archer had penetrated deep into Jochi's horde before Bekter stopped him. He wouldn't have had a chance against his older, more battle-hardened teacher, except that the soldier hesitated to attack the brother of his own general.

Bekter had no such qualms, though he tried his best to deliver a wounding rather than a fatal blow. With an involuntary grunt of shock, the old soldier went very pale and fell in a swoon from his horse. There was no way to save him. The battle swirled around them, horses crossing the ground where the wounded archer had fallen. When the armies rode on, his old teacher lay beaten into the soft ground, his bones shattered by the many hooves that had passed over him.

The sight of such terrible death turned his stomach, but Bekter refused to turn away. *I did this,* he thought. *A man I once knew is dead because of me.* This wasn't his first battle, only his first against warriors he had grown up with, who had sworn their loyalty to his brother. In despair he would have ridden from the battlefield. How could he preserve his honor when all choices led to betrayal? Did he fight Qutula or commit treason against his khan?

Neither Chimbai nor Mergen had chosen Qutula to succeed them, however. It pained him to set his arm against his brother, but he couldn't let Qutula tear apart the ulus to seize for himself a position to which he had been neither anointed nor elected. He couldn't support his brother, but he hoped they might end this war with as little damage on each side as possible. And, he decided, he'd already done his share.

So Bekter forged ahead through the chaos of battle. Swinging his sword wildly to either side, he strove to keep his new enemies at arm's length while striking none of them. His opponents knew him and gave way as he came on, but they harried him like herders, cutting him out of the herd and giving him their own direction to run.

Advancing without resistance, Bekter left his own army behind before he realized what had happened. Suddenly, he found himself surrounded by Qutula's green armbands. Qutula himself came forward, a spear held lightly in his hand. The Lady Chaiujin, openly flaunting her influence over him, rode at his side.

"My brother." Qutula's smile, more serpentlike than his lady's, sent a chill down Bekter's spine. "I wondered when you would come to me."

"I didn't." There seemed no point in glancing behind him. Qutula's followers had moved them far out of the path of the fighting. Jochi's troops couldn't help him now; he had nothing to do but to brazen out this confrontation. Perhaps Qutula would let him go back to his own side. Probably not, but as a prisoner, he'd be in a better position to help the prince if needed. Or so Bekter hoped. The light in Qutula's eye didn't encourage defiance of his will, however. He signaled for his followers to move away, out of hearing, though not out of range of their bows. The lady stayed at his side, summing up Bekter with a steady gaze that said he'd make a tasty supper.

"I seem to have strayed from my position," Bekter admitted with a self-deprecating bow over his pommel. "If you will just point me in the direction of the battle . . ."

"I'm doing this for both of us," Qutula argued, clearly impatient to be done with his brother. "We were the khan's own sons; we deserve the spoils of his death."

"He gave us what he wished us to have. His death didn't change that."

"We would have had more, if Sechule hadn't murdered him. We can still have more. You'll rule over the South in Yesugei's place, and put your hand under no foot but mine when I am gur-khan over the Qubal, as our father would have wished."

Sechule had murdered their father? The shock rocked him in his saddle. He'd heard rumors about Qutula, but he'd dismissed even those. The court had lately buzzed with gossip about Sechule's return to Mergen's bed. He thought they'd come to some agreement. Now he didn't know what to think.

"An accident, the wrong herb . . ." He denied the accusation, refused to believe she could do something like that out of malice. She was his mother.

"Don't be a fool. He made her angry, and so she killed him. So we fight for what should have been ours by right of birth." Qutula was hiding something from him, but still, if even part of what he said was true, it convinced him more than ever that Qutula was wrong.

"I won't fight with you." Dropping his sword, he moved his hands away from his sides to show he didn't mean to fight. "I am your prisoner,"

"Pick. It. Up." Qutula raised his spear.

They might have been strangers for all the recognition in Qutula's stern countenance. He meant them to fight, and Bekter knew, without a shadow of a doubt, that he couldn't kill his brother. Not that his resistance to fratricide mattered to the outcome. Against Qutula in a killing rage he would have no chance. And Qutula was very, very angry.

"You're my brother," Bekter reminded him.

"No longer." Qutula's mare shied, and he brought her savagely under control, never taking his narrowed eyes from his brother. "You'll fight, or you'll die a coward."

Bekter let his breath out in a sigh he tried to muffle between his teeth. Qutula meant what he said, but still he had to try. "If you can murder your own brother, an unarmed prisoner taken in honorable combat, then you will just have to do it. Because I won't fight you."

"Pick. It. Up."

A call to honor wasn't working. Qutula was going to kill him, and Bekter decided that he couldn't watch him do it. Better to turn away with the memory of happier times marshaled about him to comfort his last moments.

"I'm sorry," he said, thinking of all the things he regretted, not least that he hadn't paid more attention to his brother's complaints before they came to murder. Not even Bolghai could turn back time, however. So he bowed to the false Lady Chaiujin and to his brother. Then, trembling with fear, he turned his horse and started back the way he'd come.

"Then join our mother among the ancestors."

"Sechule—" Gods and spirits, his own mother. Qutula was mad. He had to be stopped.

The spear, when it struck, felt like like a punch between his shoulder blades. Bekter didn't realize, at first, that he was injured. When he tried to breathe, however, his ribs refused to rise. He could draw not even a sip of air.

"Oh!" he said, surprised by the sudden pain that convulsed his hands on his reins.

Mother. His thoughts seemed to separate themselves from his body, which grew heavier as his head grew lighter, until he slipped from his horse. He landed with his face in the mud. The wound in his back suddenly caught fire, or so it felt. No images of his brother came to him now. If Sechule were dead as Qutula claimed, perhaps she would come for him. But in his mind's eye Bekter saw the soldier he had wounded, trampled and broken and dead in the splinters of his own bones. They hadn't lied about paybacks being a bitch.

"Leave him to the crows," he heard Qutula say from the vast distance of his saddle.

Bekter heard the horses moving away, but no hoof touched him. Soon enough the battle would come this way, and then it wouldn't matter. Though he waited, Sechule did not appear to guide him to his ancestors. Bekter closed his eyes and let the darkness hold back the pain for a little while longer.

"There's fighting to the north, two armies engaged but no
tents that I could see."

The scout bowed low and Daritai accepted his report with
a nod before turning to the next. He had pitched his tents the
other side of a low rise in the grasslands so that the innocent
camp followers going about their daily work in the Qubal tent
city would not see a foreign horde threatening. They were in
easy range of any spies that Mergen might choose to send. He'd
already had news that some argument had split the Qubal,
however, and his army was mounted and ready to ride at his
command.

"And the gur-khan?" he asked the man who had been sent
to spy out Mergen-Gur-Khan's tent city. Around him his captains listened with sharp-eyed attention, adding up the odds for
their success in the quarrels of their neighbors.

"Mergen Gur-Khan is dead," the scout reported. "His
blanket-son wages war against the prince, Mergen's heir, leaving the tent city abandoned except for women and children and
those too old to fight. General Jochi has left a mere handful of
the Qubal horde to guard their tents."

"There are rumors," the first scout added to his report, "that
the heir is also dead and General Jochi fights only to hold onto
the ulus until Yesugei-Khan comes."

The news didn't surprise him. Daritai had seen the discontent simmering in the eyes of the young Captain Qutula. A
Durluken youth had murdered General Jochi's son, more reason
for him to go to war against those who now moved openly to
seize the ulus. But Yesugei-Khan had his own affairs to consider and was, anyway, far to the south.

"We'll leave the general to fight over the broken remains of
Mergen's horde," Daritai decided, "and take this city while his
back is turned. Whoever survives to claim it will be weakened
from battle when he faces our army, many times the size of his
own which will be divided and suffering the absence of their
injured and their dead."

"We ride?" his captain asked

"When Great Sun touches the mountains," Daritai agreed. They would fall on the Qubal like a great darkness out of the sunset. The shadows cast before them, stretched and weird as they passed over tents and across the avenues, would strike terror into the hearts of the city before ever a sword was drawn. With luck, he could take her with terror alone and no blood spilt on either side.

His captains bowed and began to file out of the command tent, to carry his orders to their lieutenants. They understood his purpose and would make his wishes clear: no plunder, no rape, no savagery. The Qubal would surrender to him out of fear. If he hoped to make any stand at all against his father, however, they must come to see him as their deliverer, freeing them from the chaos their leaders had brought on them.

He was alone with his adjutants and his messengers when the last of his scouts arrived, sweating and breathless from a hard ride. "Speak, and do it quickly," he told the man, who put his hands to his thighs to brace his low bow. "We ride in an hour."

"A messenger reached General Yesugei-Khan before I could intercept him." The man dropped to his knees before his prince, knocking his head upon the carpets in abject apology for his failure. "General Yesugei has now left his own camp behind and flies to the aid of the Qubal."

An adjutant stepped forward, anticipating a change in the orders given to his captains, but Daritai waved him away. "A problem we must soon consider, but not today. Unless Yesugei-Khan follows more closely than I had believed?"

"He's closer than I expected to find him," the scout conceded, "But he won't reach the tent city for another day at least."

"A tight race," Daritai mused, more to himself than to his spy. "But with the help of our benevolent ancestors, we can still win it.

"Catch what rest you can, for we ride as planned," he told the spy and strode from the tent to find his mount. They were going to pay a call on a lady. He hoped, for Tumbinai's sake and that of his family in hiding, that he hadn't judged wrong on this.

"**M**y child!" The heartbroken cry of the spirit-khaness drew Eluneke to her side. There she found the prince lying with his back to the grassy ceiling and his face staring down at his rescuers in horror. Around him howled the hungry spirits, limbless and faceless except for their small red eyes and huge, sharp-toothed mouths that slavered as they shrieked. Already they had fallen on him, tearing great chunks of flesh out of his dead body as they devoured his living spirit.

"Stop!" Chimbai drew his sword, slashing about him at the hungry spirits, but the vaporous blade passed uselessly through bloodless bone.

"Take this!" Eluneke leaped from her mount and reached into the pouch that she had brought back from heaven.

"Don't let go of the reins!" King Toad's wife reminded her. Eluneke clasped the reins tightly in one hand, and drew out the spear that the sky god's daughter had given her with the other. Along its shaft ran a dragon of silver and one of gold. The magic of the heavenly warrior goddess pulsed in her fingertips and glowed with a golden light through the spirit stuff of the khan when she handed it to him.

Chimbai took the balance of the weapon in one large hand and grinned at her. Then he turned on the spirits devouring his son. This time, when the spear touched them, the hungry spirits screamed as if heaven itself burned their fleshless souls.

Eluneke moaned a shaman's chant that the sky god's daughters had taught her. It was supposed to banish the spirits that brought disease to the sick and, while it didn't send the hungry spirits flying, it did make them more wary of her. When her pale horse became again the smooth carved shaft of her horse-head drumstick, she flung herself into the fray with a crashing blow, and another.

Smoke rose in curls where the horse-head drumstick struck the hungry spirits. They scattered, screaming in rage, only to meet the sky god's daughter's spear in the hands of the prince's father. The love of the ancestor spirit added its own pulsing silver glow to the weapon, entwining with the heavenly powers so that the dragons etched in silver and gold on its shaft seemed like living creatures, writhing in their own battle against the hungry spirits. Where the spear touched a devourer, rips appeared, shredding soul-stuff until it could no longer hold itself together, and shrieking, disappeared into oblivion.

Eluneke paused to chant a prayer for the lost ones as they vanished, that they might find healing. She feared that they had gone too far down the path of destruction, however, and were lost to the wheel of life forever.

"Don't stop! You're winning!" croaked the voices from their baskets on her robes. These souls were lost already, but she still had a chance to save Prince Tayy. Urged on by King Toad's harem, Eluneke swung her stick about her, raising it again and again to drive off the ravening mouths. At last, when she doubted she could lift her arm for one more blow, the few who had escaped Chimbai-Khan's deadly spear turned and fled, cursing all living things.

"There," she said, and blew at a strand of hair that had escaped her headdress and fallen across her nose.

"They'll be back, bringing more of their kind to fight us," the khaness warned her. "But we're safe for now."

Only then did Eluneke notice the gouge chewed out of the lady's side, and the vapors of her soul leaking like a mist from the wound.

Chimbai-Khan joined them then. A part of his leg was missing and like his wife's injury, leaked soul-stuff like smoke from the wound. His hand, where it held the spear, had burned to char, and like the spirits he had attacked with it, his arm seemed to have shredded to tenuous threads. "Thank you," he said, though she could see the pain of his wounds in his eyes.

"I'm sorry!" Eluneke reached for the spear in horror. "I didn't realize."

"Don't be sorry," he chided her as she took the weapon and put it back into the little pouch. " I'm truly grateful."

"But your wounds—"

"Are nothing," he said, "In life, I would have given body and soul to save my son. In death, I would pay no less to preserve his spirit."

"Leave us behind if you must," the khaness ruled, "but free our son." In perfect agreement on that point the khan and his khaness leaned against each other, to ease their spectral hurts.

"Where am I?" Prince Tayyichiut asked. His brows drawn tight in a confused frown, he looked to Eluneke for answers that she felt ill-equipped to give him.

"Do you remember rescuing me?" she countered. It felt odd looking up at him where he lay on the grass overhead, but she was relieved to see that the hungry spirits had had little time to do serious damage to his body. If she could get him out of here, at least he'd still have all his parts.

"I fell into Qutula's trap," he corrected her interpretation of events.

"You fought Qutula's demon-servant with all the courage I could hope for in a husband," she reminded him in turn. "No mortal could have won that battle."

"A serpent," he rememberd. "Did it—" Then he saw the khaness.

"Mother?"

"My son." The two fell into each other's arms, enfolded in the love of mother and child. Eluneke found herself torn between sorrow that she could not embrace her own mother one last time and relief that the illness hadn't turned her mother into one of the hungry spirits. Toragana was a good shamaness. Eluneke had been certain of it before, but she felt it even more so now, when her own travels in the underworld were setting all her assumptions on their heads.

Sort of like the people. Tayy was still clinging to the roof of the underworld. His mother and father, clutching him in their desperate embrace, moved as spirits within it. The resultant confusion of her senses made Eluneke slightly queasy in spite of her full heart.

Though she hated to be the one to say it, they were running out of time for farewells. "We have to go," she said. The prince had already sustained attacks in both the mortal realm and the underworld. The one left his body moldering in the ground, the other had nearly devoured his spirit. If she were to rescue him from his dire fate, she must do so quickly, while there remained enough of either to make him whole.

Chimbai-Khan clung more tightly to his son. When he turned to face her, Eluneke saw that his features were growing less distinct, all except for his teeth. Desire created hungry spirits, she realized. And Chimbai had within his reach the thing he most desired in all the worlds, his tragic loss restored to him. His son. The underworld had begun to fade the memory of his purpose, to return the prince to the living world. He stood in danger of devouring the very thing he loved.

But the khaness put a gentle hand on his ravaged sleeve and when he looked at her, she shook her head sadly, but very sure.

"You have to let him go," she said. "He doesn't belong here. If you try to keep him, you can only destroy us all."

"He is my son."

"You want grandchildren, don't you?" the Lady Temulun asked him wisely. "And what about your daughter? Who will protect her?"

"You're right, of course." Chimbai hid his face, but slowly he let go of his son and took a drifting step back. "Take care of my children," he begged Eluneke.

"I'll try," she answered him.

Tayy looked confused, as if awaking from a long sleep. He hadn't been dead for very long, but Eluneke well knew that time moved differently in the underworld. She took his hand to lead him back to the mortal realm. Then she realized that she didn't know the way.

They had made no secret of their coming, so it didn't surprise Prince Daritai to find the grand avenue leading to the ger-tent palace deserted. The women and children would be hidden away, and the old men who attended the Lady Bortu would have gathered at the palace. As for the few hundreds who guarded her—ah, there they were. Daritai raised a hand to halt the war party that had followed him to the parade ground in front of the palace. There the Lady Bortu's honor guard awaited in battle formation, some with mustaches too grizzled, and some with no mustaches at all. None of the men left behind to defend the tent city were of a fighting age, he saw.

Daritai had brought only a small portion of his force with him into the city. For the moment, they were evenly matched. The lady khaness must know that his ten thousand now circled the city, however, and were making their way to the center from all sides even as the Tinglut prince rode toward her. So he wasn't surprised to find her mounted on a caparisoned horse at the head of her guardsmen. Her towering silver headdress rattled with beads and precious ornaments as she inclined her head in a precise nod to acknowledge him.

"My lady khaness." Daritai crossed his hands over his pommel to show he had drawn no weapon and bowed a greeting in return from his saddle. "Your city is taken. I mean you no harm nor any insult, and will shed no Qubal blood if I can help it. But your guardsmen are outnumbered, my ten thousand to this small force. I would not have them throw away their lives in a vain attempt at glory."

"They needn't kill ten thousand," she pointed out. "One would do."

She meant him, of course, the leader of that army, but she was much too wise in statecraft to believe her own words. "You would be doing my father a favor," he pointed out, "ridding him of a troublesome son, and you would find my half brother, Prince Hulegu, a more exacting taskmaster."

"We've lately had one of those ourselves," she groused sourly. He figured she meant Qutula and agreed with her assessment. Hulegu was very different from Mergen's blanket-son, being his father's heir and also less than forthcoming in battle. That Qutula might share Hulegu's coldly ruthless streak of vicious self-interest, however, he had no doubt. He said nothing of this, but nudged his horse forward and rode past the lady, ignoring the angry rumbling of her guardsmen. He understood their frustration, but prayed no one acted on their emotions. He didn't want to kill an old man or a child today for throwing a rock at his head. He didn't want a massacre if they threw a spear instead.

He made it through the lady's defenses unmolested by the glaring old men, however. A young one with more courage than sense pulled a knife on him, but a sharp cuff against the boy's head sent him reeling from his horse. The distraction saw him safely to the door of Mergen's ger-tent palace.

There were ritual insults to be observed when conquering a neighbor, and defiling the home of the deposed khan was one of them. So he ducked his head low and rode his horse inside. Just a handful of his men followed.

He did it well, sustaining his dignity when his horse released a steaming pile on the carpets. As he rode past the fire-box, he took stock of the painted chests with all their treasures as he remembered them. They were his now, or would be if he could just outwit old Tinglut-Khan. When he neared the dais, however, his resolution failed him.

Densly packed around the center of the dais, the old and infirm among the Qubal nobles sat in all their finery. He counted perhaps forty or more, not one of whom carried a weapon more imposing than a small dagger. And yet, he knew, they would sit where they were and die without raising a hand before they would move a single step. At their center was the Princess Orda, bundled in a blanket with the silks of her little coats peeping through where it had slipped.

She started to smile at him, then cast a fearful glance at the nobles who protected her on the dais. A tiny fist seemed to have got hold of Daritai's throat when he thought that he had frightened her. He had a daughter and shuddered to think of his own tents seized, his own family thrown into despair by a ruthless enemy. May the spirits preserve them, he'd gotten them out safely, he thought, all but Tumbinai.

Then the little princess put a warning finger to the side of her mouth. "You're not supposed to ride your horse inside," she whispered, loud enough for all the nobles to hear. "You'll get in trouble." Her little face took on a look of horror that would have been droll if he hadn't been the cause.

Behind him he heard the rustle of silks and realized that her formidable grandmother had caused that sudden fright. For his sake, not her own. Ritual insults were fine and well in the abstract, he decided, but they made him feel foolish in practice.

"Then I suppose I should have these nice men take her outside for me, shouldn't I?" He dismounted and gave the reins to a warrior who had the good sense to suppress his grin on the way out.

"Now the Lady Bortu won't be mad at me."

The snort behind him told him otherwise, but the little girl relaxed at once. The next step would be trickier. He needed to take possession of the princess. That meant making his way past the old retainers who surrounded her. But first he had to overcome his own fatherly misgivings about hurting the people who protected her. And there was the whole not wanting to scare her thing.

He hadn't counted on the princess herself, who stood up in her little boots with their upturned toes and picked her way carefully through the rows of old nobles to stand in front of him. With her solemn, trusting eyes fixed on his, she lifted her arms to be picked up. Since that was exactly what he had wanted, he obliged.

He had not exactly feared for his life until now. Something in the very air of the ger-tent palace shifted when he lifted the princess into his arms, however. Rumor said the old khaness had strange powers of her own. His back was feeling very exposed.

"Come," he said, and invited the Lady Bortu with a glance he hoped conveyed casual command and not the vague unease he was feeling. "We can talk more comfortably on the dais."

Whatever she saw in his face, she followed him and settled herself on the right side of the dais. She didn't try to take the little girl away from him, but seemed to challenge his honor on that score with eyes too dark for comfort. It didn't matter. He set the Princess Orda down beside him and made a little den out of his arm for her to cuddle in as his own daughter liked to do. And like his own daughter, the princess tucked herself among the folds of his sleeve and peeked out at him with a hopeful pout.

"Is Tumbi here?" she asked.

He closed his eyes, unable to speak for the moment. The old woman was watching, cataloging his weaknesses, but the sudden sharp pain was too new for any practice at hiding it. "Not this time, my sweet," he told her. *Not ever*, he thought, unless he turned the Princess Orda over to his father the Tinglut-Khan. The problem was, he didn't think he could do it.

Lady Bortu saw more than he wished her to see, and perhaps understood more than he did himself about what he would and would not do and what that line might cost him. At any rate she was giving him a look he hadn't seen much in his life. Sympathy.

"Come here now, child," she called the princess to her side with brusque disapproval. "Don't tire our guest with your questions."

Princess Orda crawled out of her nest beneath his arm and curled up next to her grandmother, who smoothed her coats with grumbling sounds of normalcy. "So tell me about this Tumbi," she told the little girl, with a warning glare at Daritai to keep his teeth shut around his objections. "Do you like him very much?"

"He's nice," the princess assured her grandmother. "And when I grow up, I'm going to marry him."

"Oh, are you now, girl? And don't you think your khan may have something to say about that?"

"Tumbi could steal me away, like in the story of Quchar and Nomulun," she said, defiant in her determination.

"Who is telling you such tales?" The old khaness chided her. "Children shouldn't listen to such stories, much less make plans for acting them out when they are bigger!" She laughed to take the bite out of her scolding, however. It seemed to Daritai that Lady Bortu didn't object to the idea but tested the feelings of the little girl. Though she had seen only seven summers, the royal family of the Qubal was well known for sprouting witches on their family tree.

Daritai had seen the value of the match the first time the idea had come to him, over a Qubal murder. Unfortunately, his plans depended on keeping both of the children alive, which didn't seem all that likely at present.

"Well, we'll see what we can do, then." The Lady Bortu gave the princess a hug. "We can't have you running away like Quchar and Nomulun." With the sweet dark head tucked under her chin, she looked at Daritai, measuring up all that he was thinking. Lines of concern etched the corners of her eyes, but she gave him a little nod, accepting the bond forged by two children that would unite them as more than conqueror and conquered. He just had to get Tumbinai out of Tinglut's clutches alive.

"But first," the lady continued, and this time she spoke to Prince Daritai, though still in tones that wouldn't frighten the child. "We must stop my foolish grandson, who is causing such a fuss."

"Prince Tayy?" the little girl asked.

"No, my dear. The other one." The old grandmother patted the child reasuringly, but tears gathered in her eyes.

Daritai knew that all he had surmised and the worst that his spies had gathered was true. "Let me help you," he said. "For Tumbinai's sake."

The crows had started to gather. Sprawled in the rusty mud awash in his own blood, Bekter had accepted his approaching death. Already his mind and spirit withdrew from the terrible pain that racked his flesh. He would have liked to see Toragana one last time, though, to tell her that he'd changed his mind about older women. One of them, at least. He would miss her.

A bird settled too close to his face and he flinched away, closing his eyes tightly against the threat of its sharp beak. He was getting used to the agony in his back, but the thought of ending his life in blindness and rending pain as the creature ripped the eyes out of his living head was more than he could bear. *Please,* he tried to say, though nothing escaped his lips but a scarlet froth of blood. *Not my eyes.*

He didn't know whose mercy he would have begged, but a gentle hand wiped the blood from his mouth and fluttered softly to his cheek.

"I know, my love. You're safe now. Be still."

Chapter Forty-two

STILL EXHAUSTED, General Jochi rose from a brief nap in his campaign tent. He demanded proper rest periods for his soldiers and tried to set an example. While he pretended to sleep, however, his mind replayed the events of the battlefield behind his eyelids. Mergen's misbegotten blanket-son fought with demons at his side. The Qubal fallen lay running blood from eye and ear and mouth until they died in agony, blackened and swollen as if they had been dead for many days. Jochi shook his head, but he couldn't dislodge the images that stole his rest. Warriors went happily to their death, knowing they would fly to their ancestors in the bellies of the birds. But how would the spirits of their dead find peace when even the birds refused to eat from their battlefield?

He remembered a story about the Uulgar, who roamed a land without forests and set their noble dead, not just those of lesser rank, for the birds to take their souls to rest. It was said that when they feasted on the poisoned khan of the Uulgar, the birds died in a dark and stinking blanket that covered all the grasslands around it. He feared the same doom for his own fallen souls.

When he returned from relieving himself, Chahar was waiting. The scout had brought news that Yesugei had turned back with half the Qubal and all of his Uulgar horde to defend the ulus, but so far—

"Anything?" Jochi asked, and gestured for a drink of strong kumiss.

"The Tinglut prince sends his regards," Chahar told him, bringing no good news of Yesugei's reinforcements, then. "He's pulling out of the field with three of his thousands to rest. You have two thousands of his still to command." The captain had already stated his disapproval of joining forces with their conquerors and he didn't hide his feelings now.

"Choices?" Jochi threw the challenge at him. His officers and field servants were accustomed to this argument and went about their business preparing him for battle without comment. "Give me choices. Prince Daritai's withdrawal, even to refresh his troops, leaves us vulnerable." Like his own horde, the Tinglut had to rest. Demons, apparently, had no such weakness.

"He doesn't serve you," Chahar insisted. "His ten thousands will answer to your command only as long as Qutula remains a greater threat to his own security. Once we've dealt with the Durluken, what will prevent this Prince Daritai from turning his army against us?"

Alone, Qutula would not have stood against Jochi's forces for even a single battle. But he had seen for himself the Lady Chaiujin shrouded in a green mist and riding among the Durluken. Where she rode, the ground seethed with vipers that rose up larger than a man to sink their poisoned fangs into the warriors who rode against them.

Alone against such supernatural forces, Jochi's army would have fallen long ago. He didn't delude himself that Prince Daritai had become a friend, however.

"Just because he's polite about it, don't forget that he has taken the ger-tent palace by force of arms," Jochi reminded his captain. "The Tinglut prince holds the Lady Bortu hostage, with the Princess Orda and all the noble fathers and Great Mothers.

"Right now we need him against Qutula. And we need his goodwill toward the hostages."

A rumor was spreading that Prince Tayy had died of the bite of a serpent-demon and another that Qutula had stabbed him through the heart. The prisoners he'd interrogated spoke freely, more terrified of their allies than their enemies. They told both stories, among others. In all the tales, however, the prince was dead. If the reports were true, Daritai held the last recognized blood of the khanate.

He understood Chahar's anger. Who did they fight for, with the khan and his heir both dead? Certainly not for the Tinglut prince who had seized the ulus and only sent his men to fight in defense of his own interests. But General Jochi would fight to the last living breath in his body *against* Qutula, the murderer who had brought down the Qubal ulus.

Later, when Yesugei arrived with his combined forces and they had ended the usurper's war, then they would sort out the Tinglut prince. A niggling doubt rippled across all his assumptions, however. Lady Bortu did not seem to disapprove of the conqueror and, as his captive, she'd observed the Tinglut prince more closely than any of them. Jochi needed time to think, but Qutula gave them no respite. He'd slept with his sword still clasped to his side, so he had only to pick up his spear and let his servants put his helmet on his head. His captains were ready, his horse saddled and pawing the ground, anxious for the battle. The general kept them waiting no longer.

Yesugei-Khan sat astride a mare the faded gold of autumn grass, watching from a low-rising swell in the rolling plain. All seemed peaceful in the afternoon light of Great and Little Suns, but looking down on the shadows that crossed the gertent palace he had served all his life, he knew that for a lie. Chahar had delivered the message from his dream and departed at speed while Yesugei had prepared his army and swept down on the tent city a day behind the scout.

Mergen was dead, according to the shaman Bolghai, who had appeared to Chahar in his dream: murdered by his blanketson Qutula with the aid of Sechule, who had agreed to be his wife. Yesugei was surprised the news hadn't shocked him more. Grief, yes, he felt a terrible pain at the loss of his khan. But when he thought of Sechule without the presence of her beauty to blind him, he realized that her treachery came as no surprise at all.

Jumal had predicted Qutula's betrayal and the reports of his scouts had only confirmed the worst. But Yesugei-Khan hadn't expected to find the Tinglut installed in the palace while the Qubal fought each other for a dais they no longer owned. His scouts had counted a shifting number of Tinglut warriors, no more than eight thousands in the tent city at any time and half of them sleeping or moving to and from the battlefield.

It was clear that the Tinglut were present as an occupying force, however, and not merely as an ally. Tinglut guarded the wagons that formed a protective barricade around the tent city, and Tinglut scouts moved back and forth from the ger-tent palace to the front. His spies sent to report on the conflict had not returned, so he was left to guess what part the Tinglut played in the Qubal civil war.

But time, he had determined, was running out. His captains were ready, and he raised his arm, ready to alert the drummers and the trumpeters to sound the attack. His vastly larger army, combined of his Qubal forces and former Uulgar prisoners, would fall on the Tinglut as Prince Daritai had likely done to the Qubal. When Yesugei had driven out that threat from the rear, he would . . .

"A message!" Otchigin, who had once been a princeling among the Uulgar, but who had given his devotion and the loyalty of his horde to the gur-khan, galloped toward him. "Delivered from the Qubal city under a white banner." At his side came a rider whose beaten leather armor bore Tinglut decorations.

"I'm only interested in one message," Yesugei informed the messenger. "If Prince Daritai wishes to see Great Sun rise tomorrow, he'll return all that he has stolen from the Qubal. Including the dais of the khan."

"The Lady Bortu sends me, not my lord Prince Daritai," the messenger met Yesugei-Khan's baleful glare with wilting courage. "I bring the words of the khaness to her general, the esteemed Yesugei, named khan over the Qubal-Uulgar by her own son Mergen, who has returned to his ancestors, may they grant him rebirth fitting his station."

As greetings went, it was a mouthul, but it contained the necessary elements to confirm the sender. "Go on, then," Yesugei instructed him. Mergen, after all, had failed to listen to Jumal, and now the gur-khan was dead.

"The Lady Bortu sends this message: 'I would have my beloved general beside me. At my behest, Prince Daritai grants safe passage to Yesugei-Khan and his captains and a guard suited to his position. The prince would have me give you also his reminder, that he holds the Princess Orda in his hands and, I would hesitate to add, my own worthless life as well.' "

Insolent colt! Safe passage indeed, when Yesugei had twice as many warriors as the Tinglut. The Qubal were furthermore fighting for their home. But Prince Daritai had the princess and the old khaness, as he pointed out. He would doubtless cut their throats if Yesugei-Khan defied him.

If he were a different kind of man, Yesugei-Khan would feint an attack and let the Tinglut remove the last obstacles between himself and the dais. His own army would easily defeat the Tinglut. Too late, of course, for the prisoners, but it would add gur-khan to his title and put the grasslands in his hands, from the Shan Empire to the Cloud Country.

He was not that man, however, and dismissed the unworthy thought without even a twinge of desire. Mergen was dead, and the Tinglut prince would soon meet his own ancestors. Yesugei had no wish to follow in their ambitions or their fates. He would do as the khaness bid him, and spy out for himself how best to take back Mergen's city for the Qubal.

The young Otchigin had remained at his side and Yesugei gave him instructions. "Gather five hundred warriors under my banner, divided equally between Uulgar and Qubal. Captain Jumal has command in my absence. We pay a visit."

The tent city of the gur-khan had sadly diminished in the few weeks since he had left it. Even the most detailed reports couldn't prepare him for the sight of Tinglut warriors sleeping in a tangle of weapons and leather half-armor in the tents of the Qubal army. They could not have prevented the chill that gripped his gut as he rode down the wide avenue to the ger-tent palace behind a thousand Tinglut warriors. Columns of Tinglut brandished their swords as he passed between them and fell in at the rear, cutting off any escape.

A light rain had begun to fall, but servants had set up a dais in front of the ger-tent palace. On it, he saw forty or more of the most aged of the nobles who had stayed to guide the gur-khan in his tent city. They sat with their fine clothes beaded with raindrops, their heads raised watchfully to the Tinglut prince. At their center Daritai awaited him, a child in his arms.

A cut roughly stitched above his eye began to leak fresh red blood when he drew his brows together, leaving a lurid streak down one cheek. The prince looked hollowed out and weary as men do who have spent too long in a battle they have no hope of winning. Which was strange, Yesugei thought, because his supremacy over the Qubal city could not be doubted. He wondered what it was they fought out there where his scouts went but didn't return. The Lady Bortu stood at the prince's side but gave away no answers by glance or expression.

"Welcome, my lord General Yesugei," Prince Daritai said, reducing him to his military title. "I understand from these men and women who know you that you are an honorable man."

"I hope that I am," Yesugei answered. He hadn't expected the interview to take this direction. "Certainly I value loyalty to clan and ulus. As do my captains." Let the Tinglut invader take that as a warning. If he survived, Yesugei would fight. If he didn't, Jumal held his army and would avenge their deaths.

The child in Daritai's arms lifted her head and he saw that she was indeed the Princess Orda, though she clung to the Tinglut prince's shoulder as if she found all her comfort and safety in her captor.

Lady Bortu put out her arms, but the princess refused to go to her. "Bad man!" she insisted.

Yesugei was on the point of agreeing with the child when her grandmother chuckled.

"You have it backward, little lamb. Yesugei-Khan would rescue you from Prince Daritai."

The little girl seemed to think that was very funny, but she still wouldn't let go of the Tinglut's coat. Even slaves sometimes grew to love a harsh master, he knew, for the times when the beatings did not come. How much more might a child love her captor for ending the chaos begun by his own conquering army?

Prince Daritai sighed and rolled his eyes. Then without ceremony he dropped a little kiss on the top of the child's silky dark head. The princess snuggled in more comfortably, not in the least surprised by the kiss. "Is he going to rescue Tumbi?" she asked.

Yesugei didn't know who Tumbi was, but Daritai's eyes darkened with a pain he would have wished to keep private, it seemed.

"I hope so," Daritai answered the princess. "But first, we have to rescue General Jochi and his army."

It seemed unlikely that Jochi would bend his knee to the Tinglut. With the khan dead and Qutula in league with demons, however, Yesugei conceded he might not have had a choice until now. He had much to think about.

But the light rain had grown more persistent and the mother of two khans was getting wet. "Explanations can wait until we have allowed the old among us to get in out of the rain," Lady Bortu reminded the Tinglut prince tartly.

"As you wish, my lady khaness." Even conquerors bowed to the will of old Bortu. "If you will join us, General?"

Daritai turned and entered the ger-tent palace. One by one the elder nobles entered behind him until only the Lady Bortu remained to watch Yesugei dismount with his five hundred behind him. No Tinglut warrior moved to stop her when she came to him and put her hand on his arm. "You had your differences with my son, but I know you loved him and the ulus he led."

Yesugei nodded, accepting her words. "I won't leave his mother in the hands of an enemy," he promised, but she patted his sleeve as though he were a child and she wanted him to pay attention.

"The ancestors in their wisdom sometimes make plans for us that we wouldn't have chosen," she said. "We create nothing but grief for ourselves even to our children's children when we set our will against Fate."

"I will not believe that fate has meant the Qubal to bow to old Tinglut-Khan!" he muttered.

"Fate thinks long, my dear Yesugei. Fate thinks very long, and Tinglut-Khan is old already. Be patient. Listen. More than mortal men are moving the stones on this board. Our world may hang in the balance."

The Lady Chaiujin. Yesugei bowed his head, accepting that the greater fight would come against the khan's own blanket-son. Qutula rode with a horde of demons at his call. In the meantime, Daritai held the princess. He could do little to oppose the invader now, but he could wait, and watch, and move when the opportunity came. "I trust the Lady Bortu in all things," he assured her. She would know when he should move against the Tinglut prince.

The khaness sighed, however, and patted his arm. "We'll see," she said, and led him to the feet of the conqueror.

Guided by the spirits of his parents, Eluneke had come for him. Prince Tayy took her hand and allowed her presence to push back his terror. He had awakened surrounded by hungry spirits, unable to defend himself from their horrible mouths. Then she was with him, driving off his tormentors with her horse-head stick. Suddenly he discovered hope in the midst of his despair, and a terrible sorrow.

"Has Qutula murdered you, too?" he asked Eluneke. How else had she come to him in the underworld where his cousin had trapped him?

"Not yet," she promised, "but I don't know how long I can stay here." The toads on her costume added their opinions in urgent croaks and dainty bellows.

"Then go. Don't risk yourself for me. I'm already dead." He could move his head and his arms now and reached out to embrace the spirit of his mother. He hadn't figured out how to stand yet, but he managed to sit up. Eleuneke was upside down, hanging in the night air above him. Closing his eyes helped a little with the disorientation, but he couldn't keep them closed forever.

"I won't leave without you." Eluneke took his hand and

gave it a tug. "But I'm not going to wait around for the hungry spirits to come back either.

Suddenly Tayy was moving, though he didn't know how, or how to stop the soul-stuff that he leaked from a dozen tooth-shaped rents in his flesh.

"Gather it up in your hands and put it in your shirt," Eluneke suggested.

At first his fingers ran through it as water through mist, but gradually he got the hang of it, letting his spirit tangle itself around his fingers and wiping them off on the inside of his shirt. His success gave him more confidence.

It seemed to have the same effect on Eluneke. "You're look-ing a bit more substantial," she said. "That's a good first step, I think."

The toads seemed to agree, but they were still lost.

"This way," Chimbai said, and turned his mount around. Tayy, however, had no horse and couldn't follow.

"Come with me." Eluneke still had his hand, but she sat astride a pale horse. He climbed up behind her and they were off, across a landscape that would have turned his stomach, if he still had one, with its upside-down confusion. It wasn't only the underworld that was making him feel strange, however.

"Something is happening to me. Someone is digging up my body!"

"I should hope so," Eluneke replied tartly. "Bolghai was supposed to have started as soon as he was sure I had crossed into the underworld."

That was good news, or he knew he ought to think so. Tayy hadn't expected to be *aware* of his body after death, though. The implications made him queasy.

"Will it hurt much?" he asked. When she turned in her sad-dle with a question in her frown, he added, "The pyre, I mean when they burn me. I can take it—anything is better than being stuck here, turning into a hungry spirit myself—but I'd rather know . . ."

A little shiver passed through her, trembling against him. "I'd rather not find out."

Prince Tayy dreaded the pain that awareness would bring

when the clans burned his body, but he thought he might prefer it to this. Eluneke was going to abandon him to face the fire alone. He figured he should be grateful she hadn't left him for the hungry spirits, but it hurt more than dying had.

She was still talking, though. It took a moment for him to catch up with what she was saying. "The visions are very clear that you're going to be my husband. Since I don't plan to marry a dead man, I have to get you back to your body."

"Husband?"

"Ribbit," a small toad answered from the basket on her head. "Of course," Queen Toad said, with the toad version of a superior sniff. Tayy was surprised to discover that as a spirit he understood her.

Married. To Eluneke. Even death hadn't changed that, it seemed. He ignored the toad's condescension. Great Sun didn't shine in the underworld, but suddenly it felt like sunrise on the plains above.

He thought the light that blossomed like the bright hibiscus of Pontus was only in his mind, but the khan and khaness had drawn up their horses with wary glances around them. Eluneke brought her pale horse to a halt as well. "What is it?" she asked. The red glow on the horizon snapped like a banner of fire, growing closer as they watched.

"The court of the demon-king, on the hunt," Chimbai said. Spirits flew before the growing flame, screaming terror and despair in the windless darkness of the underworld.

Run. Tayy felt the message from the fleeing spirits and would have joined them in their race with the doom riding down on them, but Eluneke kneed her horse forward at a stately pace. His parents hesitated, fighting their own dread. Chimbai had lost none of his bravery in battle, however, and his khaness refused to leave her child. They brought their mounts around and followed the shaman-princess.

This was it, the third test that would complete her initiation. As she waited for the demon-king with his hunting party to reach them, Eluneke thought ruefully that she'd have preferred not to have the fate of worlds depend on this meeting. A minor demon she might have browbeat into revealing the secrets of the dead, and how to protect them from the hungry mouths of trapped spirits and the demons themselves, who hunted them for sport. She would have risked no lives but her own. Instead, she had to face down the king of the demons himself, with her own dead around her.

"Could be worse," the queen of the toads muttered from her perch on Eluneke's brow. "We are all of a similar rank, at least. Kings and princes all. No need to knock one's head on the ground. I would not debase myself before these malevolent creatures."

The khaness had heard and she added her own advice. "We must hold onto our dignity, but afford the king of the demons the respect due a monarch in his own realm."

"I thought the king of the demons was dead." Tayy's voice rumbled in Eluneke's ear, doing unaccountable things to her concentration. "I was there when King Llesho killed him."

"For which the new king should show his gratitude, since he owes his present status to your war," the queen of the toads agreed.

"He won't, of course," Chimbai warned them. "Any human who can kill a demon-king must be a threat to his successor."

"But I didn't do it," Tayy objected in that rumble that turned all Eluneke's insides to trembling flowers. "The god of Justice did, and he needed the help of a dragon."

"Don't tell the king that." The queen of the toads did the little bobbing thing she reserved for repeating the obvious. "It's always better to be a powerful enemy than to be the prey in a soul-hunt."

Eluneke couldn't disagree with that. She thought that was the last of it, but Tayy leaned forward to whisper in her ear, "Leave me if you must. Don't lose yourself on my account."

"Never." Her own happiness mattered little in her answer, though she refused to imagine a life without him. All of her training had taught her that she could show no weakness when she faced the demon-king. He would feed on her fear if she let him. And he would know the value of the prince to the survival of the ulus, maybe of all the grasslands.

The prince fell quiet then, which was a good thing. They had crested a rise made of the insubstantial cloud-stuff beneath them, and saw ahead the hunting party of the king of the demons drawn up against them. The demons rode in a blazing nimbus of flame, orange and yellow at its edges and a deep blood red at its center. Mountainous figures like shadows rose over steeds whose legs stretched out thick as uprooted tree trunks. Each mount had many long necks spilling from its shoulders like a writhing nest of snakes. From each neck rose a head with beady red eyes peering over a snout full of long sharp teeth curled out in all directions to tear its prey with a shake of its head.

Demons, Eluneke knew, could take any shape they wanted, or no shape at all, so she was not surprised that among the court facing her not one bore the characteristics of any other. Serpents rode coiled in saddles, and monsters rode against them that made Nogia's Bear look like a child's toy. Some took on no substance at all, their malignant consciousness glowering out of eyes of flame. She had not prepared herself for the shape the king of the demons took, however, and had to bite down on her lip to keep from crying out when he rode forward to meet her on a tall black mare breathing fire from her blowing nostrils.

"Father," she whispered, and heard Tayy whisper, "Altan!" at her back.

"No," she said firmly, to assure herself as well as the prince who rode with her. Mergen had successfully passed out of the reach of demons and the hungry spirits. The khaness Temulun had told her so. She trusted in the pyre and the prayers of the shamans who had sent Altan to his ancestors as well. And logically, she understood that the demon-king could not be two of their dead, so he was likely to be neither. But it almost shattered her when he lifted a long hunting spear over his head, pointed at her heart.

"Why have you come here, little girl?" he asked. The voice was a little off, but close enough if his face had taken her in. "Whatever your reasons, I appreciate the gift."

He was looking at the prince when he said that. With the instincts of a father, Chimbai set his steed between the demon and his dead son. "You are no brother of mine, nor are you any of our beloved dead." He no longer carried the spear of the sky god's daughter, nor could he risk further dissolution of his charred and tattered arm, but he drew the sword that he had worn on his pyre and charged.

The chaos of battle broke out then, and Eluneke would have thought they were too outnumbered for hope. But the khaness had her husband's bow and rode like a soldier, with her horse between her knees. She drew again and again, releasing a never-ending supply of ghostly arrows. A demon-steed careened past. Tayy caught the reins and flung himself into the abandoned saddle. The monster's hunting bow remained in its place at the stirrup and Eluneke saw the prince take it up and join his mother in laying down cover while Chimbai fought sword to sword.

Eluneke had her own defenses against the demon-king: her totem animals around her and her own powers as a shaman. "More valuable than iron or bronze," she riddled, and reached into her pouch for the silver dragon spear as answer. Uttering the chant the sky god's daughter had taught her to drive out demons, she set her pale horse against the king's horrible mount.

Sharp hooves rose and kicked, teeth bit. Imbued with the blessings of the sky god's daughter's horse-head drumstick, wherever her pale horse made contact with the demon-steed, it opened a terrible wound as only a prayer might do.

"Ayay-aeee!" she chanted, and her totem animals joined their croaking to her spell. The silver spear flashed in her hand, its heavenly light shining over her like a lamp in the darkness of the underworld. Wherever demons looked at it they flinched and covered their eyes.

Chimbai was down, crushed under his fallen mount. The terrified night-mare writhed and kicked, but could not escape the horrible smoking wound bleeding spirit-stuff out of her courageous heart. The khaness dropped from her roan to stand over her husband, firing and firing her arrows while the prince took up his father's sword and drove his demon mount among the onrushing soul-hunters.

Eluneke saw the fight out of the corner of her eye. They were outnumbered, and would soon be overrun, but her own battle took all her concentration. The demon-king was too powerful to be repelled by her spell alone, but he backed away from the silver spear that she wielded against him. When he saw that she would attack even when he took the form of her father, the demon transformed himself into a monster taller than a tree with horn for skin and empty pits for eyes that gleamed with a promise of agony and despair.

The pale horse, which was no creature of light or dark, but a gift of heaven and an instrument of her office, carried her close under the writhing tentacles of the demon-steed's many heads. She slashed and chanted, but he pressed her back. Soon he would be joined by his court against her.

"Remember what you are." Clinging to the basket on the shamaness' head, Queen Toad whispered a reminder.

A toad. When Eluneke discovered her totem form, she had appeared in the shape of a very small and harmless member of that species. New at her skills, she'd hesitated to claim them as her own. Since then, she had visited the dreams of the living world and the daughters of the sky god in his heavenly realm. And she now challenged the very king of the underworld for the soul of her lover, who would be both khan and husband if she succeeded. So the queen of the toads expected more from her than the paltry creature she had been.

The demon-king sat back on his fire-breathing steed, watching her with a sneer on lips already stretched by black and tangled fangs. He could have had her then, she thought, if he'd respected her enough as an opponent. But he thought of her as prey in his hunt, and preferred to play with his food. Well.

Calling on her totem animals gathered about her, Eluneke turned into a hideous toad so huge that her pale horse couldn't carry her. She leaped clear of it, remembering to keep hold of the reins when the beast turned again into the horse-head drumstick.

In her new form Eluneke stood taller than the fire-eyed

beast, and she glistened all over with the poisonous exudations of her totem race. "Excellent!" Queen Toad applauded from where she sat between the poison pits atop Eluneke's toady head. All the toad harem added their praise. But she was just one, and the demons were many. Soon the prince would be overwhelmed.

Eluneke focused her attention on the demon-king. He pretended to a condescending indulgence with her efforts to escape his clutches but she thought she detected an uneasy fear in him now. Which told her exactly what to do.

With a shouted prayer to the queen of the toads, she turned all the gathered harem into monstrous versions of themselves, an army of giant toads, each with poison ripening in the pouches above their eyes.

"Aaaayyyeeaaahhh!" she cried as her totem horde scattered against the hunting court. And then she turned and faced the demon-king, clenching the muscles that controlled her poison glands.

A hot stream of venom shot across the short distance between them, into the black wells of the demon's eyes.

"AAAhhhh!" the creature screamed. His mount reared and plunged, stung by the poison where it spattered steaming on the many heads. Eluneke fell to her knees, exhausted but in human form again, the gifts of the sky god's daughters held loosely in her hands while around her the toads, enlarged to monstrous proportion, attacked on every side. They might hold the forces of the underworld at bay a little longer, but she had failed.

She had hoped to kill, but it seemed she had only blinded the demon-king. Another attack might have succeeded, but she didn't have the strength to shape her totem form again. To escape his injury, the demon-king need only turn himself into a mist.

The demon's shape wavered.

"Nooo!"

Prince Tayyichiut plunged past her with his reins between his teeth. He slid sideways, hanging off his saddle, and with one hand he plucked the silver dragon spear from Eluneke's numb fingers.

"Aaayee-yaa!" the prince cried. His hand smoked and burned from its heavenly touch, but he plunged the spear into the fading heart of the beast.

Nothing happened.

The demon blinked, began to smile. Then confusion crossed his face. His monstrous steed bucked uneasily.

"Oh!" the demon-king exclaimed, staring in horror at the spirit-stuff boiling out of the wound. Then he was silent, already rotting before he hit the ground.

"I think the boy killed him." The queen of the toads loomed over her for a moment, then, with a little shudder, shrank down and down, until she fit into the basket-crown on Eluneke's shaman headdress. "I think we've won." Around them, the battleground had fallen silent, except for the moaning of the blinded demons running from the toads who slowly returned to their own shapes. The dead made no sound at all.

"Will he—" Eluneke stumbled on the question she started to ask the khaness. "Live" wasn't right. Chimbai-khan, and Temulun herself, had died long ago.

"His spirit remains intact." The lady rose from where she crouched, defending her fallen husband with her ghostly bow and arrow. She didn't leave him, however, but watched with drawn bow as a prince of demons in the shape of a flame urged forward his nightmare steed. He seemed uninjured, and his followers who surrounded him likewise looked fresh to the battle.

"I mean you no harm," he said, and took on the solid form of his own kind as a courtesy.

Eluneke took no chances, but clutched her horse-head drumstick in her hand, marshaling her spells to cast him out. No more convinced of the demon's goodwill, Tayy came to her aid with the dragon spear clenched in a fist of cinders. She could feel him trembling at her side, but he faced with a clear, grave eye the demons who had surrounded them. For herself, she felt as though the least breeze would pick her up like a leaf and carry her away.

"You have indeed killed the king of the demons. You have my undying gratitude for it," he said with a bow from the saddle.

"Not so undying, it seems to me," Tayy answered, and no demon among them could miss his meaning. Certainly not this one, who planned to usurp the place of his fallen king.

"The pair of you do seem to have a talent for killing my kind," the pretender admitted, admiring Tayy's handiwork with a nudge of his boot. The little that remained of the demon-king disintegrated into mist and blew away.

"I didn't kill the last one," Tayy demurred, but added, "I had good teachers. And we both learn fast."

The new king acknowledged the hit with a nod, but had his own riposte, "Not fast enough, it seems, or you wouldn't be here."

That was enough for Eluneke. She was sick of the underworld, sick of demons, and sick of fighting, whether with words or spears or her own venom. "We will be happy to leave," she said, "if you will just show us the way."

"I can send you home easily enough," the demon agreed, adding, "you don't belong here anyway. I don't even mind whispering in your ear all the secrets that shaman come here to find. Call it a gift.

"But these others are mine. They're dead, after all, and have lingered long beyond any hope of joining their ancestors in the underworld."

"The prince goes with me," Eluneke insisted, and clasped the prince's charred hand, still holding the dragon spear. "Given why we are having this conversation at all, I don't think you want him around anyway."

"I'll grant you that," the new demon-king answered, with half a smile lurking at the corner of the lips turned back by his curling tusks. "I suppose you want her, too."

They all looked at the khaness then. When it had become clear that there would be no further attack, she had dropped again to hold her husband. Chimbai's soul had almost ceased its struggle against the monstrous weight of the dead steed that held him down.

"I won't leave him," the khaness insisted.

Eluneke closed her eyes, searching within herself for a healing spell that would revive the fading spirit. Several came to mind, but none that would help her lift the weight that pinned the old khan down. When she opened her eyes again, the khaness had leaned over in a lingering kiss. Eluneke knew she ought to look away, to give the loving wife some privacy for her farewells. But she couldn't. And while she watched, the Lady Temulun took a deep breath.

At first, her lips remained pressed to those of her husband. Then, Chimbai-Khan drifted out of his ghostly form, becoming a breath. When she stood up again, the khaness held within her the vaporous spirit of her beloved khan.

"I think we're ready to go now," she said. When she smiled, a tendril of soul-stuff escaped her lips. She licked it up again and joined them before the new demon-king.

"All or nothing, then," the king bargained. "A contest of riddles. Answer this: *a string of jade beads, hidden in the branches.*"

"A snake," Eluneke answered, "The emerald green bamboo snake." The old king's daughter, who had murdered Chimbai and his wife, took the shape of a bamboo snake. Eluneke willed her horse-head drumstick into the form of a pale steed and posed her own challenge from the same height as her opponent: "Brindle-legged among the Qubal, red among the Tinglut."

"A toad," the king answered, with a tilt of his head to acknowledge the warning, and a riddle to issue another of his own: "The camel calls to its mate; far away, a light glitters."

"A bow and arrow," Eluneke answered, and countered, "Another camel opens his mouth and the tether flashes."

"Lightning," the king of demons answered and paused to think about the meaning of the riddle. Though shaman often came demanding the secrets of the dead from the demon world, he had never met one before who had climbed to heaven on a bolt of light. It said something for her skills as well as her courage. "But enough of games. Something more difficult: "Three things full at a distance, empty in the hand."

Behind her on her ghostly horse, Eluneke heard Prince Tayy gasp. The riddle was harder than the others, but her teachers had trained her well. "A dream, on waking," she said, "a greeting, returned by an echoing mountain, a tent city reflected in the dust of a mirage. And for you, three joys."

The demon king bowed his head to acknowledge her answer, and her riddle. "Though such things are foreign to my kind, I have heard the voices of the dead speaking of their lives on the path to the realms of their own spirits. Three joys must be, the rapturous sigh of a lover, victory cry in wrestling, the first squall of a newborn child. And now, for you, three lacks."

"Pillars for the sky," Eluneke answered, "A stone to cover the sea, and a girdle for the mountains." She didn't give her next riddle right away, but thought for a long time, until Prince Tayy shifted cautiously in the saddle and the Lady Temulun's eyes shadowed with despair. Then, the shaman-princess said, "A she-goat drags a tether through the gate."

The khaness blinked at her, amazed, it seemed, that Eluneke had chosen such a homely riddle. But she was counting on exactly that.

The demon who ruled the underworld frowned, thinking. He took a breath, as if to answer, and let it go again. "This is no fitting riddle," he complained, "I have heard no spirits talk of such things on their way to their ancestors."

"It's a riddle for the living, not the dead," Eluneke conceded, though she held him to his bargain. "What would spirits have to do with threading a needle?"

The demon-king's face suffused with his anger, but he gave her his secrets as he had promised, and when she demanded the way home, he said, "Rain or river, find it yourself. And don't count on my good nature if you should come back."

She bowed her head but didn't make any promises. *Not if I can help it,* she thought as he drove his spurs into the sides of his nightmare steed. Then the hunt was sweeping by them. They had left the river far behind, but Eluneke had an idea. She spat onto the ground and stepped where her spittle had fallen. Sinking upward, she found that they had traded one battlefield for another.

Chapter Forty-three

GENERAL JOCHI fought like a madman. Slashing about him with his sword, he called his captains to form their men into tight defensive circles. A serpent-demon downed his mount. Before the monster could strike again, he leaped into the empty saddle of a riderless steed which had, like himself, run mad on the battlefield. Sweat rolled off his braids and formed rivers on his brow that splashed stinging into his eyes. he ignored the discomfort, like he did the rub of his leather half-armor against the sword cut under his arm and the ache in his legs as he clung to the flanks of the horse with his knees.

They had lost already; he could hear it in the strangled screams of the fallen and smell it in the iron tang of blood running down the back of his throat. The sickly stench of their dead, untimely rotting on the battlefield, coated his tongue. His death had long since ceased to matter to him. He had served two khans, seen them both killed by treachery, and lost his son to the same evil. Jochi now courted his own murder against the monsters Qutula had raised against the Qubal ulus.

He trusted the man at a side to drive a sword through his heart when he fell, ending his suffering before the demon serpents made his last hours a horrific nightmare of suffering and living decay. He would offer the same service to any man beside him. Knowing they could depend on each other for a quick death made it possible to go on in the face of certain defeat against an enemy their weapons could not touch.

"General!" Captain Chahar reached over and grabbed the bridle of Jochi's horse to force his attention. The son of a powerful shaman, he saw too deeply into the bleak depths of his general's despairing heart.

Not yet, Jochi denied him irritably. *I haven't fallen yet.* He wanted to account for Qutula before the demons took him. That purpose alone kept him alive and fighting. But Chahar was pointing back toward the city.

Reinforcements? Prince Daritai had taken several of his thousands out of the battle to rest for a few hours, but these men looked too fresh, too unstained to be accounted by so short a respite. His few surviving warriors took no sleep at all now, determined like their general to fight past hope until they fell, which they did in staggering numbers.

Not his own thousands, then, miraculously raised up in their black and swollen bodies from the killing field. But he recognized their banner.

Yesugei. For a moment, the relief was so powerful that it unhinged all his joints, so that he almost swooned from his saddle. Yesugei had come, with five thousands of his Qubal troops and ten more thousands of the conquered Uulgar.

Drums rolled and cymbals crashed. Yesugei's trumpeters announced his arrival with a fanfare to strike terror into the heart of any foe. The serpents turned their vaporous shadow-forms on the newcomers, and Jochi saw Yesugei blanch.

Then the earth moved.

Rain was falling. Prince Tayyichiut screwed his eyelids more tightly shut against the stinging drops. He wondered for a moment why he was lying on the ground with rain leaking into his eyes.

A familiar smell of badly cured stoat pelts assailed his nostrils. Then a callused but gentle hand touched him lightly above his heart. "My prince?"

Tayy had never heard the shaman Bolghai speak so tentatively. He wanted to wipe away the water so that he could see this newly chastened shaman for himself, but his arm was too heavy; he might have been trying to lift his horse and not his own hand.

"That's all right," Bolghai soothed. "Let me do it for you."

The silk cloth that wiped his face was scented with sweet herbs. Tayy didn't object, but relaxed into the soothing touch. When the cloth went away, he opened his eyes. "Where's Eluneke?" he asked, or thought he did. But when he tried to form the words, he realized he'd forgotten how.

Just then the earth shook. Thrown from his perch on the edge of some overhang, Bolghai landed on top of the prince. Distantly, a wound in Tayy's back protested the abuse. *Now I'll have matching scars, front and back,* he thought, but didn't, immediately, recall why.

"My lord khan, forgive me." The shaman struggled upright but didn't move away. "We have to get you out of here."

Out of where? He formed the words in his mind and this time forced them past his teeth. "Where am I?"

"Where spirits rot: the dead." Bolghai answered with a riddle that would have annoyed him, except that suddenly Tayy remembered the serpent, and Qutula's sword separating the ribs from his spine as he fell. Other, more terrible things, half memory, half spirit-touched, drifted gossamer as a dream among his thoughts: dirt covering his eyelids. Hungry spirits devouring his flesh. Part of the awful smell didn't come from Bolghai at all. His wounds were swollen and rotting.

"My grave," he answered. His hand, when he looked at it, was blackened and cracked, charred to the bone. He didn't dare open his fingers for fear they would shatter into ash.

"And about time you got him out of it."

Eluneke.

Tayy looked up to find her watching him from the edge of the pit where Qutula's minions had thrown him. He'd been dead, and now he wasn't. The time between remained a lurking shadow in the back of his mind, but he was free of the details if he didn't look too closely.

He knew Eluneke had come for him. That was worth a smile, if he could remember how to do it. He must have gotten it right, because she smiled back at him. Tayy remembered his mother then, and his father.

"My parents?" he asked as Bolghai manhandled him out of the hole in the ground. "We didn't leave them behind?" How could he ever forgive himself if he'd committed such an unfilial crime.

Eluneke was shaking her head, barely controling the shudder of superstitious dread. "They're gone now. They've done their part and are eager to start their new lives together among the ancestors."

"I'll miss them." Tayy understood that he must accept their true state as his parents had themselves, but the air felt colder now that they were gone. "I think I always felt them with me."

"As I recall, they were hard to miss," she answered tartly. "You're going to need new dogs."

Tayy remembered a red head nudging his hand, a cold nose bumping his hip. Standing guard. It warmed him in spite of the rain and the chill of their absence, to know that they'd stayed behind to protect him.

While they spoke, Eluneke drew from the pouch the sky god's daughters had given her a laurel bough with the power of heaven to cure ills of the spirit. As she brushed the laurel leaves over his wounds, Tayy felt the pain of them lessen, the swelling subside.

"Can you ride?" Bolghai asked. "We are at war. General Jochi might like to know he fights for the true khan, and not merely to avenge your murder."

Khan. Mergen was dead. That made him gur-khan, assuming the chieftains voted to honor the chosen heir. Provided any survived the fighting to vote. His father had trained him for this duty and Mergen had trusted him to hold the ulus when his time came. Even the underworld had spit him out again to take up the reins untimely dropped by his father and his uncle.

"I can ride," he said. But his hand still curled like a cinder at his side.

"Take this," Eluneke said, and slipped the stem of the laurel bough into the curl of his fingers. Where it touched coals, flesh softened and grew brown and smooth as the bark of a young tree, with the flush of life running through it. Though he was not yet whole, the pain of his injuries had grown distant, and soft, tea-stained skin replaced the horrible purple and green of the serpent's bite. The bloody wound at his back remained, but deep inside he could feel the healing had begun.

Horses were brought and the shaman-princess mounted the pale steed that had carried them in the underworld. "Where you go, my khan, there I also go," she declared. "I won't lose you now."

He thought to turn her back to safety in the rear with Bolghai. But the shaman clapped his hands and smiled. "You will need your skills at banishing demons," he advised them both. "The Lady Chaiujin has brought her serpent horde to fight in Qutula's cause."

Bolghai drew from a leather thong at his side a horse-head drumstick made of the shinbone of a roe deer and flung it to the grass. Where it struck, it grew hooves and legs and a tail and mane and strong, pale haunches. With a cheerful grin the shaman leaped onto the bare back of the magical steed. "Now," he said, "begins the shamans' war!"

"**H**e killed our mother." Bekter lay in her bed, shivering with fever. Half out of his senses, he muttered over and over the impossible confession, made as a boast. Sechule had murdered the khan, and her son Qutula had murdered her in turn, and then had tried to do the same to his brother.

"I know," the shamaness soothed him with her voice. "But you are still alive, and we must make sure you stay that way." She poured a cup of healing tea from the kettle on the firebox and scattered over it a variety of herbs for reducing fever. Already she had plastered his wounds with a poultice to draw out both foreign poisons and the kind that the body grew from its own damaged flesh. Now she held his head pillowed on her breast and tipped the cup to his lips. Withdrawing it quickly when he coughed, she wiped the escaping medicine from his lips.

"Rest, dear Bekter," she crooned, lulling him to the sleep he needed more than any herbs she might prepare. In sleep, he might escape the pain of his injury, and the deeper wound of his brother's betrayal. Though his breathing remained rough, his eyelids followed the gentle command of her voice. When it seemed that he had fallen into a troubled rest, she settled his head on the cushions and wrapped the bed furs tight against the hungry spirits who might steal his soul while he slept. Then she gathered her drum into her lap and began a chant to drive out the evil vapors that possessed him.

Suddenly, the ground rolled like a carpet snapped in the breeze. The brooms clacked against the lattices of her little tent and the kettle tipped over, spilling tea in a puddle that put out the fire in the firebox. A chest fell over, cascading its shelves of charms and medicines across the cushioned floor. Happily, it fell away from the sickbed so no harm was done.

"Ahh!" Bekter cried, starting up from his bed only to fall again on his side, panting.

"Eluneke's back," Toragana observed, setting her drum down to clean up the mess from the spilled tea.

Bekter's eyes, bright with fever, sought her out with terrified questions he was too ill to shape. "Did the earth shake when you completed your training?" he whispered, which was all the voice he could manage.

She thought perhaps he was having second thoughts about a healer—and a lover—who could turn the grasslands themselves on end. But in fact, she had never known of such a thing. "Not for me, or for any shaman I have heard of," she assured him. Of course, no shaman in all the collected memory of her craft had done what Eluneke had set out to do.

A second time the earth moved under her feet.

"Why now?" Bekter clung to the carpets with clenched fists and it was impossible to tell whether terror at the earth's upheaval or his own fevered chills were the cause.

Toragana smiled, though in fact she was worried more than

she let on to her patient. "Because she didn't come back alone. And now you must drink, if you expect to get well."

Bekter's eyes went very wide. "By all the gods and ancestors," he muttered breathlessly. She thought perhaps she had erred in telling him. He was too weak from his injuries to cope with the shamanic side of his brother's war. But he surprised her. Or, she decided, she was more surprised that his answer didn't shock her at all.

"I should be there. How can I record the tale if I do not see it?" He tried to rise, but already he had set the wound in his back to bleeding again.

"If you want to live, you will keep still. You've barely enough blood in you to keep your lungs in motion as it is."

"But—"

"If things have gone as Bolghai and I hope, you will hear it from your sister and the khan her husband," Toragana assured him. "If things have not . . ."

She turned without finishing what she had begun and put on her feathered headdress with the stuffed raven perched on her brow. Bekter didn't press her to complete her prediction. They both knew that if things had not gone well, he wouldn't live to compose the tale. And no loyal Qubal would live to hear it.

The shamaness wore the robes of her office already, but gathered the tokens of her craft about her—a flute and a drum, and a broom from its peg on the lattices.

"Where are you going?"

"Don't worry. I'll send Barula to tend you." She hoped he accepted the lightness of her tone, that he didn't notice she was trembling. He was the court's most famous poet, however, and his talent for observation had recovered from his injury faster than the rest of him.

"I'm not worried about myself. The danger is out there. Where are you going?"

"To fight. And so must you in your own way. Until your wounds are healed, the danger is in here as well."

His grave eyes told her he had guessed as much, and longed to accompany and protect her.

"You've done your part, beloved Bekter." She knelt and kissed him, smiled at his surprise but quickly grew serious again. "Now it's time for the shamans' war."

"Be careful—"

She pressed a finger to his lips. "Shhh—now is not the time for caution." She used a trick of her craft to muddy his senses so that he didn't see her go.

Her horse was waiting.

"**M**y lord general!" Mangkut fought his way to Qutula's side. His captain's breath came harsh and fast, more out of fear, Qutula thought, than from any struggle with sword or spear. His serpent allies terrified his Durluken as much as they did the Nirun, though with less cause. The demons usually honored the green armbands that marked Qutula's army. Sometimes they didn't, of course, but you could hardly expect a demon caught up in bloodlust to stop for a trifle. So far, Captain Mangkut had escaped both Nirun arrows and the fangs of his allies which, considering his betrayal, was better than he had any right to expect. With Duwa dead, however, there were few Qutula would trust more.

"What is it?" He cast an impatient glance to his side, where the Lady Chaiujin had ridden through most of the battle, commanding her serpent minions as he commanded his human ones. She wasn't there, which irked him somewhat. He wouldn't call it fear, that without her the army of serpent-demons might make no distinction between himself and his enemies. Nor would he say that he needed her advice. She was his, however, and she belonged where he wanted her.

"We're under attack, Lord General." Mangkut gestured in the direction of the Qubal city, which Prince Tayyichiut's stubborn Nirun had so far denied him. This time, it wasn't the Nirun.

"Damn his soul to the mouths of the hungry spirits."

Yesugei-Khan, who should have been setting up his own court among the Uulgar far to the south, rode down on the

Durluken with his sword raised in challenge. At his back came
an army riding at full gallop in the lake formation. Qutula
watched in disbelief as the flanks of Yesugei's horde curved in
a sweep that encircled his forces together with the Nirun who
fought their desperate but useless battle against his army of
serpent-demons.

What was he doing here, now, and with what appeared to
be the whole army Mergen had sent away with him? Already
the attack had closed the circle, and moved inward, tightening
the noose.

Where was the Lady Chaiujin when he needed her?

He'd been drugged. Prince Daritai cursed himself for a fool,
half surprised that he'd woken up at all this side of the pyre
and half expecting the weight of chains on wrists and ankles.
But small untroubled fingers carded the fringes of his braids
and somewhere a little to the right of his numb backside he
heard the Lady Bortu giving orders for dinner in a soft voice.

"The general has taken his troops to the battlefield," she
said. "I assume you will want to follow."

Daritai hadn't moved. He'd kept his breathing level and
slow, but somehow she had known when he awoke. It seemed
pointless to keep his eyes closed, so he opened them. The
child, Princess Orda, gave him a secret smile. So the princess
had known as well. He thought he'd made a better spy than
that. And he still didn't know why they'd bothered to drug
him but hadn't secured him as their prisoner. Lady Bortu answered the confusion if not the questions in his puzzled
brow.

"You needed rest." She patted him on the arm—he had a
feeling she did that a lot, and that it wasn't a compliment.
"Don't worry. You've slept no longer than you required of the
men you brought with you from the battlefield. The effects of
the drug will wear off when you've had something to eat."

He was relieved to hear it, and gladder than he wished to
show when a servant thrust a tray of suet pies under his nose.

He took one and bit in. Even the rich, full bloom of sheep fat on his tongue couldn't distract him from his plight, however, or from the servants and guardsmen righting fallen chests and wrapping cracked lattices along the palace wall.

"Why?" he asked. Her eyes had grown dark and intent as a hunting eagle. They made his skin crawl, but he had to know. "You had me in your power. General Yesugei commands fresher troops in greater number than my own. Why let me go?"

"I needed General Yesugei elsewhere," she said. "As for yourself—" he found her grin more unsettling than the intentness of her gaze "—the shamans' war has begun. I have need of an escort."

She didn't wait for him to follow, but climbed down from the dais and headed for the door. The shamans' war. He knew Yesugei would fight Qutula's serpent horde, knew the general would see his warriors die in a vain attempt to hold back the demons. They were not mortal, after all, and not arrow nor sword nor spear could harm them, as he had grown to know too well. But shamans . . .There were too few in any camp, but perhaps the khaness knew something he didn't.

"The earth moved while you were sleeping." Princess Orda tugged at his hand, leading him after the khaness. "Grandmother says Prince Tayy is back." The prince, her brother, was dead.

The princess seemed intent on following her grandmother, but to where? Into some war of magic? No child would take on such a burden while he stood to prevent it. Not if it cost him his life.

"I'll go," he promised the Princess Orda, "but you have to stay here. It's too dangerous on the battlefield for little girls, even princesses."

When she looked up at him, considering his answer, her eyes showed whiteless black, like her grandmother. Daritai shuddered in supernatural dread, but he didn't let go of her hand. That seemed to decide something within her because she was looking at their twined fingers when she agreed, "Yes. You'd better hurry."

What else could he do? He bowed gravely, relieved to see

the whites of her eyes again. Then he put her in the care of her
nobles and followed the Lady Bortu, who had disappeared by
the time he reached the door. His mare was there, however, her
halter in the powerful hand of a Qubal guardsman almost as old
as the Lady Bortu herself. On the pommel of his saddle sat a
golden hunting eagle without hood or jesses.

"I think you have the season confused," he commented. Ea-
gles hunted in the winter, when the furs were thickest.

Some joke lurked in the eyes of the keeper. Daritai's hand
caressed his sword, but the laugh never reached the man's
mouth so Daritai could hardly show offense.

"The lady knows what she hunts." The keeper stepped
away.

Daritai eyed the pommel with some trepidation, unwilling
to place his delicate regions so temptingly near the powerful
claws of the unhooded bird. The creature cocked her head as if
she too were laughing at him. He thought he recognized that
piercing gaze, though he kept his suspicion to himself. He
would not have his sanity questioned.

"I trust you will behave like the lady and grandmother you
are," he muttered under his breath, and settled himself gingerly
in the saddle. She was big even for her kind; the golden head
came to his shoulder. But her eyes were for the distance. The
prince was back from the dead, the princess had said.

Wondering who had conquered whom, he directed his
mount where the eagle's gaze led him.

Lady Bortu flexed her clawed feet and settled her feathers,
amused to see the nervous glances her escort gave her
sharply curved talons. She hadn't done this, transforming into
her totem creature, since before she'd married to create a dynasty and she hadn't been at all certain that the form would
come to her when she summoned it. But Eluneke had returned
from the underworld, and the second tremor of the earth had
told her she hadn't come alone. Some demon-lord might have
followed the girl, but she'd gone to bring back Tayy and the

Lady Bortu trusted her own blood in the veins of both. The shamans' war had begun, and she owed her sons this much, at least.

Still, she'd spent a few uncomfortable minutes with the body of an eagle, berating her old retainer with the mouth and head of an old khaness. Surrender to the totem had come hard to her after all this time, longer than the lives of both her dead sons since she'd tried to summon the spirits of the earth. But finally, in desperation, she made the leap into the mind of the bird. None too soon—Daritai mustn't see her hesitate. She required his total commitment to her task.

Chapter Forty-four

Y ESUGEI HAD NEVER been a simple man. When he led the exiled god-king through the grasslands to the foot of Chimbai-Khan's dais, he had known that his world had changed forever by his actions. He had not desired fame or to mold that change to suit himself, nor did he claim a shaman's gift to read the future in the bottom of a cup. But even a man who relied solely on his intellect could see that Fate had moved in young King Llesho's eyes.

Since then, he'd seen wonders enough to last a lifetime. As a man who fought beside dragons, Yesugei considered himself free of supernatural fears. But if he had known the road on which he'd set the Qubal people would lead to this, he would have slit the god-king's throat and left the Cloud Country in the hands of the Uulgar forever.

On any other battleground he would have expected the cries of the injured to join the squeals of the horses and the shouts of the fighting men. Here, no wounded lay among the dead, which was a mercy. From inside his coat he drew out a scented scarf to wrap around his face, though it helped little against the putrefaction rising from this field. The corpses lay black and swollen as if dead for many days, and among them crawled an army of vipers, slithering here from the open mouth of a dead man whose eyes stared in horror at the stormy sky and, there, burrowing beneath the leather half-armor of another so disfigured by the venoms that had killed him that he scarcely resembled a man at all.

Yesugei pulled his gaze away with an effort. Somewhere at the center of this abomination Qutula waited with his Durluken and with his lady who commanded the serpents. He had to be stopped. His demons had to be cast back into the underworld that spawned them. How a mortal man might be expected to accomplish that he didn't know, but they had to try. Bracing himself against the horrors Qutula would throw at him, he pointed his sword. Banners dipped, and the defensive circle around Qutula tightened.

Then the earth shifted.

His horse screamed in alarm and fell heavily on its side. Yesugei jumped free before he was crushed by the weight of his mount, but his own legs would scarcely hold him. Solid ground became a tossing sea while men's senses raged against nature overset. An eathquake. He'd heard of them from travelers. The hungry dead beat against the gates between the realms of the living and the underworld, they said. Demons reached through the shattered earth to swallow cities whole.

They had enough of demons in front of them. Better the underworld should open up and take these snakes back where they belonged and leave living men in peace. He waited for another tremor, but none came. His horse struggled to its legs, unhurt but shivering and rolling the whites of its eyes as it stood its shaky ground.

A khan could show no less courage than a dumb beast, or a general attend any less to his training. So exhorting himself, Yesugei leaped into his saddle and raised his sword again.

"Ayee-yah!" he cried.

The signal passed down the line of his captains, who watched him to shore up their own flagging courage. The order flowed from the captains to the thousands who took their lead from the officers charging at the head of their troops.

The horde surged forward. They would sweep this landscape of despair and drive out the human monster who had raised a demon army against his father the dead khan. And then Yesugei would take care of Prince Daritai. But a foreign conqueror seemed like a very small thing as his horse plunged toward the supernatural forces seething death in front of them.

"Rise up, damn you! Rise up!" Qutula called to his army of serpents. His men, those who had survived both the serpents and General Jochi's attacks, fell back in terror. Chief among his Durluken, Mangkut circled his horse, panic stretching his lips in a grimace as he looked for a way out of Yesugei's trap.

"Do you think the good general will allow any Durluken to live if he wins?" Qutula snapped at him. Duwa's execution had taught him not to invite open rebellion. Where a man would not go at command, however, he could be pushed indirectly, with threats. If Mangkut cast a glance at his general's sword before he turned his horse into the invading horde, he might be forgiven.

"Go, you curs!" the Durluken raised his sword to answer Yesugei's challenge. "No man can stand against us! The spirits will clear the way to the very ger-tent palace of our own true khan!"

Qutula, who would be khan when the battle ended, acknowledged their devotion as his Durluken called his name for their battle cry. They were too few to stand alone against the many thousands Yesugei-Khan led over the killing field, but his lady would be pleased to see human warriors fighting beside her serpents. It was worth expending a few more lives for the pleaure of viewing the general's bloated corpse, he thought, and led his own thousand into the fray.

Swaying in his saddle from exhaustion, Jochi led his warriors at an angle that brought him to Yesugei's horde on the very edge of the writhing sea of vipers. Each general reached over his horse to clasp the arm of the other in greeting.

"I didn't think you would come in time."

"We're here," Yesugei answered his greeting. "To what use against such a foe, I cannot say."

Demon-serpents snapped and hissed on every side of them, great fangs longer than his finger striking out again and again. Jochi raised his sword and slashed at a demon's head while his men cried out in terror and loathing before they died. Horses reared up screaming in pain, throwing their riders as mortal vipers struck at their fetlocks and then at the exposed faces of their riders.

Like all Mergen's officers in the recent magical wars in the Cloud Country, Jochi had paid the shaman Bolghai for blessings and protections placed on his sword. So far, he hadn't killed any of the Lady Chaiujin's demons with it—he thought only Chahar had managed that—but they tried to avoid his blade at least, as if it caused them pain. Few among the thousands tithed to the khanate would have such weapons, however.

"Cut a path!" General Jochi shouted above the din.

Yesugei, whose sword also enjoyed the shaman's blessings, nodded that he understood.

Then, with their captains to either side, the generals turned on their demon foe, slashing to right and to left and in front of them, clearing a path down which the horde would follow with one goal. They would find Qutula and force him to send the serpents back where they came from, or he would die. *Die anyway,* Jochi thought, and distracted himself from the ache in his sword arm by imagining the varied and painful ways they would kill the murderous traitor.

Somewhere out in that landscape from hell, a mind was ordering the serpents. The generals soon found themselves separated from each other, and then from their captains, surrounded by venomous attacks on every side. Jochi hacked and slashed, his teeth gritted in a terrible grin of concentration. The serpent to the right and to the left of him felt the bite of his sword and fell back.

Another raised dripping fangs in front of him. He struck again, but distracted by the new attack, he didn't notice the serpent-demon rising up head-tall behind him until he felt an acid pain slice the back of his neck. Twin knives, it felt like, each longer than his finger sunk in to the hilt, severing his spine. The viper shook him like a rattle while it loosed its venom. When it dropped him, he fell to the ground in agony, and uttered one great, raw-throated scream as his living flesh began to bubble and swell. The fangs had severed his spine, paralyzing him. Soon, thankfully, he felt nothing at all, though a glance told him that the wounds erupting on his blackening flesh still festered and bled. He closed his eyes, then, waiting for death, and prayed. But death, it seemed, would take its time today.

It was time. The demon who went by the stolen name of Lady Chaiujin cursed the human who had quickened her egg and his war that had embroiled her people in his devices. She cursed the human shape, grotesquely distended by the growing egg, which trapped her. And she cursed her offspring, which wanted out *now*.

She had lost her horse somewhere on that vast field of black-and-purple death. Not that it mattered. She couldn't ride; her body screamed at her to squat in the mud and release her egg. She told her body to shut up. Standing rain-soaked in his battlefield, with her coats caught up in her arms and the rain pouring down from the horns of her headdress to drip like beads from its silver chains, she cursed Qutula for living and her father the demon-king for dying. She cursed Chimbai-Khan for good measure, though she had murdered him herself and felt neither grief nor remorse for it.

Her warm dry nest of stolen silks lay far on the other side of this abandoned killing field. The battle had passed on to fresh ground, leaving her behind with the dead. She took a step, another, pulled each foot out of the blood-and-rain-drenched, sucking mud and put it down again. The simple process of getting to the place where she could let down her egg took more strength than she had to give. The serpents who curled among the corpses at her feet gave neither help nor comfort. It wasn't in their nature or hers.

"Father!" she screamed as the urge to rid herself of the egg overpowered her.

It hurt, it hurt. She wasn't going to make it back to the warm, dry place she had prepared so carefully. Like all her plans, this one, too, had gone so wrong. She should have been khaness by now, wrapped in silks to comfort her pain, and in command. Or home, but her father was dead, the gates of the underworld closed to her now.

"Aaahhh! Aaahhh!" She couldn't wait, couldn't stop it, and the serpents picked their heads up and tasted the air when she screamed. They were hungry and knew their own, and its young. But this egg would be too big a mouthful for any of them.

"Leave me alone!"

She was their queen in the mortal realm, and so they pretended disinterest, slitherering away leaving wave tracks in the mud. She bent, tucking up the skirts of her coats so she could squat in the rutted earth. Heavy with rain, the rich cloth sagged and drooped, escaping her hands to drag in the mud. She struggled with it, gave her knees permission to fold under her.

Ah, there. The mud was soft, after all—almost comforting. The egg pushed harder. The human body she'd been forced to wear like a badly fitted coat these weeks clenched in rejection of its passenger. She hadn't expect this, the size of the egg, or the pain as it fought its way through, making an enemy of the creature who had given it life.

Then it was out, gone, not a part of her anymore: a leathery sac half buried in the mud. No one would find it here. No one would think to look. There were so many dead, after all, purple and black and noisome, their guts swollen and their eyes eaten out by the serpents.

Once she had had plots to rule the grasslands, and an egg by which to claim them. But the egg wasn't a part of her anymore. And quickly she forgot. Cool and sleek and green again, the Lady Chaiujin no more, she left her own waving pattern in the mud. Away, away, away.

Chapter Forty-five

NOT ALL THE NIRUN had gone to fight Qutula at the front. Prince Tayyichiut found himself in the company of half a dozen of his own guardsmen who had stayed behind at Bolghai's insistence to watch at his grave. Now they brought his horse and Tayy found that he could ride. He felt little changed for having been dead, though his Nirun shied from looking at him when they didn't think he would notice. Still, the wounds were healing with magical speed, those of the demon-serpent taking longest, while the damage from the hungry spirits showed now only in the shadowed memories in his eyes.

Eluneke rode her own ghostly steed at his right. She'd lost the argument with her totem animals, who wouldn't stay behind. Led by the queen of the toads, who crouched in her perch atop Eluneke's headdress, they insisted on joining in the shamans' war to end the sway of demons on the land. Bolghai rode at his left, beaming at his student and his patient, who had returned from the land of the dead.

The battleground was before them, ringed about in Yesugei's lake attack formation. Tayy kneed his horse in the ribs, urging it to a gallop and the circle opened to admit his party with a cry of terror and joy.

"Ayyeee-yah!" he cried, a salute and call to battle. Then he plunged ahead, heedless of the dangers that rose up from the steaming grass to accost him. He'd been dead, and had come back not alive, exactly, but in some altered state which brushed aside such things as serpent-demons like they were shadows. He carried his father's sword. Brought back with him, a gift from the underworld, the weapon shared in the properties of the living and the dead and cleaved head from body where it fell among the serpent-demons. The monsters, already dead, fell writhing among their more lowly brethren in the mud.

At his side, Eluneke raised the dragon spear of the sky god's daughter, made for this very purpose. With it, she drove the demons as she had repelled their kin in the underworld. Her drumstick horse, another gift from heaven, reared up kicking and biting to trample serpent-demons underfoot.

Bolghai, with his more humble gifts of magic fought beside her while driving ahead, Prince Tayy heard the scream of one of his guardsmen. The man fell with fangs lodged in his side. "You can't help him," Bolghai urged. "You can only win and make his death worthwhile."

Only the the danger to the whole ulus—and its survival— could make the struggle worth the cost. So many lay dead so horribly, without the pyre to free their souls. Hungry spirits haunted this ground. Tayy shivered in remembered dread, but Bolghai was right. He could mourn later. Now, he had to win.

Across the battlefield, the banner of his general, Yesugei-Khan, flew ahead of a dark tide of riders. There were too many for the demons to dispatch at once. Among the mystical ene-mies were Qutula's Durluken; Yesugei's thousands concen-trated their attack on those human warriors while his captains strove hopelessly to clear the ground of demons. Prince Tayy swung his sword and charged, driving the serpent-demons be-fore him. *They are mist, they are nothing,* he told himself. And they fell back, cringing away from his deadly sword. But there were too many.

"There!" he cried to his companions. General Jochi—he rec-ognized the father of his own dead captain—strove against too many serpent-demons rising up like a vapor all around him. Even with a sword protected by spells he couldn't hope to see through the number who attacked him.

Tayy turned to the rescue with Eluneke beside him. She began to chant, low at first, then with a voice growing stronger and more commanding. From her costume jumped the toads who had accompanied her through heaven and the underworld, and underfoot, more toads joined them. As Eluneke recited her spell, they began to grow, their skins glistening with venom, until they were taller than the horses, taller than the demon-serpents who rose on vaporous tails to strike. The toads leaped into battle, their huge tongues flicking like whips, spraying the demon-serpents with venom. The enemy fell back.

They were too late. A viper rose and drove its fangs into the back of the general's neck. Tayy flinched, remembering the touch of those razor teeth against his own throat, the burning agony of the venom pumped into his veins. But there was no one to rescue Jochi, nor any to light a pyre to release his spirit. His spirit would take the long way home, carried in the throats of the carrion birds who feasted on every battlefield.

Tayy wept as he fought, and where his tears touched his enemy, they burned with the acid of his grief and fled screaming their own demon despair.

Yesugei understood now. This was why Daritai had looked the way he had, why he had thrown his conqueror's horde into the fight alongside Jochi's Qubal. The serpent-demons revolted him as much as they terrified him. There were too many, and mortal weapons did them no noticeable harm. But if he let up even to wipe the sweat from his eyes, he would fall as Jochi had done.

Jumal!" he called his young captain to him and gasped out his command, never ceasing to lay about him with his sword.

Jumal was too good a soldier to protest, but Yesugei saw the dismay on his face and understood that, too. Mergen had sent his captain to the rear before and now Mergen and Prince Tayyichiut were both dead. They couldn't change that, couldn't change the outcome against an army they could neither wound nor kill. They might strive until the last man fell to protect the ulus, but someone had to live to tell the tale.

"Find the Lady Bortu," Yesugei gasped between strokes of his sword. "Save what you can."

The boy—no more, but a man tested in the fires of supernatural battles—nodded a salute and turned to obey. Then something amazed him so that he almost lost control of his horse. "My lord!" he cried, and Yesugei turned, followed the direction where Jumal pointed his sword.

"By all the gods and ancestors, it cannot be!" he whispered.

"It is him, though," Jumal confirmed, though neither needed the confirmation of the other. "Prince Tayyichiut, brought back from the dead. And the serpents seem to be running from him."

Not that. The stories of Tayy's death must have erred. But the hairs on Yesugei's neck rose as they did before lightning struck. The serpents, who had shown no fear of any mortal, now fled before the prince and the unearthly green-and-gold fighters who leaped at his command.

"Send young Otchigin to the palace with a third of the horde," Yesugei amended his orders. Though he was as embattled as he'd been a moment before, hope now strengthened his arm. Jumal accepted the order with a grim smile and rode off to do his general's bidding.

Yesugei had no time for idle thoughts then. The serpents, driven now by their own desperate fear, threw themselves against the mortal army in a frenzy of slashing fangs. As his sword rose and fell, rose and fell, however, a chant set the rhythm of his arm: *the prince has returned. The prince has returned.* The prince had returned from the dead to save his people.

There she was! It had been a good guess that the earth, shaking, had been coughing up her apprentice, but Toragana hadn't been sure until she actually saw Eluneke next to her prince, riding through the drizzling rain across the muddy battlefield. So the visions so long ago now proved true. Dead, and living again, though it remained to be seen what Eluneke had actually brought back with her from the underworld. Death changed people. But Toragana had no doubt that the prince and the shaman-princess would soon become khan and khaness, as the visions had predicted. First, of course, they had to end the Lady Chaiujin's war.

Toragana had practiced her healing arts far from the court of khans, so she bore no weapons. She had a horse, however, and rode to the battle with her magic about her, and the broom she had danced with long ago. She swept the ground with it, driving the serpents before her. Where the broom struck a demon, smoke rose and the creature smoldered with soggy flames. Soon they were keeping their distance. The toads recognized her and let her through, so she made good time drawing up to Bolghai and his royal party.

"Glad you could join us," he said with a cheerful smile.

Toragana turned up her nose at him. She would have sniffed her displeasure with his levity, but the miasma of death and decay that rose from the battlefield assaulted her nostrils in spite of the wintergreen salve with which she had treated her upper lip. She would take no more of this foul air inside herself than she had to, and certainly none just to make a point.

"Keep your eyes on your charge," she cautioned him. Up close, the prince was looking a little . . . mad. And the rain fell harder.

Furious, Daritai rode out with four thousands of his Tinglut warriors, the better for a few hours' rest, to relieve the thousands he'd left under General Jochi's command. He'd had an understanding with the general. But with Yesugei-Khan's return at the head of an army of Uulgar and his own Qubal horde, he figured it was time to renegotiate. If any of them survived to sit a dais again. Sourly, he considered the golden eagle riding to war on his saddle pommel.

"I hope you know what you are doing, old woman."

She turned her predator's dark eyes on him and gave one long, slow blink, the meaning of which eluded him. Then she lifted on strong wings and circled, circled lofting higher with each turn, until he had lost sight of her in the sparkles that Great Sun scattered across his eyes. Snakes, he remembered. The great golden birds ate snakes. Maybe the old woman would be worth something in the fight after all.

He hadn't counted on the whole family having shamanic powers when he'd considering marrying his son to the little Qubal princess. The old khan wouldn't like it. No Tinglut royal had ever shown such tendencies. Mostly they kept their heads down and hoped Tinglut-Khan didn't notice them. He was bound to notice a neighbor returned from the dead, however. The thought might dampen his ardor for conquest.

Things were looking up. Or would be, if any of them survived the serpent war. Shamans' war, the old woman had called it. General Jochi was nowhere to be seen and Yesugei-Khan was surrounded. Daritai drew his sword and called his men to the aid of the under-Khan of the short-lived Qubal empire. But someone arrived before him, driving the serpent-demons like smoke before him. The boy prince, Tayyichiut, surrounded by shamans and with his own sword raised, slashed into the fleeing demons.

So the old woman had been right about the returned from the dead thing. Or, more likely, not dead at all but merely stunned until his shaman roused him from his stupor. It was a good trick, and the boy knew how to make an entrance. Daritai would need more evidence before he would believe the boy had returned from the dead, but the demons were afraid of him. That certainly meant something.

And so did the toads bigger than horses who had invaded the field. Back the other side of a war with demon vipers, Daritai might have turned and fled at the sight. Now, he wearily asked himself the only question that mattered: whose side are they on?

Damn it. Damn it! He'd killed his demon-cursed cousin, put a sword in his back, and then covered him with dirt. So what was Tayy doing back again, riding across the battlefield like he owned it? He didn't look like a ghost. Qutula's own half sister was riding next to him. She seemed solid enough and she'd brought their own army of monsters. Where was his Lady Chaiujin when her precious serpents were shriveling up and running away from the spear the girl wielded like a warrior queen of Pontus?

Qutula figured that between his Nirun, the Tinglut, and Yesugei-Khan's horde, Prince Tayy had almost thirty thousands to call upon, not counting his toads, against Qutula's paltry handful of thousands under captains he couldn't count on or trust. He needed the Lady Chaiujin to turn back her minions and force them to fight. Where in all the demon hells of the underworld had she disappeared to?

She always came back to him. He had her mark . . . but the serpent tattoo was gone, had disappeared from his breast weeks ago. Though she'd ridden at his side, and sat with his captains at his councils and lain with him in the dark, he hadn't felt her presence beneath his skin for too long. *I'm losing her.* The thought filled him with rage. He'd lost everything, and his lady serpent-demon as well.

He'd once dreamed of punishing her, when he was khan. Perhaps that part of the dream was beyond him, but his cousin was here, now, and he'd stay dead this time, if it took a hundred arrows to put him in the ground. Qutula turned his horse and called his human fighters for one last rush. He would take down the prince, finally and forever. Qutula's serpent allies would rally. Yesugei would fall. Daritai would crumble. And Qutula would hold all the grasslands within his clenched fist.

Demons didn't bleed, but the ichor they were made of burned Tayy's hands where it splashed over the crosspiece. It was eating his blade, but there were fewer of them now. Eluneke had accounted for a goodly number, and old Bolghai.

The shamaness Toragana had made good account of herself with her broom. Even the toads fought, driving the serpent-demons back with their venom, which flew from the sacs above their eyes like arrows.

If he wanted to fool himself, he could believe they were winning. But for every serpent-demon accounted for by his shaman army, there were a hundred warriors rotting in the light of Great Sun and his little brother.

Jochi was down, the toads were abandoning the field, their venom depleted, and Yesugei was struggling, with his captains close in to protect each other's flank. Tayy would lose the last of his standing generals if he didn't reach him in time.

"Just one more, just one more, just one more." The chant took his mind off the ache in his arm, it gave him a rhythm to each jab and slash of his ghostly sword long after sense told him to just give up. "Just one more . . ."

Yesugei wasn't clear yet, but the supernatural assault had lessened and his lake attack was drawing tighter, pressing the Durluken into the center. And Qutula . . .

The sound of horses drew his attention and he almost missed his mark, but the demon under his sword was slithering away, abandoning the field like his fellows. And Qutula had taken its place, sword upraised, while at his side Mangkut rode high on his stirrups, aiming an arrow over his horse's head. Tayy turned into the fight, ruining the Durluken's shot. With a screech of steel against steel, his sword met Qutula's, their blades screaming against each other.

Lady Bortu executed an awkward turn before the natural sense of flight returned to her, then she glided in a wide looping circle, rising, rising. The ground fell away beneath her and she soared. She'd forgotten over the years the pleasure in stretching her wings, in catching the wind and rising, rising, until she had disappeared against the clouds. The rain beat against her wings, but she brought her predator's mind back to her task. Nothing must distract her: not the pleasure of flight or her regrets. Her children were dead, the ulus in chaos at the hand of her own grandchild. It had been for nothing that she had given all of this up so long ago.

Below, the ground was rutted and churned. Rivulets of blood-pinked rainwater splashed off the dead and formed gullies in their lee. Down there, the reek of death would be overpowering. Up here, she could pretend the dead below didn't signal the end of the Qubal people.

Another circle, tighter this time, a little lower. The rot from the battlefield floated up to her on the air, but she didn't let it drive the raptor's brain. Around again. She would leave Qutula to her grandson, Tayyichiut-Khan, whose life would make the stories that his grandchildren would tell their children, if he lived. The khaness had one goal in this fight: the serpent at her family's breast. And there she was. The Lady Chaiujin.

Sweat mixed with rain and stung his eyes. To spare even the moment to blink or wipe them would have meant death, however, so Tayy ignored it, as he ignored Mangkut who awaited the outcome with drawn arrow. It was harder to set aside the jarring ache that rang up his arm with each slash averted, each pointed lunge parried, so he embraced each shock as proof that he was alive. Eluneke rode beside him, her spear accounting for as many as his sword, but she was engaged at his flank and couldn't help him. He moved in for a strike.

He'd been fighting too long while Qutula had watched and commanded, but had raised no sword in warrior's work that day. His cousin was fresher. His cousin was stronger. His cousin hadn't been dead a few hours before.

The muscle in Tayy's arm bled their own fire in protest, but he commanded it to rise and fall anyway. If he died, the serpent-demons would return; the putrifying dead of Qubal and Tinglut and Uulgar would litter all the grasslands, until only the serpents remained.

As his cousin's horse danced out of range, Qutula shifted his attack, cutting at the legs of Tayy's mare. She screamed and fell, the tendons severed. Tayy leaped from his saddle and rolled free, but came up empty-handed. He'd lost his father's ghostly sword in the fall.

"Fool." Qutula smiled, but it wasn't a friendly sight. He settled his sword more comfortably in his hand and prepared for his swing.

Weaponless, Tayy wondered if this was the end Fate had in store for him. Qutula had already murdered him once. Had that been his intended destiny all along? But no, he didn't think the gods and ancestors would have sent him back just to die again. And he didn't think he'd come back entirely the same. He had shown the same powers that his shamans possessed, to kill the demons.

The rain fell in rivulets down his face, but that didn't matter. He had a plan. It would probably kill him, but he'd pay that price, to save the Qubal. . . .

"My lord!" Eluneke, freed of her battle, reached a hand to him and he took it, leaping up behind her on the pale horse.

"I love you," he whispered into her ear, and then Tayy reached out with his hand and heart. But he was too tired, or perhaps had never had the power that had seemed to follow him from the underworld.

"Let me help." Eluneke closed her hand in his. Between them, she had clasped the dragon spear of the sky god's daughter.

Tayy felt the power then, flowing not only from Eluneke, but rising in himself, gathering between them. He needed only to be reminded of how it was done. Together, they called the lightning.

Tayy felt the spark grow between their hands. He pointed the spear at his cousin.

"My lord," Eluneke whispered, a signal that she was ready. Then Tayy released the god's fire.

The spear shattered. Thunder cracked like heaven itself was falling on their heads. Qutula's eyes were wide with terror as he was lifted out of his saddle. The sword in his hand melted and ran sizzling in liquid drops to the ground, where it pooled in strange shapes with the blood of the fallen locked in its heart.

Qutula's horse was dead, blasted and charred. And Qutula lay with his eyes open to the rain, the sign of the tree burned across his unbeating heart. Dead.

Lightning forked in the air, reaching for some target on the ground, but Lady Bortu ignored it. The snake was her target. Bortu had never feared the contest itself. But she had feared unmanning her son in front of the ulus by fighting his battles for him. She had feared a war if she confronted Qutula over his lady. She had feared, most selfishly and with the greatest dread that, once she discovered them again, she would lack the strength to let her shaman powers go. And one by one, she had lost the fight for each of the things she had hoped to save through her inaction. It hardly mattered if she lived, as long as the false Lady Chaiujin died. But if she did survive, she would never give up flying, or her totem form, again.

The golden eagle swooped out of the blinding light of Great Sun, careful not to cast a shadow that would alert her prey. She had sighted the emerald green bamboo snake swimming across a basin of rainwater carved by the frantic beating of a dying man's boots against the muddy ground. And there, passing on, the demon left the slithering trace of her serpent body in the bloody slime.

Silent and deadly in flight, Lady Bortu snatched out with her sharp-clawed eagle's feet and grasped the serpent tight under the jaws. The demon writhed and twisted, but her fangs couldn't reach the eagle's horny legs. A loop of the sinuous green body coiled and tightened around the golden eagle and they tumbled in the air, plunging toward the battlefield while Lady Bortu struggled to free her wings. She didn't dare let go her hold on the serpent's jaws—the Lady Chaiujin's venomous bite would kill her instantly—but squeezed more tightly in her clawed feet as she flexed her powerful shoulders in abortive flight.

"You'll die with me," she spoke to the mind of the serpent as she had spoken once to her granddaughter, showing the demon her own vision of the ground coming up at them. Serpents have weak eyes, but the clear and deadly images Bortu fed her dismayed the creature. She loosened her coils and the eagle lifted, but not soon enough. They tumbled to the ground together.

Lady Bortu righted herself, but the Lady Chaiujin had vanished. Failing to murder her captor and fearing the death of her serpent body, the demon turned into a thick green mist. Bortu had seen the like before, however; she used her wings to beat the vapor into the ground, where it must take on a shape or melt into the mud.

She expected the creature to rise up in her human form, but instead the serpent writhed on the ground, her curved and hungry fangs reaching for the eagle. Bortu struck first.

"Awk!" Rising on powerful wings, she lunged at the serpent. Her powerful beak clamped over the scaly neck and gave a shake.

Snap! The false Lady Chaiujin lay dead between the jaws of the Lady Bortu's totem form. The golden eagle shook her head a second time just to be certain, then with her clawed feet carefully shredded the carcass. And if Bortu was careful to avoid the poison glands in the creature's pitted jaws, the meat was quite tasty, really. Quite tasty indeed.

Tayy had forgotten the marksman with his arrow but when he looked up, the man had fled. Which was fortunate, since he didn't think he could lift a hand in his own defense. He hadn't heard Mankgut go, and when he looked around, he was surprised to discover that the fighting still went on. A cocoon of silence had descended around him with the lightning. Steel clashed against steel, men cried out to exhort their comrades, or screamed in pain as they died, but none of it reached him.

He thought he ought to be helping to route the serpent-demons, but the silence was such a relief that the tension had fled his weary bones. He found himself sitting in the mud beside his dead cousin and didn't know how he'd gotten there.

Nothing seemed to hurt in the way an injury ought, though, so he sat, surprised that the wind seemed to have gone out of him so completely. He still hadn't wiped the sweat and the rain from his brow. His arms were covered in demon gore to the elbows, however, and the stuff burned when it touched his skin. It could wait until he had a clean corner of cloth to mop himself with.

It wasn't as bad as the burn on his hand. When he finally managed to raise it enough to check the damage, he saw the sign of the tree had burned into the palm. The trunk started at his wrist and branched out across his fingers. He wondered, with a remote part of his brain, what it meant, but couldn't get past the one thought that drove out all others. Rest. He could . . .

"They're gone."

He couldn't hear her, but she touched his shoulder and he read the words on her lips when she repeated them. Eluneke looked filthy and tired and as covered in the ichor of the demon-serpents as he, but blessedly, blessedly unhurt. It took a moment for the meaning of her words to sink in. Then he looked around. The demon-serpents were gone. Even the mortal snakes called to battle in aid of their demon brethren had slithered from the field.

From somewhere on the battleground Toragana had appeared, and Bolghai. Yesugei followed. Each looking as weary and filty as he, but Tayy saw no injuries except, he thought, to the soul.

Bolghai touched his ear. "She's dead," he said, grinning. Tayy realized he could hear again and figured out the answer to that riddle easily enough. The false Lady Chaiujin, who had caused them all so much pain. Toragana had tears in her eyes and left them quickly to minister to the dead and the wounded.

He closed his eyes and let Bolghai bring him to his feet and steady him.

"My lord gur-khan," General Yesugei said.

Gur-khan. Tayy opened his eyes again, but of course Mergen wasn't there. Slowly, he realized that Yesugei meant him.

Prince Daritai was there as well, eyeing the general warily.

"Tayyichiut Gur-Khan," he said, and bowed as one of slightly lesser status to one of greater rank.

He wasn't sure what Daritai was doing here, but figured he ought to be grateful for the help. "You may tell your father that the Qubal gift him with the death of the creature who caused the loss of his daughter, the beloved Lady Chaiujin of the Tinglut." He gave a little bow of his own, as one who has received a service of an ally and has repaid it with one of equal or greater value. "The false Lady Chaiujin is now dead."

"Was she . . . ?" Prince Daritai lifted his hand in a small gesture at the battlefield, all he could do, it seemed, now that the need to wield a sword had ended.

"We can talk as we ride," Tayy offered. He didn't think he could stand any longer. Someone had put his own mare out of her misery, but there were riderless horses enough on the field and Bolghai gathered one up for him and saw him into the saddle.

"She murdered Chimbai-Khan and his first wife as well," he said as they rode, with Daritai on his left and Eluneke, who had never left him, on his right. "By the serpent-demon's influence, my uncle the gur-khan died as well. Be grateful you never met her."

Daritai nodded, partly to acknowledge the answer, but just as much, Tayy thought, because he was stunned by exhaustion. They would have to deal with the whole conquest and invasion thing soon enough, but Tayy had a feeling they'd work that out in time.

"Come back with me," he said. "Take your rest while our living sort their dead."

Daritai nodded again, but the intelligence was returning to his eyes. "We have much to discuss," he said.

"In time." Tayy nudged the mare under him to a walk and let her go home at her own pace. Daritai followed. "After we've cleaned the dead off our hands, we can have a thought for politics."

With their dead by thousands on the ground they traveled, he couldn't find it in his heart to think about politics at all. But politics had put the dead there. Politics would end it now or see them falling on one another in another war, if he had not yet learned the lessons Mergen had died for. Yesugei seemed pleased with him so he figured he must be doing all right.

"Huh. There she is." Daritai grunted. He was looking up into the sun and Tayy shaded his eyes to follow his gaze.

A speck. A bird. The golden eagle landed shakily on the pommel of Daritai's horse and then slid off into his lap. The Tinglut prince winced, and then the eagle turned into Tayy's grandmother.

"My Lady Bortu." Tayy refused to show his surprise. So did she.

"You're looking well, grandson. Death seems to have been good for you. But I think your lady wife would like it if you didn't try it again."

"I live only to please my lady wife," Tayy agreed. He'd meant it as a joke when he said it, but the words unfolded like a flower in his heart. Eluneke's smile felt like a kiss.

Chapter Forty-six

W HEN THEY HAD honored their dead, Tayy ordered the camp moved, and further declared that the Qubal would bend their course in future so that they might never camp by the little dell on the river again. So it was with some sorrow that he made his last visit before he took horse. Eluneke, who would become his wife at their next camp, accompanied him, her face as wistful as his own.

"Prince Daritai is waiting to say good-bye," she reminded him.

"He can wait a little longer." The Tinglut prince, accompanied by his own survivors of the recent shaman's war and a handful of Qubal thousands, carried with him a betrothal contract between his own son Tumbinai and the Princess Orda. Tayy would have preferred to wait until after the election for gur-khan, but Daritai needed the leverage of the proposed marriage to free the groom, held hostage by his grandfather. The princess was determined that no harm come to her beloved Tumbi.

But first, Tayy had his own good-bye to make. "This is where we first spoke to each other," he said, and took Eluneke's hand in his. He'd lost his best friend to this river in his first battle and found a new one in the god-king Llesho. Here he'd lost his father and started on the adventures that led him through slavery and near-murder to the Cloud Country. He'd come to know his wife here.

In this little dell, the tent city and all its tribulations seemed far away and he could forget, for a moment, the many dead they'd lost here. He could remember, for a moment, the happy times. But too much sorrow brought bad luck to a place. He was glad to be leaving it behind.

"Ribbit!" King Toad showed himself with his crown of leaves. "So you're going at last."

"Yes, we're going." Eluneke took up the conversation with her totem.

King Toad bobbed his head, not to show submission, since he would never admit the superiority of a human khan, but to acknowledge the wisdom of this decision. "I can't say we'll miss you—humans make it hard for the toads," he said in the language of the toads. "But you've given us plenty of stories to tell. For that we'll be grateful."

"I'm glad." Eluneke bowed to show her respect, but he was gone before she straightened again.

"I guess it's really time," she said.

He nodded and took her hand, and together they climbed out of the dell for the last time, back to the ulus where they served as khan and, soon, khaness. Before they left the shelter of the trees, however, Tayy leaned over and kissed her. She kissed him back, and the pine needles were soft and smelled like summer.

The egg had grown thin and stretched as the offspring grew within it. Arms, pink and green, moved. Legs kicked. An egg tooth sharp as a knife cut into the leathery case. Pink fingers with pale green scales along their backs clutched at the shell and pulled as the egg tooth did its work and then dropped off in the splinters of the casing. The ground was soft and warm. The grass tickled his nose. The child looked up into a blue-and-golden sky and gurgled happily. Then he rolled over, dug his toes into the dirt, and crawled away.